Page of

Swords

BY BEN REEDER

Page of Swords

Copyright © 2015 Ben Reeder/Irrational Worlds

All rights reserved. No part of this publication may be reproduced, distributed, or transmitted in any form or by any means, including photocopying, recording, or other electronic or mechanical methods, without the prior written permission of the publisher, except in the case of brief quotations embodied in critical reviews and certain other noncommercial uses permitted by copyright law.

This is a work of fiction. Any resemblance to real persons or entities is strictly coincidental.

Cover art by Angela Gulick. Model photo by Machine Fairy. Model: Siroj Steems

Other books by Ben Reeder:

The Demon's Apprentice series:

The Demon's Apprentice

Page of Swords

The Zompoc Survivor series:

Zompoc Survivor: Exodus

Zompoc Survivor: Inferno

Zompoc Survivor: Odyssey (2015)

Also from Irrational Worlds:

On the Matter of the Red Hand

Rationality Zero

The Herald of Autumn

Coming soon!

Of the Dark and Desolate Sea

A Hand against the Wind

Slave of the Sky Captain

Dedicated to my heroes, the men and women who serve our country in uniform, abroad and at home. Because of you and people like you, books like this can be written and enjoyed. Thank you for your service.

And to my girlfriend and my Mom, the two most important women in my life. You both believed in me and encouraged me when I would have doubted myself.

Acknowledgements:

New entries in italics.

No author ever writes entirely alone, or at least this one doesn't. While I was *first* working on Page of Swords, I found myself saying things I never imagined I would before, usually phrases that included the words "my second book". But most often, I found myself saying "Thank you".

To the True Believers who read through the early copies and caught the little things I missed, many thanks. Especially to Todd and Kat, who saw things in my characters that went deeper than I expected, but were still true.

For Laura Davis, my most excellent editor, who made sure things ended up being more than alright, and for her daughter who helped me create Dani and get her right.

Greg Price, thank you for giving me Steve Donovan to work with.

Last, but by no means least, thank you to my publisher, Peter Paddon for having faith in a first time writer, and thinking my writing compares favorably to the Dresden Files. *May your journey to the Summerlands be easy, Peter and may your next life be a good one.*

Thanks to Angela Gulick for another awesome cover, and to Machine Fairy and Siroj Steems for the model photo used. Also, thanks to Amanda Ables, my newest beta reader and reality checker.

And as always, my eternal gratitude to the readers who make The Demon's Apprentice series successful.

Chapter 1

~ Love is the enemy of reason and the death of discipline. All that does not serve is swept aside in its heedless path. For good cause do the elders curse it. Oh, how we need it! ~

Henriette de Bernardis, 18th c. wizard

By eight on Friday night, my weekend was already dying an ugly death. My favorite moping place, the back booth at Dante's, gave me a great view of the dance floor and the stage. It was perfect for those nights when I showed up to Dante's without Shade. For the fourth week in a row. Suicidal Jester seemed to hover over the crowd as they played one of their own songs, "Maddened Heart," and Mike Destine was moaning the lyrics into the microphone:

Where are you now? In the middle of the dark,

In my mind's fevered eye, I see you laid down,

In grace pale and stark. My maddened heart watches over you,

And you can't know, you don't know to care, but I don't care!

His voice rose to a scream on the last word, and the lead guitar matched him as it launched into a solo. In the crowd, I could see a familiar mane of flame red hair as I found Shade. She had her arms up in the air as her hips writhed like snakes, dancing with her eyes closed to a rhythm it seemed like only she could hear. Shiny black boots flowed up over her knees and clung to her thighs, leaving a few inches of pale white skin showing before a painted-on black leather miniskirt wrapped itself tight around her hips. The top of her skirt disappeared under a black satin corset that was laced up the back; the only color in the outfit came from criss-crossing lines of blood red ribbon cinching her into it. Even though she was dancing by herself, I knew she hadn't come alone, and that twisted the knife in my weekend a little more.

"Dude!" Lucas yelled from across the table. I could barely hear him over the music. "Maybe she brought him here for some kind of Pack business or something!"

He'd taken off his denim trenchcoat, showing off his black t-shirt that read, "I have epiphanies." Strands of black hair brushed his eyebrows and the tops of his new glasses, narrow-lensed with half rims. He'd gotten titanium frames and high impact lenses after his old pair had been broken for the second time around Yule.

Beside him, Wanda was in a red top with black hearts all over it, wearing a red choker trimmed in black lace and red lace fingerless gloves that hugged her elbows. Her new pentacle, a silver star flanked by crescent moons, rode over her shirt. Her mom had given it to her when she'd started her year-and-a-day training as a Wiccan dedicant, and it never came off, no matter how much crap she caught about it at school. Below the table, she had on a red and black plaid skirt and red lace stockings that matched the gloves. One of her heavy wedge-heeled boots was on the seat beside me, black with red flames coming up off the soles.

"What kind of *business* is she doing in a *mini-skirt?"* I yelled back.

"But Chance, she's so into you!" Wanda said.

She tried to give me a reassuring smile as she brushed a few bright red strands of hair away from her cheek. The red framed her faltering smile and the rest of her hair, a black line that ran just below her ears, swung as she nodded. Always the optimist, Wanda never thought Shade would date anyone else.

But my thoughts always went back to the last kiss Shade and I had shared at Imbolc last month. One of the problems with trying to date a werewolf is the danger of having your face eaten while you're making out, and that had come damn close to happening when we'd tried to move past kissing. But the memory of just kissing Shade made my lips tingle, and reminded me of what I couldn't have. She'd told me after that she needed an alpha. Something I wasn't, and short of a werewolf bite, I never would be.

"She's here with another guy, and she's dressed to thrill. I'm pretty damn sure she's not here on business, and it looks like she really not that into me. So stop trying to cheer me up, okay? Besides, it's better this way." I said the last quietly.

I tried to want her to be happy, but it hurt like all the Nine Hells just to see her. I wanted her to be happy with *me*, but that didn't seem like it could happen. So, I figured the best thing to do was avoid her. Made it easier to keep my hands to myself that way. And, it made it easier for her to find what she needed.

"Yeah," I lied to myself a little more. "It's better this way." It was Friday . . . yay. I tried to let the music wash over me and forget everything else for a little while.

"Are you the guy who does magick?" a girl asked as I was losing myself in the music. She'd almost had to yell to make herself heard over the pulsing beat of the band.

I tried not to grimace and looked down from the stage show to look her over. She was kinda pretty, I guessed, but I could only see the right side of her face. The left side was covered with a curtain of brown hair streaked with black. Half of an oval face peered at me, the one visible brown eye giving me the same once over I was giving her. I figured she was fifteen, the same age as me, maybe sixteen, probably a sophomore. A faded peace symbol was stretched across the front of her dark blue t-shirt, tight enough that I could see she had at least one piercing her parents weren't supposed to know about. Her dark gray hoodie hid most of the other side, so I couldn't tell if she had a matched set or not. A pair of tight black jeans rode low on her hips. All this girl lacked to make her a complete Emo chick was the dark eye make up. Her black-tipped fingernails tapped against the tab of her hoodie's zipper as she waited for me to answer.

"What?" I yelled back.

I gave Lucas and Wanda a quick glance across the table in our booth, and caught a nod from Lucas. He seemed to know the girl.

"You're Chance Fortunato, right?" she leaned forward. "You're the guy who does magick!"

The song ended just as she yelled it out, and people around us turned and stared at her while the rest of the crowd cheered. I gave her a glare as Dante's filled with sound. The girl pulled an empty chair up to the end of the table and sat down.

“Do I have a sign over my head that says 'I do magic tricks!' or something?” I asked as the band picked up with cover of Linkin Park's *Shadow of the Day*.

Nobody covered Linkin Park like Jester, and it was one of my favorite songs, which just pissed me off even more. More than the fact that she was right. I did know magick. Lots of it was black sorcery, but I was learning some new stuff. Her being right didn’t piss me off as much as the fact that she was yelling it out in public. I wasn't exactly on the Conclave's good side these days. They didn't care why I’d worked for a demon, just that I had. My demon master had called me his apprentice; I called me his slave. Guess who the guys in white robes believed? Go figure.

“My friend Robbie told me you broke a love spell some psycho bitch cast on him a couple of months ago. You gotta help me out.”

Her story fit, the name was right, and the time was pretty close. I leaned back in the seat and crossed my arms so I could favor her with a glare that should have peeled a couple of layers of skin off her face. As she matched my look, I remembered Dr. Corwyn telling me after the fact that I shouldn't have told the guy I'd broken the spell. It sucked when he was right, especially since that was most of the damned time. My weekend wasn't going to end well.

“And?”

“I need your help. I think . . . someone put a spell on my girlfriend.”

I closed my eyes in exasperation. I was actively trying to *avoid* being noticed. I should have told her no. I should have lied and told her anything but the truth, and part of me *really* wanted to.

Instead, I asked her, “What's your name?”

“Danielle.” The word fell off her tongue like she was spitting it out, just a little too familiar but a little too formal, too. Like it was a name she only used sometimes.

“What's *your* name?” I asked again. “The one your friends call you.”

She took a quick little breath and her mouth closed up tight for a second before she answered. It told me a lot about her. Most kids my age believed in a lot of urban myths. Only not all of them were myths. Danielle probably believed that giving me her name gave me power over her. That one was partly true. Giving me her personal name, the one that she used in her own head, was very potent, and she seemed to know that. Little alarm bells started going off in the back of my head.

“Dani,” she said softly.

“Dani,” I repeated as she hunched across the table from me.

The way she said it had a masculine ring to it. And she had mentioned 'her' girlfriend like a guy might, a little possessive. Yeah, this was who she was.

“Okay, what's up?”

“Crystal, that's my girlfriend, didn't come to school today. We were pretty serious and all until last weekend. After the Love In Chains concert, she got all moody and weird. Said I was going to leave her. She didn't talk to me at all on Wednesday, and by yesterday, she'd ditched the rest of our friends, too.” She stopped and put her hands on the table for a minute, looking at them like they were someone else's. “She wouldn't let me touch her.”

“And all of this adds up to 'someone put a spell on my girlfriend' how?”

“I felt it.”

“You . . . felt it.”

“Sometimes, I just know things. Crystal just . . . *felt* wrong. Like it wasn't really *her* anymore. I think that asshole Julian cast some kind of spell on her.”

"And you want me to break it for you," I told her.

Her face brightened a little, even though I hadn't said yes, and she dug into her pocket as she started to talk again. "I've got some money. I can pay you fifty bucks, maybe a little more, but that's all I got."

Old reflexes kicked in at her offer, but I stepped on them hard. I wasn't pimping souls for a demon any more, and I wasn't going to turn a quick buck on another kid's problems. I put my first two fingers up in a gesture I copied from Dr. C. She clammed up and went still.

"I can't take your money. I can't really do anything unless I can actually see your girlfriend face to face. And I'm not a detective. If you don't know where she is, I can't help you." Everything I had said was true, but I still felt like an ass when I said it.

"Please, you *have* to help me!" Dani said as she leaned forward. "I know how to find Julian! Could you break the spell if you could see *him*?"

Her hand snaked forward and gripped my forearm. There was a flash of contact, even through the sleeve of my sweatshirt, and suddenly I was pretty damn *sure* I'd find Crystal where I found Julian. Other images piled on top of each other, too fast to make out all at once, but the sight of Crystal's face was the one that seared itself across my memory.

We recoiled at the same time and stared at each other. I was pretty sure I had felt what she was feeling, but there was also a part of that flash that wasn't her at all. She blinked a few times, and her face went a little green. My aura wasn't very wholesome, and if she'd seen as much of me as I'd seen of her, she'd definitely gotten the worse end of things.

I closed my eyes and took a breath, then let it out slowly. There is a moment after you open your eyes before they refocus. I could hold that moment and let my Third Eye see the world. I hated doing it in a crowd, but I had to know what it was that had attached itself to Dani. Her aura was bright pink with innocence at its core, but there were stains on it, dark places from her past that were still screwing her up. I could see the energies of the crowd coloring her aura at the edges, a sure sign of a naturally empathic person. It didn't go deep, though, mostly playing along the surface and sliding off like water on oil. I figured she'd learned to shield herself somehow. It was that or go nuts, for most empaths. But as strong as her defenses seemed, something had stuck to her aura.

A pale, powdery green smear ran across her chest, right over her heart. It explained a lot. I let my senses refocus on the physical world again and shook my head. All of that had only taken a few seconds, but like most of the times I used my mystic senses, it felt like I'd been at it a lot longer.

“Chance, are you okay?” Wanda asked me from across the table.

Lucas was sliding out of the booth toward Dani, who was swaying in her seat. My boot caught his leg before he cleared the edge of the seat.

“I'm okay, and don't. Touching her'll only make it worse.” I slid to the edge of the booth and waited for her to steady herself.

“Holy crap. You're really screwed up,” she said after a moment.

“Yeah, I get that a lot. It's hard for your friends to lie to you, isn't it?”

“How did you . . .”

The thing about having a reputation for doing magick is that people assume you have this whole list of powers you really don't. I could see her mind working through the usual assumptions, thinking I could read her mind, or that I just *knew* stuff. Totally bogus, but it saved time.

“You're an empath. I'm . . . something else. Look, where can I find this guy Julian?”

“He's usually on the Square. Are you gonna break the spell?”

“I'll do what I can, Dani, but no promises. Can you come with us and point him out?”

“Yeah,” she said with a cold smile.

“All right. Meet us outside.”

She got to her feet and leaned forward for a moment like she wanted to hug me or something, then she turned and headed off into the crowd.

“Dude, why did you do that?” Lucas asked. “She probably screwed around on her girlfriend or something and she wants you to make her fall in love with her again.”

“No, there's something there, guys.”

“There is?” Wanda asked. “She felt weird, but not, like, wrong. Like she was sick or something.”

“Yeah, she had something on her aura, a trace she picked up from a spell on someone she loves.”

“Then you *really* need to back off, man! Dr. C told you not to do any magick outside the sanctum, remember? Take it to him or something.”

“I'm just going to go take a look, Lucas, I promise. I don't want the Conclave's wizard cops on my ass, either. If it's something, then we tell Dr. C, deal?”

“You better, man, or your ass is walking all the way home,” he said as he slid out of his seat. For all his grousing, he still had his car keys out.

We were halfway to the door when I stopped in my tracks and felt my heart just sort of go hollow.

Shade was dancing with a guy. Not just dancing out on the floor. Jester's female lead, Sindy Sinn, was moaning the lyrics to an old Madonna song, *Crazy For You,* and Shade had her arms around about six feet of tall, dark, and, I figured, handsome. Her body pressed against his the way I wanted her pressed up to mine. The whole night turned to crap in front of me as she looked up at me and smiled. I wanted that smile to be for me. Not at seeing my heart breaking. I turned away before she could see me die any more inside and headed for the door. I really, *really* wanted Julian to be as bad as Dani made him sound. I needed to hurt someone tonight.

Chapter 2

~ There's always a bigger fish. ~ Qui-Gon Jinn, Jedi Master

Lucas' car was a beat up Honda Civic that had to have been made sometime before they put the patent on dirt. He'd named it the *Millenium Falcon*, and it looked the part. It was his pride and joy, and he'd put a lot of work into it on weekends and the odd afternoon. It was faster than it looked, and it almost never seemed to break down. That was good enough for me.

We pulled up near the Square and gave up on finding a parking place anywhere close by. We settled for a spot near the top of one of the newer parking garages next to the Hollywood Theaters, and rode the cramped elevator down to ground level.

The Square was about five minutes away, but the Friday night hustle added another fifteen minutes to the trip. Dani hunched in on herself, trying not to touch anyone as we went. With Lucas and me in front, and Wanda at her side, she did okay. We stopped as we came up on the west side, next to the old Sears Building, and I took a quick look around. On the street level, everything looked pretty much normal. A handful of smaller *fae* drifted in and out of the clustered groups, pixies, sprites and faeries working the crowd. Their normal *glamoury* kept them from being noticed by the people around them as they swooped around their heads. The Goths were grouped around one of the concrete benches that lined the edge of the Square itself, with the Emos on the opposite side. Closest to us, I saw the cluster of homeless men, with their backpacks and duffel bags beside them, bundled in old army jackets or faded windbreakers.

The Square itself was less crowded than the sidewalks around it. The weekend partiers, mostly college students and hipsters, filled the restaurants and bars that lined the open space and, even from the edge, I could see heads turning away from the middle of the Square. Most of them were a little sluggish, a little clumsy, and more than a little drunk. As I scanned the crowd for some sign of Julian, a white stretch limo rounded the corner and started around the Square. A girl in a blue dress popped out of the sunroof and screamed, "Loooosers!" at no one in particular. She ducked back into the limo pretty quickly when someone threw a beer bottle at her.

“Gotta love it,” Lucas remarked, as I shook my head. “Hundreds of people on the quest for the perfect hangover.”

“You mean the one that includes a strange person in your bed the next morning?” Wanda asked dryly.

“That'd be the one. So, where do we start, Chance?”

“I don’t know what he looks like. I'd have to look for his aura . . . and I *really* don't want to do that here.”

“He’s usually at the coffee shop,” Dani said.

She pointed off to my right, at a small shop with a sign over the door that read 'The Mocha Method.’ It was busy, like any business downtown on a Friday night, but it was also the only place that was full of high school kids. It was the kind of place where I would have done business a few months ago.

“Not a bad thought,” I said as I pulled my backpack off my shoulder and unzipped it. “Wait here, we'll be back in a few minutes.”

“Dude, you said you weren't gonna do anything,” Lucas moaned.

“And I'm probably not.” Inside the heavy nylon pack was my working gear. The telekinesis wand I'd made last year while I was trying to find Mr. Chomsky's killer. My new leather-bound journal, a Yule gift from Lucas, and an Ariakon paintball gun of my own. Dr. C gave it to me at Yule because he was pretty sure that was the only way he'd get his own back from me. For what we were doing tonight, the TK wand was all I could get away with, and most likely (hopefully), I wouldn't even need that. I tucked it in my jacket pocket, re-slung the pack, pulled out a cinnamon Firebomb and popped it in my mouth.

“If the Conclave catches you though . . .”

“I'll be more dead than if some half trained warlock catches me with my pants down?” I asked. The cinnamon was starting a pleasant burn on my tongue as I turned and headed toward the Mocha Method. I couldn't hear Lucas and Wanda behind me, but I knew they were only a couple of steps back. Lucas' hand fell on my shoulder as I reached the door.

"Be careful, okay?" The worry was plain on his face, and Wanda wasn't looking too happy about it either.

"You've got my back, man. I can't be much safer than that. Save it for the other guy."

Before he could say anything else, I pulled the door open and stepped into the shop. The first thing that hit me was the smell of coffee, and then I caught the wave of sound. A dozen different conversations, all going on at once, hit me like a wall after the intermittent sounds from outside. The barista counter took up half the wall to my left, and a row of tables lined the wall all the way down the right side. A couple of small tables sat in the front half of the place, and I could see a few tables in the back, too. That was where I would be if I wanted to be all dark and mysterious. The people in the front tables looked dark enough, but it was mostly a social thing. Half of them looked like Goths, the other half just wore black trenchcoats and tried to look more depressed than everyone else. But none of them had the feel of serious Darkness to them. I felt my mouth turn up in a pleased grin at that.

The back of the shop beckoned. If Julian was here, I was betting he'd be in the middle of the knot of dark clothes and spiked hair I saw around one of the tables in the back. Most of the audience were girls, with enough black on to suck half the light out of the room. As I made it to the edge of the little crowd, my skin started to tingle, and a familiar pressure began to build between my eyes. Dark magick.

Normally, I would have hated being right. But tonight, I was spoiling for a fight.

I earned a couple of dark looks and a few remarks about my character from the girls around the table as I pushed in closer. Those, I could handle. The sight of what was happening at the table was what made my stomach turn.

The guy sitting at the table wore a white t-shirt with a red goat's head in a pentagram plastered on it, and a blood red beret perched over a mop of greasy black hair. He had a round, almost baby-faced look, but there was a coldness to his eyes that made me want to reach across the table and hit him. He was shuffling a deck of black-backed tarot cards, and playing the girl sitting across from him.

"I must tune the cards to your energy, first. Give me your hand," he said as he laid the cards down on the table and put his hand out to the girl, a tiny blond in an off white lace and satin dress.

She reached out and put one lace-gloved hand in his and looked at him with wide, trusting blue eyes.

"Concentrate on your question to the twilit forces, and we will show you the truth. I must warn you . . . it may not be what you want to hear. Do you have the courage to continue?"

I had to hand it to him; he was good. The odd word choices gave his act an air of the exotic, and by 'allying' himself with an outside force, he was taking any blame off himself if the reading didn't give the results his mark expected.

She hesitated for a moment before she gave him a jerky nod.

"I want to know if—" she started to say, but he put his other hand up and shushed her.

"Do not speak your question until I have given you the answers you seek."

Legit readers did the same thing, only they were trying not to load their readings with advance information. If he was using dark magick, it wasn't a question of *if* he was conning her, it just was a question of *how*. In fact, I would have bet every dollar my father had ever stolen that the he'd pulled same bit with Crystal.

I closed my eyes, concentrated for a second, and opened my defenses just enough to allow my aura-sight to fall into place. When I opened my eyes again, I could see the auras around the table, mostly purples and blues in this crowd. Across from me, I could see Wanda's aura, a bright, vibrant yellow that looked like sunlight through leaves. I gave her a smile and turned my attention on the wanna-be warlock.

Julian's aura was murky, not as bright as the rest of the auras I could see, with narrow bands of dark green and red in running through it. He had a lot of envy and anger going through him. Aside from being a little faded, he was pretty much a normal guy, except for the thin, glowing tendril of pale green that drifted from his tarot deck and flowed up to the middle of his forehead. Another tendril ran up the girl's arm and wrapped itself around her neck, flowing up until it plunged into her left temple. Her aura practically screamed of despair, tinged with a pastel shade that I had named 'suicide blue' after seeing it on the walls during one of my first trips to Twisted Oaks Asylum.

A pulse ran along the energy strand connecting them, and Julian reached for the deck. My eyes went to it, and I saw the image of a tarot card face floating above it. The card was the four of Swords, showing a man resting on a sarcophagus and holding a sword by the handle, with the point laying at his feet. On most decks, there would be three other swords hanging sideways above him. This one showed them with the points hidden behind the man's body. It didn't really show that they were stabbing the man on the sarcophagus, but a depressed girl would see what she wanted to see, or, more accurately, what she expected to see.

I shuddered as I recognized the design. Julian was using an enchanted Despair Deck.

"The Four of Swords," he said before he turned the card over.

There was a gasp from the crowd as he turned the card face up.

"You are seeking some sort of . . . respite: a reprieve from a painful situation."

The girl's face fell as she heard her troubles suddenly spoken aloud, as Julian gave her a direction for her thoughts to move in. She might not have been on the verge of suicide before, but the deck's magick probably just made her believe she was. The next card was the Tower, a card of uneasy changes. Despair Decks didn't have to change it much to give the worst possible interpretation.

The tendril of energy pulsed again, and I saw Julian's aura glow a little brighter while the girl's dimmed in response.

"Your life has become turbulent, there are . . . changes? No, not changes . . . a disturbance: turmoil. Your world has been uprooted."

Tears were streaming down the girl's face now. I'd seen enough. I wasn't going to let him prey on her any longer. It only took me a couple of steps to shove my way to her side, and a quick glance at her purse told me her name: she had it written with another name all over a small journal. She flinched when I touched her shoulder and squatted down beside her, but her eyes were on mine, and I wasn't letting go.

"Listen to me, Giselle," I pitched my voice soft, so she had to concentrate on what I was saying over the crowd. "He's a fake. I'll prove it."

"Hey, you're disturbing the energies of the aether!" Julian said angrily. "Your negative energy is making things worse for her, asshole."

"The next card is the Chariot." This time, I was louder.

Giselle's eyes went wide as I reached for the deck with my right hand, and Julian grabbed my wrist. The tingle of minor talent coursed along my skin. Our eyes locked as I reached into my jacket pocket for the TK wand.

"*Verto*," I whispered as twisted my wrist in his grip.

One of the things Dr. C had been teaching me over the past few months was how to fine-tune my control over a single spell. The new trigger word made the wand send a tiny surge of telekinetic energy rolling across the table instead of a destructive blast.

Everyone, including Julian, was looking at my right hand as I twisted my wrist and pointed my index and middle fingers at the deck. All eyes followed my gesture, as the TK wave touched the deck and flipped the top card over, revealing a man in a chariot with two black horses galloping full tilt with the reins flying across their backs.

"Back off, asshole," Julian hissed at me.

I stood up, and Julian came up with me. His grip slipped off my wrist when I yanked my arm away.

"You do *not* want to end up on my bad side," he threatened.

"The cards are marked," I said, ignoring him. A low mutter drifted from the crowd. "The next card is the ten of Swords." This time, Julian kept his hands to himself, and I flipped the top card without any resistance from him. As the card slid across the table, I laid my hand down over the rest of the deck. The mutter turned into a rumble of disbelief, and the crowd started to break up. Julian's tricks weren't so cool now that they knew they were being tricked. I turned to Giselle; it was time to undo some of the damage he'd done.

"It's a card of betrayal. But any idiot can look at you and see you've just had your heart ripped out and stomped on. You wouldn't have found any answers here. Just Julian leading you on, telling you there was a curse on you or bad karma from a previous life or some other bullshit, and how only he could understand and help you. You want hope, all you gotta do is go look in a mirror. There are plenty of guys here who'd love to get to know you better . . . and help you forget about Chris."

"How did you know my name? And about Chris?" Giselle asked.

When in doubt, be cryptic, I could almost hear Dr. C saying in my ear while I matched Julian's glare with one of my own.

"I have my ways," I told her. "Now, if you'll excuse me, I need to deal with this charlatan."

She backed away with wide eyes, and I fought to keep a straight face. There was no telling what explanation she would come up with by tomorrow morning, but for now, Lucas was at her side, getting her out of the shop through a side door. We exchanged a nod as they headed for the door, and he held up his keys to tell me where they'd be waiting.

"Get your hands off my deck, asshole," Julian spat, "or you've got a mage war on your hands." The deck's enchantment was trying to work its way into my head, but my defenses were holding it off for the moment.

"What were you planning on fighting it with? This?" I held the deck up and grabbed the enchantment poking at my aura with a thought.

"*Tribuo suus viris ut meas,* "I uttered, and Julian gasped as I broke his control over the deck.

"Next card is the Page of Swords," I told him and flipped the Page face up.

He stared at me in disbelief as I held the card up for a second, then slipped it into my back pocket. Vague memories of the Page of Swords card and a moonlit room tugged at the back of my thoughts, but I pushed them aside for the moment.

"What are you doing?"

"If you think you're mage enough to take this from me, you can have control of your deck back."

I tossed the rest of the deck down on the table and headed for the front door. Even the last lingering touch of the deck made me want to wash my hands as I left. I pushed the glass door open and stepped into the cooler outside air.

The group that had been lurking around Julian was watching the door from the Goth benches, and the group of Emos were wandering across the open concrete plaza for a better look as I walked toward Dani. She fell in step beside me.

"So?" she demanded.

"I hate to admit it, but you were right," I said. "He probably did cast a spell on Crystal."

"But . . . but . . . did you break it?"

"No."

"Why not?"

"Not that easy."

"But you're going to, right?"

"You'll see."

"What are you gonna do now?"

"Is he following us?"

This cryptic thing didn't always work as well for me as it did for Dr. C. Hell, it didn't always work for him, either. Now I understood why he got the look on his face he sometimes did.

Dani looked over her shoulder, then turned back quickly. "Yeah. What now?"

"Now we find a quiet place to wait for him."

"Then what?"

"I'm gonna kick his ass a little. He'll whine a lot. I'll kick his ass a little more, and then he'll tell me where your girl is. It'll be fun."

We headed into a dark alley between two buildings and found ourselves out on St. Louis Street. A quick left turn took us to where I wanted to be: the opening of another alley, right behind the parking garage the *Falcon* was in.

Seconds later, I caught sight of Julian peeking around the corner, and I made little bit of a show of looking around like I was looking for a place to hide. As I ducked into the alley, I felt a touch on my arm, and I nearly ran into the wall as a flood of feelings and images ran roughshod over my thoughts.

Dani staggered a few steps away from me, her own face screwed into a pained grimace.

"Sorry," she said. Obviously a well-practiced phrase for her.

"Damn, don't do that!" I muttered before I could think about it.

"Your mind's no freaking picnic, either."

"Yeah, well. Come on. He's right behind us."

A dark alcove loomed on our right, and I pointed her at it. We squeezed into it without touching and waited. Julian didn't disappoint. Only a couple of minutes passed before he came stomping down the alley, muttering to himself. I waited until he had passed us before I stepped out behind him with my fingers laced together and hammered him in the back of the head. He staggered and fell to his hands and knees, and I was on him before he knew what was happening. My hands were bunched in his belt and jacket before he could do more than shake his head, and I bounced his face off the side of a dumpster. He slumped to the ground and tried to get his arms and legs back under control.

"Now that was disappointing," I said with my best I'm-about-to-eat-you grin.

It took a little work to get him turned over and on his feet, but I got him up. His eyes struggled to focus on me, and he reached for my hands. I pushed him against the wall next to my hiding place, but he still struggled, so I bounced the back of his head off the bricks a couple of times, then a couple more times because it felt good.

"Chance, stop," Dani said softly. "You're hurting him!"

"Kinda the point. Omelet, eggs, you know the drill. So, Julian, that funky little deck of cards you have . . . where did you get it?"

"Bought it off the Internet, man," he said as his eyes focused on me.

I didn't need to use my mystic senses to know he was lying. His head made a satisfying thumping sound as I slammed his shoulders into the wall again.

"You know, you should lie to me more often. I kinda like this part. Now, let's try it again, with the truth this time."

"I got it from a guy on eBay!" he said. I struggled not to play handball with his skull some more.

"Don't lie to me!" I yelled. I punched him in the ribs to make my point, then slammed him against the wall. "Those decks can't just be sent by mail! Someone has to give you control over it. You both have to *be there!* Who did you get it from?" I demanded again, this time almost yelling in his face.

"It's none of your damn business, man! It's my deck!"

"It's my business when you pimp souls for a fucking demon!" I drew back and slapped him hard. He hit the wall and slid down a little ways before I caught him. I hauled him up and slammed him against the wall again to make sure I had his attention.

"He would have left a mark on you, laid his hands on you somewhere. He marked you as his bitch, dumbass!"

I pulled the front of his shirt up. His chest and belly were clean, no demon marks. I pulled him away from the wall and turned him around, then pushed him hard against the wall again. There was a rush of air as I knocked some of the wind out of him and pulled his shirt up over his shoulders.

His back was clean, too.

Where was the mark? A demon's mark would have to be somewhere he could have touched easily, and if he didn't know it was there, it had to be on his back. Demons didn't give gifts. They made deals, and they always came out ahead.

"Where's your mark!" I demanded. I grabbed his right arm and turned it, looking along the inside.

"Demon? What mark?" Julian asked. "What are you talking about, man?"

He was afraid, maybe too afraid to be lying.

My hands were shaking as I turned him back to face me again.

"Ask him about Crystal!" Dani interrupted. She stepped up beside me and put her face close to Julian's. "Where is she, you son of a bitch?!"

"Who?"

"Her girlfriend, dumbass. Girl named Crystal."

"I don't know what you're—"

The rest of it was lost as the world went sideways for a second. When things stopped jumping around in front of my eyes, I was on my back about ten yards away from Julian, and there was a familiar ache along my left side, the kind of pain that came with a broken rib.

Another guy stood between me and him, looking over his shoulder and pointing at the mouth of the alley.

"Run!" the new guy said. "I'll take care of this scumbag."

With the light behind him, I couldn't make out his face, and his hair fell down far enough to cover up any details I could have gotten from his profile. He looked big, and the arm that he had stretched out behind him was pretty thick. It was the baseball bat in his other hand that really got my attention, though.

Julian didn't need to be told twice. I saw elbows and assholes as he sprinted for the street.

Dani screeched, "NO!" and took off after him as he ran.

The new guy turned back toward me, and I could almost feel the hate coming off of him.

"I was hoping I'd find you again," he growled as he hefted the bat.

I scrambled to my feet and took a step back as he closed on me. "Do I know you?"

"No, but I know you." He took a quick step forward and swung the bat at my head.

One knee hit the ground as I ducked under the swing, then I leaned back and swept his legs out from under him as he staggered into the follow-through. There was a clatter as the bat hit the pavement, and a meaty thud as he followed it down. I grabbed the bat as I got back up and backed away. Guilt turned my arms to lead, and I knew I couldn't hit this guy. Not if he had a legitimate beef with me from my past. And there were too many people who could say that.

"Look, if I did something to you before, I'm really sorry. I didn't have a lot of choice, okay?" If I was hoping to calm him down, he wasn't buying. He put his hands back behind his head, drew his feet to his chest and sprang to his feet.

"Not to me, scumbag." He came at me again.

This time, he was a little more cautious, fists up, on the balls of his feet, his eyes on the center of my chest. The first punch came from somewhere west of Seattle, and it was too easy to duck under. The uppercut that followed it, though, caught me square in the chest. When I could breathe again, he was standing over me, and he had that damned bat again.

"Wait, please," I managed to gasp out.

"I'll give you just as much mercy as you showed Riker," he said.

My left hand dove into my jacket pocket as he drew the bat back for a swing. Riker McKane had deserved what I'd given him, which was nothing worse than a couple of sprained wrists. There was no way I was taking a beating over him, especially since I'd actually done him a favor by stripping him of the charms I'd put on him in the first place. The leather-covered barrel of my TK wand slipped into my hand as the bat started to come down, and I tried another one of the new spell triggers.

I croaked out, *"Obex!"*

A barrier of force sprang up a split second before the bat broke against it, and collapsed as the impact came in the moment before it stabilized. With no spell to fuel, the magick suddenly had no place else to go but backwards, and my vision went white as I took the feedback of the failed casting. It went red as I took the boot to the ribs, then I felt myself bounce off a wall.

I'd heard that when people were having near-death experiences, they saw things. White lights, dead family members, angels. Some people thought they were hallucinating, some thought they were seeing the spirit world. The second group was right. The mind lowers certain defenses when it's in shock, and the Third Eye opens up. Maybe it's a survival thing, maybe it's just a lack of oxygen. All I knew was that I heard the clang of a bell, and this time, I saw a bright line of white light in front of me. Then I saw the darker image of a person's aura behind it, and I held the wand out in front of me and groaned, "*Ictus*!"

The dull ache behind my eyes turned into a needle of fire as my vision went white again, and the memory of the bell was replaced by a hollow ringing in my ears.

Chapter 3

~ To survive a fight, come well-armed and bring friends. ~
Lazarus Moon, Master Mage

The first thing I was aware of was the sound of my name being called. My vision was still one big blur of white, but I could hear something over the static sound in my ears now.

"Lucas!" My voice was still weak, and talking felt like someone had put my head under a jackhammer. Raising my arm felt like picking up a bus. It hit the pavement after a few seconds, and all I could do was lay there.

"Dude, what's with your eyes?" Lucas asked from beside me.

I felt his hands on my shoulders, and suddenly, reluctantly, I was sitting up. That lasted for all of two seconds, then I felt myself slumping forward.

"What about my eyes?" I asked as Lucas propped me back up.

"Dude, they're glowing! You're like a damn puppet with the strings cut! What the hell happened to you?"

"Spell backlash . . . and I got the crap beat out of me."

"You all right?"

"Just broke a rib is all."

"Only you, man. 'Just broke a rib.' We better get you to Dr. C's place." I felt hands plucking something off of me. "You've got splinters and wood chips all over you."

"Baseball bat . . . Lucas, there was another guy!" I blurted out. The surge of adrenaline helped me move my arms, and I turned toward the last direction I knew he'd been.

"Still is." The slugger's voice came from my left. "Get away from him, kid. He's . . . dangerous."

"You don't sound so sure there, asshole," Lucas quipped. I felt his hand on my backpack as he spoke.

“I can feel evil, and I could feel it coming off your friend in spades earlier.” Bottles and cans clattered on the ground while Lucas pulled my pack open.

“It wasn't me you were feeling,” I said.

“Your actions told me something different.”

“You don't know Chance, dickhead. He's not evil.”

“He's more likely possessed. Or he's got you fooled. Do you remember anything about the last ten minutes, Chance?” Slugger asked. Lucas' hand moved around slowly in my pack for a few moments, then I felt him grab something. I was guessing he had the Ariakon.

“More than you'd like. Who in the Nine Hells are *you*?”

“My name is Steve. Steve Donovan. Look, I can't feel anything off of you now, but I did earlier.”

“That was Julian, dumbass,” Lucas scoffed. “He's gone: no more evil. Get it?”

“But he was . . . he attacked him!” Steve's voice sounded closer, and I could hear the scrape of his shoes on the pavement.

“And you attacked Chance. That makes you just as 'evil' as my friend here. Now, stop right there.”

My pack got lighter as I felt Lucas stand up.

“Look, there's no need for violence here. Put the gun down and we'll figure this out,” Steve said slowly. Never mind that he’d been ready to cave my head in a few seconds before. He sounded like a cop in a movie to me, trying to take control of the situation by sounding calm and reasonable.

“You need to know anything else from this guy, Chance?” Lucas asked.

“Tomorrow's lottery numbers?” I said quietly.

Lucas chuckled, and I heard Steve's boots on the pavement. The Ariakon coughed twice, and I heard two splats.

"What the—" Steve said. "That's just a paintball . . . gun . . ." he got out before I heard him hit the ground.

The next thing I knew, Lucas had his arms under mine. He struggled to get me to my feet, in spite of my attempts to help.

"Come on, let's get you out of here," he said.

"You didn't have to knock him out, ya know."

"Yeah I did. He wouldn't have just let us go. Besides . . . it just felt good."

"Seriously though, I owe you one."

"No, you don't. Now, shut up and move."

My feet started doing what they were supposed to after a few steps, and I started seeing colors other than white. By the time we made it to the elevator, I could start to make out shapes and I was grateful that the damage I'd done wasn't permanent. The last thing I needed was to go blind from a failed spell. The elevator dinged open, and we stumbled out. If I squinted, I could make things a little less blurry, but it made my headache worse, so I gave that up as a bad plan.

"Lucas!" Wanda's voice came from behind us as we made it to the end of a row.

I could see a blur that was about the right shape and color for the *Falcon* ahead of me, but Lucas turned to look back the way we had come from. I saw two people-shaped blurs headed in our direction, one wearing the same shade of red as Wanda's outfit, and another dark blue blur that looked the same color as Dani's clothes.

"Is he okay?" Wanda asked as they got closer. "Great Mother! What's with his eyes?"

"Yeah, mostly. Just a couple of busted ribs and some spell backlash."

"You guys call that okay? 'Just' a couple of broken ribs?" Dani's voice trembled on the edge of hysteria.

"Chance's seen a lot worse than that before," Wanda said with a hint of pride in her voice. "Come on, let's get him to the car."

"But what about Julian? We have to break the spell! I need to find her!"

"Listen, sister," Wanda snapped. "Chance got his ribs busted up looking for your girl. Look at him. Even if he knew where she was, he's in no shape to do a DAMN thing!" Her voice rose to a yell at the end. It bounced around inside my head like a ball bearing in a tin can. I moaned and waved my free hand at her to shush her.

"He'll find her," Lucas added. He hustled me along a few more steps. "And he'll break the spell. But. Not. Tonight."

"He's lucky he's got such good friends," Dani said. I barely heard her. For all the response she got from Lucas and Wanda, they might as well not have heard her at all.

"Yeah, I am."

"Don't talk, dude. We're here."

An off-white blur moved inside the car. I heard the sound of a door unlocking. Lucas lowered me gently into the passenger seat of the *Falcon* and laid the seat almost all the way back.

"Is he all right?" Giselle's voice skidded across my eardrums.

"He'll live," Lucas told her. "We need to get him to some help, though. You gonna be okay?"

"Yeah. I came with some friends, I'll catch a ride home with them. Thank you for showing me . . . what Julian was."

"Hey, no prob. That was mostly Chance."

Lace hissed against satin on my right. A gentle, vanilla-scented hand touched my cheek.

"Thank you," Giselle whispered in my ear.

Soft lips caressed my cheek, then she was gone.

Chapter 4

~ Things can ALWAYS get worse. ~

Common proverb among magi.

After that, things were a little fuzzy. I was aware of Wanda's face hovering over mine, and her hands on my face, warm through her gloves. Light pulsed against my eyelids. People around me talked quietly. One of the *Falcon's* doors opened and closed. Then, there was just the pattern of light and darkness, Wanda's touch, and her voice calling on her Goddess. My eyes snapped open when the car stopped. Wanda's concerned face was still there.

"Chance, we're here," she said.

"Where's here?" I asked. My headache had faded from a spike of fire to a dull pounding behind my eyes. No more blurriness.

"Dr. C's place. Can you see yet?"

"Yeah. I think I can walk, too."

"Your eyes aren't glowing anymore." She sounded relieved, and I shared the feeling.

"Yeah, uh, Chance?" Lucas didn't sound so happy.

I leaned up experimentally. My head didn't fall off my shoulders or threaten to explode, so I came up the rest of the way. My ribs threatened dire consequences if I moved again, but I ignored them.

Lucas wasn't one to jump at shadows. After dealing with an empathic Emo girl and a guy who claimed he could sense evil, though, I was ready to start asking him to. His gaze was on something in front of us, and I looked out the windshield.

"Oh, sweet Venus," Wanda whispered softly, sounding like a prayer had been answered.

Shade's silver Mustang was parked down the street. Not quite a shadow. Not quite a danger. Just another spike through the heart of an already-crappy night. The driver's side door opened, and while the dome light was on, I could see Shade was alone in the car. She stepped out, still in her outfit from earlier. Even in high-heeled boots, she was graceful as she walked.

My hand fumbled for the door latch, and I spared a grudging glance to find it so I could get out. The cool air on my face helped my headache, and it helped me get other things under control. By the time she made it to the car, I was my usual surly self again.

"Where's your boyfriend?" I asked. Yeah, I was smooth.

"He's not my boyfriend, Chance. Tonight was . . . I wanted to talk to you about it, actually, but *someone's* been avoiding me. Please, Chance, I need my *gothi*. I need *you*."

Hearing her say that ripped something open inside me, and suddenly, all I could think of was having her in my arms. Right here, right now. In spite of what she'd said at Imbolc.

"Anyone missing or dying?" It sounded harsher than I'd intended, but it was all I had.

"No, but there's a—"

"Then it'll have to wait. Someone *is* missing, and there's a warlock involved. I gotta talk to Dr. C. We can talk about whatever it is later."

So help me, she ducked her head like a whipped puppy. I felt about an inch tall right then.

"Okay," she almost whispered. "Please, Chance, I need to talk to you about this." She brought one hand up and laid it on my chest. "Please."

Another word from her, and my resolve was going to crumble.

"Later, okay?"

She nodded and took a step back from me. I headed for Dr. C's front door with the loud sounds of Lucas and Wanda getting out of the *Falcon* behind me. I could hear them talking to Shade as I opened the wrought iron gate and headed up the walk. Hells, they still thought she and I had a shot at being together. In spite of my own wishful thinking, I knew better.

Dr. C's place was the perfect house for a wizard. If I could have lived anywhere other than my mom's house, it would have been here. I didn't know Victorian from Gothic from a hole in the ground, but this place just oozed history in spite of the new paint job. Windows jutted out from the sides in sitting nooks, and the eaves were scalloped. The roof sported chimneys and lightning rods, and a big, beveled-glass window that looked out from the attic. My combat boots sounded loud on the wooden porch, and if a screen door could sound warm when it squeaked open, this one did. The house itself seemed to welcome me the first time I set foot in it six months ago. Since then, it had only seemed more and more like a second home to me.

The door opened with a gentle thump. Something felt *off* as soon as I stepped across the threshold.

“Dr. C?” My voice got swallowed up by the silence.

Nothing looked off in the foyer. The lamps were still on, still shining warm against the dark gloss of the wood paneling. The coat rack held two unfamiliar coats though. My hands went to my back, and I realized my paintball gun was still in my backpack . . . out in the car. After the backlash of magick earlier, I wasn't eager to toss spells around. Just thinking about it made my head pound even harder. I still had my wand in my jacket pocket, though. And, I had a new toy that might take the edge off of the first couple of spells I might have to cast.

I stuck my right hand into my front pocket. Snuggled in with a couple of cinnamon Firebombs was my touchstone. I'd only managed to get it to hold a store of magickal energy this afternoon, and evidently, just in time. With it, I wouldn't have to draw on my own energies, which were still pretty small, or on external magick, which took a greater toll on the body to focus. Besides, drawing on one of the ley lines that ran through the house would only warn whoever was here, if they were the least bit sensitive to magick. The touchstone activated with my touch and a thought.

“In the library, Chance,” Dr. C's muffled voice came.

I breathed a sigh of relief. At least he was okay. With no more reason to worry, I deactivated the touchstone and went across the foyer and down the hall to the twin doors of the library. The doors opened with their usual whoosh, and the smell of old books hit my nose.

Dr. C was behind his desk with one of his thick tomes in front of him. He had his favorite black sweater on, and his glasses were perched halfway down his nose. Over the top of the chair I usually sat in, I could see the dark skin and neat cornrows of the man sitting across the desk from him.

"I know you have company sir, but I need to talk to you. There's a girl missing, and I think there's a warlock involved."

"You mean, aside from yourself?" a cold voice came from over my left shoulder.

A cold line of steel pressed ever so gently against my throat. I turned my head slightly to see who was talking. He was big, an easy six feet with an inch or two to spare. Corded muscle ran like ropes across his arms. A black t-shirt was doing its best to cover a broad chest that I bet women loved to throw themselves against in moments of passion. This was muscle meant for doing things, not for flexing. His brown hair was tied back from his tanned face, and his brown eyes were serene. He stood like there was nothing wrong in the whole world, like there was no hurry to do anything. My eyes went to the heavy silver ankh pendant on his chest, the symbol of the Sentinels.

From the corner of my eye, I saw the other man stand. He wore the same black shirt and fatigue pants, only he was carrying a pistol in each hand, instead of four feet of sharp steel. One was pointed at me, and the other at Dr. C. Another ankh pendant was gleaming against his shirt. Yeah, this weekend just kept getting better and better.

"Cross, T-Bone, he's not a threat," Dr. C said. He hustled out from behind the desk, and came to my side.

I recognized the names. When the Conclave wanted someone really dead, really bad, they called these guys in. Todd Cross and Thaddeus "T-Bone" Banner. The Right and Left Hands of Death. Dulka had taught me to fear them second only to him, and if I'd been in better shape, I would probably have tried to run.

"I beg to differ," the man with the sword rumbled.

"Oh, relax, Cross. He's injured, and his aura is scrambled to hell and back. Chance, what happened to you, son?"

Dr. C was the only person other than my Mom who could call me that and not piss me off. I shrugged and tried to keep my game face on in front of the strangers. Cross lowered his sword, but T-Bone's guns stayed on us.

"Guy hit my TK shield before it was completely, um, stable."

"With what? A bus?" he asked incredulously.

He put one hand in front of my face, and I could feel his aura against mine. As he moved his fingers slightly, I could feel my own aura responding. My spine twinged as he put his other hand over the small of my back.

"Baseball bat. But he was really, really strong, sir."

"I'd ask how that happened, but I'm afraid we have bigger problems now."

"Yeah, I kinda noticed the Hands of Death. What's up?"

"They're from the Conclave. The High Council sent them to ask me a few questions. About the *Maxilla*."

"We got a few more questions now," T-Bone said. He had hints of inner city in his speech, and an accent I couldn't place. His head snapped to his right when the thump of the front door opening reached us.

"You're about to have a few questions of your own to answer, gentlemen. Unless I miss my guess, two very normal teenagers have just entered this house. Presumably, Chance's friends who gave him a ride. Seeing two men brandishing weapons in my library is going to lead to an awkward situation."

Dr. C ran his hand up behind my back. The last of the headache faded as I felt energy centers in my body realigning.

“You two are going to have to come with us, then. The High Council wanted to speak with you anyway. Finding *him*,” Cross pointed at me, “was a bonus.”

A pair of taps came at the library door, and the weapons disappeared like magick.

“Once, upon a midnight dreary, while I pondered weak and weary, over many a quaint and curious volume of forgotten lore,” Dr. C quoted with a smile.

Lucas pushed the door open. “While I nodded, nearly napping, suddenly, there came a tapping, as of someone gently rapping, rapping at my chamber door,” he finished the quote from Poe's poem 'The Raven.' Wanda stepped in behind him. They both stopped when they saw strangers in the room.

“Sorry, Dr. C,” Wanda said. “We didn't know you had company. We'll come back later. Come on, Chance.”

“Actually, I was just about to drive Chance home. Why don't you two go on. I'm sure he'll call you tomorrow.”

They looked to me. Once I gave them a nod, they backed out quickly. The front door thumped closed a moment later.

“No questions,” T-Bone remarked. “They're either really dumb, or they know more than they should.”

“They've seen enough to know that Chance and I deal with unusual things sometimes. Things the Conclave ought to have dealt with instead. Now, if you don't mind, I need to gather some things that may answer some of the Council's questions.” The pair exchanged a look. T-Bone shrugged, but Cross looked like he'd just swallowed raw lemons.

Dr. C didn't wait for his nod to pull a pair of leather-bound journals from the drawer of his desk and grab his staff from the corner of the room. Like all magi, his staff was as much an expression of who he was as it was a symbol of his rank. Dr. C’s was a dark wood, unvarnished and worn-looking. A rough-cut crystal was set at the top, amid a tangle of roots. One of his wands was also tucked into the top, and a small bag dangled from leather straps.

Runes and sigils were burned into it down its length, and a metal cap covered the bottom.

We left through the side door off the kitchen. The night air was cool and damp on my skin after being in the warmth of the house.

"If Shade's here, I hope she doesn't do anything rash, like try to rescue us," Dr. C said softly. "That would only make things worse for us." My eyes went to the street. Shade's car was still parked down the street, and I felt my gut go tight in sudden fear.

"No, she's smarter than that," I said.

"Good. Your mother should be here for this, Chance. You can ask for her to be present, you know," he said as we got to the curb.

"No!" I snapped. "I don't want her to know about . . . what I did. Not ever. I'd rather die than let her know. She'd hate me."

Dr. C put his hands on my shoulders as our two escorts exchanged a look.

"Listen to me Chance. Her presence might just save your life. Whether you like it or not, I think she should be there. Anyone who cares about you would make sure she was there. I think you underestimate how much she loves you."

"No one could love me that much, sir." I pulled away and got in his beat up Range Rover.

He shrugged to Cross and T-Bone and got in. Cross led the way on his motorcycle, a big Harley, while T-Bone followed in an old blue Torino. Dr. C and I didn't say a word to each other as he drove.

I don't know what I was expecting for the meeting place of the High Council of the Conclave of Wizards. I sure as all Nine Hells didn't expect them to choose the Hamblin Tower. Dr. C smiled at the look I gave him as we pulled up under the black building's shadow.

"You were expecting an abandoned warehouse or a dilapidated church? We're wizards. Where else are we going to meet but in a dark, forbidding tower?" He got out of the truck before I could come up with a smartass answer and reached in the back for his staff. I followed him to a side entrance. It got harder to actually look at the

Tower the closer we got to it. On impulse, I stretched my senses toward it, and felt them slide off of it. A quick peek with my Third Eye showed me the red aversion runes that hung in the air at the building's four quarters. Glowing white ward runes hung behind them, and at the cross quarters as well. They hammered at my senses as I got closer to them. With the level of power I was feeling, the only way anyone was going to get inside the Tower tonight was with a ward stone, or in a bucket. I didn't have the first one, and I didn't want to explore my career options as goo. My feet stopped as I made it to the edge of the warded area.

"What?" T-Bone asked.

"The wards."

"What about 'em?"

"Can it, T-Bone," Cross grumbled.

"Aw, hell," T-Bone said. He grabbed me roughly by the shoulder and shoved me forward.

Before I could even think to be scared, I felt the ward slide over me like a thousand pins were being pushed against my skin, then I was on the other side.

"Man, I hate doin' that," he said.

My eyebrows furrowed into a glare. "You could've fried me!"

"Who d'ya think set those damn wards, kid? Santa Claus? We can take someone across. We just don't like to if we ain't got to."

I looked back and saw Cross step through. Dr. C was right behind him with a plastic keychain in his hand. The last faint blue discharges of the ward were arcing away from his aura as the ward stone let him in.

"Why didn't you just give me one of those?" I asked T-Bone.

"'Cuz you're a known warlock. He's not." He gave me a cold smile before he turned to Cross.

A few seconds later, what he said sank in.

“Wait a second! What do you mean, a known warlock?” I had to jog a couple of steps to catch back up to him.

If the Hamblin Center wasn't what I'd expected for a meeting place, the sound that hit me when the elevator doors opened on the twenty-first floor kept my expectations of mages off balance. Laughter, a murmur of conversation, and music flooded my ears when the doors dinged open. Two blue-robed magi stood outside the elevator with silver staves that were topped with ankhs. Sentinels. The cops of the mage world. I'd been looking over my shoulder for ankh staves and blue robes for months now. The one on the left was an older Asian man with a crew cut laced with silver among his black hair. On the right side was a younger woman, with streaked blond hair caught up in a severe ponytail. Both of them wore their ankh necklaces openly as well, signifying that they were on duty. The ankh symbol was like the police badge in the cowan world.

Cross and T-Bone took my arms and pushed me out of the elevator. We stepped into the hallway, and the two Sentinels flanked us as they turned me to the right and through a pair of open double doors.

The room went quiet; even the musicians stopped playing as they led me into the room. At least two dozen magi stared at me. Most of them wore suits, but I saw one sari and several plaid shirts in the room. They all gave me the same look, though. I'd expected hostility, but not the predatory glee I saw burning out in the crowd.

A rotund man in a shiny brown suit stepped out of the crowd. He wore his thinning brown hair plastered back against his skull, and his pudgy lips quivered into a cruel smile. His staff was a smooth, white wood, with a faceted ruby on the tip. A straight line of glyphs was engraved in silver down the length, and four green gems were set into the gold band below the crystal at the top.

“Gentlemen, congratulations on capturing this warlock. But surely bringing us just his head would have done.”

A few of the magi behind him laughed nervously, but most of them just looked sour.

“Shut up, Polter,” T-Bone growled. “Corwyn vouched for 'im.”

The chubby mage frowned and his jowls quivered. If he was going to say something, he changed his mind awful quick. His eyes focused on something above and behind us, and his smile slid back into place.

“We'll see how much *that's* worth,” he said. “Master Draeden, it seems your faith in the Hands’ ability was well placed. Their judgment, however, appears to be lacking.”

I looked over my left shoulder and saw a man coming down the sweeping staircase behind us. He was wearing a blue suit, with a white shirt and a red silk tie. They looked even more expensive than the ones my father had custom tailored. He carried a plain white staff that had obviously seen some use. His had a round crystal set in the top, and the runes in his spiraled down its length. His wavy hair was a dark auburn, and his face was angular and lean, with a hooked nose. It looked like the kind of face that would only smile when he was torturing puppies. His eyes, though, were what made me look away. They were a cold blue, and I was sure I didn’t want to know what was going on behind them.

“My faith is not given lightly, Andrew,” he said with a chill in his tone. His voice was calm, deep, and commanding, with an accent that spoke of New England. “Before you cast doubts on *my* judgment in placing it in the Hands of Death, perhaps we should wonder why Wizard Corwyn chose to vouch for this young man. I'm sure he has good reason.” Draeden turned and walked up on me like a tiger on easy prey.

“You'll pardon me for being forward, Master Draeden, but there is *no* good reason to vouch for a warlock. This one especially.”

“Dickhead.” The word slipped out of my mouth before I could think twice about how dumb I was being.

Polter's hand was even faster than my tongue, though. The room went white, and I was sliding backward down the doors I'd just come through with the sound of the slap still ringing in my ears. I was getting awful tired of being knocked around tonight.

I surged to my feet to start doing some ass kicking and ran into Cross's open hand against my chest. T-Bone held Polter in place as I pushed against Cross. It was like trying to press against a building. As if to show me how useless it was to keep fighting him, he straightened his arm. Slowly.

"Don't," he said low enough that only I could hear. I blinked and looked at him. His eyes were dark as thunderclouds, but it didn't seem like he was pissed at me. I let up, and he lowered his arm.

"Could you at least have made it look like you had to work at it?" I asked as I looked down at his arm. He gave me microsecond grin, then turned back with his usual sour look. Polter stopped struggling against T-Bone when Cross stepped up beside his partner. One meaty hand came up to point at me.

"You will not speak in the presence of your betters, *warlock!"* He spat the last word like a curse he couldn't wait to get out of his mouth.

"The only person in this room I call my better is Dr. Corwyn, you overstuffed son of a bitch!" I snarled. It was all I could do to keep myself from smashing my fist into his fat face.

A hand fell on my shoulder, and I recognized the feel Dr. C's aura.

"That's enough, Chance," he said. He didn't sound mad or even disappointed, but I knew right then I was embarrassing him. All of the anger drained out of me, and I bowed my head.

"I'm sorry, sir."

"Don't be. Master Polter was out of line in laying a hand on my student. He and I will address that later. Master Draeden, I believe as the accused, Chance is to be sequestered."

"Indeed, Wizard Corwyn. Though the usual forms must be followed."

"Is that strictly necessary?" Dr. C asked.

"Given the boy's temper, and reputation, I feel it would be safest for all involved. Cross, if you would please see to the boy?"

“What's he talking about, Dr. C?” I asked.

A second later, Cross' right hand smashed into my face. I staggered back a couple of steps before my knees gave out and I fell on my butt. My eyes were having trouble focusing, but I could hear everything just fine.

“Man, you’re losin' your touch,” T-Bone quipped.

The two Crosses swimming in front of me just looked at their fist for a second. “Sorry, kid. It usually doesn't take more than once.” Both of him merged together as he took a step toward me.

“Ow,” I finally managed as his fist fell again.

Chapter 5

~ None may sway the Hands of Death on their Path. ~

Charter of the Conclave

The left side of my face hurt like Hell. Why didn't I ever run into people who hit like sissies? My left eye barely opened when I tried to look around, and there was some kind of rough cloth over my face. I couldn't move my hands from behind my back, and I felt a familiar cool metal band around my wrists. Spellbinders. The Council wasn't taking chances with me. If they weren't talking about killing me outright, I would have been impressed with myself.

"Sorry about the eye, kid," Cross's calm tenor came from my right. "It usually only takes one shot." The cloth over my face lifted free, and he squatted beside me.

"Yeah, I get hit a lot," I grumbled.

"I know. I saw your scars. Here, hold still. I usually have more time when I knock someone out. This should take care of the shiner."

He reached out and put some kind of smelly ointment on my cheekbone. He was surprisingly gentle as he rubbed it into my skin, in spite of the thick calluses on his fingers. A cool feeling spread from where the gel touched my cheek, and the pain faded. I held still, paralyzed more by uncertainty than obedience.

He'd seen my scars. For years, Dulka had drilled into me that they were something to be ashamed of. That if anyone from our world ever saw them, they'd know my secret. That I was a demon's slave. I was embarrassed about them, but hiding them magickally was something I'd never do. Dulka had tried to get me to do it plenty of times. Refusing to do it was one of the only ways I had to defy him.

"Why are you doing this?" I asked.

"When I'm more than likely going to kill you in a little while?"

"Uh, yeah. Thanks for the reminder, by the way."

“Cross used to be a paramedic. Mosta the time,” T-Bone said from behind me, “when the Council calls us, someone's gonna die. Cross likes to even things out when he can. Old habits.”

“If I can save a life instead, or help to heal an injury, I will,” Cross said.

My face didn't hurt any more. I scrunched up my left eye and drew the corner of my mouth back to see if the swelling was still there. The skin didn't feel so tightly stretched, and my eye was getting easier to open.

“So, you only kill when you have to, is that it?”

“Only if I have no other choice. At all. Then, yes, I do. Without hesitation.” He stood up.

The room we were in looked like a private dining room with the tables gone. The walls were a comfortable beige color, with tastefully bland paintings of the city decorating them. Now that I was looking around a little, I saw T-Bone sitting in a padded, straight-backed chair with his back to a floor-to-ceiling window. Behind him, I saw the lights of the city laid out like a net of stars. With the lights down, and no one waiting for the order to kill me, I could see it being a nice place to take a girl. Cross' last comment had pretty much been a conversation killer for me, so I leaned back against the wall and waited.

It was only a few minutes later that a soft tap came at the door.

“Once upon a midnight dreary,” I whispered.

Cross cracked the door a little and blocked it with his body.

“Master Draeden wants to speak to the warlock,” a woman said from the other side.

Cross nodded, closed the door, then turned back and gave T-Bone a nod. I was on my feet before I knew it, and out in the hall. They led me through the kitchen then up a set of stairs, and a minute later, I was being ushered into another dining room. This one was a lot bigger, with a bar off to my right as I came in, and a raised section in the middle of the room. Brass railings went around the edge of the raised part, and fake green plants around the base set it further apart. Draeden was sitting in a pale green chair on the dais, looking comfortable and in charge. A covered round table sat on his right, and one of the straight-backed dining table chairs faced him.

"Thaddeus, I think we can trust the boy far enough to remove the spellbinders," he said. Beside me, T-Bone growled, but he didn't move.

"Sir, with all due respect, I don't think that's wise," Cross replied.

"Your concerns are duly noted, Todd. I am, however, the head of the Council. I believe I can be allowed a little *hubris* in thinking that I can handle a teenaged warlock."

The manacles came free. Draeden raised his eyebrows and gestured at the door. Both of them grumbled at that, but they stepped back, and I heard the door close behind me. Somehow, I felt more vulnerable with the two of them gone.

"Come on up here, son. We have a lot to talk about." He took a sip from a glass of wine as I stepped up onto the dais with him. "Have a seat."

"I'm not your son, and I'll stand, thanks."

"As you wish. Well, I must say, you do present a man with quite the dilemma. Your soul is as black as they come, but if I'm to believe what I read from two wizards of otherwise sound judgment, you aren't evil. Rumor speaks of you defeating your demon Master, a feat of which even I am not capable. Yet, you seem no better trained than the worst apprentice. Most of the Council is screaming for your head, but the sentiments of a few have changed due to your youth. And they don't know what they want to do with you, either."

"What am I supposed to do about it?"

"Give me a reason to keep you alive."

"Give you . . . okay, let's try this: I didn't ask to be *sold* to a *freaking demon*!"

"So, you weren't a willing apprentice?" The tone in his voice caught me up, and I wondered where the trap was.

"Technically, I was a familiar. A slave kept for doing magickal work."

"The version your old master tells has him releasing you for being a poor student."

"Yeah, let's go with that. Cuz demons are so honest. But why are you so interested in saving my ass? You don't know me like Dr. C does."

"Two reasons. First, but hardly foremost, I *do* know both Chomsky and Corwyn, and they have expressed their faith in your character. Both of them are well respected, if not entirely well liked, which also tends to endear them to me more than a little. The second is a bit more complicated. Do you know what a weird is?" he asked.

Finally, a question I had a snappy comeback for.

"I prefer startlingly odd, myself." I only got a frosty smile at that, so I knew I'd dropped a bomb. Draeden got up and went to the table. With a flick of his wrist, he sent the white tablecloth covering it billowing away. My stuff was spread out in front of him, and several books lay open at the end of the table. Suddenly, I felt like I was standing in the room with no clothes on. My TK wand and new touchstone were there, and the last three of my cinnamon candies. The Page of Swords card was under my wallet. My amethyst scrying stone lay next to them. Draeden picked up my touchstone and smiled.

"My first touchstone gave me fits. It took me a month to get one to hold. How long did it take you?"

"Nine weeks," I admitted.

He reached for the tarot card. "It's a noun," he said casually.

"Huh?" I can be a brilliant conversationalist sometimes.

"A *wyrd*. Spelled with a Y. A thread of destiny that affects the past from the future, and the future from the past. All time and fate is interconnected, but sometimes, certain strands of Fate exert a stronger influence on one particular life than they do on others. Your fate is touched by a particularly strong wyrd. One that is connected to all of our fates in turn. I can use that to delay the Council's vote, but only until the spring equinox."

"That's less than a week."

"The wyrd's influence only extends until then. By then, you will either have fulfilled the task set before you, or you will not."

"If it's destiny, won't it work out either way?"

"A wyrd only influences your fate. It does not control it and it in no way guarantees success. Rather, it points the way to a desirable outcome. If you take up the task, then it can become a guiding force. Very little can stand in the way of a man who accepts his wyrd. The Norse had a saying. 'Wyrd often saves the un-doomed man, so long as his courage holds.' So the question becomes, do you have the courage to face your wyrd, and take up the task given you by fate through this Council?"

"Dude, I've faced a werewolf and a demon. I think I can handle whatever this is."

"Bold words. I can take them as assent then?"

"Hell, yeah."

"Excellent. Now, we'll go out and—what now?" He snapped as someone knocked on the door.

A young mage in a brown robe stepped in.

"Master Draeden, a supplicant. She wishes to address the Council."

"Why are you asking me? She has the right to address the Conclave and the Council any time it convenes. You know that!" he snapped at the mage.

The mage looked meaningfully at me, then back at Draeden.

"But . . . the warlock, sir."

"The Council is capable of dealing with more than one issue in a single night. She'll just have to be patient, and wait until after we've dealt with him. Now, go and let her in."

The mage bowed out and closed the door. Draeden frowned and shook his head, a lot like I'd seen Dr. C do after dealing with idiots.

"You were saying something about going out and doing something?" I prompted him.

"Are you in such a hurry to risk your neck, Mr. Fortunato?"

"I've got a curfew." That got a smile from him.

"Well, we should hardly keep your mother waiting, should we? Now, we must delay the vote until your wyrd has run its course. Master Polter will no doubt be leading the charge to have you executed post haste, and Corwyn alongside you for harboring you. Many fear his influence. It will be up to you to inspire more sympathy than fear in the hearts of the Conclave as a whole."

"Up to me?" I asked. "You might not have noticed this, but I'm not the best at the whole hearts and minds thing."

"Two wizards have vouched for you, boy. They did so based on your actions, not your words. Play to your strengths."

The doors to the room opened at his gesture, and T-Bone turned to face us.

"About damn time. You better get the hell out there. The natives are gettin' restless."

We heard a low murmuring from outside.

"Damn that Polter," Draeden hissed. He nodded to T-Bone and strode off down the hall.

T-Bone grabbed my arm and dragged me along.

"C'mon kid. You all right?"

I gave him a curious look. What the Hell did he care? If things went bad, he was going to have to kill me tonight.

"Yeah, I guess." He nodded back and pushed me ahead, into the center of the big room we had first come into.

The middle of the room was clear now. They'd set tables end to end in a semi-circle facing the stairs, leaving a broad open area.

There was an opening at the mid point of the tables, right across from the door I had come out. I turned to look behind me.

Draeden was making his way up the sweeping staircase on the left. Sentinels lined both staircases, and I saw twelve hooded mages in white robes along the rail at the top. Draeden took his place at the open spot in the middle of them, making it thirteen. Polter's girth was unmistakable on his right. Draeden shrugged a set of black robes into place, and pulled the hood up and picked up his staff. I was left staring at the purple-edged opening of his hood, my most powerful ally now hidden and anonymous.

"The High Council of the Conclave is convened," Draeden's voice boomed.

The whispered conversations behind me stopped, and T-Bone moved to the bottom of the stairs on the left. Cross stood across from him at the bottom of the right hand stairway. That left me alone in the center of the room, facing the whole Conclave, High Council and all, on my own.

"This special session is called to deal with the matters of the loss of the Maxilla, and the matter of the warlock Chance Fortunato, captured this night and brought to face the justice of the Council," one of the Sentinels read from an unrolled scroll.

"Justice is the Conclave's highest priority," Draeden said after he'd finished. "Chance Fortunato, you are brought here to face serious charges. That you did knowingly and willingly enter into the apprenticeship of one of the *asura*, to wit, the demon Dulka, a Count of the Second Order of the Fifth Circle of Hell, and did knowingly and of your own free will, assist your Master in the enslavement of not less than forty seven innocent souls. That you did also, at the behest of your Master, use dark sorcery to break the Laws of Magick, to wit, the frequent use of spells to bend the will of another, and the use of magick to bring profit at the cost of the cowan. You stand also accused of the setting of no less than two hundred curses. There is no doubt that you did perform these vile acts. What say you in your own defense, bearing in mind that your own testimony may be brought to bear against you?"

"I didn't 'knowingly and willingly' enter into anything," I started.

"Oh, were you *tricked*?" Polter mocked. "Poor little warlock, he didn't *know* he was trading his soul to a demon!"

A few people laughed at that, and I felt something break open in my head.

"*I was SOLD, you stupid son of a bitch!*" I screamed. The words came out raw, and I couldn't stop them. "My own father pulled me out of bed the night before my seventh birthday, took me out to the garage and threw me into a circle with the demon he'd summoned! I was his price so the demon wouldn't take his soul until he died! He got rich, and I got shafted, and now you assholes are trying ME for what HE did to me."

"You could have refused him," a woman to Draeden's left said in a harsh, reedy voice. "Death was always an option."

"The boy was only seven, Master Hardesty," another woman said, this one near the right end of the line of Council members. "He was young, impressionable, and we can clearly see the impact it made upon him."

"The choice was his, and he chose to protect himself, Morrigan. I believe the forty-seven souls he enslaved would agree with me on that."

"I wasn't trying to protect myself, lady. He threatened my mother."

"And we're supposed to believe that you did what you did out of some kind of noble self-sacrifice?" Polter sneered. "That you profited nothing from your deal with your Master? We know the temptation of dark magick, warlock. We know all too well the lure of its power. You can say nothing that will convince me, or any member of this Council, that you did not enjoy every spell you cast, and secretly thrill to every bit of control you exerted, every moment of pain you inflicted on those innocent souls."

I was so angry I could barely even put words together. This bastard looked like he'd never met a menu he didn't like, and he was accusing me of enjoying what Dulka made me do. I saw Draeden's hand move to his face, and he brought his index finger to his lips like he was shushing me. His advice from earlier came to me. Actions, not words. Play to my strengths. Courage.

"You want to see just how much I *enjoyed* doing what I did? All the *rewards* I got for being a good slave?" I spat.

I grabbed the bottom of my shirt and pulled it up. The hem caught on something, and I yanked against it. Fabric ripped as I tore it away from my body and threw the scraps on the floor in front of me. A dozen gasps came from behind me, and a woman gave an anguished cry. I looked down at the scars on my chest and upper arms, then back up at Polter before I put my arms out and turned around to show them the roadmap on my back. I turned a complete circle and gave Polter the full weight of my stare.

"You lied to me!" I heard a woman sob behind me, and my blood froze in my veins. There was one thing I feared more than death, more than the High Council, even more than being taken back by Dulka, and it was happening right then and there.

My Mom knew I was a warlock.

Chapter 6

~ Even Demons flee before the just wrath of the Romany. ~

Mage proverb

"Mom, I'm sorry," I told her as she walked into the cleared area with me.

I felt terrible about lying to her, but then, her knowing the truth had seemed worse at the time. Now, she knew it all, but only as a spectator. If I should have told anyone, I should have told her. But if there was anyone in the world I *didn't* want to know about my past, it was also my mom. Even though she was crying, she looked pissed. But then, I figured I deserved that more than a little.

"We'll discuss this later, Chance," she said.

I shut up.

When she spoke again, it wasn't to me. "I came to you eight years ago about this. You told me that there was nothing you could do. You told me my son was safe!"

"We told you that your son had not been abducted, and that your husband was not doing him any harm at the time," Draeden said. "We spoke the truth. There was nothing we could do to return him to you. He had not been abducted, and no harm was being done to him at the hand of his father. Unfortunately, we did not know the circumstances of his service to the demon at the time. In fact, we did not know he had been forcibly sold into servitude until this very night."

"We failed them," an older sounding man said. His voice seemed tired. "We failed you both, miss."

"Nonsense!" Polter said. "We can't let ourselves be swayed by sympathy over a few scars and a sob story. The boy would tell any lie to save his life. And his mother would say anything to save her child!"

"I'm not sure which I find more disturbing, Andrew," Morrigan said. "That you would accuse this woman of lying, when Master

Draeden has just corroborated her claim, or that you are still so eager to kill this boy when it's possible he may be as much a victim here as anyone."

"There is another issue to consider, ladies and gentlemen of the Council," Draeden said.

Polter's mouth closed so fast I could almost hear his teeth click together.

"With any issue of justice, I seek guidance through divination. What was revealed to me gives me reason to do a thing unheard of in our history. First, there is no record of an accord between this young man and the Red Count. Given his testimony and the ample evidence we have seen etched upon his flesh, we cannot rightfully accuse him of being a true warlock. Secondly, this decision is currently not in our hands. This boy has a wyrd attached to him." Draeden pulled the tarot card from inside his robes and tossed it.

It spun slowly toward me, until it finally landed on the floor at my feet.

"Are you certain, Master Draeden?" Polter asked.

I reached down and picked the card up. The Page of Swords stared up at me, frozen in place as he offered a sword to someone unseen. I looked up to see Draeden skewer Polter with a look that even his hood couldn't hide.

"Quite certain." There was enough ice in just those two words to stop global warming. "The wyrd, combined with the claims the boy has made, are enough to give me more than a moment's pause. My scrying indicates that the wyrd will run its course, for good or ill, by the Equinox. Given the new evidence we have, I propose that we allow the boy to prove himself, through an Ordeal. None of us can say this was his choice…not with any credibility, at any rate. All we can know is who is he is now, and if his desire to follow the right path is sincere."

"Master Draeden," the tired sounding old man said, "we have never set an Ordeal in such a case before. Warlocks are judged by vote of the Council alone."

“Would you have voted for immediate execution of this boy at the beginning of this night, Master Moon? I believe all of us would have, without hesitation. Yet now, how would you vote?”

“I would vote . . . with my conscience, Master Draeden.” I got the sense from the tone of his voice that he was trying to say he’d vote in my favor without saying it out loud.

“As would we all, Lazarus. My friends, we have served for many years as members of this Council, and in all our time, we have not seen a case such as this. If we are to vote as our morals dictate, we must know the heart of the young man before us. This boy has a task to perform, and by it, I think his true character will be revealed. I put it to this council that Chance Fortunato *must* be allowed to complete the task set before him by the Fates. Only by this can he be judged fairly, and Fate be served as it demands. Who among us favors setting this boy's task as his Ordeal?”

Five green balls of light floated out over the floor. Draeden nodded gravely.

“And who opposes this course?”

Four red balls shot out quickly, Polter's brightest of all. A sigh of relief died on my lips as a fifth red globe sailed out slowly.

“There can be no abstentions in this,” Polter said. He gave a glance to the two Council members who had not voted, and I saw them exchange a glance, then one more red globe floated out over the floor, and Draeden sent a green globe of his own. Still a tie, and the last vote I could count on had been cast.

“Caleb, you know how you must vote in this,” Polter said, and I saw the remaining mage's hand come up.

“Which one a' you's gonna kill the boy then?” T-Bone's voice cut through the tense silence.

“You know the answer to that, Hand,” Polter answered as he gave a dismissive wave of his hand.

“I don't think *you* do, though,” Cross replied.

“Silence, Cross. We are weighing an important decision here.”

"A decision you think someone else is going to carry out. Before you cast your final votes, Council, know that you would be best served not do so." Cross's voice was as hard as steel.

"*Silence*!" Polter shouted. "Master Draeden, will you tolerate such insolence?"

"Indeed not." Draeden said. "Shut up, Polter."

The entire chamber gasped, and a couple of people laughed. Not me, I swear. I had to cough, really.

"What?" Polter gasped. Draeden nodded to Cross.

"You thought nothing of making the decision to kill this boy, Andrew Polter," Cross said. "But it is not you who would bear his blood on your hands. As the Left and Right Hands of Death, we are the *final* word where such decisions are made. We, and we alone, have the right to carry out a death sentence . . . or to refuse it."

"And if you all vote to kill him tonight, with a wyrd on his ass, without givin' him a chance to prove himself, we're gonna tell you *exactly* where you can stick it."

"May this Council ask why you would refuse, T-Bone?" Draeden asked politely.

" 'Cuz if what this kid says is true, the Conclave couldn't protect him when he needed us to. He may have done a lot of bad stuff, but Hell, he was just a kid! None of you were there helpin' him. When it came down to it, he did what none of you could. He got himself outta some bad shit, and now you're comin' along and tryin' to punish him for stuff he shoulda never had to do."

"The purpose of the Conclave is to protect the cowan and the mystic population from harm by the misuse of magick, and from the *asura*. Where were you, Master Polter," Cross pointed at my chest, "when these wounds were inflicted on this boy? What did *you* do to stop this?"

Dead silence met his question.

"Then you will understand if we follow your example in this, and do just as little where you are concerned. The boy deserves the opportunity to prove himself. He's had enough taken from him by our negligence. It's time to let our inaction benefit him."

"So, yeah, until the Equinox, no one's dyin' and the kid gets a shot to prove himself. Any questions?" T-Bone asked.

Silence continued its reign of terror until Cross spoke again.

"I believe the floor is yours, Master Draeden."

The mages behind us muttered as Draeden pulled his hood back and leaned forward.

"All that remains is to set the task. Chance Fortunato, this Council commands that you return the sword known as the Maxilla and fulfill the fate set by your wyrd. Do so before the Equinox, and you will have completed your Ordeal to this Council's satisfaction."

"But . . . Master Draeden!" Hardesty said. "The Maxilla is Wizard Corwyn's responsibility! We summoned him to answer for its loss!"

"There is also the matter of harboring a warlock," Polter said with a malicious glee in his voice.

"We'll just have to wait until the Equinox, then, won't we? By then, I think both matters will be resolved sufficiently to make a final judgment."

"Chance, don't do this," Dr. C said from right behind me.

As usual, I hadn't heard him approach. I gave him a glare.

"Already agreed to," I told him, then turned to face Draeden. "Like I said earlier, Master Draeden, I'll do it."

"Excellent, Chance. Cross, T-Bone, would you see that his things are returned to him?"

Draeden turned and disappeared into the halls of the upper floor. The rest of the Council followed him, but Polter stayed long enough to give me a lingering glare. His expression faltered when Mom caught sight of him, and he scuttled back from the railing.

"We're going home, Chance," Mom's voice was tight. I followed her with a heavy heart. It was one thing to face the Council. This was worse. I was pretty sure that death was a lot easier than facing the wrath of Mom. Cross met us at the elevators and handed over my stuff without a word. I slipped my jacket on as I stepped into the elevator with Mom and Dr. Corwyn.

"Mara, I'm sorry you had to find out like this," Dr. C said.

Mom's hand landed against his face with a crack that made me jump. She barely came up to his shoulder, but he stepped back when she took a step toward him.

"You took my son as your apprentice without my knowledge, *Mister* Corwyn. You lied to me, and you encouraged Chance to continue to lie to me. Enraged doesn't even *begin* to describe my feelings right now. For now, it's best if you didn't talk to me. In fact, moving out of the country for a few years might not be a bad idea."

"I understand if you're angry with me," he said. "But don't be angry at Chance. He's the victim here. Any error here is mine entirely."

"Dr. C, please, don't. Mom, I'm sorry."

"We'll talk about this when we get home. Not before. As for you, Corwyn . . . just don't talk to me right now." The doors dinged open, and Mom dragged me out of the elevator and into the parking lot.

I rode back home with my faced pressed up against the window of Mom's van. Right then, my world sucked about as bad as it could. Dying on the Equinox seemed like the least of my problems. Mom knew about my past, and I was having a hard time deciding which part was worse, her knowing, or how she'd found out.

All the bad things I had done were out there for her to see. At least, the ones the Council knew about. She knew I'd been a demon's slave, though. She'd guess the other things I'd done, the things the Conclave didn't care about . . . the things that had been done to me. If she knew about the Conclave, it was a safe bet she knew how twisted demons could be.

I couldn't look at her, but I heard her knuckles pop on the steering wheel. She took every corner like a personal insult and every time she stopped, she stomped the brakes hard. We pulled up into the driveway and stopped with a short yelp of rubber on pavement, then Mom was out of the van and heading for the door at a quick walk.

I jumped when the door slammed, but I didn't move for a moment. Facing Dulka had been easier than getting out of the van to face my Mom. Finally, I opened the door and made my way through the cool March air, shivering as I tried to wrap my jacket around my shoulders like so much shredded dignity. The door loomed closer with every faltering step, and my gut churned. I would rather have done just about anything else as I watched my hand reach for the doorknob. The door pulled away from my hand before I could reach it, and Mom's brittle voice emerged from the still-dark room.

"Get inside, son." She still called me 'son'? I stepped into the darkness and pulled the door shut behind me.

"Mom, I'm sor—"

"Why didn't you tell me?" she whispered. I swallowed around the lump in my throat. I struggled for a long moment.

"I didn't want to stop being your son," I finally said. The answer surprised me, and it made me feel naked now that it was out there. I heard Mom sit down in her favorite chair in a rustle of fabric on fabric. The silence in the room got heavier and heavier, and finally, I found something worse than being yelled at by Mom.

"Mom, I'm sorry."

"Don't," she said. "Just . . . don't."

The lamp by her chair clicked on, and she got to her feet again. My eyes went to the floor as she came up to me. Her hands touched the scars on my chest, and I followed her fingertips as she went from one ugly line to another, light touches that I had never expected to feel on those wounds. I had never wanted her to see them, never wanted her to know about them, but now she knew, and I could never hide that shame from her again. I fought back tears as she sobbed once.

"When your father took you from me, I was always afraid I'd never see you again, at first. Then, I started to think that you wouldn't want to see me again, that he would teach you to hate your weird, controlling mother." Her voice wavered as she spoke, verging on tears.

"Mom, no, I never . . ." my throat closed around the words before I could finish them.

"When you came back to me, I was so happy, because I finally had my baby boy back. I had my sweet Chance back, and I thought I'd get to see you grow up to be a man."

Her words hit me like hammers, each one a punch in the gut.

"Please, Mom . . . I didn't mean to! Please, don't be mad?" I pleaded.

I hadn't felt so desperate since I'd broken Mom's best china. I had begged and pleaded with her not to send me away, not to be mad. Back then, it had just been a stupid plate, and everything had been okay. But now . . . no amount of begging was going to change things. Somehow, I was certain, things were NOT going to be okay. How could they?

"But . . . these aren't the marks of a boy. You grew up while I wasn't looking, while I wasn't there. You didn't have the childhood I wanted to give you, son, and I'm sorry that never happened," she said unsteadily. "My little boy is gone . . ." her voice broke completely then, and she let out another strangled sob.

"I didn't mean to come back broken, Mom. It just happened." My own voice broke, and I lost the fight against my tears. They streamed down my face as I finally looked up at my mom.

Her hands came up to my damp cheeks, and I saw how sad her eyes were. I had done this to her, and I hated myself for it. Then her expression changed, and I saw something flash across her face that I would have hated in anyone else: pity.

"Oh, Chance! This isn't your fault, sweetie. I'm not mad at you. Chance, I love you, and I'm never going to stop."

"Promise?" was all I could manage.

"With all my heart." Something inside me crumbled.

I wasn't sure how long I bawled my freaking eyes out, and I wasn't up to trying to guess. There was just a point where I was aware of being on my knees in the living room, with my mom's arms tight around me, and the sound of her own fading sobs in my ears. I was holding on to her like a drowning man would a life preserver, and I loosened my arms when I realized how much smaller she seemed than I remembered.

One of her hands came up to stroke my hair, and her voice sounded in my ear.

"Chance, honey, I'm sorry I let this happen to you," she whispered hoarsely.

"No, Mom. It's not your fault either."

"So, are we going to blame this all on your father?"

"Yeah. Pretty much." We pulled back a little and I gave her a weak smile. "I'm sorry I lied to you, Mom. Please, I need you to forgive me for that."

"Son, there's nothing to . . . but you don't see it that way, do you?"

I shook my head.

"Of course I forgive you. I never told you what I knew, either. Can you forgive me for that?"

"Yeah, no problem, Mom. But why didn't you tell me? I mean, I was a warlock. It wouldn't have been a big deal to me."

"I didn't know that sweetie. The world I had to step into and . . . learn to accept when I went to the Conclave was so different from what I knew, I was pretty sure I'd lost my mind. I tried once to tell a friend about it, someone I thought would understand it. She was a Wiccan high priestess, and she knew more about mysticism than anyone I knew. But when I told her about the Underground, and the

Conclave, she thought that I was telling her about a past life. I tried to tell her this was all here and now, that it was very real, and do you know what she told me, honey? That past life visions can *seem* very real when they happen, but that we need to remember that nothing in them can hurt us, and to wrap ourselves in white light, and so on. Can you imagine what I thought my apparently normal teenage son was going to say?"

"If you ever have one, I'll ask him. But, how did you know, Mom? About tonight?"

"Your girlfriend came over to tell me. You never told me you were dating a cheerleader, sweetie."

"I'm not, Mom. Did she tell you that?"

"She didn't have to. I could see it in her eyes."

"We're not dating."

"She obviously doesn't think that. She was practically in hysterics when she knocked on the door."

"It's . . . complicated, Mom." I stood up and offered Mom a hand.

"It always is when you're fifteen. Are you going to be all right for a little while? I need to go pick up your sister from Wanda's." My nod seemed to reassure her a little. "There are leftovers in the refrigerator."

Fifteen minutes later, Mom was pulling out of the driveway, and I had a plain black t-shirt on. The clock over the sink showed the fat little chef's big hand on the eleven, and his short hand on the six. Outside the window, the neighbor's white garage was turning grey in the predawn glow, and the birds were warming up for their morning performance. I was supposed to be getting up now, not rummaging around for a replacement for dinner.

Mom's fridge yielded a decent substitute for dinner and breakfast in the form of cold *moussaka,* a blend of potatoes, onions, and beef mixed into a casserole. It was better hot from the oven, but it reheated well enough in the microwave that I called it good.

I was halfway through my first bowl when I heard Shade's bike pull up in the back. I looked out the window in time to see her stop on the narrow grass strip between the edge of Mom's chain link fence and the asphalt alleyway. She flipped her visor up with one hand, but she didn't straighten from the handlebars. Even from across the yard, I could see the doubt on her face, even though all I could see was her eyes and her slightly upturned nose. It didn't hurt that she looked incredible in black leather. But seeing the uncertainty in her eyes kicked a switch on in my head, and I was out the back door before I knew it.

"Am I welcome in the home of my Pack's advisor, *gothi*?" she asked, her tone formal. The brittle edge to her voice felt like a knife in my stomach. I answered by opening the gate for her and stepping back.

She got off the bike and pulled her helmet off and unzipped her jacket. I never got tired of watching all of that red hair come tumbling free. For a moment, I stumbled for some way to say just how welcome the sight of her was, but there wasn't enough poetry in the world to do it right.

"More than welcome," was the best I could come up with. She stepped into the yard and gave me a long look.

"I thought I was going to lose you tonight," she told me as her hand came up to touch my face. "And the only thing I could think of was that I'd been dancing with someone else tonight and hoping you'd be jealous and stop ignoring me. I didn't want that to be the last thing between us."

"I know I've been a prick lately, too . . . I'm sorry." We stood there for a moment. Neither of us knew what to say, or what to do. Things weren't quite right between us, but we didn't know how to fix that, either. All I knew was that I wanted to.

"I can't stay long, Chance. I have to get home before my parents wake up. I just needed to see you again. Make sure you were okay. There's something I need to tell you, too. It's complicated. The Branson pack sent a beta to court me. He wants to claim me as his mate, Chance, and I don't want to let him."

"Then tell him no!" I said a little too loudly.

She smiled and touched my cheek. "It's not that easy. He needs a rival, or he has undisputed claim on me. Even if . . . I've already chosen my mate."

"Shade, you're not some piece of meat; he can't just pee on your leg and say you belong to him," I argued. "Can't one of the Pack say they're dating you or something?"

"I don't like any of the rest of the Pack enough to date them. And none of them are willing to back talk me. I need a guy who doesn't always agree with me. Someone I can lean on sometimes. So, you can see why I need my gothi." Her eyes closed as she finished. She tilted her head a little and opened her eyes slowly to give me one of her enigmatic looks.

If I had a thought running through my head before that, my hormones chased it down and killed it. When she leaned in and kissed me, I was completely useless for anything but kissing her back.

"Uh, yeah," I managed as she pulled back and left the memory of her warm lips against mine.

She'd asked me to do something, I was sure, but I couldn't remember anything before she kissed me. All I could think about was how the lines of her breasts pressed against her grey t-shirt while she put her helmet on, and the way her pants stretched across her bottom when she got on her bike. Then I was staring into her big gray eyes as she pulled her riding gloves on.

She gave me a slow wink before she flipped her visor down and started the bike.

At some point, I must have wandered into the house, because the next thing I was aware of was Mom's voice.

"Honey, your feet are damp," Mom said to me, and I left memories of kissing Shade to come back to the real world.

Now that she mentioned it, my feet were a little chilly. Darker cloth showed where my jeans were wet, and my socks were crisscrossed with tan and green blades of grass from where I'd walked across the back yard. My eyes went to the window, and I could see the silvery sheen of dew marred by my path to the gate and back. I didn't really remember walking back in or sitting down at the table, but there I was.

"Yeah," I said again, my entire vocabulary suddenly reduced to one word. "Shade came by to make sure everything was okay."

"That explains the stupid grin," Dee quipped. I shot her a look, but she'd developed an immunity to my glares months ago.

"Honey, you should get some sleep," Mom said as she took my plate to the sink. "You've been up all night."

"He was out past curfew, Mom!" Dee protested. "Why isn't he in trouble?"

"Oh, honey, your brother . . ." she stopped, and her eyes went to me. She wanted to spare Dee the worst of it, but lying to her wasn't going to cut it.

"I used to do some bad things, Dee," I told her.

"Like the bad things I used to dream about?" Dee asked.

"What bad things, sweetie?" Mom asked.

"My bad dreams, Mom," Dee said, like that explained everything.

"What bad dreams?" I asked, taking up the mantle of cluelessness from Mom.

"Your sister used to have nightmares about you being hurt. I thought . . . hoped . . . they were just night terrors, or bad dreams. But now—"

"They were real?" Dee asked, looking scared.

"Not any more," Mom crouched beside her and put her hands on her shoulders.

"But the man in the dreams . . . he used to say he'd hurt you if Chance didn't do what he said," Dee cried. "Chance always did, but he still—"

"I kicked his butt, Dee," I said. Me, cocky? Nah!

The look she turned on me, though, took me aback. "Really?" she said. That one word sounded so fragile, so trusting that I felt my chest go tight.

"Really. Big time." I'd never been proud of my violent streak before. But Dee's smile made me more proud of kicking Dulka's demon ass. I'd beaten him months ago, but I hadn't felt . . . *victorious* until just now. There was nothing in the world I wouldn't do to earn that look from my little sister again. I was my sister's hero right then, and I never wanted that to stop being true.

"Chance, get some sleep, we'll deal with the rest of this tonight."

I really wanted to lie down and close my eyes, but I didn't have the time to waste. The Council wanted me to find that stupid sword, but all that was on my mind suddenly was Dani's missing girlfriend. Julian had seen her with me, and if he'd really done something with Crystal, he might go looking to tie up the loose end.

"I'm fine, Mom. I have to—" I started to say. The rest of it was swallowed up in a jaw-cracking yawn.

Mom favored me with a raised eyebrow. "You need your rest, son."

"Just don't let me sleep too long, okay?" I said as I stumbled toward the stairs.

I heard her promise to get me up before too long. Then I was in my room, and the spot on the floor beside my bed looked pretty damn inviting. I pulled my sheets and pillow off the bed and curled up on the floor. A couple of hours of sleep would be nice. I'd just close my eyes for a little bit and . . .

Chapter 7 Saturday Afternoon (Five days left)

~ Magick serves life. It is not to be used to kill. ~

Third Law of Magick

My fist connected with someone as I came awake. My attacker stumbled back as I came up swinging. My next blow, a blind backhand, missed completely. I took a second to look around wildly. Their back was to me as they caught their balance against the wall. Someone was yelling. It only took a couple of steps for me to cross the room and grab their shoulder. I drew back to hit them and spun them to face me.

“Chance!” Lucas cried out.

My fist froze in place behind my ear as I stared at him wide-eyed and panting. The yelling had stopped, and I realized that it had been my voice I was hearing. By reflex, I looked around to make sure no one was behind me.

Wanda stood framed in my doorway, round-eyed and panicked-looking in a full purple skirt and matching bodice and blouse with billowing sleeves. No one else was in the room, but I heard the pounding of feet on the stairs, and Mom calling my name.

“I'm fine, Mom!” I answered. “I'm fine.”

Lucas was going to have a beauty of a shiner, though. Already, his left eye was swollen and red. Blood trickled from his nose and threatened to drip down onto his Miskatonic U t-shirt.

“Dude, I'm sorry,” he said. “I didn't think about—”

I cut him off with a shake of my head. “I'm working on that. Sorry about the eye, man.”

He gave me a crooked grin and dismissed the apology with a wave of his hand. Wanda was beside us then, tissue in hand, and Mom was a split second behind her.

“Chance, what happened?”

“I, uh, woke him up,” Lucas said sheepishly.

Mom looked at me, then at the floor beside the bed. Her eyebrows came together in a curious frown.

"No, Mom, I didn't fall out of bed. I . . . I can't sleep on one. And . . . I have . . . I'm jumpy when I wake up sometimes."

"Bad dreams?" Wanda asked.

"There's another kind?" My watch beeped, and I glanced at it to see that it was almost seven o'clock at night. "Mom, you said you wouldn't let me sleep too long!"

"Your idea of too long and mine are a little different, young man." She was even more resistant to my dirty looks than Dee was, but that didn't stop me from giving her one.

"Dude, you gotta fill us in on last night! Shade already told us what she knows, but she wasn't there." Lucas was fairly bouncing, and even Wanda was getting her smile back at the prospect of good gossip.

"In a minute, man. I smell like a dead yak. Get out so I can take a shower!"

Mom shooed them out for me, but she gave me a look as she closed the door that told me we were going to be having a long talk later.

Twenty minutes and a hot shower later, I was downstairs in clean black jeans and my black wolf t-shirt. Everyone was in the living room, waiting for me. Lucas stood up when I came in and held my backpack out. The metal plates along the back were scratched up pretty bad, but it looked like they had protected the rest of the pack.

"So, what's the plan?" Wanda asked.

"We have to find Dani. Julian saw her with me, so I have to make sure he hasn't gotten to her."

"You think he'd try something?" Wanda's voice was tight with concern.

"I don't want to take the chance that he won't. Especially if he thinks we can connect Crystal's disappearance with him."

“Someone’s missing?” Mom demanded. “What does this have to do with the sword?”

“Yeah,” I said. Lucas helped with the details as I laid out what had happened before we went to Dr. C's place.

“If you’re trying to find her, how are you going to find the sword, honey?” My mom, always the practical one. I took a breath to explain, and saw a flash of white. Like an afterimage from looking into a bright light, I saw the image from the alley again, the bright line of white with Steve's outline behind it, and the sound of Dani's voice in my ears again. I shook my head to clear it and staggered against the wall.

“Dude, are you okay?” Lucas asked.

Mom was out of her chair and holding me up before I knew what was happening.

“Great, now I'm hallucinating. I'm okay, but I think I picked up something from Dani. I keep seeing something from the alley. I think it might have to do with the wyrd.”

“You said she's an empath. D'you think you picked up some of that?” Wanda asked me.

“Only one way to find out,” I said. “But first, I have to find her.”

“I think I can help with that,” Lucas offered with a sly smile.

Half an hour later, we were pulling up behind Mitternacht's Books, in the older section of downtown, on Walnut Street. Mom hadn't been too keen on me even leaving the house, but she *really* didn't like the idea of leaving Dani out in the cold with a warlock knowing she was on to him. She'd settled for feeding us before she let us out the door, and reminding me that I had other obligations to meet.

We slipped into the storeroom through the loading door off the alley. I'd always loved the way Lucas' grandfather's shop smelled, especially the storeroom. The scent of old paper and leather was the first thing that hit my nose, then the subtle scents of incense and herbs. The old man sold a lot more than just books. Lucas led us between the book-laden wood shelves to the small office near the store room entrance. He slipped into the little mesh cage and behind the tiny wooden desk.

"I thought your grandfather's office was that big open section up on the second floor, with the desk and filing cabinets," I said.

"It is," Lucas explained. He pulled a battered spiral notebook out of a drawer and started leafing through it. "He does all the books up there, takes care of the money and stuff, and orders books. This is the shipping and receiving office. I take care of all the inventory when it actually gets here, and I ship out all the mail orders and newsletters from here. And . . . here she is. I thought I recognized her. She ordered the new book in the Vampire Sisterhood series last month. Danielle Scott, address on Park Lane. That's almost rich territory." He scribbled it down in his notepad before he slid the notebook back into its drawer.

"So, this is your office," I observed. He got up and pulled the door closed behind him.

"Yeah. One smart remark, and you're walking." I help up my hands in mock surrender. He gave me a benign smile and headed back toward the door.

"Smart move," Wanda whispered as she went past me.

"Yeah, I'm just made of brilliant," I shot back.

I slipped out into the store itself to pick up a few things, then I followed across the bare concrete floor, back out into the alley behind the shop.

"So, I get the part about the trial, and the ordeal thing you told us about," Wanda picked up the thread of our conversation from the ride over as we pulled out into the street. She twisted in the seat so she could face me. "What I don't get is how you're supposed to find the sword. I mean, is that the wyrd thing you have on you? Or is that just what the Council wants you to do?"

“I'm not sure about any of it, really. If it is the wyrd, I was already supposed to find it anyway. If it's just what the Council wants me to do, I may be seriously screwed. But I can't leave this alone. Julian is a warlock, I can feel it. But he doesn't have a Mark on him like I used to. I don't get that.”

“Maybe Dr. C can help,” Lucas offered.

I gave him a growl in response.

Even thinking about Dr. C just then got my blood up. I'd told him I didn't want my mom involved, and I had things under control. Why had he insisted on sending Shade to tell Mom? What really got me confused was that I didn't want Mom to be mad at him for not telling her, no matter how mad I was at him for actually making sure she knew.

There was no way I could describe the two-story house we pulled up in front of as anything other than cute. Pale blue vinyl siding and white trim made the front look like someone had yanked a piece of summer sky down and laid it on the front of a house. The grass was neatly mowed, and somehow they had managed to keep the brown even, so that it avoided patches of dead grass. It had been raked to within an inch of its life, and it looked like leaves didn't dare fall on that lawn.

We crawled out of the *Falcon* and took a moment to stare at it and acclimate ourselves to the growing sense of middle class normality that the place just seemed to ooze.

“Is it just me, or are you guys hearing the theme to 'Leave It To Beaver,' too?” Lucas asked.

That got him a blank look from Wanda and me, especially me.

He shook his head and muttered, “Cretins.”

“Betcha anything her Mom's baking cookies,” Wanda offered.

“Hey, my mom bakes!” I protested.

“Chance, your mom bakes stuff like honey cakes for the Equinox, and *marikli* bread. We're talking brownies and chocolate chip cookies, here.” Even as she said it, Wanda smiled.

“Oh. Normal people,” I mused. “Heard of them.” I started up the walk, but Wanda got in front of me.

“It's a girl's house, so maybe I should do the talking? Besides, you um . . . you kinda scare normal people, Chance.”

I looked down at myself. The black t-shirt with a tribal wolf's head, black jeans and laced-up combat boots weren't too scary. Even my scuffed up brown bomber jacket seemed pretty average.

“It's your eyes,” she explained as I looked back up at her. She trotted up the walk as I looked back at Lucas.

“She's right, you have this look like you're half way to pissed-off all the time. And you have your mom's eyes, dude. Like you see stuff about people that they don't want you to know.” Which was pretty accurate, actually. The shoulder length black hair and my slightly olive skin probably didn't help, either.

Wanda gave us a wave from the door, and we headed up the walk.

Inside, the house was just as normal as the outside. Beige carpet and white walls with family photographs showing three smiling people waited for us. A tan, smiling blond woman sat next to an equally tan dark haired man in most of the pictures, with Dani looking increasingly less and less pleased to be in the pictures as her image got older. Off to my right, I saw a dining room that looked like it didn’t get regular use. The table gleamed with an almost mirror-bright finish, with a fake flower centerpiece, and four chairs that sat on carpet with no wear under them.

The woman from the photos was in front of us, talking on a cell phone and giving us the eye. Between the three of us, I could see her wondering if we were going to loot the house or something.

Wanda led us up a set of carpeted stairs to a door with a single decoration, a white wooden sign that said “Danielle's Room” in black block letters that hung dead center at eye level. She tapped softly on the door, and called Dani's name. A moment later, the door cracked open, and Dani peeked out at us for a second before she opened it further and gestured at us to come in.

A Green Day poster looked down at us from her ceiling, and the members of Fallout Boy stared out from over her headboard. A bag from Hot Topic dangled from the corner of her bed. Her bed sat in one corner of the room, a four-poster with white lattice work all around it except for a space in the middle, and rumpled black sheets. Lucas perched himself on the corner of her desk on the left side of her bed.

"How did you find me?" Dani demanded.

Lucas raised his hand. "You come into the shop all the time."

"What do you want?" Her tone was cold and guarded.

"Look, you came to me for help, remember?" I said. "I'm just holding up my end of things."

"Look, I made a mistake, coming to you. It was . . . it was just a misunderstanding, okay? She'll come around in time."

Wanda gave me a skeptical look and tilted her head at Dani. I shrugged and plowed ahead.

"Look, if you've found her, cool, but there's more going on here. Julian really is a warlock. He's probably going to come after you next, and I don't want to leave you out in the cold. Besides, there's another reason I needed to talk to you."

As I explained, her eyes narrowed, and I could see her expression getting more and more guarded.

"Of course. The first one's free. How much is this going to cost me?"

"I can make a protection amulet that'll shield you from most spells he can cast from a distance with what I have on hand. You don't have to buy anything special. The other part, though, I need your help with. Ever since last night, I've been—"

As if on cue, the world was replaced with the image of a small wood building, surrounded by trees and brush. There was a bright flash, and I staggered back against the wall with the after image of a sword burned into the back of my eyes.

As the room swam back into view, I saw the bulky figure of the guy from last night framed against a door to a bathroom.

"Don't accept anything from him!" the guy was saying. "There's always a price with black magic."

"Well, hey there, Slugger," Lucas said with a vicious smile. "Back for round two?"

"Dani, don't listen to him," he went on. "He's just trying to pull you in."

"What are you talking about?" I asked him. "*She* came to *me* for help."

"I came here to warn her about you. Looks like I was just in time. I've known what you are for months, Fortunato. Yeah, I know your name. I know a lot about you. I've talked to your victims, I've even been to your little website. I know how you operate." His voice was filled with venom.

I stood up straight and gave him a dark look.

"No. You don't." I walked across the room toward him. "You don't know a damn thing about me, asshole. Until you do, I suggest you shut the hell up."

Only the memory of his strength kept me from swinging at him. That, and we were in someone else's house. Trashing her place would have been kind of rude.

"I know enough not to be sucked in by your lies," he spat.

"Do you feel evil from him right now?" Lucas asked. "Do you? I told you last night, he's not evil!" He stepped between Donovan and me, body tight and ready to spring. Wanda moved to his side.

"His actions say different."

"What are you going to believe? My actions six months ago, or your evil detector now?"

His brows crawled together and his mouth went crooked. Deep thought might not have been his strong suit, but he *was* thinking. It was a start.

"Okay," he said after a moment. "So, maybe you're not evil. But you still use black magic. That's a fact." He crossed his arms and gave me a defiant look.

"It's more of a plaid magick, really," I told him.

"Kind of a tartan, really, if you're going to be giving it a color," Lucas grinned.

"Now you're being childish."

"I won't tell you how to swing a bat, you don't tell me what color my magick is. Deal?"

That got me a grudging nod.

"Good," Wanda said with an acid tone. "Now that the two of you are done splashing the walls with testosterone, maybe we can get back to helping Dani out?"

I frowned at her, and caught Steve looking about as annoyed at her as I felt. Our eyes met, and I gave him a raised eyebrow. He shrugged, and our bruised egos called an unspoken truce in the name of male solidarity.

"I don't know who to believe here," Dani said.

"Dude's heart's in the right place, it's just his brain that's misplaced," Lucas offered.

"I know where it is, and it's a wonder he can sit down," Wanda said.

"Guys, chill. Look, Dani, I can protect you from pretty much any spell he can cast. He can't do anything without a circle, I'm betting."

"How can you be so sure?" Dani asked.

"Because if he had more serious mojo going on, he would have been able to fight me when I took his deck last night. But if we're going to find Crystal, we have to find Julian."

"I can help you with that," Donovan said.

Lucas and Wanda gave him a disbelieving look, while I went more for a skeptical scowl to balance things out.

"He goes to the same school I do. I asked around. There's a place where the trenchcoat crowd hangs out, near the Square."

"All right, then," I said as I shucked my pack. "I'm gonna make you a protection amulet, Dani, then Lucas and Wanda, I need you guys to get her out of the house for a while, until we can find Julian."

"But won't the amulet do the job?" Dani asked, as I pulled the bag from Mitternacht's out of my pack and sat cross-legged on the floor.

"Between that and your home's threshold, it'll stop the bulk of the spells he could cast. But he'll probably target the places he thinks you'd be with things other than spells. And this is the safest place you can think of."

"But if she's not here, won't he just—" Donovan started.

Lucas shushed him as I set out the silver amulet and supplies I'd bought from his grandfather's store. Moonstone, a double-terminated quartz crystal, sea salt, sage, and cedar were set on the floor, and I pulled my own tools from my bag. My black-handled athame, my abalone shell, and my white working candle would have to do for a protection amulet on the fly.

I lit the tea candle with my Zippo, so anything I lit from it would come from a more pure flame, and picked up the silver amulet. I'd chosen a Celtic cross for Dani, an old symbol with meaning for both Christians and pagans. Its true meanings were long lost, at least to most people, so they tended to apply their own. For my purposes, that worked just fine. The circle around the intersection of the arms would provide the right shape for the protective ward symbols, and the ends of the four arms would hold the runes for body, mind, heart and spirit.

I lit the end of the sage bundle and the cedar needles, then set them to smolder in the shell. The wooden handle of the athame warmed to my hand when I picked it up. I drew on the touchstone in my front pocket and added the other two stones in my hand. Magick surged through my arm and the sound it made in my head was beautiful. For a moment, I just sat there and enjoyed the feel of it flowing through me. But all I could spare was a moment. All that magick needed a place to go, something to do.

I willed the power through the copper blade of the athame and pulled the protection ward symbols from my memory. In my mind's eye, I saw them as I wanted them to appear on the amulet, blazing with blue light, then tapped the power of the moonstone and the quartz. Both stones had a strong protective energy about them, and by channeling my magick through them, I added a little bit of that aspect to the amulet. My own instinct was to draw it out with pure brute force, but I found that the stones added their own aspects easily enough. My eyes closed on their own as I felt the magick just . . . flow.

Nothing I'd ever done before could have prepared me for the rush of power that coursed through me. Always before, I had pushed and wrestled with magick, making it do what I wanted through sheer force of will. The words of my spells, the symbols, all of those had channeled power to do what I told it to do. This spell seemed to flow on its own, as if it knew what needed to be done and couldn't wait to get to it. The symbols seemed to reverberate in my head, each one like a note of beautiful music as I imagined it, all coming together to in a melody that brought tears to the eye and made the heart beat faster. My hand moved on its own, and it seemed like the symbols were leading me through their own creation, instead of me setting them in place.

Magick filled my head and washed over me. I could feel the hair on my arms stand on end as my whole body tingled with the touch of something wondrous. The last of the symbols coursed through me and found its place on the top arm of the cross. I set the athame down, but the spell didn't seem to be done and I didn't really want it to end. My hands cupped the amulet and magick kept flowing into it. The backs of my hands felt warm, as if they were being held from below by a pair of gentle hands. I didn't understand what I was doing, but something did, and I wasn't about to argue with it.

As if that agreement was all that the outside force was waiting for, I felt a gentle nudge against my palm. My hand opened and I felt the cross lift away from my palm, caressed by an intricate pattern of mystic energy that I could see even though my eyes were closed. A blue-white glow was visible through my eyelids, and I finally opened my eyes. The glow faded and the amulet slowly descended until it lay warm, smooth, and perfect, on my palm.

Dani was looking at me with a look on her face of disbelief, mingled with hope. Lucas had a huge grin on his face, while tears streaked down Wanda's slack face as she touched her pentacle reverently. Donovan was frowning like he'd just seen a gorilla sing opera.

"This is yours," I told Dani.

She reached for the amulet as I held it out and plucked it delicately from my hand.

"What's the price of your *gift*?" Donovan asked as she slipped it over her head.

"It's not a gift," I said. My voice felt distant, disconnected from me. "It was never mine to give. It was always hers. I just . . . carried it for her for a while." The words sounded right, even though I didn't really understand where I was getting them. I had the feeling that there was more to what I was saying than I understood. All I knew was that it felt like my mind was quiet for a little bit, like someone had turned the volume way down on my thoughts.

"Wow, Chance," Wanda whispered. "Is it always like that?"

"No. This was . . . this was different." I gathered my stuff as I spoke and tucked it away in my backpack.

"That was beautiful. I could feel it . . . here," she put her fingers over her heart. "It was like . . . hearing the voice of the Goddess."

"I think we all felt it," Lucas said.

Dani gave an enthusiastic nod, while Donovan's head inclined reluctantly.

“I still don't like it, but if the only way to fight dark magic is with more magic, then it'll have to do for now,” he said as I got to my feet. “I've got my bike here. You can ride with me, Chance.”

Lucas inclined his head at Donovan and gave me a meaningful look. He still didn't like the guy. I wasn't sure about him myself, but he was a lead on Julian. I'd have to take that risk.

“Take Dani with you, Lucas. Hell, take her to Dante's or something. Just make sure it's some place she wouldn't normally go. Steve and I will go find Julian.”

Half an hour later, Steve and I were getting off his bike. He'd told me it was an '83 BMW K100, which meant a big bunch of not much to me, but he was proud of it. He'd parked us at the top of the same parking garage Lucas had chosen last night. While he locked the helmets to the bike frame, I went to the edge of the garage and looked out over the Pittsburgh district’s upscale version of downtown, which at the moment was pretty much limited to the theater and the other parking garage.

“We need to talk,” Donovan said from behind me.

“When a girl says that on TV, it's usually a break up,” I said without looking at him. “But our relationship hasn't gotten there yet, so you're just scaring me now.”

“I'm serious. You have to stop using magic. It can only have one source, and we both know it's not a good one. I'm not saying that to judge you. I just have to warn you, that's all.”

“Gee, thanks. So, when are you gonna stop using yours?” I asked.

“Chance, I don't use magic. If I did, I wouldn't be saying anything to you,” he said earnestly.

“You really believe you've got room to talk, don't you?”

“Of course I do. The Bible forbids dabbling in those kinds of things.”

"You knocked my shield spell down with a freaking baseball bat, man. That thing's tough enough to stop cars, and you're strong enough to drop it with a Louisville Slugger. You can sense 'evil' from people, and that ain't magick?"

"Well, no," he said, but his voice wasn't as confident as it was before.

"Why not? Does it have a label on it somewhere that says 'Made in Heaven' or something? Cuz it sure isn't normal!"

"Because I use it to fight evil." He was grasping at straws now, and I started to feel like a heel. I'd gotten him to where he was thinking again, though.

"So, you don't know where it comes from, but the way you use it makes it right?"

He hesitated, and I pressed on.

"Magick is a tool, man. We both use it. I know where mine comes from. You don't. And believe me, I know a lot more about evil than you do." I turned and headed for the stairwell. His footsteps sounded behind me a moment later. Another thought occurred to me as I took the steps down, and I stopped on one of the landings to face him again.

"Your parents don't disappear for a couple of days each month, do they?" I asked. "Right around the full moon?"

"Wouldn't matter if they did. I'm adopted," he answered with a shrug.

"I was thinking you might be a born Were, but that still doesn't explain the Spidey sense for evil."

"This only started last summer," he said. "If it was something I was born with, wouldn't it have started earlier?" I nodded.

"Just a thought," I told him as we hit street level." We can figure it out later."

Saturday night was just as busy on the Square, so we skirted around the west side and crossed College near the same alley we'd met in the night before. Steve took the lead from there, heading north down Boonville until he hit the railroad tracks at the bottom of the hill. We made our way along the alley that paralleled the tracks until we saw flashing red and blue lights. Blue and white New Essex P.D. cruisers were parked in a semi-circle, and two silver Essex County Sheriff's patrol cars blocked the street at each end of the arc of PD cars.

"Cops," Steve grumbled.

"Thanks, Doctor Obvious, I would never have known."

Steve's pace slowed but I never let mine falter. The quickest way to get a cop's attention was to act nervous as soon as you saw them, I'd learned. Besides, it wasn't like I had anything to hide at the moment. It was an odd thing for me, and I wanted to enjoy it a little. As we got closer, I saw a familiar figure emerge from the crowd of uniforms. An easy six feet tall, with dark brown skin and a lean frame that I knew from harrowing experience could run faster than me.

The last time I'd seen Demetrius Collins, he'd been standing over the body of the alpha werewolf I'd just killed, ready to tell the police he'd shot the man in self-defense. I owed the man big time for that. His curly black hair was cut shorter now, not much more than stubble next to his skull, and he wore an off-the-rack tan suit instead of an officer's uniform. Light caught the badge at his belt, and I saw the round sheriff's deputy's star instead of the P.D. shield he used to wear. Officer Collins was Deputy Collins now, it seemed. I filed that away for later as my eyes went to a gap in the wall of black uniforms.

A guy in a blue jumpsuit was taking pictures of something on the ground, and in the flash, I caught sight of a crimson beret on the ground. The photographer stepped back and motioned to a uniformed officer, who covered something on the ground with a white sheet.

The camera's flash went off again, this time lighting up a section of the concrete retaining wall, and my blood froze in my veins. Sigils in an ancient language crawled across the wall in a circle that almost seemed to move in the micro-second burst of light from the camera.

"Damn," I muttered as we kept walking. I could see red starting to stain the sheet on the ground.

"Who d'you think it is?" Steve asked as he got a better look at the scene.

"I'd bet it's . . . it *was* Julian."

"Well, then, that solves most of our problems," Steve said flatly. "With him dead, the spell he put on Dani's friend will be broken, and things can get back to normal."

"It's Dani's girlfriend, man, and I don't think it's that simple."

"Her . . . girlfriend? As in, you know, *girlfriend* girlfriend?" Steve's eyes went a little wider as I gave him a nod to confirm what he was putting together.

"Yeah, but the thing is, someone had to give Julian that Despair Deck, and I'm betting that same someone's behind both Crystal's disappearing act and Julian suddenly getting a bad case of dead. So, no, our problems are *sooooo* not solved."

We got closer to the scene, and I saw a knot of black trenchcoats gathered near one of the cruisers. There were a couple of faces I recognized from the night before, and it looked like one of them recognized me. His hand came up with a finger pointed right at me. Collins looked over his shoulder and I could see his face fall as he reached for his belt with his left hand.

"So, what do we do now?" Steve asked.

"Well, you need to look surprised."

"Why?"

"Because I'm about to run," I told him before I turned and broke into a sprint. Several voices yelled for me to stop, and I could hear shoes slapping pavement behind me as I rounded the corner of the nearest building. Dr. Corwyn had started me on a training regimen almost as soon as I became his apprentice. Aside from a rep-heavy weight routine, he had me run every morning and after five months of it, I was pretty fast. More importantly, I could keep up a sprint for several hundred yards.

As I poured on the speed on the straightaway, I risked a look back over my shoulder. Collins was pulling ahead of four cops and he was gaining on me. I hurdled a low brick wall and put on a last burst of desperate speed before I got to the end of the building. There was a slap as leather soles hit pavement, then the crunch of someone running across gravel, and only one someone. All I had was a split second to look over my shoulder before I was around the corner. It was Collins, looking pissed, with the group of cops nearly a hundred yards behind him shaking their heads.

With the building blocking the view of the rest of the cops, I took a few more steps and shucked my pack off. My fingers found the zipper for the small outer pocket and yanked it open. Inside was a *neglinom* charm that I'd taken from a necromancer a few months ago. I slipped the cord through the carrying loop at the top of the pack and threaded the amulet through the free loop to secure it as Collins rounded the corner.

He never broke stride as he tackled me, and we went spilling into the dirt.

"Damn it, kid, now I *have* to arrest you!" he snarled as he grabbed an arm and pushed my face into the gravel. "You just had to make it harder on yourself, didn't you?"

"Yeah, it's a teen thing," I said into the ground.

He yanked my right arm out and planted a knee in my back.

"Need to ask you a big favor, Collins."

"Now ain't the time, kid," he told me as the handcuffs ratcheted around my right wrist.

"Need you to take my backpack and hold on to it, man."

He grabbed my left wrist and pulled it behind my back.

"Why the hell would I do somethin' stupid like that?" he demanded.

I felt the steel of the cuff start to close around my wrist and I knew I only had a couple more seconds left to convince him.

"Because it's got everything you need to convict me of Julian's murder in it."

My left hand stayed free for another heartbeat.

"Aw, shit," he cursed. "Did you do this?"

"Hell, no!" I said indignantly.

"Had to ask, kid. Last son of a bitch you killed really needed it." His knee came away from my back, and he hauled me to my feet. "That whole savin' my ass part didn't hurt either."

"Kind of worked out good for both of us." It only took a couple of steps to grab the pack and hand it to him. "The amulet'll keep anyone from noticing it, but it doesn't work on video cameras."

"Like in an interrogation room. What if I lose track of it?"

"It only works on one sense: sight. You've held it, so it's real to other senses for you."

"I still have to arrest you." He took my left wrist and hauled it back behind me again. The harsh scrape of the cuff closing echoed in my ears.

"Yeah, I know. And Collins? We gotta stop meeting like this."

"Can it. You have that whole right to remain silent thing goin' on. I suggest you exercise it, because anything you say can be held against you. You've got the right to an attorney. If you can't afford one, one will be provided for you. You got all that?"

"I got it."

"Good, now shut up and act like a troubled teenager."

Chapter 8

~ Never underestimate the power of the occasional good deed. ~

Sammael & Berith employee manual.

"It doesn't look good for you, kid," the guy playing bad cop said. His I.D. card read 'Simms, D.' "Lots of witnesses saying you and the victim got into an argument the night before he died. We got the victim telling all of his buddies about this, um," he flipped through his notes, "whaddya call it?"

"A notebook?" I asked, pointing at the battered little pad he was holding. What was it about cops and mangled notepads? I wondered if there was a hidden closet somewhere that had them already half beat up and bent.

"You think you're smart, don't you, boy?" he asked. I gave him a level look.

"I think I'm innocent. Well, not guilty, at least." I leaned back and studied my reflection in the two-way mirror that took up most of the wall behind Simms. Collins had given me a couple of scrapes down the right side of my face when he'd tackled me, and the ripple in the mirror made them look pretty crooked.

The interrogation room was the same shade of gray it had been since the first time I'd been hauled in when I was ten, probably even the same paint. Only the door broke up the wall on my right, and the video camera in the black plastic bulb over my left shoulder gave the only other detail to the room.

"All right, so your buddy Julian was talking about something called a mage war going on between you two. For something like this, you're probably going to be tried as an adult. And with your rap sheet, there ain't a jury on the planet that won't convict you in ten seconds flat."

"Except for the part where I didn't do it."

"Yeah, why am I having a hard time buying that?" He gave me a smile that dared me to convince him.

“Probably because that'd mean you'd have to think.” I saw him move, and willed myself not to flinch when he lunged to his feet and slammed his fist down on the table. As it was, I still jumped. Just a little. Purely for dramatic effect.

“Dave, chill,” Collins said over my left shoulder. He stepped up beside me and hitched himself up to sit half on the table's corner where he could face me. It was time for the good cop to give me a little hope, stand up for me and show me how I could salvage things.

“Look, kid, make it easy on yourself. If you did this, 'fess up, and we'll try to keep this in the juvenile court. If you didn't, you're going to need a damn good alibi. Word is, you're big into magic, and your files full of some pretty weird stuff. Stealing medical waste, grave robbery, animal sacrifices, you name it. My partner's right, it's looking pretty bad for you right now. You can help yourself out—” he was interrupted by the door swinging open.

“I gather that I haven't missed the actual custodial interrogation?” a smooth, cultured voice said from the hallway. My eyes went to the open door, and went wide.

“Well, well, well,” Simms sneered. “You got Kyle Vortigern representing you, boy? Now I know you did it.”

Vortigern stepped into the room like he owned it. His charcoal-colored suit even matched the paint. If I was any judge, it was handmade, probably by someone on Savile Row, and it probably cost more than half the salary of most of the cops in the building. He was the kind of lawyer who won, and won big. The kind of guy guilty people with lots of money hired to make their problems go away. People like my father. Usually, he wouldn't have been caught within a hundred miles of an interrogation room. His black hair was slicked back against his head, and his eyes, a cold sapphire blue, took in the room with all of the disdain of a prince in a pigsty.

“Your assumption of my client's guilt warms my heart, gentlemen,” he said with a frosty smile.

Another man came in behind him and gave me a dark look. Where Vortigern commanded the eye, Tad Zucherman just tried to fill it. The word that always came to my mind when I saw him was beefy. He might have been someone's All-American Boy once, but now, he looked like he'd been living on a steady diet of lemons and salt. His mouth puckered in a permanent scowl, and I had never seen his eyebrows separate. It looked like two caterpillars had a head-on collision over his nose.

"Well, Fortunato, I'd wondered when you'd turn up again," he said, by way of greeting. Zucherman had been my juvenile officer. Between my father and Dulka, he'd never been able to get anything to stick on me.

"Good to see you again, too, Mr. Zucherman."

"Gentlemen," Vortigern said. "I'd like a word with my client."

All three cops trooped out of the room like guilty children.

"What in the Nine Hells are you doing here!" I said as soon as the door closed. I had to keep my hands under the table to keep him from seeing them shake. I already owed him enough for helping me get free from Dulka and work things so that my mom had custody of me.

"Protecting my investment, Mister Fortunato. You still owe me a favor, and you cannot repay it to me if you are serving twenty five to life for the murder of a pissant warlock." He sat across from me in the chair Simms had just vacated. "We should start by establishing your alibi for the time of the murder, which I can do for you well beyond a reasonable doubt. All I need to know is where you were at the time, and I'm sure multiple witnesses can be found to establish your presence there."

"I was asleep at home until about seven. My mom and my friends can vouch for that. After that, my friends and I went to a girl's house, then I went to the Square to find Julian."

"We'll leave out that last, but I think that once we've established your alibi, you'll do well to keep a somewhat higher profile than you normally do. You'll need to avoid your usual haunts and practices, anything that could link you to this." He stood and went to the door before I could say anything.

"You done?" Simms asked from the hallway. "Good, cuz we got us some more questions. Now that you're all lawyered up, kid, I hope you're ready for a long haul." He stepped in past Vortigern and took his chair back.

Collins and Zucherman followed him in, and Simms laid a thick file folder on the table and smiled at me like he was about to eat me. Kyle closed the door slowly and paced to my side with measured, tightly controlled steps.

"My client has an alibi for the entirety of this evening, Detective Simms. I will produce witnesses who will testify to his whereabouts. Including several of your own officers, if need be."

"That's great, I'm sure he does. But you know, there's one thing I was hoping you could tell us. Where were you on December sixth? How about February second? Or January seventeenth?"

"I fail to see the relevance of this line of questioning, officer, and must therefore advise my client not to answer."

"You want relevance, counselor?" Simms said. "How's this for relevance?"

He pulled a photo from the file and slid it across the table at me. Another followed it, and a third. Each one showed a circle of Lemurian runes. The first one was done on a linoleum floor, the second against a brick wall, and the third, against a concrete surface.

I felt the blood drain from my face as I looked them over. The photos were in black and white, but I knew that the rune circles would have been the dark brown of dried blood.

"Circles of unusual-looking symbols? Really, Detective Simms, is the rank of detective so easily earned these days that any simpleton can achieve it?" Vortigern put his index finger against one of the pictures and turned it so he had a better look, then tilted his head to give Simms a condescending glance.

Simms didn't glare back at him. Instead, he looked to Collins, who had taken his usual place in the corner under the video camera. He shook his head and came around to stand beside his partner.

"Each of these was found around the same time these kids went missing," Collins said. He slid three more pictures across the table at us.

The first thing I noticed was the fact that they were all different races. An Asian boy, one black girl, and a round-faced Hispanic girl with a sweet smile looked back at me from yearbook and family photos. I recognized two of them as former clients of mine from when I worked for Dulka. One was a wanna-be sorcerer who'd never given me his real name, and the other was a girl named Monique Dawes who had an abusive ex with a talent for violence. I'd done a handful of protection charms for her back before I'd escaped. The third girl I didn't recognize.

"Each of these was found within half a mile of the last place they were seen," Collins continued. "Your client was seen with two of them on several occasions. His email address was on both their computers, attached to messages about magic spells and charms. We have a consultant on the occult who verifies that these things are legit, and they're the kind of thing your client is known to have dabbled in."

He was lying about the last part. Very few people might have been able to place Lemurian sigils, but no one, short of my father or Dulka, could have associated me with them.

"These look like the markings I saw next to Julian," I said. My voice didn't carry far, but it didn't have to.

Simms grinned like a loon.

"So, you recognize them, don't you? You didn't think we'd catch on to you, did you boy?"

"My client has admitted to no such thing. He is merely making an observation based on things he saw at a crime scene earlier this evening. The connection was made by you, Detective, by laying down information in front of him in a case he is not a part of."

"Bullshit!" Simms barked. "Your boy here as good as confessed to doing this when he saw those pictures!"

"It's the same reaction you'd get if someone handed you a bottle with a bio-hazard label on it and told you to be *reallllll* careful with it. If you know what these symbols mean. I didn't do any of this . . . but I can help you find whoever did."

Simms and Vortigern both tried to talk over each other.

"No deals, you little son of a bitch!"

"Mister Fortunato, I must ask you to reconsider!"

"Both of you! SHUT! THE HELL! UP!" I screamed. Dead silence fell. I pointed to Collins. "I'll talk to him, off the record."

"Your lawyer stays, too," Collins said. I didn't like it, but I nodded. Simms and Zucherman headed for the door after he gave them a nod.

"Captain Cronkite's gonna hear about this," Simms muttered.

"Call him," Collins said. His voice was level and cool, and I saw Simms' face lose a little of the bravado.

The door shut, and Collins turned and looked over his shoulder at the mirror. A couple of moments later, I saw a light go on behind it, revealing a video camera on a tripod, and an otherwise empty room.

"What about that one?" I asked with a gesture over my shoulder at the black bulb near the ceiling.

"Video only, no sound. It's the best you're gonna get."

"Are you quite sure this is prudent Mister Fortunato?" Vortigern asked.

"Prudent? Probably not, but it's the least stupid choice I figure I can make."

"I tremble in anticipation at the prospect of hearing your logic in this decision," Vortigern said.

"Sarcastic much? All right, here's the deal. I don't know who your occult expert is, but I can bet that they haven't seen these before. They're from the *G'Honn* Fragments, and they're written in ancient Lemurian."

“How can you be sure?” Collins asked.

“There are only thirty one of the G'Honn Fragments known. I've seen four of them, and I know for a fact that only one of them has ever been in human hands. It was recovered during the Crusades. The rest of them are either accounted for or lost.”

“Who has these things?”

“I highly recommend you not answer that, my boy. You may commit more egregious offenses in the process,” Vortigern said.

“Can it, he already knows. Mostly demons, a couple of vampires. I think a drake has a couple, too.”

“A drake?” Collins asked.

“A young dragon,” I said.

“So, how do you know how to read this forgotten language?”

“Demon's apprentice, remember? Besides, it's not forgotten. You just *really* don't want to meet anything that speaks it.”

“So, what's the deal with these? I need details, kid, something to impress the captain with and get you off the hook for this. Something I can verify.”

“Okay, first off, these outer rings would have been done in blood, but not the blood of the victims. The victims' blood would only be in this little circle here,” I pointed to a spot to the lower right of the central sigil.

Collins scribbled on his note pad.

“The rest of it is animal's blood. Probably pig or something else unclean.” I looked closely at the three pictures and started noting details.

“I fail to grasp how giving the police details only the person who performed these rituals would know amounts to being the least stupid choice you can make,” my Infernal lawyer commented.

“Shows I know what I'm talking about,” I muttered as I went from photo to photo. “If I offer to help, and tell them things even their occult expert missed, they know I’m the real deal.”

“Thereby establishing your credentials beyond a reasonable doubt and proving that you are acting in good faith,” Vortigern said with something like approval. “A bit more generous than I prefer, but somewhat more effective in the long term.”

There were markings around the edge of the circles that made something in the back of my memory twitch. Each circle had the same symbols in different places. I rolled my sleeve up and looked at the fading Lemurian blood tattoo I'd carved into my right biceps almost a year ago. No symbols crawled along the outside of the miniature circle.

“What the hell!” Collins said. “Kid, how am I supposed to keep you out of this as a suspect with shit like that tattooed on you?”

“As a former insider who left the cult, one who is offering to turn his knowledge of its inner workings to its downfall,” Vortigern offered smoothly.

I arranged the photos in front of me and looked at the symbols again, then rearranged them.

“Is this the right order?” I asked Collins.

He shook his head and reversed the second and third pictures. “That's the one we found in January, and then the one from February.”

“Right. Mars was in retrograde until the end of February. These are planetary symbols. The darker ones set the circle's place in time from when they were done, and these empty ones, see how they're all the same? They must be where the planets are going to be later. Like . . . when the whole ritual's done. This is part of something bigger, a ritual that's still going on. ” I looked up to see Collins' face go dark.

“What kind of ritual?”

“I don't know. A big one. If Julian's death is a part of it, then it's got at least one more piece to go before it's done. Big rituals like this usually have nine or thirteen parts, and they don't go off quietly. They're messing around with reality, so you get the standard 'portents of doom' thing going on as they get closer to being finished."

"Like hordes of locusts and raining fire?"

"Yeah, like that. Lots of warning." I gave him a mocking smile.

A knock sounded on the door.

"I take it this is sufficient to clear my client?" Vortigern asked with a perfunctory smile.

"Yeah. I'll ask to have him declared as a confidential informant. We can keep his name out of the public records between that and him being a juvenile." As he collected the pictures and closed the folder, as the tapping came again on the door, this time more insistent. He crossed to the door and yanked it open.

"The kid's mom's here," a new voice said. "And she's pretty pissed."

"First you, now my mom. Who called you, anyway?" I asked Vortigern, after Collins left. The door was standing open, which pretty much meant the interview part was over. I got up and headed for the doorway, and he followed.

"The police. Mr. Zucherman called the last contact number he had, which was that of your father's attorney. He appears to have informed your juvenile officer of your new representation, to wit, myself. I, however, did not contact your mother. Even I am loath to incur the wrath of a protective Romany mother without *very* good cause."

"So, what do I owe you for this?"

"In mundane terms, this is *pro bono.* I am merely protecting my investment. There will come a time when you return the favor." He was smiling when he said it, and that bugged me more than any price he could have named.

Mom and Dr. C were waiting for us at the exit. I knew right then who their occult expert was. I also knew he was the same guy who had called my mom. Mom was in a pair of black sweats and a white t-shirt, with her hair pulled back into a thick ponytail that hung down to the middle of her back. She had her purse slung across one shoulder, a big hand-woven monster made with black, blue, and green yarn in alternating rows. Dr. C looked only a little rumpled, in tan cargo pants and a light jacket over a blue polo shirt. He had an overstuffed satchel slung over his shoulder, probably filled with books. Collins was talking to them as we came to the thick glass door.

"Look, when we get out—" I started to say, but Vortigern was no longer at my side. "Now that wasn't just creepy," I muttered to myself as I opened the door.

Conversation stopped as I stepped into the lobby. Three pairs of eyes turned to me, and I got the feeling I had been the topic of conversation. And of course, Mom had to choose that moment to give in to her maternal instincts.

"Son, what happened to you?" she said as she swooped in on me.

My mom's mothering wasn't the usual wadded up tissue or fussing. She reached out and put her fingers on the left side of my face, her thumb on my chin, and tilted my face so she could see the scrapes.

"I fell," I told her as her right hand probed the raw skin. I tried not to wince, but it hurt like all Hell.

"Mm-hmm," she said. In mom-speak, it meant she didn't believe it, and I was expected to know it and be suitably chagrined. Her head only turned slightly, but I felt her gaze slide off of me and fall on Collins. "What really happened to my son, Mr. Collins?"

"It would have to be like he said, Miss Murathy," Collins replied. "Cuz if he got those scrapes while he was running from the police, we'd have to charge him with resisting arrest. Your son is too smart to do something like that."

He slid my backpack off his shoulder and handed it to me. Mom frowned as it shimmered into sight for a moment. He made his excuses and headed back into the depths of cop-land, leaving me between Mom and Dr. C.

On my own.

Coward.

I looked at Mom, who stood few inches shorter than me, and felt like she had a foot on me. She shot a sharp glance over my shoulder at Dr. C, then she turned the full weight of her glare on me.

"All right, son. You tried it your way and ended up in jail. Now you're going to do it Mom's way. I don't want to get called away from the house again this weekend. Am I understood, young man?" She was trying to sound like she was scolding me, but the worry I heard in her voice was worse than any ass-chewing she could give me.

"Yes, ma'am," I told her. Again, her eyes went to Dr. C, and I wondered just what they'd been talking about before I came out.

"For the rest of the weekend, you are grounded. You're to be at Dr. Corwyn's researching the Maxilla, or at home eating, sleeping, or helping with chores. Nowhere else. Trevor, you are not to let my son leave *your* sight unless he's where *I* can see him. If he's not trying to find what he's supposed to be looking for, he should be doing whatever other lessons you have for him, or something else that builds character and isn't fun. Do *you* understand me?"

"Of course, Mar- I mean, Miss Murathy. Chance will be very productive this weekend, I can assure you."

"He'd better be. I will see you at home, young man," Mom said. Her hand came up to my face again, and she shook her head. "What am I going to do with you, son?" she said with a sigh. She cupped my cheek and pulled me forward to plant a quick kiss on my forehead before she turned and walked for the glass doors leading outside.

I turned to Dr. C.

"All right, let's go. We have a great deal to do tonight." He led the way out to the parking lot and his beat up green Range Rover.

The ride back to his place was quiet. Between being mad at myself for worrying my mom and still being pissed at Dr. C for revealing what I was to her, I didn't have much to say. I watched the rest of the world slide by my window and wondered if I wanted to be out there, or what.

Chapter 9

~ To know, to will, to dare...to keep silent. ~

Oath of the Magi.

Most people seem to think being a wizard is all about casting spells and being cryptic, but, really, most of it is really *boring*. A big chunk of it is research. Reading old books, cross-referencing them against other books, and then double-checking all of that against other sources. Then, for the big finish, writing down your own conclusions in your own journal, detailing what you did and how you did it so that someone else can repeat the process with your notes in a hundred years. Yeah, I was in for a glamorous life. That's why mages get invited to all of the good parties.

The thing is, it worked. There was a lot of useless crap to sift through, but I ended up learning a lot about the Maxilla. It had a history that went back a long way. I'd never heard of it while I belonged to Dulka, and for good reason. An old Arab mage from back before the Romans were a big deal found out that it could kill a demon for good. I'd never heard of anything that would actually kill a demon up 'til then. The most a mortal could ever do to a demon was send it back to whichever of the Nine Hells it was originally from. That tended to piss them off, but it wasn't much more than an inconvenience. Not the Maxilla. It just flat *killed* demons. Dead for all time. No wonder they didn't talk about it. Religion didn't seem to matter, either. No matter which of the Nine Hells they came from it killed them just as dead.

Not all of the sources I found agreed. A Greek scholar said that only a holy warrior could use it, but one of the early Phoenicians talked about it like anyone could use it. It had popped up in the hands of heroes of most religions, from the early Greeks to the Mesopotamians, even before the Hebrews told the story of Samson. All the sources I could find in Dr. C's library did agree on one thing. No matter what name you used for the Divine, the Maxilla was the concentrated wrath of God, straight up Old Testament-style ass-kicking in a box. It had brought down kingdoms, allowed warriors to kill dozens of men in battle on their own, and slain some of the scariest-sounding monsters I'd ever read about. It had only fallen into the hands of agents of Hell twice. Both times, it had been found somehow, and heads had literally rolled. But while it was lost to Hell, the world had really, really sucked. The first time had been before the rise of Lemuria, and the second time had kicked off the fall of Rome. No pressure.

But all of that was about the sword's past. What I needed was its present. The best source for clues on that was going to be in the journals of its last guardian. Dawn was about half an hour away when Dr. C handed me a thick, leather-bound book with the previous year stamped in gold on the front, and the title "Journal, Sydney Chomsky." My chest went tight and my jaw clenched as I ran my hand over the leather cover.

I'd known Mr. Chomsky for about a day before he was killed by a rogue werewolf. It happened a few days after I had escaped from Dulka, and I'd been pretty screwed up. Not the usual teenage angsty version, either. I was verging on the homicidal maniac brand of dark and twisty, with an unhealthy dose of low self-esteem for good measure. Okay, I was *still* pretty neurotic, but now I was just moody and hard to get along with. I could pass for a normal teenager most days. Mr. Chomsky had managed make me feel like I was worth something in only a few hours. He'd made me feel like I wasn't just a warlock. His death had also given me a purpose when I really needed one. It was kind of disturbed, but I've only ever seen normal from a distance anyway.

Reading his journal was going to be like getting to know an absent, idolized father. It was tempting to start at the beginning, but I had a job to do. I started at the back, and hit paydirt almost right off. The last entry was dated the same day I started at Kennedy High School, and mentioned the sword by name. I went back a few entries and found another one, and started there, in the hope that it would help me make some sense of the last entry:

> *Thursday, October 15: The Maxilla has awakened. I know of no other way to describe it. Had I not been its guardian for the past thirty years, I would have missed it. But there is no mistaking the eldritch glow of the blade, nor the pulse of pure,*

divine power emanating from it. If my theories about the blade are correct, it has just called a Seeker. That can only mean one thing: it will be needed, and soon. There are divinations that will reveal more, but at the moment, I must admit I am afraid. The Maxilla hasn't called a Seeker since 1938, and then even the death of Heidler's Demon was not enough to keep the entire world from plunging into war. What threat is so dire that the sword needs a Wielder now?

The date was the day before I escaped. I fought down a sense of panic, and wondered if someone somewhere was spouting off some cryptic warning about the slave who was not a slave passing through fire to walk among men, who would walk without walking or something equally hard to understand until it was too late. The next entry was two days later:

Saturday, October 17: My sources tell me that the representative from Samael and Berith who arrived here three months ago was on the move last night. Could this have something to do with the fire at Truman High School last night? It sounds like I need to make a trip to the Underground tonight and put my ear to the proverbial ground. It's been too long since I had a taste of Patrick O'Gill's darkling ale anyway.

Sunday, October 18: Note to self: stop at six pints. The headache is worth it, though. And not only for the ale itself! Word traveled fast, and what word! Someone has been spreading it about that the demon Dulka, whom I had long suspected of working here, was beaten last night in a magickal duel of some sort, by its apprentice, no less! All of this is rumor and suggestion, but I think that before long, the demon is going to start spreading a new story that will help it save face. If that happens, I will be sure that the first story is the accurate version.

Addendum, 8:00 PM: The Council has already sent word to be on the lookout for the fugitive, and has labeled him as a warlock. I disagree with their ruling. Polter will undoubtedly be pleased, but I have to wonder if an apprentice who beat his master is as bad as they think.

Monday, October 19 (barely): I have been awakened from a sound sleep by the activation of the external wards on my sanctum. I will set wards in the neighborhood tonight to mark anyone who is watching the house. If they are in close proximity to me, I will know. For now, the Maxilla is safe.

The last entry was the day I met him, and I had to take a second before I could go on.

Tuesday, October 20: Whoever is seeking the Maxilla is no mage, of that I am certain. The wards were activated, and the aura of the person who tripped them felt . . . familiar. Addendum: This day was particularly frustrating and heartbreaking. All day, I felt the ward marks nearby, but I could not pin them down. Finally, during my fifth period class, I felt them strongly enough to feel certain I was in the same room with the would-be thief. I also sensed the taint of the Infernal Realms in my classroom, and wondered if my new student might be the culprit. Unfortunately, he wasn't.

I have rarely been so saddened as I am now. The boy, Chance, must be the 'warlock' the Council is seeking. Despite the fact that his aura is tainted by dark magick, I sense that he is not evil. He is deeply scarred, wounded in ways that make my heart break to imagine. That a mere child should be subjected to things that could so deeply stain his soul . . . we failed him. The Conclave is supposed to stop this sort of thing before it happens. Not hunt the victims down years later to punish them for what we let them become. He is bright, but woefully ignorant in so many ways. I can see the glimmers of a gentle, good spirit in the boy, hidden beneath the armor he has built around himself.

The identity of the would-be thief is no less distressing. Alexis Cooper, one of our most talented athletes, bears the marks of my wards on her aura. The girl is a cheerleader! She plays on the volleyball and basketball teams! She seemed to share the interests of many of her classmates, however juvenile and shallow those might be. How can she be involved with this? I will set a tracking spell on her this afternoon, and see where she leads me.

5 PM: I can't stand by and let the Conclave have this boy. I have to give him the chance to redeem himself. If only to satisfy my own guilty conscience, I'm going to take him as my apprentice in secret, and see if he might be able to make something of himself.

The last words played across my mind like the last few steps before jumping off a cliff, and suddenly, it was like Mr. Chomsky had died all over again. The book closed in front of me, and Dr. C pulled it out from under my numb hands. While his back was turned, I scrubbed the back of my hands across my eyes and tried to look like I was all business again. He put the heavy leather-bound tome on the desk and took a moment to clean his glasses before he turned back to face me.

"Well, that was almost useful," I said dryly. The sniffle at the end killed the smart-ass in that comment, and pushed it toward the borders of teen angst. My eyes itched and my brain felt like my head was two sizes too small for it.

Dr. C covered his mouth like he was going to yawn, and the next thing I knew, my jaw was cracking in a yawn that I thought was going to swallow my head.

"It's a start," he pronounced while I was trying to shake my head clear. It only took me a few seconds to get that he was talking about all the research I'd just done. "I think it'll have to do for now. Let's call it a night. Get your backpack. I'll take you home."

Yeah, home. That place where Mom was pissed at me. Maybe I could just walk on broken glass or chew some razor blades. It would hurt less.

Chapter 10 Sunday Morning (Four days left)

~ A mage's restraint stems from those they love. Threaten the family of a mage, therefore, at your peril, or better, from a range far removed. ~ Rasputin, 1922

The morning sun was an ugly shade of cheerful when Dr. C pulled up in front of my house. Even with my shades on, it hurt my eyes enough that I was cursing the merry, glowing day-ball from the second I got out of Dr. C's Range Rover and all the way up the front door. The dim interior was like a salve on my bloodshot eyes when I slipped inside, and whoever was playing the drum solo on the inside of my skull decided to take it down a notch. I slipped my sunglasses into my jacket pocket and ran my hand over my head as I tried to relax my back and get my shoulders down out of my ears.

"Wizards," I muttered. "They can suck the fun out of anything."

Never mind that I was training to *be* a wizard and grow up just like Dr. C. All-nighters were supposed to be fun. There should have been pizza and green, caffeine-laden soda, nacho cheese chips, and good music. And people. That was how it had been during midterms. Hell, I would have given a lot if all I had to do was make it through a day of midterm exams. Instead, I had a head full of information I didn't have the first clue what to do with, a death sentence from the High Council hanging over my head, and a pissed-off mother to deal with. The first two I could handle. But only an idiot would cross my mother when she was mad.

"Chance?" Mom asked from deeper in the house. "Come to the kitchen, please, son."

Well, so much for slipping in unnoticed. Still, I reminded myself, I did go and get myself arrested last night. I should have figured on getting more than a little punishment, and it sounded like Mom was going to be getting an early start on that. My feet felt like lead weights as I shuffled across the hardwood floor toward the kitchen. There wasn't an ounce of the usual comfort in the house as I went. No lights on, not even the smell of food, which was almost always in the air. Mom always cooked breakfast. Except today. Even my usually loud and bouncy little sister seemed to be in on the silent treatment. Extra chores or an ass-chewing should've been nothing compared to some of Dulka's more enthusiastic punishments, but a broken arm would have been easier to deal with than the look on Mom's face last night.

My feet stopped on the kitchen tiles, and I got a cold feeling in the pit of my stomach as I saw Mom sitting at the table. Her left eye was swollen and her bottom lip was puffy. A man stood behind her with one hand on the side of her neck. Mom looked terrified, and the guy had a smug look on his face. For a second, I had no idea what to do. Every bad thing I had ever dreamed of was suddenly coming true right here in my mom's kitchen and I was almost totally paralyzed with fear for her life. Some of Dr. C's training must have stuck with me, though, because as immobilized as my brain was, I still found my left hand closing around the TK wand in my front pocket. My right hand balled into a fist, and the guy behind Mom chuckled.

“You need to chill out, kid,” he said. “Unless you want to bury your mother today.”

While he was gloating and exerting his control over the situation, I looked him over. He was pale with gaunt features that were sharp enough to cut yourself on. There was a redness around his dark eyes and his straight black hair hung to his shoulders like he'd just left the stylist or something. He wore a long black trenchcoat and a black, worn fedora. I thought I caught a glimpse of a logo on his t-shirt, but I couldn't make anything out for sure. I waited for a few seconds and watched his chest rise and fall with a breath. He wasn't one of the undead, then. Sunrise didn't affect all of them as badly as people thought, but *none* of them breathed reflexively. The fact that he was on the wrong side of a threshold was also telling, even assuming he hadn’t tricked his way inside.

“You okay, Mom?” I asked.

“I'm fine, son,” she said, then gave a little gasp of pain as Fedora's hand closed on her neck. I made a mental note that ignoring this asshole pissed him off.

“You're here to do one thing, boy,” he hissed. “Listen and answer.” His cadence and the slightly formal way he talked was another clue. This guy obviously spent a lot of time on the other side of the Veil. Wording was incredibly precise and manners were everything. Even being rude to someone required specific forms. For example, calling me ‘boy’ as an insult.

“That's two things,” I said. “And you're an idiot if you think I'm gonna let you walk away from this.” His hand closed a little tighter on Mom's throat.

“Yeah? You might want to ask yourself where your little sister is before you do anything stupid.”

The question hit me like a kick in the gut. From an elephant. It also told me something about him. A lapse into normal speech…he hadn’t been born behind the Veil. He’d been born mortal, and if he was still breathing, odds were good that most of my mystic arsenal would work on him.

“She'd better be okay,” I snarled.

“One word from me, and she'll be dead. So shut up and listen.”

“I'm listening,” I said. I had to, until I came up with a better plan. This guy held all the cards, and he knew it. I'd been in the same boat for eight years under Dulka, and being back there, even for a few moments, made me madder than almost anything else. But as angry as I was about that, it was chump change compared to the mad I had going over him hurting my mother. It took all the discipline I'd learned under Dr. Corwyn to harness that rage and focus it into the cold, calculating force I needed it to be.

“That's better. Now, tell me how you came to interfere in my Lord's affairs.”

“By accident!” I said sarcastically. “Since I don't know who your 'Lord' is or what his affairs are.”

“Oh, of course, you just happened to interrogate one of my Lord's servants by sheer coincidence,” he sneered. My brain raced, which after my weekend, meant it moved at a slow walk.

"Pretty much. You mean Julian? That wanna-be warlock? He worked for your boss?" I let out a bark of laughter even as my sluggish brain tried to remind me that there was something about this that was important. "Your boss must have some pretty crappy standards."

"Shut up!" Fedora barked. Mom flinched and went pale at the outburst. "I warned you, boy, about your behavior. You're already a suspect in Julian's death. You won't be able to explain a second corpse in your own home. If I raise my voice one more time, your sister dies."

I let my eyes narrow at that and did my best to keep my feelings off my face. *Gotcha!* I thought. Dee was in the house somewhere. Now, all I had to do was get Fedora off Mom and keep him quiet while I freed Dee before his buddy could hurt her. Yeah, this just got easier and easier as I went along.

"Hey, I answered, just like you said. Not my fault you didn't like the answer."

"Now, you will shut up and you will listen, if you value your family's lives. My Lord demands that you cease your meddling in his affairs. If you do not, you will return home one day to find your mother and sister much . . . changed. Are my Lord's wishes clear?"

"I think I get it," I told him as I worked out my plan.

His grip loosened on Mom's neck and he straightened, leaving me a clear view of his upper body.

"You're pretty important, then?"

"I am my Lord's most trusted and powerful mortal servant," he said. "He does you too great an honor in sending me to deal with you."

"That's good. Because if you're the best he's got, I've got a message for you to give him."

My left hand tightened around the TK wand, and I silently thanked Lucas for all those hours spent watching Star Wars, and for the idea for the particular variant of the telekinesis spell I was about to use. He'd even convinced me to practice it on a pumpkin last Halloween. It worked, but the question was, how well?

"You aren't worthy of his time, mortal." Boy, Fedora had a case of Master-worship going on with his Lord. And, he'd given me a good straight line to cast my spell. Who was I to waste it?

My right hand came up with my index finger out, looking almost casual. "I find your lack of faith disturbing," I said in my best James Earl Jones impression. It wasn't a very good impression, but it was the effort that counted in my head.

I felt the tingle of magic course through my body and down my arm, and Fedora blinked for a moment as his brain tried to make sense of what I was saying. The skin on his neck dimpled in a second later, as a ring of telekinetic force closed around his throat. Then, his hands left my mother's neck and went to his own. He tried to speak, to yell, but all that came out was a choked gasp as he staggered back against the wall behind him. Mom was out of the chair and moving across the kitchen like a shot as soon as his hand left her neck. As soon as she was clear, I turned and sprinted for the stairs.

My feet cleared the steps three and four at a time, and I was at the top of the stairs in three bounds and headed for my sister's room at the end of the hallway.

"*Obex!*" I hissed halfway down the hall, which got the shield spell up a split second before I hit the door to Dee's room.

The shield slammed into the thin wood of the door and knocked it open with a bang, knocking it clear of its hinges in the process.

Time slowed to a crawl as I charged into the room, but all I got were quick impressions. Dee was in her desk chair. A big, heavily tattooed guy in a mesh shirt and black pants with lots of buckles and straps was standing over my sister with a wicked-looking knife. He looked at me with wide eyes, then his knife hand started to move in a vicious arc toward my sister.

I reacted the way any fifteen-year-old would if his family was in danger: violently. Only I'm an apprentice mage and a reformed (mostly) warlock. When I resort to violence, I do it with a lot of power to back me up.

"*ICTUS*!" I yelled, and poured every ounce of magick I could muster into the spell.

There was a bright flash, then a wall of noise struck me in the chest as the kinetic force of the spell left my hand. Then, there was the memory of the air pressure in the room dropping and rising, a sound like a side of meat being hit with a wrecking ball, and a crunch from across the room.

When my eyes would focus again, all I could hear was Dee screaming from about a mile away. I was on my butt, and there was a big, thug-shaped hole where Dee's window used to be. My breath misted in the air in front of me and the walls of Dee's room were covered with a thin layer of white frost. I crawled forward on aching arms to Dee and saw that she'd been tied to her own chair with duct tape. I fumbled my balisong out and tried to cut her hands free without cutting her hands *up*.

When she was free, she hit me in a flying tackle and held on for dear life. Words and sobs poured out of her as I tried to stand with her weight in my arms. It took me a couple of tries, but I got my feet under me and staggered to the jagged remains of Dee's window.

The guy was lying next to the neighbor's house with his limbs pointing in painful-looking directions. I was pretty sure arms and legs weren't supposed to bend in that many places. And I was also pretty sure I'd have a hard time explaining the vaguely person-shaped crater in the neighbor's second-story siding. Maybe no one would notice. Like, if the police sent over a blind cop with the IQ of an eggplant.

"Dierdre!" Mom cried out from behind me, and suddenly my sobbing sister was being pulled from my arms.

She adhered to Mom with an almost audible sound, but the crying stopped almost immediately.

"Is the guy I did the Darth Vader kung-fu grip on still in the kitchen?" I asked Mom.

She gave me a nod as she backed away.

"Call Detective Collins!" I told her as I stalked through the splintered door. "And Dr. C!"

"All right, son, but why are you shouting?" Mom asked.

"I'm not pouting, Mom!" Dee said from her shoulder. "I was just scared!"

I gulped at the thought that I might have just made my sister deaf, and my ears popped. Mom's almost frantic-sounding giggle was a little clearer, and I breathed a sigh of relief. The overpressure from my spell had probably done the same thing to Dee. It was a lot like a change in altitude. Now I could talk to Fedora without distraction.

I went back to the kitchen and found him still struggling on the floor. If I'd been much longer coming back, he probably wouldn't have been struggling at all. As it was, his lips were starting to turn blue and his eyes were starting to look a little glazed. I squatted next to him and tried not to let him see how painful that was. A wave of my hand released the spell, and he sucked in a gasping lungful of air.

"So, you're the best he's got?" I asked again.

Fedora's right hand was on my throat before I could even see it moving. It felt like a band of iron strapped to my neck. He flowed to his feet and held me up off the floor, and it was my turn to start choking. He'd caught me being overconfident and stupid. Dr. C would never let me live that down.

"I am indeed," he snarled.

I smelled the coppery tang of blood mixed with the moldy odor of grave dirt as I tried to get air into my lungs. I'd completely underestimated Fedora. He might have been a living person, but that didn't mean he couldn't bench press a house. Hell, I had the hots for a werewolf; I should have known that.

"And I will take word of your insolence to my Lord. That you are a mageling will not matter to my Lord one bit. Your mother and sister are still going to suffer for a long time before I give them the death they're going to be begging for when I'm done with them. And you will wa-AHGH!" he yelled as I stuck the point of my balisong into his armpit and settled the score between us.

He dropped me, and the knife slid free as I fell. I reversed the blade in my grip and slammed it into the top of his foot, then staggered to my feet. I left the knife sticking out of his shoe, but it didn't pin his foot to the floor and he came after me. His hands fell just short of my throat as I lunged back. I ended up against the wall next to the fridge when he came at me again. My left hand slammed the freezer door in his face and knocked him back. Blood ran freely from his nose as I closed the freezer and kicked him square in the privates. I had yet to meet a living being that didn't double over when I hit them there. While he retched and moaned, I grabbed the collar of his trenchcoat and dragged him to the back door, then opened it and thrust him a little ways ahead of me.

"You *never* threaten my family!" I yelled. Then I slammed the door on his head.

He brought an arm up, and I slammed it in the door a few times instead. When it was bendy in places an arm shouldn't be bendy, I stuck his head back against the door jamb and brought the door against it a couple of times, then shoved him out into the back yard. His hat was on the floor next to the door, and I flung it out to land next to him. He rolled onto his back and snatched my knife out of his foot and threw it at me. It went wide, but it stuck deep in the door.

I came off the back porch with a growl that started deep in my throat. He was already scrambling away when I hit the grass, and he was in a staggering run before I could get to him. That should have told me some scary things about him, but I was too pissed off to care just then.

"Tell him that, asshole!" I yelled after him. "Never!"

He disappeared down the alleyway, and I stood there for a few seconds, wondering what to do next. Mom and Dee were safe, and the bad guys were taken care of. I vaguely recalled something important was going on inside, and that I needed to be there instead of on my knees in wet grass. And when did the part about not standing happen, anyway? For that matter, my fuzzy brain was wondering why my hands were shaking and why I was cold all over. It was warm inside, the part of my mind that handles things like that reminded me. My monkey brain had its own set of priorities, and at the moment, monkey brain made sense. I got to my feet and staggered toward the house. Somewhere along the way, everything got really bright and my head felt like it was going to float off my shoulders.

If I had just passed out, the next hour or so would have been a lot more pleasant. Instead, I was pretty much aware of being nauseated, cold, sweaty, and generally in shock. All my brain could handle was impressions. Dr. C laying me down on the couch, cops and paramedics going back and forth, a light shining in my eyes, and something liquid, cool and sweet, being poured down my throat.

"It's the body's natural reaction to a disruption of its normal processes," I heard Dr. C saying a queasy eternity later. He was sitting on the coffee table with a cup of something red in his hand. "Expending so much of his personal energy like he did caused a reaction that's like a combination of heat exhaustion and shock. Plus, once his personal stores were depleted, the spell drew most of the kinetic energy out of his body before it drew from the room around him." That explained the frost on the walls.

"He'll be all right soon, won't he?" Mom asked, though I thought it sounded more like a demand.

"Yes," Dr. C said. "It's nothing permanent. In fact, if he'd remembered to use his touchstone, he probably wouldn't have exhausted himself so badly."

"Oops," I said softly.

"Chance, honey," Mom said softly as she came to my side, "How are you feeling?"

"Like a train wreck," I managed as I struggled to sit up. For a minute, the room spun and my head pounded, but I figured laying back again would just give my head an excuse to explode or my stomach enough reason to heave my ankles up through my teeth, so I sat there and waited the worst of it out. “Isn't this where someone was supposed to tell me not to sit up?”

“Experience is the best teacher, my young apprentice,” Dr. C said, sounding sage and a little Sithy.

“Ah, Darth Smartass. You are strong in the Dork Side of the Farce, my Master,” I shot back at him.

“He'll be fine,” Mom said levelly. “If he learns to watch his language.”

“What did you tell the cops, Mom?”

“The truth. That I didn't see what happened upstairs. By the time I got there, he was already outside. And if they ask you about it, I expect you to tell them the truth as well.”

“That I cast a spell and knocked him thirty feet?” I whispered.

“That you ran into the room, yelled at him, and he left through the window,” Mom said with a crafty smile. “Let them come to their own conclusions about how he managed the rest.”

I looked at my mom with a whole new level of respect. It was the absolute truth, but it didn't reveal anything. The police would explain away what didn't fit, and no one would even think about magick. Of course, that begged the question of the example we were setting for Dee. Which brought my thoughts to wondering where my little sister was.

“Telling the police about the bad man in her room,” Mom told me, when I asked.

About then, one of the paramedics came over and checked me out, and gave me a clean bill of health when I didn't seem to be on the verge of collapse. Once he was satisfied that I had just been coming down off of an adrenaline rush, he closed up his bag and made for the door.

That just left Collins and his partner in the house. Simms came out of the kitchen with a frown on his face and gave me a glare.

“He's your informant, you talk to him,” he said sourly over his shoulder.

Collins appeared in the doorway behind him and gave him a curt nod. Simms didn't waste any time getting out of the house.

"So, what really happened here?" Collins asked, his notepad disappearing into his coat pocket.

Dee's head appeared around the corner, then she darted to Mom's side and clung to her like Velcro.

"Off the record?" Dr. Corwyn asked.

"Yeah, off the record."

"Pretty much what we told you," I said. "Except there was magick."

"So the guy in your sister's room didn't jump out the window," Collins said dryly.

"No, I threw him out of it with a TK blast. And I got the other guy with a kind of choke hold."

"What kind of blast?"

"Telekinesis. TK for short. Same thing I used at Camp Werewolf last October. They told me to stay out of their master's business, but I don't know who they work for. I think they were talking about Crystal's disappearance, because they asked me why I shook Julian down Friday night. They already knew he was dead, and they thought I was still a suspect."

"We haven't given the press any names," Collins mused. "Wonder how they knew that?"

"Maybe he saw you bust me. One thing's for sure. He wasn't a normal guy. I got a blade into him twice and he still didn't slow down."

"So they were trying to get you to back off," Collins said with a smile. "Means we hit a nerve. Okay, here's the deal, we're gonna get you, your mom, and your little sister in protective custody, get you set up in a safe house or somethin'. Then we're gonna keep pushing this."

“No way,” I interjected. “I have stuff I have to do. And I can’t help you find this guy from a safe house.”

“You can’t help us find him if you’re dead, either, and no way I’m lettin’ that happen.”

“He can stay with me,” Dr. Corwyn said quietly. He turned to my mom. “If that’s acceptable to you, Mara. My home is warded, and I can take more precautions while Chance stays with me.” Mom gave him a hard look before she answered.

“I’m still not happy with you, Trevor, but Chance is right. He can’t hide and still do what he needs to. If I had any other option, I’d take it.”

Dr. C lowered his eyes and turned away. “I know.” Dr. C wasn’t the kind of guy to use two words when he had another fifty that sounded better. Something about this whole thing was eating at him.

Mom took Dee up to get some stuff together, and Dr. C sent me upstairs to do the same. I stopped at the doorway to my room, and my mind just kind of locked up. Since October, this had been my safe place, the first place that I could call ‘safe’ for years. Up until then, everything I had in the world fit into a gym bag with room to spare. Mom barely made ends meet, and I didn’t have a lot of stuff, but I didn’t want to leave any of it behind. It was *mine*. Hairy monkey brain pounded its chest in defiance for a moment, until I tranq’d it from a distance and started thinking over its prone form.

Since things had to be taken care of one way or another by midnight Wednesday, I only grabbed enough clothes for that long and my stuff from the bathroom, including my favorite towel. Finally, I dug my stash of magickal gear out of the hiding spot just inside the door of my closet. Almost six months of scrounging had netted me enough foci for half a dozen spells, and I had all of them primed and ready to be charged.

As I pulled the meager supply of magickal gear out of the hole I had made in my closet, a tarot card and a slip of parchment fell to the bottom of the hidey-hole with a soft tap. I flipped the tarot card over to see the Page of Swords facing up at me, and Mr. Chomsky’s last message. I tucked them into my back pocket as bits and pieces came together in my head while I stowed the rest in the hidden section I'd made months ago in the bottom of my Truman high school gym bag. Finally, I dumped my clothes and stuff on top of it all.

"Grab a couple of books," Dr. C said from my doorway. "And don't forget your laptop."

"I'm not very good at this," I told him as I tucked the computer into its case. "You'd think I would be, you know. I'm half Romany; most of our history is one long journey."

"You shouldn't have to be, Chance. You've been adrift too much as it is. We'll get you back home as soon as possible." He took my bag and computer and headed downstairs.

I spent a few seconds looking around at my room. If things went bad, I was never going to set foot in here again. It was a thought that really, *really* sucked. It stayed in my head as I went downstairs and into the kitchen.

There was blood all over the place. Bloody footprints smeared the linoleum and a trail of round drops ran beside them to the door. Another smear of dark brown covered the freezer door where I'd slammed it into Fedora's face. There were bits and pieces of him all over the room, more than I needed to track him. I'd told him that threatening my family was a bad idea. Now it was time to show him why.

I met Dr. C out front with my duffel bag over my shoulder and a handkerchief with Fedora's blood on it in a plastic bag in my jacket pocket. Mom and Dee were loading their bags into the trunk of an Essex County Sheriff Department patrol car as the door closed behind me, and we met in the middle of the lawn.

"Be careful, Chance," Mom said sternly. "Listen to Trevor, and find that sword. I want you back home before your birthday."

"I will, Mom," I said. I wanted to promise her I would, but promises had extra weight behind them when a mage made them; even an apprentice like me had to be careful about giving my word. The consequences for failure weren't pleasant.

Dee put her arms around my middle and squeezed tight for a full minute. "'m scared," she muttered into my stomach. "What if someone else comes?"

"No one will be able to find you. And someone will be with you all the time."

"Don't want anyone else. Want you there."

My eyes stung and my chest went tight with that strange rush of feelings I'd been starting to get used to again over the past few months. I knelt down so our eyes were almost level with each other.

"Dee, I want to be there so much," I told her. "But I can't be. The people who came today . . . that was my fault. They came because of me. So you and Mom have to go somewhere . . . away from me for a while, okay?" My voice broke, and Dee's eyes welled up with unshed tears. She held up her hand with her pinky crooked, and I hooked mine through it.

"If the bad people come . . ." she said softly, and let the sentence hang.

"I'll be there," I finished as I put my arms around her and hugged the stuffing out of her. It was a promise I didn't mind making, not for Dee.

Mom gave me a hug of her own. Over her shoulder, I could see Simms watching us from the other side of the patrol car with his arms folded across his chest. His mouth twisted like he'd just swallowed a lemon before he started toward us.

Dr. C put his hand on my shoulder as Simms led Mom and Dee to the patrol car, and gently steered me toward his green Range Rover. He waited until they turned the corner at the end of the block before he pulled away from the curb. I looked to my right, trying to etch the vision of home into my brain as we pulled away, and hoped I'd get to see it again. Collins' blue Neon slid in behind us. The sun was still bright, the sky still blue, and the morning was still too damn perfect. How was I supposed to be all moody and angst-ridden in this kind of weather? I felt a good brood coming on, and I needed gray clouds and rain to set the scene.

Sunday evidently hadn't gotten the memo, because it kept up the brood-killing ray of sunshine bit. Not even a cloud dared show itself against the azure sky as we drove along.

"I'm sorry Chance," Dr. C said as we crossed Viaduct Avenue.

"What for?"

"Letting you get involved in all of this. The Maxilla is my responsibility, and I let it slip right through my fingers. And your family almost paid the price for my negligence today."

Grown ups. Always apologizing for the wrong things. Here he was, giving me the *mea culpa* for losing a sword that wasn't stolen, but not for showing my Mom how screwed up I was. *Thanks, Dr. C.*, I thought. *You're a huge help.*

"It wasn't your fault," I told him. "Those guys didn't come to my house because of anything you did, sir."

"You're starting to sound like me," he said as he pulled to a stop at a red light. "I know, it was their own choices that led them there, but whoever they work for is obviously willing to go to great lengths to protect it." His free hand gestured as he shook his head.

"No, I mean no one has the sword."

"You're right, logically, I shouldn't be blaming mysel—" He stopped mid-word. "What?"

"No one. Has. The sword," I said slowly. "It wasn't in the case. Mr. Chomsky moved it before he was killed."

"How do you know that?" he asked. I dug the note and the tarot card out of my pocket and held them up. He spared a glance, then smiled. "Typical of Sydney to leave a note. So, why didn't you mention this before?"

"Mr. Chomsky hid it for a reason. I figured if the magi thought it had been stolen, and whoever wanted it thought the Council still had it, everyone would go looking in all the wrong places for it. Seemed like the best way to keep it safe at the time. After that, I just kind of . . . forgot about it."

"It was probably the best thing you could have done," he told me after a few moments.

The light changed and he didn't say anything for a few seconds as we kept going.

"Sydney's journal said it had called a Seeker. I think when you picked up that card, you answered that call."

"So, it didn't choose me; I was just in the wrong place at the wrong time."

"Or the right place, at the right time. I don't think it was completely random, Chance. If you didn't at least have a shot at finding it, the wyrd would never have attached itself to you." He gave me what I guessed was supposed to be a reassuring smile, but I wasn't buying it. How was I supposed to find a magickal weapon that didn't *want* to be found?

Dr. C's words came back to me. It *did* want to be found. It had chosen a Seeker: me. I'd picked up the card and the note thinking I was protecting the sword's hiding place. In a weird way, or more accurately, a *wyrd* way, I'd taken on Mr. Chomsky's job as the Maxilla's caretaker when I'd done that. My eyes went to the card in my hand. Up until then, I'd been thinking I'd been forced to take this on. The truth was, I'd put myself on this path months ago when I'd made the decision to keep protecting the sword in Mr. Chomsky's place. The Maxilla had been Mr. Chomsky's responsibility, and he'd died trying to keep it safe. I might not have chosen to become the Seeker back then, but I'd made the choice to protect the Maxilla. Evidently, it had also accepted me as its protector. Now, the only way to protect it seemed to be to find it. And to do that, I had to become the Seeker. If he'd still been alive, I was pretty sure Mr. Chomsky would have already agreed to the wyrd because it was just what needed to be done.

I looked out at the painfully blue sky. Finding the sword would also prove to everyone that Mr. Chomsky had made the right choice when he'd taken a chance on me. The thought left a calm feeling in its wake. Maybe I needed to prove that to myself, too.

Chapter 11: Monday (3 days left)

~ We respect the symbols of cowan governments. Where they fly their flags, we Accord to be neutral ground. ~ Philadelphia Compact, 1779

School was a blessing. I rode in with Collins, which probably saved Dr. C's life . . . or mine. One more hour with him, and I would have been exploring new opportunities as an axe murderer. My head pounded and my eyes were dry and gritty from too little sleep. Collins veered off as I headed across the lot to the tree Lucas and Wanda were waiting under.

"Dude!" Lucas called out as I crossed the grass, "Where were you yesterday?"

"We went by your house and no one was there!" Wanda added with a note to her voice that edged on panic. "Are your mom and sister okay? What happened?"

"We had some uninvited guests over Sunday morning," I told them softly once I could get close enough to answer without having to shout. "Cops have Mom and Dee in a safe house somewhere, and I have Collins playing shadow on me."

"How do you go from being arrested Saturday night to your family being in protective custody this morning?" Lucas asked.

"You know about that?" I asked.

"Everyone in the whole damn school knows about it," Lucas grumbled. "So does everyone at Lincoln Heights and Truman."

"Julian's friends were spreading the word before they even got you in the squad car. You were uh . . . you were even on YouTube," Wanda added apologetically.

"YouTube, great," I grumbled. "Dr. C's gonna have kittens."

"So, dude! What happened?" Lucas demanded.

I laid it out for them, starting from Saturday night until I ended up over at Dr. Corwyn's place. "After that, it was pretty boring. Research, training . . . maybe a little sleep when Dr. C wasn't looking. I made a couple more touchstones last night . . ." I let the sentence trail off under the roar of a motorcycle pulling up to the curb.

A heavy knot formed in my chest as I watched Shade swing her leg over the back of the big Harley and pull the black bowl helmet off. She had on a pair of faded jeans that were tight in all the right places, with a black leather jacket over a red t-shirt. Her gray eyes were hidden behind a pair of wrap-around sunglasses. As she turned her head toward me, I got to see her smile. For a few seconds, I imagined that smile was because she was happy to see me.

"Shade!" the guy on the bike barked. Her eyebrows dropped down below the top of the glasses when he reached out and grabbed her arm. He pulled her around to face him. "Don't you turn your back on me!"

Wanda called my name as I got to my feet and started toward them. Monkey brain was shouting suggestions as I stalked over, and some of them didn't sound half bad. I could see that Alexis was saying something to the guy, but I couldn't hear a word of it. She looked pissed, though.

"I don't give a damn if you're the queen of the goddamn Nile," the guy on the bike said as I got closer. "You still show me some respect. You got it?"

He was a pretty big guy, with black hair and a line of fuzz down his jaw he probably called a beard. He pulled the pair of sunglasses off his nose with his free hand and leaned forward. He had a strong jaw under the last few ounces of baby fat on his face, and a nose that looked like it had been broken more than a few times. His eyes flashed gold, a sign I'd learned to recognize was his wolf showing.

"You okay, Shade?" I asked softly.

"Yeah, I'm fine." The words were clipped and tense and said she was anything but fine.

"Go away, little boy. My girl and I are having a private conversation." He gave me a dismissive wave with the sunglasses.

“No, you weren’t,” I said slowly. “This conversation stopped being private when you grabbed her.” He turned his gaze on me like a gun sight, and his lips pulled back in a silent snarl.

“Get the hell outta here before I break both your arms, punk,” he growled.

“Deek, stop it. This is Chance; he’s my gothi. He’s just doing what any member of my pack would do if some asshole grabbed their alpha.” Shade’s voice left enough venom in the air to kill a rhino, but Deek just smiled.

“So, you’re the demon’s apprentice. You don’t look like much.” He smiled as he looked me up and down. “Keep your pack in line, Shade, or you’re going to end up losing a couple of members before I take over.” Even as he was talking a line of crap, he let go of her arm. To my right, I could see Collins coming our way. I should have let it ride, but monkey brain staged a bloody revolt and took over my tongue.

“Keep your hands to yourself, or you're gonna end up losing a limb,” I said. I could almost feel the macho oozing out of my pores. Somewhere in the back of my head, monkey brain hooted its approval.

“Both of you stop it!” Alexis hissed. “Deek, if you're trying to impress me, it isn't working, okay?”

“You know you need a strong man, Shade,” Deek said as he pointed the arm of his sunglasses at her. “Strong enough to lead your pack . . . and strong enough to tame you. I'm the only man strong enough to do that. This little warlock isn't half the man I am.”

I fought down the urge to pull my wand and blast this bastard across the parking lot, mostly because it would be too messy and piss Shade off even more than she already was. Mercy and compassion didn't even cross my mind, and I scheduled a little time during my mid-life crisis to feel guilty about it. If I lived that long, I figured I'd have about eight seconds to spare around then.

Deek reached out and put one finger in the middle of my chest with enough pressure to leave a bruise.

“That mouth of yours is going to get you killed,” he said softly.

The sound of a camera clicking to my right brought both of our heads around. Collins lowered his cell phone. His badge was hanging around his neck, and he made sure his gun was visible at his hip.

“That's assault,” he said with a smile. “And if you've got a warrant, I can find it.” He wiggled the phone at Deek. “I've got an app for that.”

Deek laughed in his face. If he expected Collins to be intimidated, he was in for a lot of disappointment. I'd seen him face an alpha werewolf a few months ago, and no beta with an attitude and a Harley could match that level of badass.

“Try something, cop,” Deek sneered. To his dismay, Collins just raised his eyebrows and turned to me.

“Is he one of your crowd?” he asked.

“Like King,” I told him.

“A Were, huh? I've got ammo for that,” Collins smiled. Deek’s sneer slipped a little.

Shade put her arm around my waist and laid her head on my left shoulder. Her eyes closed for a moment, then she opened them and looked at Deek.

“You need to go,” she told him with a tone in her voice that was an obvious dismissal. Deek's face twisted into a frown, and he leaned forward.

“We'll talk later,” he said before he started the Harley.

From the way he said it, it didn't sound like talking was all he thought was going to happen. He pulled away from the curb, and I expected Shade to pull away from me. It had been weeks since she’d been this close to me for this long, especially not in public.

“You're an asshole,” she said without moving.

"And you're a pushy bitch," I told her with a smile as I put my left arm around her waist. It felt good to do that again, and I didn't want to let go.

"What was that all about?" Collins asked.

"Beta from out of town," Shade said.

"Trying to put the moves on Alexis," I added. "Not part of the same problem."

Collins nodded and slipped his badge back under his blue polo shirt.

"Try not to make any more people want to kill you, okay?" he said before he headed back to the side of the school. Shade did pull away from me at that.

"Who's trying to kill you now?" she asked.

"No one. You say that like it happens all the time or something. It's been at least . . . three months since someone tried to kill me." I started toward the double doors of the school. Lucas and Wanda got up as we passed, both glancing toward the street like Deek might be coming back.

"So the girl selling the love talismans doesn't count?" Shade taunted me as she kept pace with me. Behind me I could hear my two friends chuckle at my expense.

"She only *threatened* to kill me . . . on Facebook," I muttered the last.

"And on Twitter, twenty blogs, her friends' websites, and in a dozen emails. She just didn't get around to *trying* to kill you before the cops got her." Then we were inside, and it was too public for us to talk about our real lives any more. At least outside we had a little space where we couldn't be overheard by anyone with normal hearing. But even with the hall almost empty before the bell, we weren't supposed to risk being overheard. In here, we stopped being a warlock and an alpha werewolf and had to be normal kids. Well, normal-ish. Okay, weird kids without any magickal mojo.

"Did you spend the whole weekend with Deek?" I asked quietly as we headed for our lockers.

"You know I didn't, Chance," Shade hissed in my ear.

"He dropped you off, Alexis. It's like watching you with Brad all over again." I could feel her stiffen beside me, even though we weren't touching.

"Would you rather come pick me up on your bicycle?" she asked. I took in a sharp breath at that, and I gave her a dark look and reached into my bag of comebacks for something really scathing. All I pulled out was a bitter, "Fine, whatever," before I turned away from her and stalked toward my locker.

I heard Wanda's boots behind me, but I didn't wait for her. She caught up to me and stayed quiet as I opened my locker and pulled my Algebra book and notebook out. I felt her eyes on me as she leaned her back against the locker next to mine and fiddled with her pentacle. It was just out of place enough with the punk Catholic schoolgirl look to remind me how serious she was about her beliefs. The pentacle never varied, no matter what she wore.

"What?" I growled.

"Apologize to her, Chance," she said quietly. "You need to be the one who does it first."

"Why? She was the one who hit below the belt," I said.

"With the bicycle thing?" she asked. "Look, I know you hate when people remind you about the money thing, Chance, but you did just play the Brad card on her. You *both* need to say you're sorry, but you have to say it first."

"Again with the 'Why?' question," I said as I closed my locker.

"Because Brad never would," she said with a mysterious smile.

"Sometimes, Wanda, you make me want to— *unh*!" I grunted as someone rammed an elbow into my side and knocked the book and notebook to the floor. The rib Donovan had busted Friday night flared from a dull ache to a spike of pain that felt like it shot through my whole left side.

I vaguely heard snickers and whispers as a trio of Shade's old cronies strutted by.

"Freak," the one closest to me hissed.

I steadied myself with my right hand against the locker and fought to breathe for a second or two, then knelt to grab my books. Just as I was about to lay my hand on them, an expensive sneaker slid into view and kicked them down the hallway. A hand pushed my head down further for a second as I heard an insincere "Oops, sorry about that, loser," from above me.

When I looked up, I could see the retreating back of a letter jacket over a pair of designer jeans. One of Brad's teammates, if the perfectly styled, dyed-blonde hair was any clue. The guy looked back over his shoulder at me and raised his middle finger.

I raised my own hand, then stopped. I didn't want to end up in front of Principal Ravenhearst's desk again, and I sure as all Nine Hells didn't want my mom to have to face off with another high-priced lawyer threatening to charge me with attempted assault. It was part of the downside of having a rep as the guy who supposedly knew magick. Even a bluff could get blown into something more serious. Besides that, Dr. C would have had me doing extra training for a week again. *That* was the down side of being the guy who *actually* knew magick.

I snatched my folder up from the ground, but not before it had collected several sets of footprints. Wanda met me halfway with my Algebra book and a conciliatory "Assholes." I nodded and we headed for class. My Monday wasn't starting out much better than my weekend had ended.

The pain in my ribs kept me awake through Algebra class. After learning hundreds of hexes, curses, and spells, all of them having variables that had variables of their own, math was simple. Once you solved for *x*, it didn't change if the month was different or if the stars weren't aligned right.

Wanda's advice echoed in my head all through first and second period, between the whispered comments and the snickers when Mr. Strickland asked me something about Prohibition. I had to admit I didn't know which state was the first to outlaw alcohol in its constitution, or when.

English was easier, but Phys. Ed kicked my ass. You try running laps with a busted rib. Having a girl on my mind and a double handful of words I wanted to take back even if it meant I had to eat them raw didn't make things any easier.

I dragged myself into the cafeteria with the same sense of dread that I'd learned to get used to this semester. Off to my right, I could see Brad with his new group of cronies, his arm around the girl of the month, Chelsea Tyler. She looked like she'd been poured from the same mold as his last six girlfriends: blond, skinny, and tan. The rest of the girls at the table were pretty much the same. The guys were all wearing the same shirt in different colors or patterns, and had enough product on their heads to start their own salon. I avoided their table by habit, but I could still hear the laughs as they spotted me. Once Brad had figured out that Principal Ravenhearst was just waiting for an excuse to expel me, he'd made it his personal mission to make my life hell. New rumors about Shade and me floated around every week, and I knew I'd given them plenty to work with Saturday night.

Shade wasn't at the table I shared with Wanda & Lucas, so I made my way over to my only other allies and friends at school: the Pack. Mark Tyler, Shade's beta, looked up at me and offered his hand as the other six gave me head nods or raised hands and quiet greetings.

"Hey, Tyler. You seen Alexis?" I asked. At school, they didn't use pack names, so I hadn't called Tyler by his.

"Yeah, she said she was going to the library." I nodded and headed for her favorite hiding place.

The library at Kennedy High School was the biggest of any of the high schools in the area. It took up two stories and had its own stairwells at the front and back. It also had one in the back corner that almost no one knew about. It didn't really come out near anything, and most students didn't make it very far from the computer stations near the front, anyway. I found Shade in her favorite spot, on the bottom steps at the first landing. Her hair draped down on either side of her face and cast her eyes in shadow. Even in the dim light of the stairwell, she looked incredible to me. She didn't slide away from me when I sat down next to her, and I took that as a good sign.

"I'm sorry about what I said this morning," I said. "That wasn't cool."

"I know Wanda told you to apologize," she said back. All I could do was shrug. "But . . . you were right. I do feel like I did when I was with Brad. Like I'm just a trophy girlfriend or something . . . an accessory." I winced at that. I'd called her those things when we first met.

"Shade . . . I'm really sorry I ever said that stuff. I'll apologize to you every day for the rest of my life if you want. I hate it when I say stupid shit and hurt you."

"Why did you ask me if I spent the whole weekend with Deek?"

"Because I was busy being an idiot."

"No, Chance, please, don't do that. Tell me why. Please? I need to know." She looked at me with those gray eyes, and my heart just flipped over. All the things I had wanted to say all day vanished in a wave of jumbled feelings, and I found my heart right back where it had been this morning.

"Because when I thought about you being . . . with him, you know? It just made me all crazy inside. All I could think of was that I wanted to be the one with you all weekend. I wanted to be the guy you wanted to kiss. I wanted to be the guy you were dancing with. I wanted to feel you in my arms, wished you wanted me . . . wished you looked at me like I imagined you looking at him. And it hurt to think of you with anyone else, because of the way I feel about you. Every time I see you any more, I feel it, right here," I touched my chest. "I just wish you wanted to be with me as much as I want to be with you." The thoughts came tumbling out, and it felt like I'd just laid my own heart down on the concrete between us.

She ducked her head for a moment, then she leaned in and wrapped her arm around me, and mine went around her shoulders automatically. Her head nestled into the hollow of my shoulder, and the smell of cinnamon filled my nostrils.

"You know I *was* a trophy for Brad . . . and worse for King. And Deek . . . when he looks at me, it's like Brad all over again. Like I'm just property. I don't want to be any man's whore ever again, Chance, but that was what I felt like all weekend. But this morning . . . I wanted to believe that you just wanted *me* because . . . well, I'm not sure why I wanted you to want me. But ever since you didn't let me . . . you know . . ." She stopped, and I turned and kissed the top of her head.

She'd tried to thank me for killing Dominic King and setting her and the rest of the pack free the only way she knew how: by offering to sleep with me. Telling her no was the second hardest thing I ever did, after escaping from a demon count. Monkey brain reminded me daily how stupid it thought I'd been to turn her down, and there were days I agreed with it. Okay, *most* days I agreed with monkey brain. But not right now. Not when she was too embarrassed to even say it.

"Yeah," I whispered softly to her, "I know."

We held each other in silence for a few more seconds before she said anything else.

"It's like you're the one guy who isn't trying to date me to get into my pants, and half the time, I can't figure out if I want to sleep with you because I know you'll let me say no, or if I like this whole 'I don't do casual sex' thing you've got going on too much. But this weekend . . ." her voice trailed off.

"What about this weekend?" I asked.

"Friday night, I wanted you. All weekend long, I wished it was you I was with. This morning, all I could think about was seeing you."

The next thing I knew, she had twisted so her weight was across my legs. Her arms went up over her head, and she tilted her head back. The move pulled her t-shirt up to expose her belly button, and

I laid my right hand on the bare expanse of skin. She trembled and let out a soft sound somewhere between a sigh and a whimper, then she lifted her head and gave me a coy look with gold eyes. Her skin was warm and smooth under my hand, and I wanted to feel more of it. I put my left arm behind her head and pulled her up to me. I meant to just pull her close, but her arms came up and she turned it into a slow kiss.

Her lips came away from mine a few moments later, and I opened my eyes. Hers were half closed, and her lips parted just a little. All I could think about was kissing her again, and my gaze went back to her eyes. They were green now, as her wolf faded back into the background. Even as I watched, the color faded to her normal gray. Her mouth lifted into a smile, and we kissed again: slow, probing, our tongues touching gently, lips moving against each other as we explored the kiss together. She caught my lower lip between her teeth and pulled back a little before she let go. Then she leaned in and rubbed her lower lip against my top lip for a moment as a prelude to another kiss.

Finally, she pulled away, and I forced myself to focus again as she straddled my legs and looked down at me with her own hands on her thighs. I laid mine on top of them to keep them out of forbidden places as she hunched her shoulders up and cocked her head. For a few seconds, she looked away from me. Then, she turned her eyes on me, her lower lip between her teeth and her hips moving as she squirmed a little on top of me.

"I do want to be with you, Chance," she finally said. "I want it as much as you do. I need *you* to be my alpha."

"Your alpha?" I asked. "You mean, you want me to . . . you know, be a werewolf?"

Her shoulders slumped as she sighed. "No, I mean be alpha male to my wolf. Treat me like . . . I'm yours. Be a little aggressive with me. Let me know you're the one in charge sometimes; that I don't *have* to be the strongest person in the room all the time. And I wouldn't mind if you were a little . . . possessive."

She reached up with her right hand and pulled her hair away from the left side of her neck as she tilted her head to the right. My eyes went to the exposed stretch of pale skin. Slowly, she leaned toward me until I felt her breasts press against my chest and her hair on the right side of my face and neck.

"Bite me," she said softly. I looked up at her in confusion for a moment.

"I don't . . ." I stammered.

"Please, trust me . . . please . . . I need you to do this. I have this wolf in me, Chance. She needs this as much as I do."

Her words were like fire in my head, and I put my teeth to her neck. Her stomach clenched against mine as I closed my mouth on her skin.

"Harder!" she hissed through clenched teeth.

I clamped down a little, and almost pulled back at how difficult it was to keep from biting as hard as I could.

"Harder!" she said again, and I let myself do it. She hissed and trembled as my teeth dug into her skin, then slumped against me.

I let go and put my arms around her as a whirlwind of feelings tumbled inside of me. I looked down at the purpling marks of my own teeth on her neck and felt a surge of pleasure at the sight. Immediately, I slapped the feeling down. What kind of guy was I if I enjoyed hurting her? The part of me that liked the sight seemed to draw back, and I felt it slide into its hidden place again. As it slithered into the dark shadows of my thoughts, I felt a fierce exultation. *Mine,* I felt more as a possessive urge than as a coherent thought.

"Shade, your neck," I said as I reached up and touched the bite mark. Her hand covered mine gently, and she smiled at me with her eyes blazing gold. There was a hunger in her look that made me wish we were anywhere else but here.

"Thank you," she whispered. The kiss almost made me forget what I'd done, but not quite.

"You better cover that up," I tried to tell her, but she just smiled and shook her head.

She stood and pulled me to my feet. "Werewolf, silly," she giggled. "It'll fade in a few minutes. Come on, we need to get out of here before we end up naked or something."

I did a mental facepalm. I pulled my shirt straight while she ran her fingers through her hair. Mine just took a good shake to get back to normal, then we slipped through the library and made for the cafeteria.

I was halfway through French when the whisper of magick against my senses snapped me out of the semi-doze I'd slipped into. As I tried to focus my senses on it, it felt like it slipped away, and I suppressed the urge to utter a few choice Infernal curse words as I realized that I was hitting some sort of concealment spell. Something was lurking in *my* school and, after Sunday, I wasn't feeling particularly happy about having the bad guys screw up one of the few normal things in my life, even if it sucked half the time. Besides, the last time, they'd caught me by surprise. I was looking forward to a little payback.

I pulled a green stick of chalk, a wood handled dip pen, and a vial of dragon's blood ink out of the spell supplies in my backpack and quietly set them out on my desk, then drew out a blank sheet of paper. As everyone around me worked on conjugating verbs, I dipped the pen in the vial and carefully drew out an Eye of Horus and enclosed it in two concentric circles. Between the inner and outer circle, I wrote out the phrase *Demonstra, quae abscondita est.* As the ink dried, I slipped my balisong out and shaved some chalk dust off the thick piece of chalk under the desk, catching it in my hand. Once I had enough, I dropped it on the symbol, then put my tools away.

The next part was the hardest. Under my former master, Dulka, I had learned how to cast a spell using an object as a focus for the energy. I'd needed pretty durable things to store the energy, and I always had to use the right tools and inscribe the correct symbols at the right time, in a circle, and so on. It made for potent spells, if I had the time and the supplies. He'd taught me that way to keep me crippled as a spellcaster. But Dr. C had been teaching me all kinds of new tricks over the past six months. Including how to imprint a spell on something that wasn't so sturdy, like paper, and release it a few minutes to an hour later. The trick to written spells was in the symbols and in how the magick was stored in them.

I took one corner of the page and whispered the Latin phrase I'd written in the circle as I folded it over. The tingle of magick spread from the center of my chest, down my arm, and into the page. Then I repeated the process with the other three corners. The trick wasn't in the words; it was in the complex spell matrix I had to hold in my head as I spoke the words. The symbol acted as a battery to store the energy, and each fold acted as a sort of barrier to the magick to hold it in until I said the release word.

"*Ligare,*" I whispered after I made the fourth fold.

My hair fluttered in the wash of excess energy that drained off of it and I could feel the hum of magick in it as it strained to contain the spell. It was far from my best work. Dr. C would have made me redo the whole damn thing if he ever saw it. I slipped it into my pocket and made sure I had my TK wand in my hand before I asked Mrs. Molierre if I could have the bathroom pass.

The halls were empty as I stepped out of the room. For a moment, I considered how stupid I was being. Here I was, facing the Powers knew what on my own, with nothing but attitude, a half-assed revealing spell that might blow up in my face, and my tried-and-true TK wand. Of course, I'd faced an alpha werewolf with about as much, and my old demon master with less, but both times, I'd had more time to prepare. I wasted a few seconds wishing I'd been able to figure out a way to sneak my paintball gun out of the class with me, but gave it up after a few steps. I didn't want to be distracted if whatever was hiding in the hallways decided to jump me.

I stretched my mystic senses as I went, but I couldn't feel anything over the hum of hundreds of people on the other side of the wall to my right. Even I could cast a decent enough concealment spell to stay invisible under those conditions. It would be like trying to not be heard in the mall: too damn easy. What I needed was a moment to concentrate, and feel for the difference in the energy, the bubble of 'not' that I couldn't see so I could find the target for my spell. As I headed down the hall, I saw the curved fish-eye mirror near the corner, and got a smile on my face as a flash of inspiration hit. Maybe I didn't need to hit whoever it was, if I could catch them in the mirror. It was a small surface, but it let me *see* a huge area.

As soon as I got to the corner, I ducked around it and pulled out the folded spell. I sensed the slight distortion as something came into the mirror's field of view as I held the vibrating piece of paper up toward the mirror and uttered the release phrase, "*At vero!*"

The paper disintegrated in a sparkling flash as the energy consumed it, and the chalk dust flew at the mirror. A distortion wave spread out in a circle with a warbling sound, then reality settled down. In the mirror, I could see the chalk slowly coalescing into a human form, then it fell away from the mirror to reveal a woman in a black shirt with an oversized ankh necklace around her neck. A Sentinel. What the hell was a wizard cop doing in my school?

The woman stopped in her tracks. For a moment, she looked down at herself, then her head turned to face the mirror. Dark eyes bored into me like a pair of black holes, sucking any emotion into them.

"What the hell?" she said. I was just as surprised. Sentinels were some of the best mages out there. They had to be, given what they did. But somehow, I'd managed to penetrate her concealment spell.

"How did you do that, warlock?" she scowled.

I gave my best nonchalant shrug.

"By accident?"

"Why did you assault me?" she demanded.

I realized I was hearing her voice in my head and that bugged me. But I had a bigger problem to deal with. Attacking a Sentinel was pretty much an instant death sentence from the Conclave.

"Because I didn't know you were running around invisible at my school!" I told her. "And aren't you supposed to not do that? This is neutral ground, or did you miss the big flag flying out front?"

Neutral ground was pretty serious stuff, since the flag in front of it essentially claimed the school as a public place, off limits for anyone to claim as their turf. The best the Conclave could do was operate undercover, like Dr. C did. Overt agents like Sentinels were completely forbidden, or so I thought.

I took a few steps closer to the mirror so I could see her better. She was pretty ordinary looking, brown hair, dark eyes, and a plain, round face that was easy to forget.

"You're still a fugitive from the High Council's justice," she said. "Even with the Council's indulgence to pursue your Ordeal, anywhere you go, I have leave to follow."

"Let me guess . . . you can't do squat to help though, can you?"

"No, I can't. My orders are only to follow and observe, unless you do something that goes against the Laws."

"Why?" I asked. "It's not like it'd be hard for you to find me now."

Her face went blank at my question. I'd done my share of poker face moments to know she was trying not to give something away.

"Who told you to follow me?" I demanded. Her eyes narrowed, like maybe she was considering her options before she answered.

"I . . . can't tell you which Council member ordered me to follow you. Or why."

Something in her eyes told me she wasn't lying, but there seemed to be more to what she was saying. Something I wasn't getting. I took another step closer, so I could see her for real, but when I came around the corner, I didn't see her. She was still visible in the mirror, though. In the mirror, I could see her eyes tracking back to the reflection, and a knowing smile spread across her bland face.

"Would you mind getting out of my head?" I asked.

"That isn't my doing. It's your spell. I hid myself from sight and hearing, but I didn't consider a reflection. You didn't break my concealment; you just stumbled around it. You're hearing me through the mirror. It seems we both learned something today."

"Yeah," I grumbled. A wave of my hand dispelled the casting. "Not sure I'm real happy about it, though."

When I told Dr. C about it during sixth period, he reacted about like I figured he would.

"Those pompous, back-stabbing pricks!" he hissed. "My bet is that Polter is behind this. He'd love nothing more than to catch you breaking one of the Laws. And sending in someone else to do all the work is just his style. Round face, brown hair, kind of young, I'd bet?" he recited my description of the Sentinel.

"Yeah, pissed off look. You know her?"

"Maybe. It could be Jane Dearborn. I'm betting the Council heard about your trip to the jail this weekend. That would be enough for Polter to convince them to set a Sentinel to watch your every move. Still, that shouldn't slow you down much, since you're not planning on breaking any of the Laws any time this week . . . right?" He gave me the raised eyebrow at the last, and I gave him a shrug to mess with him. He stalked away muttering about me getting him killed.

I needed to ditch the Sentinel to go after the asshole who had threatened my family. Collins was probably going to go orbital when he found out, too. If he found out. I waited until Dr. C was a couple of tables away before I leaned forward over the table and gestured for Lucas to get closer, too.

"Need you to text Donovan. Ask him if he can meet me at Finley Park around three," I whispered to him. He gave me a grim look.

"Are you sure, dude?" he asked softly, even as he pulled his cellphone out of his pocket.

"Yeah, I'm sure."

For a guy like Lucas, who saw his whole future revolving around his GPA, what I was about to do was almost blasphemous. He thought in terms of years. There was a missing girl out there, and her life might only be measured in days. Or even hours. With the Council's Ordeal to finish by Wednesday, I could relate.

I was going to have to skip class.

Skipping class is easy if you're a normal kid. If you're an apprentice mage and you happen to have an illegal *neglinom* charm you beat up a necromancer to get, it's a breeze. Skipping class without being caught by a teacher, a Sentinel, and a street-smart cop? That's a little harder. I had to step into wood shop so my Sentinel saw me go in, then get the *neglinom* charm on and slip back out without bumping into anyone, and I had to do it before the door closed to start the period. The trick was in the timing.

Once I got out of the class, I still had to make it to Finley Park by three, which meant I had to run. *Neglinom* charms are good at making you forgettable, but that's only if you're not drawing attention to yourself by doing something like running. So, once I was clear of the school building, I made my way across to the stadium and jumped the drainage ditch that ran behind the football field. Once I was on the other side, I slipped the charm off and broke into a jog. Finley was about half a mile from the school, and I made it there only a couple of minutes after three.

Donovan was waiting by the skate park on the east side of the park. Half a dozen skaters were already there in jeans and zippered hoodies, all of them giving the big guy on the motorcycle the wary eye from under their hoods or backwards baseball caps. Me showing up didn't make them jump for joy, either. Combat boots, jeans, and a leather jacket didn't fit with any one group, and I wasn't wearing my hair in any style that said I was a jock or a Goth or whatever. Besides, as I found out on Friday night, I was already getting a rep as the guy who knew magick.

Dr. C had told me once that outside of a very few friends, I'd probably never really fit in anywhere because I was a mage. He'd called it being "distinctly Other." I didn't think about things other kids thought about, didn't talk about what they talked about, and wasn't interested in the things they were interested in. Even when I ditched seventh period, I wasn't just hanging out with friends or something fun. No, when I skipped school, I did it to avoid a mage cop and find the guy who'd threatened my family. I shook my head as I realized I lived in a completely different world than the kids around me.

"Sorry I'm late," I said as I walked up.

"No problem, man," Donovan said. "What's up?"

"I need to track someone down." He nodded.

"Lucas told me about Sunday morning," he told me as he tossed an extra helmet my way.

"Good. Less explaining. Head for my house," I said as I slipped the plastic bowl over my head.

"Aren't you gonna catch a lot of crap for this?" He asked a few minutes later as we sped down a side road.

"Only if I don't make it back in time," I answered.

He leaned forward and poured on a little more speed. A few minutes later, we were pulling into the alleyway behind my house.

I slid off the back and handed him the helmet, then I knelt down and took my backpack off. From inside it, I pulled my indigo chalk, my *athame* and *boline*, and the baggie I'd tucked the handkerchief with Fedora's blood on it into.

While most seeking spells were supposed to be able to be done from anywhere, I'd always had the best luck when I cast them near the last place what I was looking for had been. Even if it didn't make sense to anyone else, it made sense to me, and all magic was fueled by the caster's will. If I believed it would work better this way, it would.

It took a minute or two to draw the casting circle and to get the symbols inside it right. I closed it with a whispered "*Circumvare*," and felt the world seem to go silent around me. Really, it was just the absence of all the rest of the background noise against my mystical senses, but my brain told me it got quiet. I held my amethyst over the blood-stained cloth and uttered the spell, willing the connection between my little crystal and the blood beneath it.

"*Velle, virtutem quaero, videtur tacta, XXXllust tenere*!"

As the last word sounded, I felt the power of the spell build, and the pendulum started to move in a slow circle, getting faster with each rotation. After the seventh time, I nudged my boot across the chalk line and broke the circle. The pendulum stopped spinning and leaned to the south-east. I hopped the steps down and crossed the yard at a jog.

"What the hell is that?" Steve asked.

"No time for questions. Game's afoot and all that!" I called out as I straddled the bike again. I slid the helmet on and held the amethyst out where he could see it. "That way!"

"Straight?" he asked over his shoulder, pointing to the garage we'd have to plow through to follow it.

"That way-ish, then. You know the drill. We follow it until we find it, and hope we do it quick!"

"Your 'ish' is my command, sahib," he quipped before he gunned the throttle and we headed down the alley.

The stone held true as we hit a southbound street, only moving a little to the east as we went. When we saw a sign for the freeway, I pointed it out to him, and he nodded. Less than a minute later, we were on Highway 71 east with the wind in our faces and cars sliding by on our right as he took over the fast lane. I had to lean back and cup the pendulum in my hand between his back and my body to keep it from getting blown all over the place.

The pendulum started to swing south, and I tapped Steve's shoulder when it got close to pointing all the way to my right. He yelled something into the wind and the bike leaned to the right.

Three lanes of asphalt slid by under us, and I fought to keep my cool as he cut across the path of a semi with only a few feet to spare. We hit the off ramp at speed, and I felt myself slide forward on the seat as he braked hard. The front of the bike dipped down as we slowed down, and I pointed to the right. The light was green, so he took the turn without stopping, and we headed down Republic Avenue. The pendulum swung to the left as we went, until it was pointing across the fifth red light we came to at a club called Inferno.

"Jackpot," I muttered as it swung to keep Inferno on point as Steve crossed through the intersection. I pointed at the club, and he nodded, then circled around until we were turning into the parking lot.

Inferno was all white concrete and glass in front, with a neon marquis. The club's name in flaming letters showed on the sign, then spun away to show that the club was closed for renovation until Thursday. It dropped to announce Love In Chains was playing Friday, opening for Personal AntiChrist. Then it came back to the Inferno logo.

"*Ego sum inter illustrator,*" I whispered as I got off the bike and pulled my helmet off. *I am among the enlightened.*

A series of vampiric glyphs flared to life above the doorway. I could recognize vampire glyphs, but I only knew the meanings of a few of them. The two I did understand were enough to make my blood turn cold. The first one was common to any territory claimed by a clan of vamps, basically saying, "This is our feeding ground, don't hunt here." The second one was a cabal mark, and it was one I recognized.

"What is it?" Steve asked as I hissed a curse. He'd come to stand beside me while I was staring at the glyphs.

"This just got complicated," I told him. "This is a vampire clan's feeding ground. Which means the messenger boy we followed here works for one of Lord Thraxus' minions."

"Which means exactly what?" Steve asked. He turned to face me, and his eyes flicked to the marquis. I gave him a hard look.

"Which means we can't just go in there and start with the smackdown like I want to. Not unless we want every vamp in the city after us with sanction to drain us dry."

"There's evil in there, Chance, I can feel it. It's like a thousand ants on my skin. I've never felt it this bad before. We can't just walk away from this." His jaw set and his eyebrows settled like thunderclouds.

"Steve, we *have* to. As much as I want to go in there and shed the light of day on every single one of these bloodsuckers, we can't. You have to understand how sanguinary politics works. This guy isn't far down the ladder from Thraxus, maybe a lieutenant or even a trusted lieutenant, depending on how literal you take the Evil Overlord list. And I'm in the know, uh, *inter XXXllustrate*. Which means I can read the glyphs over the door and I know who this guy answers to. If I do that, then Thraxus has to hit me back hard."

"I know the risks, Chance," he said. "I'm a big boy. I can take care of myself."

"No, you don't. If the lord of a cabal comes after you, you're the *last* person he kills. He starts with your friends, then he kills your family. Painfully and slowly, and he makes sure you know it was all your fault. If he's feeling generous, they'll stay dead. Then he comes for you, when he's sure you know everyone you ever cared about is dead because of you. If he does anything less than end your bloodline, it looks like he can't take care of his own people, and that makes him look weak. Then he has to worry about waking up with a stake through his ribs, or at the bottom of the Marianas Trench in a coffin full of concrete. You may not give a shit about your family, but I have a mom and a sister I've already put in harm's way. So help me if *you* put them in danger, I will kill you so hard your own mother will forget she ever had you."

I looked up at him and felt the pull of a Horus gaze about to begin as our eyes locked. I resisted it, but I could see that he had glimpsed something in my eyes. He looked away for a second, then backed up. He may have had six inches and the better part of a hundred pounds on me, but there was no way I was backing down.

"All right, we play it your way. But for the record, I won't play by their rules forever." He got on the bike and tossed my helmet at me. "A man has to take a stand somewhere."

I stepped up to him and put a hand on his shoulder.

"We're not playing by their rules," I told him. "They're playing by ours."

***

"He went *where*?" Dr. C asked. He had that barely calm tone to his voice that Mom's sometimes had when she was trying her best not to freak out. He leaned back in the leather chair and looked at me from across his desk like he was trying to stare through me.

Behind me, I could hear Cross and T-Bone suppressing chuckles. As amused as they were, I was so busted.

"Inferno," Cross rumbled after a few seconds. "It's a vampire-run club just off Republic. They use it mostly as a blood tap. Not a bad source of revenue, either."

"Why?" he asked me directly, the first words he'd spoken to me since we'd gotten back to his place and found Cross and T-Bone waiting for us.

"I was following the guy who attacked mom and Dee," I told him. "I was testing a theory."

"Don't try that with me, Chance. You're already on thin ice with the Council, and sneaking off isn't going to help at all. Besides, *if* your theory is correct, this had nothing to do with the Maxilla."

"Somethin' tells me it does," T-Bone said. "Or at least, it's got somethin' to do with the wyrd. Kid might have gone off the rez, but every divination we did said he was doin' what he was supposed to."

"You should have come to me, Chance," Dr. C shook his head. "I can't help you if you won't let me. And you put yourself in a great deal of danger. Do you know who owns Inferno?"

"Thraxus." I smiled at the reaction the word got out of Dr. C; the frown on his face turned into an eyebrow-raising look of surprise.

Behind me, I heard T-Bone give a satisfied little grunt. Cross swore softly under his breath.

"I keep forgetting who you spent the bulk of your childhood with," Dr. C said quietly. "I should have realized you'd know that."

"Yeah, and there's more. Thraxus has a pet demon, Furcas the Impaler."

"How'd he manage that?" Cross asked. I shrugged.

"Just that badass, I guess. Neither one of them talks about it. Still, Dr. C, I have to go talk to Thraxus. One of his people threatened my family. If I don't at least show up and make some noise about it, he'll do something worse next time. At the very least, I need to figure out why he sent Darth Fedora to talk to me." I put my hands on his desk and leaned in. "Please, Dr. C. I'm going to go do it whether you say I can or not. I just don't want to waste time sneaking out of the house is all."

He leaned forward, put his elbows on the desk, and steepled his fingers so that he was looking at me over the tips of his fingers.

"Exactly how likely is he to put you on the menu?" he asked after a few moments.

"Not very, since you know where I'm going. If I take someone else along, the chances of him having me for dinner drop a lot more. Harder to explain two missing people. I'd take those two," I pointed over my shoulder, "but he wouldn't let them inside. Same goes for you. But I think I know who I *can* take that will keep him on his best behavior."

Chapter 12

~ Lie. Cheat. Threaten. Intimidate. All of those things are accepted, even encouraged, among the vampyri. But never steal, and never bluff. ~ Killian Moon, monster hunter

Two hours later, I found myself standing in front of the very big, very old mansion that everyone thought belonged to a very rich man named Cassius Cromwell. On paper, they were right, but Cromwell was Thraxus' White Mask: his legal presence in the world. Everything Cromwell was, he owed to Thraxus, including his long life. I'd never been inside Chateau Thraxus, but rumor had it that the place had been built in the early 1800s. There was supposed to be a grand ballroom in there somewhere, and a theater complete with projector booth. Under the moonlight, the beige limestone was more of a pale gray, with squares of light peeking through the façade.

I'd ridden out on the back of Steve's bike, with T-Bone and Cross following us. Donovan fidgeted as we waited for the third person in my little adventure to show. I figured he could feel the evil that lurked inside the Cromwell Mansion from the road, and taking him inside was going to be tough on him. But he was one of two people I knew who would stand a good chance of getting out alive if things went to Hell.

I smiled as I heard the throaty buzz of Shade's Ninja a few seconds before I caught sight of her headlight coming around the corner. Then another sound intruded, a rumbling growl from a bigger engine, and I saw another headlight behind her. She pulled in behind T-Bone's Torino, and the bike behind her followed suit.

"Nice Harley," Steve said in open admiration.

I was about to say something when Deek pulled his helmet off and stood there like a hero in an action film. While he stood posing for effect, Shade came up to me with a frown marring her brow. She reached up with her left hand and pulled her hair away from the right side of her neck and pulled the collar of her shirt aside with her right hand. With a dark look back at Deek, she tilted her head to the side in invitation. As much as I wanted to repeat what we did during lunch, I hesitated.

"Please?" she whispered.

She gave me a sultry smile and I gave in to the urge. As my teeth clamped down on her soft white skin, she gave a soft moan and arched her back a little to press against me. I let go a lot faster this time; she stepped back with her eyes closed and sighed softly. When she opened them, they were gold.

Behind her, Deek was glaring daggers at me. Great, on top of going in to a vampire's lair, I had a pissed-off beta to deal with.

"What's he doing here?" I demanded.

Shade looked over her shoulder at him, then gave me a smile.

"Pouting," she said. "He followed me on his own, Chance. He's not part of the Pack, so I really can't tell him what to do." Deek came up behind her and glared at me over her shoulder.

"Right. I *so* needed this night to get more complicated."

"Back off and things'll go a lot smoother for you," Deek said. He went to put a hand on her shoulder, and she shrugged it off.

"Go home, and things'll stay attached," Shade growled. He gave her a frosty smile and stepped around her.

"You can't tell me what to do, and neither can he. I can smell vampires in that house, and I'm not letting him take you in there on his own. I'm going with you. Deal with it."

He turned and gave me a level look. The problem was, he had me and he knew it. The mystical world lived by its honor, and if he was Shade's guest, she couldn't do anything to stop him. And unless I wanted a bunch of Weres pissed at me, I couldn't either. All he lost by acting like an ass was another invitation.

"It works to your favor by taking him with you," Cross said quietly from behind me. "If they eat him, it might look bad for Shade, but it also risks war with a second Pack. Thraxus is powerful, but he's not a fool. He won't risk making that many enemies at once."

I glared over my shoulder at him, then turned back to face Deek.

"Fine, you can come," I spat. "Once we're inside, this is my show. You do exactly what I tell you to do. First off, vamps are big on hospitality. Just by going in, we're agreeing to the courtesies of the Accords. That means we're nice to our hosts. They're also big on debt. Gifts are never just gifts. If we eat or drink anything they offer us, we give them the right to feed on us. If they give us something, and we accept it, we have to offer something in return. You can turn something down, but you have to do it the right way. Leave that to me."

"Vamps like to make you flinch and they'll push your buttons, it's like a game to them," T-Bone said. "One of 'em gets in your face, smile. Don't let 'em think they got under your skin."

Steve nodded, and Shade stepped past Deek and took my hand. The beta snorted as we turned and headed across the road to the gate. We barely got off the main road when a vamp in a black suit appeared in front of us.

"You are not welcome here," he hissed at me. He was flashing fang at us, which meant he was taking us seriously enough to be rude.

"Your Master's people weren't welcome in my home, either, but that didn't stop them." I told him. "His house is open to me until things are even between us."

He lowered his lip over his teeth and glared at me.

"Big words for a demon's little bitch," he said. I took the blood-splattered handkerchief out of my pocket and tossed it at him. He rolled his shoulder to avoid letting it touch him, and I scored the next point in the game.

"Take that to your Master, and see if I tell the truth. Then, when we get inside, call me that again."

He picked it up off the driveway and held it to his nose, then he frowned at me before he disappeared.

As soon as he was gone, I let my hand fall on the butt of my paintball gun. I'd come armed to the teeth, with my paintball gun strapped to my left leg, my wand and touchstone in my jacket pocket, and a handful of charms wrapped around my right wrist. Going in to a cabal master's lair with anything less than an arsenal on you was considered an insult if you didn't know them personally, and Thraxus and I weren't that close.

Ten minutes later, the gate opened on its own. Everyone looked at me, and I started walking up the driveway. It was still a hundred yards or so to the house, and common courtesy would have been to send a car down for us whether we started walking or if we waited. The trick was in how long it was before he sent them.

"So, if he sends a car down, we don't get in," Deek said.

I nodded. It wasn't that simple, but I didn't have time to explain. Headlights lit up the ground in front of us, and I struggled to keep my face neutral. Everyone followed my example when I stepped to my right and waited at the side of the drive. A few seconds later, twenty feet of white limo followed the twin cones of light on the ground. It pulled up until the driver's side window was even with me, and the tinted glass slid down with a hum. Behind it was a blond woman with ample curves in a shirt whose top three buttons had probably never seen a buttonhole. The ones below that strained to stay on the shirt, as they fought to contain what was beneath them. I tried not to stare, but it was like her cleavage had its own gravity. I wondered if even light escaped from it as she turned smoky blue eyes on me and smiled with full red lips.

"I'm at your service, if you require a ride to the house," the young woman behind the wheel said. The way she wrapped her voice around the words made it sound like she was offering another kind of ride entirely, and I was sure that was supposed to be the message I got. After all, what else do you send to tempt a fifteen year-old boy?

Beside me, I could feel Shade tense.

"Our host's offer is both gracious and timely. I'm afraid that we can't accept his generosity right now, if only because it wouldn't be .

. . proper, under the circumstances." The words were slow and clumsy coming out of my mouth. I'd been talking like a normal person for the past six months, so the slightly formal cadence of the Veiled world took a little work to get back into.

"If you should change your mind, the offer remains . . . open." She shifted slightly in the seat, and I could see her knees move under the skirt. Yeah, that was about as subtle as wrecking ball.

I stepped back, and she gave me a lingering smile as she pulled away. Shade's glare was a weight on my skin as we waited for her to pass us by on the way back.

"That wasn't exactly turning her down," she growled as she fell in beside me again. Deek chuckled, and earned himself equal time under her scrutiny.

"I'm still a little rusty, okay? The Graces are a very precise art. It takes practice to get good at them, and more to stay good." I glanced her way to see if she was going to let it go, but her face hadn't softened any. Her hand tightened on mine, possessively, however, and I took it as a good omen.

We made it the rest of the way to the house, and the door opened as we mounted the marble steps. The same guy from the gate was waiting for us, framed in the doorway like a man-shaped hole of darkness against the light. We still weren't exactly invited in, which meant that I would lose most of my power if I crossed Thraxus' threshold without being asked in.

"So, am I still a demon's bitch, or are you going to take my stuff and make me come in uninvited?" I asked as I got to the door. His eyes narrowed and he stayed in place for a second as we played the game and tried to see who would flinch first. The first option meant he'd have to close the door on me with an open complaint against his Master. His life would last about six seconds longer than his career as a doorman if he took that option. If he took door number two and made me come in unarmed and uninvited, it said to the whole world that his Master considered me a threat. He really had only one option, but the way I'd played it, it made him the one offering it, instead of me asking for it. To his credit, he smiled and stepped aside. He'd chosen door number three. In vampire politics, it meant I was slightly ahead in the game, since I wasn't one of them. They hated making concessions to mortals.

"My Lord asks that you come in, and he offers safe passage to you and those with you, if you wish it," he said. My mouth twisted up into the half-grin my mom hated. Two things offered at once, the first of which I could expect as my due because I had a complaint against one of his people. The second, however, would leave me in is debt if I took him up on it.

"We accept his invitation, but safe passage is not required. This is a matter of honor, I'm sure we will be able to handle things between us . . . amicably enough." The doorman smiled, knowing I'd allowed his earlier insult to pass in order to leverage him into letting me keep my weapons. If he was on the dumb side, he would think he'd scored big on me and lose a lot of respect for me. If he was smart, he'd know that a little pride was a small price to pay for surviving the night. He stepped aside and gestured with one hand for us to step past him.

Shade, Deek, and Steve followed me in. Over my shoulder, I saw them look around in awe. The foyer itself was huge, with a pair of white marble staircases on either side that led to a balcony. A pair of gilt double doors loomed on the far side of the balcony, with another pair below. White double doors on either side led into other sections of the house. A pair of statues missing the arms stood on either side of the foyer, and paintings framed in gold hung on the walls. I didn't know Rembrandt from Bob Ross, but I was willing to bet all of them were originals, and worth more than some pieces of real estate. Red carpet that was thick enough to lose small pets in was laid in a path from the door to the staircases and the other exits from the room. A heavy chandelier hung in the middle of the room, and antique looking chairs and tables sat in corners, making the room look more welcoming than it was.

The most disconcerting thing about the room, though, was the vampires scattered around it. One lounged in a chair on the ground floor, in a tux that looked almost a decade out of date. Another leaned on the banister of the right-hand staircase, wearing a leather jacket, a black t-shirt, and jeans. A third, a girl in a little black dress, lounged at the top of the stairs. It took me a moment to even notice them, and that bothered me. Young vamps had a hard time blending in with people because they forgot the basics. They would spend a long time not breathing, or they'd smile with their mouths open. But older vamps, while they could remember the basics better with years of practice, had a whole different level of creep factor when they weren't putting on the act. They had a way of just going *still* that made it hard to forget that you were in the room with a walking corpse. Dead people just don't fidget or move randomly.

Steve was stiff and pale beside Deek, and Shade's hand trembled in mine, though I couldn't tell if it was from fear or ferocity. Don't get me wrong; I was having a hard time keeping it together myself. When the doors on the balcony opened, I had to fight the urge to grab my TK wand from my pocket. But then, Steve and I were probably sensing almost the same thing. I could feel the demonic presence press against my mystic senses, and I was sure Steve was getting major evil vibes off the blue-skinned demon that stepped out on to the upper level.

It wore black robes that concealed most of its body, but its face was easy enough to see. A ring of small spines stuck out of its head and encircled its skull above the ears. Two larger horns curved away from its cheeks and around its face to end up a few inches apart, in front of the raised ridge of cartilage around its nostrils. A bony ridge separated the nostrils and stuck out a little, giving a two-dimensional illusion of a nose. Red eyes with vertical slits stared down at us for a moment, and I got the feeling this was one pissed-off demon.

"Come," it said with a voice that sounded like it was chewing rocks. "The Master awaits you."

Our escort led us up the left hand side of the stairs, and the female vamp moved to stand to the right side of us as we came up. She eyed Steve up and down, then stepped up to him with a hungry look in her eyes.

"We like this one," she said in a dry hiss. "It smells delicious. Fear and impotent anger. We think we'll take it." She lunged at him, and the big guy moved.

I saw his arm as a blur, and the sound of flesh hitting something solid resounded through the foyer. The vamp flew away from him and hit the wall with a thud, then bounced off and hit the ground. Cracks spider-webbed away from where she hit, with the largest one behind where her spine had impacted. She tried to get back to her feet, and I tried to stop Steve. Both of us were too slow. He was on her in a heartbeat and had her held up in the air with one hand around her throat by the time I got to his side. The woman's smile was fading as his fingers dug into her throat.

"Choking her is of no use," the blue-skinned demon said as he reached for Steve.

I jumped between them and raised my hands.

"Not trying to choke her," Steve grunted as the vamp started to struggle against his grip. "Trying to break . . . her neck!"

Her struggles became more desperate at that.

"Steve, put her down!" I said over my shoulder to him.

"No!" he barked. I turned, came around on his offhand side, and grabbed his face to make him look at me. His whole face was red from the effort he was putting into the death grip he had on the vamp, and veins were starting to pop out on his forehead. His eyes were distant, as if he was seeing a completely different world than the one I was standing in.

"You're going to get Crystal killed if you do this!" I said.

His eyes focused on me and his arm lowered. The vampire scuttled back, and I saw the blue demon come around to his side. I had a bad feeling that things were about to start sucking.

"You dare bring a Nazarite among us?" it grumbled.

"A what?" Steve and I asked at the same time.

It did a double take and stared at us for a second.

"You truly do not know what he is," it said. We shook our heads, and it gave us a disdainful look. "Perhaps it is best that we allow this to even the balance of things a bit between you and this august house."

I weighed that in my head against what I still had to do. I hated to give up even an ounce of the little bit of leverage I had, but if I didn't, I'd end up with a pissed-off vampire lord and nothing to show for the trip out here.

"A bit," I agreed.

"She was foolish to antagonize one whose first instinct is to kill. Especially an untrained boy."

"I apologize for acting in ignorance," I countered. "I should have known better."

We bowed slightly to each other: an acknowledgement between equals for the moment. He turned and led us through the double doors, and into a broad hallway.

The doors at the end opened before us, and we found ourselves entering a grand ballroom. I sensed a mix of vamps and humans and other races. One cold presence on the edge of my senses seemed to belong to a woman with jet black skin and oversized fangs drinking something out of a skull. Her red eyes looked at me with the kind of hunger that I usually reserved for my mom's cooking. She smiled around her fangs before she turned away, and I was relieved to see the flame-red ponytail that ran down her back to her tailbone. Rakshasas didn't usually like to spend a lot of time in U.S., so I was guessing a temporary guest. I looked around and guessed at maybe a hundred people in the room, or to be more accurate, less than fifty 'people' and the rest people-ish.

Then my attention turned to the focal point of the room: the pale guy sitting on the raised platform on the far side of the room. Even though the platform was less than a foot high, it seemed like it was much higher. The man himself was bald, with ears that were pierced along the outside with multiple silver rings and a slightly elongated jaw. Sunken eyes were shadowed by heavy, dark eyebrows, and his fingers seemed too long, even without the claws on his fingertips. The plain, black jacket he wore looked Chinese, with a straight collar and buttons that were slightly off center.

People milled about below him, vying for his attention, trying to get a scrap of his time. The demonic major domo made that part easy for me.

"My Lord Thraxus," he boomed.

The room went quiet.

"I present Chance Fortunato, apprentice mage, and advisor to Shade, alpha of the Diamond Lake Pack."

The crowd moved away from Thraxus' chair as he stood to face me with his arms spread slightly.

"Ah, the Red Count's escaped apprentice. Welcome to my home, young man." He gestured for me to come forward with a smile.

I stepped to the edge of the low dais, and he reached down to put one hand on my shoulder, then he turned to usher me onto it as he moved toward the back of it. A pair of French doors waited at the back.

"Furcas, please have the musicians strike up an air. Mr. Fortunato and I have a small bit of business to discuss," he said over his shoulder as we headed for the doors. "Your friends will be seen to, never fear," he said softly as I looked back over my shoulder. "So long as they have a modicum of good sense, they will leave here in the same shape they arrived." His voice was a warm tenor, smooth and controlled. I gave Shade a nod, and she let Furcas usher them to one side.

"That's reassuring," I replied as the doors opened before us at a gesture from him.

"It's meant to be," he smiled as we stepped out onto the balcony. "Your lack of respect is hardly endearing." Below us, I could see the lights of New Essex spread out in front of me like a net of sparkling jewels to the southeast. I put my hands on the stone balustrade.

"Looks like you have enough people trying to kiss your ass already," I said. "And, I like to stand out." To my surprise, he started laughing.

"It's refreshing," he said after a moment. "I don't think there is enough room to attach another pair of lips at any pass. Pleasantries aside, let us address your claim of trespass. Your proof is a few drops of human blood you claim belongs to one of mine, on a handkerchief. Hardly convincing." He said it with a smile, with a hint of menace under the light tone.

"There's more where that came from. It's spread pretty randomly around my mom's kitchen. If a half-trained apprentice like me can follow it to Inferno, then imagine what a fully trained mage could do with a few drops. Or even a wizard like Trevor Corwyn. Besides, you opened your gates to me based on those few drops of blood, so you know they can be traced back to you."

I didn't turn away from the city as I spoke, but I glanced his way to see his eyebrows twitch and the corners of his mouth tighten.

"Inferno . . ." he said softly. "If you followed him to Inferno, then he is one of Etienne's creatures. Etienne is one of my eldest children, thus one of my most trusted. I give him a great deal of leeway, apprentice Fortunato. Your accusation is serious, and you have given me no reason why I should think Etienne sent his servants to you without provocation. Guilty or no, if I go to him, he will have some explanation prepared. The burden falls upon you, whom I have known for less than the span of an hour, to give me cause to mistrust the childe I sired almost three centuries ago."

His stare hit me like a brick. There was no mistaking the threat in his tone this time. This wasn't a hint or an implication; it was a promise of a messy, painful death if I screwed this up. So I took a moment to think it through.

"Dulka said once that you had five of the G'Honn fragments. The cops are investigating a bunch of disappearances . . . kids, mostly fringers, Goths, Emos, outsiders. Some runaways, a few just loners. The kind of kid most people outside of family wouldn't miss. And guess what they found near where each kid was last seen?" I pulled the pictures Collins had given me out of my pocket and laid them down on the stone railing.

"It's Lemurian," Thraxus commented flatly. "But very few would know it was from the G'Honn. You might, but the connection between this case and you, apprentice, is still far from clear."

"The girlfriend of one of the missing kids came to me, asking me to break a spell on her girlfriend. She's a sensitive; she could feel the enchantment. I tracked it back to a guy named Julian. He ended up dead the next night, right under one of these," I tapped the photos. "Guess who their prime suspect was? So, I cooperated with the cops, because I'm too pretty for juvie. The next morning, two guys showed up at my house, telling me to stop interfering in their master's business. My guess? I got closer in one night than the cops have in five months. These guys work for Etienne, and the only thing he'd know about that I've been up to lately is this. And from what you just told me, if anyone would have a shot at the only collection of the fragments in the area, it'd be your boy Etienne. How's that for a connection?" Thraxus looked at the photos for a few moments before he replied.

"Disturbing," he said. "What does the Conclave know of this?"

"Squat. Corwyn is focusing on something else right now. I should be, too, but . . . well, I'm not."

"Yes, there are larger concerns on the minds of many right now. And what do you expect me to do, little mageling? Confront Etienne and risk an internal conflict now, when the drums of war are sounding on the horizon? Promise you the big, bad vampire will leave your mother and sister alone? Maybe I should slap him on the back of a hand with a ruler and chastise him for making me so vulnerable to exposure, based on the words of a half-trained mage and disgraced demon's apprentice!"

He stalked toward me as he spat the words out, and his eyes started to glow red. He ended on a fang-baring snarl, and I took a step back. Sometimes, you just have to flinch to keep the game from escalating, and I did it without a moment's pause. Besides, he was *really* scary right then. The trick to flinching is in your recovery. Dr.

Corwyn had taught me a few months ago that in social situations, you could take your opponent's attack further than they wanted it to go.

"I know your hands are kinda tied in all this, Lord Thraxus," I said softly, using a little verbal judo. If he wanted to play up how he wasn't going to do anything, then it was time to make it look like he *couldn't* do anything. "And I'm not really asking you to do anything, because I know you can't, not as things stand. Hell, I'll even let this first attack slide for now. What I want is consent to confront him if he does it again." His eyes faded back to their normal lifeless gray, and he cocked his head to one side.

"Why should I grant you sanction against him if you fail to heed his warning?" he asked with a smile.

"Because I'm not getting the Conclave involved," I countered. He gave me a slow smile.

"Because you dare not," he mocked. "Your so-called evidence linking me to this is thin, at best."

"Not if you keep protecting him. I let this slide once and it just looks a little fishy. But if you cover for him twice . . . even the dumbest Conclave mage is going to believe me if I lay this down in front of them." His eyes narrowed to slits and his upper lip curled away to reveal razor sharp fangs.

"What you ask cannot be easily granted to one outside of the clan. All I can promise is that I will look into it." He turned away from me.

In the distance, I saw lighting flash, and tall, fluffy clouds lit up from the inside like an explosion in freezeframe.

"So, I'm just supposed to take your word for it, and hope he doesn't do it again?" I asked.

His dry chuckle reminded me of leaves burning.

"That is the best you humans can ever hope for from the *vampyri*," he said.

"Then here is the best you can hope for from me. If he tries to attack me again, I *will* go after him. And I won't stop until he's dead. I told his boys this, and I'll tell you: You do not fuck with my family."

I never saw him move.

One moment, I was laying down a threat, and the next, I was on the ground, looking up into his eyes. His hand was around my throat, holding me down, and all I was aware of was fear. Cold, bone-chilling fear. I was paralyzed by it, with no thought but to cower before his terrible will. There was no escape, no thought; there was just the certainty that horrible things were about to happen to me and there was nothing I could do about it.

On the heels of that fear came something else, something colder. If I couldn't stop him from ripping the flesh from my bones, then I could still hurt him. Maybe I could drag him with me to whichever Hell was waiting for me. I reached into the icy well of hate that followed fear and touched one of the few spells I could do on my own.

"Ingus Infernum," I croaked past the band of steel that was wrapped around my throat.

Hellfire ripped through me and blossomed into bluish black flames around my hands. Thraxus was gone before I felt the power surge through me, and I sat up to see him across the patio. I wanted nothing more than to wipe the smile off his face.

"Stay your wrath, mageling," he said calmly. "I guaranteed your safety. I merely needed to be sure you could make good on your promise."

I stopped and let the magic fade, but I kept the glare on him at full strength.

"And?" I said. "What are my odds?"

"For most of your kind, I'd say you stood no chance whatsoever. You, I would give slim to narrow odds. But magi have a way of bending the odds to their favor. And you . . . I feel the touch of Fate upon you." He gave me a half smile that didn't really give anything away.

"Yeah, I've been getting that a lot lately," I told him.

"You're familiar with the etiquette and courtesies that rule our world, little apprentice. You came here knowing what you would get from me. While you play the Great Game well enough to survive, it does not suit you. Let us dispense with the façade. I take your claims seriously, but until I know more, or Etienne oversteps his bounds with you again, I can make no promises. If you truly are willing to . . . how did you put it? Let the first offense slide? If you are willing to do that, then the balance swings in your favor, and the debt will be mine for the moment."

"For now, it'll do."

I got a slow nod for a reply, and he turned back toward the doors to his ballroom. In the distance, thunder rumbled across the sky. I glanced over my shoulder in time to catch a cascade of red lightning as it streaked along the bottom of the approaching cloudbank. As I passed him, he placed a hand on my shoulder.

"You should hurry home, child. There's a storm coming," he said quietly.

No, that wasn't ominous or anything.

Chapter 13

~ Cowan technology is nice, but it will never replace good old fashioned magick. ~

Caleb Clay, Master Mage

Cross and T-Bone were gone when we left. The trip back to Dr. C's place on the back of Shade's bike was a thrill ride. With her Were reflexes, she made moves that left me wondering what had just happened. She zipped in and out of traffic at speed, and leaned deep into impossible turns. Deek barely kept up with us, and Steve fell in behind him until we came up on the exit off the freeway that would take us to Dr. C's street. A semi pulled on ahead of us with a line of cars behind it. The smart thing would have been to slow down and get into the exit lane behind them.

Shade looked back over her shoulder then leaned forward over the handlebars. I followed suit as she twisted the throttle and we surged ahead. Deek's bike roared behind us as we passed the cars, then the semi was sliding by on my right, the trailer's bottom edge even with my eyes. Up ahead, I could see the exit, and my eyes went wide as I realized how close she was going to be cutting it. Then there was nothing on my right but air and the headlights of the semi's cab. The bike leaned hard to the right, and I watched each letter on the tractor's grill slide past as I looked over my shoulder.

We cleared the front bumper by about six inches, then the yellow crash barrier zoomed by on my left, and we were heading down the ramp, the bike growling its displeasure as Shade downshifted. The growl and deep rumble of Steve and Deek's bikes faded as they headed for the next exit. We pulled to a stop at the light, and Shade looked over her shoulder at me. She was smiling under her helmet, and there was a fierce heat in her gaze.

"I like it when you hold me like that."

"Like what?" I asked, trying to keep my bravado up. I was scared, but I was smiling too.

"Like you're never going to let go," she said.

The light turned green, and she gunned the bike. I held on tight, even though the ride wasn't as wild. For a few minutes, I managed to forget everything: the Maxilla, Dani's missing girlfriend, the Ordeal, all of it. All there was in the world was Shade on the bike in front of me, the heat of her body though her shirt, the gentle rise of her breast on the top of my hand, and the wind on my face as we rode through the darkened streets.

We pulled up by the side entrance to Dr. C's house, and I wrapped my arms around Shade and drew her to me for a moment before we got off the bike. We slid off, and both our helmets bounced in the grass as she slid into my arms again, and her lips melted against mine. Her tongue darted against my lips as she let mine chase it, and my hands went in opposite directions from the middle of her back. I felt her grab a thick handful of my hair at the nape of my neck, and I followed suit. Her grip went slack once I closed my fist on her hair, and she pulled back for a second. Her eyes were still closed, and her lips parted as she let out a tiny gasp. I tried to pull her mouth back to mine, but she pulled back a little with a playful smile on her lips. Her eyes sparkled in the soft light.

"You have to earn the second one," she said.

I tried to pull her to me, and she came, but she turned her face to one side, avoiding my lips with a giggle. I tried to follow, and she only let me brush her lips for a heartbeat before she twisted away.

"Take it if you can," she taunted as she squirmed in my arms.

She ducked her head forward, and tried to bury her head under my chin. The part of me that I'd touched that afternoon woke up, and I gave her a growl of desire as I fought to keep it in check. The shiver that ran through her at that destroyed my will, and I tightened my hand in her hair then pulled her head back slowly. Her eyes were wide and trusting as she came up to face me. Then I lowered my head and put my teeth on the soft skin of her neck.

She trembled in my arms as a growl rumbled up from my chest, and I heard her whimper softly. Then her arms closed around me, and I felt her hold on to me like she was never going to let go. Something warm fell on my neck, then Shade's trembling gave way to tremors from her stomach, and I realized she was crying. I pulled away, but she just held on tighter.

"Don't let go," she sobbed. "Please, just don't let go!"

I held on to her with everything I had.

"Did I hurt you? Did I do something wrong? What is it?" I asked quietly. My hand came up and stroked her hair. In the middle of wondering what I'd done wrong, I noticed how good her hair felt under my fingers, and how much I enjoyed her reaction to it. Hot tears coursed down my neck, and my cracked ribs flared pain up my side as she held on to me tight, but there was nothing in the world that was going to make me let go of her a second before she wanted me to.

Finally, she pulled back and looked up at me. Her face was damp, and a single tear rolled down her cheek.

I caught it on my thumb and wiped it away gently.

"Whatever I did, I'm sorry. I didn't mean to—"

She shut me up with a kiss.

"I don't know why," she said softly. "I felt good. Safe . . . and then . . . I was just . . . crying. God, I'm such a screwed up mess. I don't even know what you see in—"

It was my turn to shut her up with my kiss.

"A lot. Don't even go there. Please, you're beautiful, and we get each other. Tonight, there's no one else I would have wanted at my back, and right now . . . there's no one else I want in my arms. When I'm with you, Shade, it's like nothing else exists. I can forget about all the screwed up stuff in my life for a while. When we're together . . . even as messed up as I am, as screwed up as my life gets sometimes, I'm happy." I kissed her forehead and closed my eyes.

"We don't exactly have normal problems, do we?" she asked.

"No, we don't," I agreed. "We better get inside."

She nodded, and bent to pick up our helmets.

“Collins is here,” she said as we hit the steps to the porch. It wasn’t a surprise, since he was taking shifts watching over me. “There’s another cop down the street.”

She nodded toward the dimly lit side street, and I could barely make out a car parked well out of the nearest streetlight’s range. It was hard to forget Shade was a werewolf, with amped up senses and enough strength to bench press me . . . while I was on her bike. It was harder sometimes to remember she was a teenager.

Her hand slipped into mine as I touched the ward stone on the iron railing on the steps, and let her through. Dr. Corwyn had ramped them up from just setting off an alarm to lethal levels if they weren’t deactivated. If anyone came on the property and tried to get inside, they were in for a fiery welcome or the shock of their lives, depending on where they tried to come in. I opened the door to the kitchen and we slipped inside as I felt the wards reset themselves.

We stopped long enough to grab a couple of bottles of Coke from the refrigerator before we headed for the library. Shade reached for two of the bottles beside the fridge, but I put my hand on hers and shook my head.

“Don’t. Those are Dr. C’s. He doesn’t like his cold.” I got a look from her at that, and I shrugged.

“Weird,” she said as she popped the cap off hers with a casual flick of her thumbnail.

I set mine against the handle to one of the drawers and brought my hand down on it to get the cap off. Both went into the wire basket by the door that Dr. C used to collect them, and we made our way down the hall toward the open double doors of the library.

“Just give them a few more minutes, Demetrius,” Dr. C’s voice came from inside the door. “They don’t get the chance to just be teenagers that often. And if this all goes wrong . . . he might not have many more moments like this.”

“That ain’t right,” Collins grumbled. My chest went tight again when I heard what they were saying, and I had to stop for a second to get my breath back before we went around the corner and entered the library. Dr. C was behind his desk, still in the white button down shirt he'd worn to school that day. Collins had changed into a black t-shirt. He wore his gun in a shoulder holster with spare clips under his right arm.

"I'm back," I said. "Did I make curfew?"

"Barely. And you're welcome."

"Did I miss something?" I asked.

"You could say that," he sighed. "I got Draeden to pull the Sentinels off of you, but there was a price. Cross and T-Bone had to back off, too. On the plus side of that, they were assigned to watching over your mother and sister."

"I'm okay with that," I said.

"It isn't how I would have preferred things to go, but it'll work. How'd it go with Thraxus?" Dr. C asked.

"About like I expected. Thraxus didn't commit to anything without more proof, but he did admit he owed me for letting the first attack go. If his boy Etienne does anything else, he pretty much has to give me sanction to go after him. So, now all I have to do is figure out how to prove he's got Crystal without doing a B and E to actually see for myself. Or I can just wait to see if Thraxus actually digs anything up on his own."

"How likely is he to do that?" Collins asked. I took a sip of my Coke while I gave it some thought.

"Actually, he probably will. I think he knows Etienne's up to something and whatever he does is gonna get laid at Thraxus' feet. In the meantime, I also have to figure out how to find where Mr. Chomsky hid a sword that doesn't really want to be found."

I set the Coke on the big oak desk and went to the bookshelf. Something was nagging at the back of my brain, and I pulled out one of the references I'd gone through Saturday night.

"Divinations are still proving fruitless," Dr. C offered. "And nothing in Sydney's journals has given us any clues about where he hid it. I'm going to check some of the Conclave's archives tonight to see if I can find anything about where it would be likely to be found. There may be a more theurgic based spell to reveal it, given its origins."

"Maybe you should try finding the old fashioned way," Collins suggested.

Dr. C waved one hand at the bookshelves in exasperation.

"I've already tried! We've come at this from every angle we can!" he snapped.

"You've come at it like a wizard. If magic isn't working, then maybe you need to come at it like a cop."

"I'm not exactly a detective," Dr. C said.

"I am," Collins countered as he pulled out the bent note pad and pen from his back pocket and started scribbling things down. "Get hold of Kale and Romanoff, too. You're gonna need a few things." He ripped off a page from the notepad and handed it to me. "Don't ask questions, just get this stuff," he said.

Two hours later, Lucas and Wanda were sitting beside me in two of the other chairs, and Shade was curled up on the floor in front of me with her arm over my leg. Collins had a dry erase board up on the wall behind Dr. C's desk, and a card table laid out beside the desk itself. In red marker he'd drawn a line with little hash marks with dates. On the left, the first read "*10/15 – Maxilla awakens (?) Seeker chosen. Seeker = CF*"

Then he'd written:

10/19: Wards hit. 1st attempt to steal. Maxilla safe.

10/20: Chomsky IDs AC as perp. IDs CF as demon's appr.

10/21: Chomsky murdered. TJC arrives. Case still in possession. TJC never actually sees Maxilla.

10/23: Case stolen.

10/24: CF finds case opened. Maxilla not in case according to note by SC.

He'd drawn a blue bracket between the entries for the 19th and the 21st, with a mark in the middle pointing at the 20th. A line led from it to another entry that read "*Maxilla hidden*". On the right side of the board, he'd put up a map of the southwest quarter of Missouri and the southeast quarter of Kansas, with an area circled in red that centered on New Essex.

The table had a thick file on it and a box with red stamps that read "EVIDENCE." Dr. C perched on the edge of his desk looking irritated as Collins taped up a sheet of paper under the timeline with highlighted entries on it.

"Okay, so the journal did tell us something," Collins said as he turned around. "From Chomsky's journal entry, we know he was asleep until late Monday night, when the wards were activated. That's the last mention he makes of the Maxilla. We know from his journal and from witnesses that he was at school all day Tuesday. Chance was the last person to see him alive, at about three-thirty that afternoon. We know he was killed sometime Tuesday night. That opens two windows of only a few hours when no one knows where he was."

"About midnight Monday night to seven or so Tuesday morning," Lucas offered, "and Tuesday afternoon to Wednesday morning, right?"

"Right," Collins answered. "The investigation into his murder is still open, so I pulled the evidence we had on it. Detective Roberts pulled his bank statements, and we have him using his debit card to buy gas just south of Springfield around one o'clock Tuesday morning."

"How does all of this help us find the Maxilla?" Dr. C asked.

"It doesn't help us find the Maxilla. Concentrating on the sword only led to dead ends. What you have to do is focus on the guy who had it. We're gonna find where Chomsky went to hide it."

"What's the big circle?" Wanda asked.

"That's the distance he could have traveled in about three hours. His time out of pocket was about six and a half to seven hours. That gives him about three hours out, half an hour to hide the sword, and three hours back, then half an hour to change and get to the school."

"We know where he was about one a.m. or so," Lucas said as he got to his feet. "So, if we find out the exact spot on the map, we can do another circle with a two hour radius, and cut our search area from about what, seventy thousand square miles to about thirty one thousand?" He looked to Dr. C for confirmation and got a nod.

I shrugged, since beyond knowing area of a circled equaled pi times r squared, I needed a calculator. I was just glad it cut our area from freaking huge to just really, *really* big.

"Okay, Kale, you and Romanoff are here with me, working the evidence. Corwyn, you knew him best. Take Fortunato and Cooper and go check out Chomsky's room for evidence. Anything he might have had with him that night, you go over it with a fine-tooth comb. Anything you find, bag it, tag it and bring it to me."

"We're not detectives," I said, gesturing between Alexis and myself.

"Girl's a werewolf, kid. She's got better senses than any of us. And you got pretty good instincts. Between the three of you, I figure you'll find something. Evidence kits are in the hallway. Wear your gloves and keep your mouths closed. Tie your hair back, too."

We trudged out into the hallway and Shade handed me a ponytail holder.

Mr. Chomsky's bedroom was on the east side of the house, the largest on the second floor. Dr. C had taken the one next to it, but as far as I knew, he hadn't gone in it except for a few times when he had to. I'd never set foot in the room. The door opened and we stood there for a few seconds. I heard Shade inhale through her nose while Dr. C let out a soft sigh. He wasn't looking forward to this, I could tell.

I stepped across the threshold first and took a long, slow look around the room. The bed was a double, with an iron headboard and foot board, and a thick, dark green comforter. A dark-stained wood dresser sat against the wall to my right, and a bookshelf took up part of the wall to my left, with a chair and a small table set next to the window that looked out over the front of the house. There wasn't a door for a closet, but I saw a tall wooden wardrobe on the far wall from me.

I wandered over to the dresser and looked over the few things he'd left on it. A silver bowl held change and half of a roll of Lifesavers, along with a couple of quartz crystals and a pair of mismatched cufflinks. I tried to imagine what might have happened that night when he came home from hiding the Maxilla. I heard Dr. C and Shade step into the room behind me, as I saw in my mind's eye how things might have gone.

Chomsky steps into the room. He's in a hurry. He has less than an hour to get changed and get to the school for first period. Conference period. He goes to the wardrobe to get out of his dirty clothes . . . he sets something next to the wardrobe before he takes his shoes off and peels his clothes off. Even he isn't sure where he's been.

I shook my head and looked around the room. Vague impressions lingered in my head, and I felt something in my hand. I opened my hand to see one of the quartz crystals lying on my palm.

"In there," I said with a gesture at the wardrobe.

Shade nodded and opened the doors, then squatted down to look inside. She reached in and poked around, and presented me with a wonderful view.

Dr. C nudged me as he went by, and I gave him a dirty look before I went back to sorting through the stuff on Mr. Chomsky's dresser. Fountain pens, three wristwatches, two pocket watches, and two pocket knives went through my hands without so much as a tingle. Only the touchstones seemed to trigger any response from my mystic senses.

"I think I found something," Shade's muffled voice came from inside the wardrobe. She stood with a pair of rumpled pants dangling from one hand, and a pair of weathered hiking boots held in the other. "I smell pollen on these, and some kind of dirt. And . . . fish."

I grabbed a couple of the paper bags Collins had given us and held one open for her while she dropped the pants into it. Dr. C held the second to catch the boots, and sent her downstairs to deliver them to Collins.

"We're missing something," I muttered.

"You're right. Something feels off, like there's something we should have noticed. But what?" Dr. C said. He sounded as frustrated as I was.

"I ask that question every day, sir," I said. "But I'm fifteen. The answer's usually something stupid like 'taking out the trash' or 'Shade changed her hair.' I'm pretty much out of my league here."

"You're not doing so bad," he said back as he looked around the room. "Collins is right, you've got good instincts. You didn't do so bad finding Sydney's killer. He didn't want to be found either. Come on, let's go back downstairs, get a little distance and a different perspective." He put a hand on my shoulder and pointed me toward the door, but I took one last look at the room before I closed the door behind me.

When we got back to the library, Lucas was just stepping back from the map on the dry erase board. A new circle was drawn in blue inside the larger one, and a sticky note was near the center of the smaller circle. I stepped up beside Lucas and looked at the whole picture, timeline, map and bank statement. Collins was sitting at Dr' C's desk with Lucas' laptop open. He looked up at me as I stared at the board.

"You look like my oldest niece with a jigsaw puzzle," Collins said.

"I'm trying to figure out how you got all of this from the same journal I read."

"I didn't. I mean, yeah, about half of it I got from the journal. The rest is from Holly's notes and the statements she took. A lot of detective work is learning how to look at a crime, and get a picture from what a bunch of different people tell you, then figure out what really happened. The rest of it's evidence. Main thing to remember, people lie, but the evidence don't."

"Right, so you think we're going to find Mr. Chomsky's favorite fishing spot from his pants and shoes?" I asked.

"Seeds and plant residue would tell us what he walked through, and soil samples can tell us almost exactly where he's been, so yeah, if he went fishing, we'll know where."

"In case you missed it, we don't exactly have our own crime lab here," Wanda gestured at the walls. "And Cindy Walker's dad is a cop. He says it takes weeks sometimes to run down forensic evidence."

"We do have the science labs at school, though," Lucas countered, then gave me a grin. "And two wizardy types who can probably do some of the same thing, only with divination. Remember how Chance figured out King killed Mr. Chomsky?"

"Whoa, don't go turning us into Sherlock Holmes, dude," I said.

"I was thinking more of Bruce Wayne, only without the cowl and neuroses. Well, without the cowl, anyway. You already have the anger issues down."

"Who's Bruce Wayne?" I asked.

Lucas gave me a look like I'd just committed some kind of sacrilege.

"You don't know who Bruce Wayne is? Batman? The world's greatest detective?" he asked.

"Oh, yeah . . . wait, Batman's a detective?" Everyone looked like me like I'd just belted out a show tune at a funeral.

"Mother of All, save me from the unknowing. Lucas, lend him every comic book and graphic novel you own," Wanda ordered. "Educate the poor boy, so he doesn't embarrass himself like that again."

He gave her a thumbs up, and Shade came over and kissed my cheek.

“I’d love to see you in a cape and tights,” she whispered in my ear. “You’ll always be my superhero.” The sound of her voice in my ear sent my hormones into overdrive, and I had to take a deep breath before I could think straight.

The sound of a cell phone’s insistent chirp broke into the room, and Collins reached for the case on his belt as he headed for the door. He was gone for less than a minute, and when he came back in, he still had the phone to his ear. He pointed at me then crooked his finger for me to come with him. Dr. C was on his feet as Collins grabbed his jacket and headed for the door.

“Text the address to me,” Collins said before he hung up.

“What’s going on?” Dr. C demanded.

“Need the kid to come with me. They found another circle.”

My blood ran cold when I heard that, but I headed back into the library and grabbed my own jacket and told the others where I was going. Dead silence fell when I told them they’d found another circle. I kissed Shade and went to head for the door. When she stood up, I stopped and turned back to her.

“I’m coming, too. Shut up and listen to me, Chance,” she said when I shook my head. “You know the magick part, but I can smell and see things you can’t.”

Our eyes locked, and we tried to stare each other down. I tried to find a flaw in her argument, but I couldn’t keep my thoughts straight while I was looking her in the eyes. I didn’t really want to, but I looked away first.

“All right, but stay out of sight, okay?” I said quietly.

“Better forgiveness than permission; I got it. I’ve got your back.”

In spite of myself, I smiled at her before I headed back out into the hallway. I heard Dr. C’s voice, low and intense, as I got closer.

“He’s in enough danger already. Besides, I’m the department’s occult expert. I should be called in on this. Leave Chance out of it.” I stopped and listened, not wanting to step in the middle of things.

"Look Doc, I know you're trying to do what's best for the kid, but if they found another one of these damn things, then someone else's kid's missing. And Chance is the expert on this, not you. So, yeah, I'm gonna call him in on this one, because he's the best shot I got at bringing these kids back home safe. It's a crime scene, so there'll be deputies all over the place. He'll be almost as safe as he is here."

"He'd better be," Dr. C said.

I stepped into the foyer and slipped my jacket on, playing oblivious to the tense looks they were exchanging.

"I'm ready," I said. "I'll be back soon, Dr. C."

He looked like he wanted to say something, but he only gave me a nod before I headed out the door and back into the night.

The ride over in the unmarked police cruiser was all business. Collins laid out how to handle myself at a crime scene, basically "Look, don't touch" and to keep my mouth shut until he asked for my opinion.

He headed into Old Town, which used to be part of Joplin. Not the best part of town to be in after dark. Come to think of it, before dark wasn't much safer. Crumbling, abandoned businesses stood next to rubble-filled lots, and if there were flickering lights in some of the supposedly empty storefronts, no one was complaining. The closer we got to the railroad tracks, the more buildings I saw with heavy iron bars over the windows and doors, and the fewer signs that weren't years out of date, faded or covered in graffiti. Most of the businesses that weren't abandoned had NCK tags on them. On some of the buildings, though, I saw another mark, usually in the upper right hand corner of the wall, where a person couldn't reach. The Night City Kings ruled this part of town, but they shared it with a vampire clan whether they liked it or not.

"Vampire marks," I told Collins as I pointed to one. He nodded and gestured to the glove compartment.

"Get me some pictures of it when I stop. One up close, so I can see detail, and a couple from further back. Make sure you get the bottom of the building in the shot, and something I can use for scale, so I know how high up it is and how big it is."

He pulled over beside one of the buildings, and I took three shots of it with the digital camera I found in the glove box. I tried to get the dumpster behind the building in the shot, and ended up catching part of it. When I handed him the camera, he thumbed through the pics and nodded before he handed it back to me and pulled back onto the road again.

"You ever think about being a cop?" He asked. "You got the instincts for it, and you got the heart."

"Lately, I've just been hoping to survive the week. I haven't had much time for thinking about career day, you know?" I watched him nod, and wondered why he'd asked.

"Yeah, I kinda noticed that. So, why are you working this missing kid thing?"

"Because Dani asked me to. I figure, if she was coming to me, no one else was taking her seriously. And I know what her girlfriend's going through."

"Guess if anyone would . . ." he let the thought hang there, unspoken for a moment.

I nodded.

Up ahead, the blue and red strobes from the top of a police cruiser flashed against the sides of buildings. We pulled up to see a lone cruiser parked in front of an apartment building, with the officer standing by the front door. Collins grabbed the mike to his radio and reported us as ten-something. When the dispatcher's static-y voice came back, he opened the door and stepped out.

After a few seconds, he gave me a gesture and I got out and followed him toward the skinny cop standing by the door. His uniform hung off of his shoulders, like it had tried to swallow him and hadn't quite finished the job. His nametag read "Perkins." Nothing about his face screamed "cop" to me. I was getting more of a serial killer vibe off him. He had a nose that seemed too big for his narrow face, and watery blue eyes that never seemed to stay on one thing for very long, like he wasn't actually looking at anything so much as looking *for* something. And something about him just made my skin want to crawl.

"Whadda we got?" Collins asked. Perkins started, like we'd just appeared in front of him or something.

"Yeah, uh, the super found some kind of circle down in the basement, in the uh, laundry room, I think." He gestured over his shoulder with his thumb as he talked, and Collins looked through the doorway for a second.

"You clear the scene?" Collins asked. Perkins nodded quickly.

"Oh, yeah. No one down there. I closed the area off and called you and the forensics team. They ought to be here any time. What's he doing here?"

"Consultant," was all Collins said before he went through the door with me on his heels.

As much as I wanted to be as far away from Perkins as I could, my shoulders itched at the idea of having him behind me. Still, it was better than standing next to him, and every step made me feel better. When we got to the stairwell, Collins pulled out a white ball of something out of his jacket pocket and handed it to me.

"Foot covers and gloves. Once forensics clears the scene, if I give you the go ahead to enter the scene, you put those on. It's like I said in the car, you don't touch anything you don't have to. You don't pick anything up, you don't move anything. Something catches your eye, you point it out to me. I'll tell you if you can move it or whatever. We clear?"

"Yeah. Point, don't touch, and stay the hell out of the way." I got a smile and a nod, then he turned and went down the stairs. I didn't miss that he undid the snap on his pistol, though.

Inside, the building was showing its age. The walls were starting to show cracks in the faded brown paint, and the black and green spotted linoleum was chipped and showing concrete in places. The concrete steps were smooth under my shoes, with brittle rubber strips glued along the edges. Aside from the sound of our feet hitting the floor, the only thing I heard was the hum and occasional pop of the fluorescent lights overhead. My nose told me that something was moldy down here, and that this place had been too long without being disturbed.

Collins hit the bottom of the stairs and turned to his right. His footsteps were mostly muffled by the threadbare green carpet, and the creep factor went way up for me as my feet hit the ancient carpet.

A few steps away from the taped off door, Collins turned and held up one finger, and I stopped in my tracks. He nodded before he put his hand on the butt of his gun, then covered the rest of the distance and leaned forward to peer around the edge of the door. After a few seconds, he ducked under the tape and stepped inside, then ducked back out and let out a relieved sounding breath.

"See what you can see from the door," he told me.

As soon as I got to the doorway, something felt off. I could see one edge of the circle to my right, the rest hidden by a wall that separated the laundry area from a more brightly painted section. The reddish brown circle was a dark stain against the faded yellow. I gave him a shrug and a shake of my head.

"Can't see enough of it."

"Didn't think so. What's your gut tell you?" he asked.

"That something isn't right about this one. I just don't know what." I shrugged.

"All right. Cover your feet and follow me. Step where I step, and keep your hands in your pockets," he told me as he pulled his own covers out of his pockets. Once he had them on, he put on a pair of latex gloves, but he shook his head when I pulled mine out. "You don't touch anything until after the forensics team gets done. All we're doing is getting a little closer so you can see the circle."

He ducked under the tape again and held it up so I could get under too. The foot covers made a hissing sound against the floor as we walked forward, and aside from the hum of the lights, that was all I could hear.

“Yeah, this isn’t creepy at all,” I muttered.

“Quiet,” Collins whispered. “But yeah, this is creepy.”

We got to the corner and the whole circle came into view against the yellow wall. The area it was in looked like it had been set aside as a play area for kids, with grass painted along the bottom of the wall, and a happy looking sun smiling down from one corner. All I could be grateful for was that the moldy smell had gone away, though the not quite pine fresh smell wasn’t a lot better. More and more things about the circle started to look wrong the longer I looked at it. The outer symbols were in the wrong place. The placement not only felt wrong, I got that they weren’t fitting a pattern. Something clicked in my head about the other symbols, and I filed it away to tell Collins later. But something else had been bugging me, and it couldn’t wait.

“All the other circles . . . they were all outside, right?” I asked.

After a few seconds, Collins nodded.

“And you had kids missing nearby.”

“Yeah, I checked on the way over. I’m not sure if we got lucky, or if no one reported them. Maybe a homeless kid or a runaway,” he said, but he didn’t sound convinced.

“No, this circle’s all wrong. The planetary symbols are all messed up, and the internal ones are . . . well, they’re just random. And I’m not getting any kind of hit off this like I should if there’d been any magick done here. And it’s not . . . round like the others. Well, not the right . . . as big of round . . .” I started to say something else, but I was having a hard time thinking of the words.

Besides, Collins had split into two, and I didn’t really know which of the two Collinses I should talk to, and neither one would hold still long enough for me to focus on anyway. That was when my legs stopped working.

While I wondered when I’d decided to lay down, my brain was trying to tell me that I hadn’t closed the door when I came in. That was important somehow, maybe because it was closed now. But I had more important things to do, like fall into the well of black . . .

Chapter 14 Tuesday Morning (Two days left)

~ Every mortal has a weakness. Exploit their frailties whenever you can, and never let them forget that the vampyri are in every way superior to them. ~ Radu cel Frumos, 1471

My head hurt. And my mouth felt like someone had laid ten year-old carpet on my tongue two days ago. And I was blindfolded. Again. This shit was getting old. I turned my head and tried to get my bearings, and figured out I was upside down. My feet felt like they were tied together, and my hands were held behind my back by something rough, probably hemp rope, if I was any judge. The carpet feel on my tongue felt like it belonged to some kind of cloth shoved into my mouth. Great, blindfolded, bound, and gagged. Either the people who had knocked us out knew I was a mage, or they didn't want me to see them. I pretty much counted on the first, given the way the past few days had been going. The other I hoped for, since people really only care if you can see them if they're afraid you'll be able to ID them later. That meant there would probably *be* a later for me. If I was right.

Other sensations started to make it into my little bubble. First was the smell. Blood, animal crap, and death. My guess was a slaughterhouse. There were a lot of empty ones near the railroad tracks and the Southtown docks. No matter how long it had been, the stench of death never seemed to leave them completely. My father owned a couple for disposal of the occasional inconvenient corpse. I figured it was the "in" thing among the well-to-do scumbags.

Rats scurried around somewhere, and I heard the blare of a train horn somewhere off to my right. I heard the creak of ropes, and counted at least two beside the one wrapped around my ankles. There was a whisper of conversation, then the chirping flutter of wings. Our hosts had just revealed themselves.

"Detective Collins," I heard a familiar voice croon. Darth Fedora. "How good of you to finally join us. Do you know why you are here, detective?" He clipped the last word into a mocking note.

Collins turned the air blue when he told him what he could go do with himself.

I heard the smack of skin on skin, and the grunt of pain that told me Collins had just been slapped.

"I didn't think so. Your kind rarely understand anything."

"My kind?" Collins growled.

"Yes . . . mortals. Especially the unenlightened. You are about to be awakened, *cowan*. There is more to the world than your science can imagine. My Master is that which makes the dark so terrifying to you. He is *vampyr*, *nosferatu*, all that you fear beyond the grave. And he is displeased with your meddling."

"So have his lawyer sue my ass," Collins said.

That earned him another slap, this one loud, probably harder.

"He is above your laws. You will not speak again. You will listen, and you will obey. This is my Master's will." As Fedora hissed at Collins, I felt the shimmer of a familiar power hammer at my mental shields.

"To hell with your master's will," Collins said.

I chuckled into the gag when I heard Darth Fedora curse. Another slap sounded before he spoke again.

"You will halt your investigation for seventy two hours, detective. Beyond that, you have my Master's permission to resume your enquiry. If you disobey him, your family will face dire consequences."

"What family? I'm not married, got no kids." Collins laughed.

"What you do have, Detective Demetrius Collins, is a sister and three little nieces. Kendra, Kesha, and Kayela. It would be a pity if one of those precious little girls disappeared." I heard something rustle, then Collins made a strangled sound.

"Yes, detective, that would be the youngest, Kayela, wouldn't it? You see, even Detroit is within the grasp of my Master. You will obey him. You will not interfere further. Do you understand?"

There was a tense silence that dragged on for almost a minute.

"Do you under—" Fedora started to say.

"Yeah, I understand, asshole," Collins cut him off.

I couldn't even imagine what it cost him to say those words.

"Karl, come on! Someone's coming!" I heard another voice call out. This guy sounded farther away.

"I'll just be another moment," Darth Fedora said.

I tried to pin the name Karl on him, but it just didn't stick in my head. I heard footsteps coming toward me, then the blindfold was pulled away.

"You still don't seem to have learned your lesson, warlock," Fedora said as he loomed above me. He was still wearing the same pants and trenchcoat, but his shoes were new. No sling for his arm, and not even a limp from where I'd put my balisong through his foot. Damn it, life was really a bitch sometimes. Still, when he squatted down to look at me at eye level, he was out of easy reach.

Since I couldn't talk, I hitched my body around so he could see my hands as I flipped him off from behind my back.

"Defiant to the last. The only reason the two of you aren't dead is because you are both too visible to dispose of conveniently. There will be consequences for crossing my Master. Think on that, warlock."

His foot lashed out and caught me in the ribs. My vision went red from pain, and by the time I could see clearly, he was gone. Asshole had gotten in the last word and he'd taken a parting shot. I hated it when they did that.

"You okay, kid?" Collins asked.

I turned to face him and show him that I couldn't answer.

"Dumb question, huh? Okay, I'm gonna try to get my hands free. You just take it easy." I gave him an eyeroll.

He did something behind his back, and the next thing I knew, his hands were free and he was working on the rope around his ankles with one hand still in the cuff. I had to stifle a laugh when he got his feet loose, because he hit the ground like a side of beef. He got up slowly, then looked around.

I made a noise of protest when he headed for one of the butchers' tables instead of coming over to get me down. He picked up his pistol and ammo, then grabbed his badge and wallet before he scooped up what I figured was my stuff and came back toward me. My feet came down first, then he got the gag out before he went to work on my wrists.

"I hate that son of a bitch," I muttered when he handed my stuff back to me. I pocketed everything but my wand and a cinnamon candy. When I felt the sweet burn on my tongue, I gave him a nod.

"Didn't this happen last time I went somewhere with you?" he asked.

"Yeah, but last time, I was the one who got you loose. I think we're even now."

"Guess so. At least there's no werewolves chasing us this time. All right, stay behind me," he said. He held his gun low, with both hands on the grip.

"I'm at least as well armed as you are, man," I said.

"You're still a kid, and I'm still a cop. Besides, being in front of the guy with the gun ain't a good idea." He started for the cargo door, leaving me to either follow or look like an idiot. I followed, damning adult common sense and experience.

We were about ten yards away when the door blew inward. We both dove for the floor. Collins came up behind a column, gun up and pointed toward the door. I propped myself up on my elbows for a second to see who was coming. The jagged hole where the door used to be let in a flood of light. A lone figure stood silhouetted there, one hand holding a staff out to his left, his right brought up about to his shoulder and surrounded in a nimbus of blue.

"Okay, that was impressive," I said. I brought my own little TK wand up and prepped the shield spell in my head. If this guy was going to start something, the least I could do was make it past round one.

"Chance?" the man in the door said. I stared in disbelief for a moment, and fought a flood of emotion that I was pretty sure I was supposed to be too pissed to be feeling just then.

"Dr. Corwyn?" I asked. "What are you doing here?" The blue corona of magick faded from his hand, and he took a few steps forward.

"Well, I was here to rescue you, but it looks like I'm a little late for that."

"That's okay, you're just in time for the daring escape," I quipped. Hey, it was either joke, or get all stupid about him riding in like the damn cavalry. I figured I still had a couple of days left of being mad at him about the whole Council thing, and Mom finding out I was a warlock. But when he came up and grabbed me in a bear hug, I wasn't sure what to do.

"God, I was so worried about you," he growled. "I'm glad you're safe."

"Me, too, sir," I murmured into his shoulder. It felt weird, but I hugged back, maybe a little harder than I meant to.

"I don't think they were gonna hurt us," Collins added when Dr. C stepped back. "They just wanted to send me a message. Besides, they had the kid gagged the whole time, so we weren't in any real danger." I gave him a glare, but instead of dropping dead on the spot, he just laughed.

"What was the message?" Dr. C asked as he turned and ushered us toward the splintered door he'd just come through.

"Back off," Collins said.

"Or bad things will happen to his sister's kids. Dr. C, we have to help him out. It was Etienne's servant again. Collins is doing his job, this isn't his fight!"

"Like Hell it ain't!" Collins barked. "He made it personal. This ain't about a paycheck anymore."

"Both of you, calm down. First of all, Chance, *we* don't need to do anything about this. *You* do. Etienne has acted against not only you, but a public servant. Thraxus won't like that. Go see him tonight, and yes, Demetrius, you need to go, too. That should really rattle his cage."

We stepped out into sunlight, and I realized we had to have been out for several hours. My mouth felt a little less like cotton, and the light started an ache behind my eyes. Collins let out a groan to match mine as we stood there trying to let our eyes adjust.

"My head is killing me. Wonder how long we been out?" he asked.

"It's about six forty-five," Dr. C answered.

"It was almost one when I got the call, so about four hours or so," Collins said. "They must've hit us with some kind of gas or something." I couldn't stop the snort of laughter at that. "What's so funny?"

"I've been knocked out three times since Friday night, and this time hurt the least."

"I think that, given the circumstances, you're going to be skipping school today, Chance. And so am I," Dr. C said soberly. He led the way down the steps toward his Range Rover. "For that matter, I wouldn't be surprised if Lucas and Wanda come down with something, too. I left them at the lab when Alexis called me."

"So, she's okay?"

"Yes. When no one came out after an hour or two, and no more police showed up, she got suspicious and went in. She tracked your scents to the sewers, then she called me. I sent her to keep an eye on Lucas and Wanda while I was gone, and from there, it was a matter of zeroing in on you with a simple pendulum divination, and coming to your rescue."

"So, no one knows I got cold-cocked and trussed up for four hours," Collins said after he climbed into the Range Rover's back seat. "I hope my car's still there."

The first few minutes of the drive to Collins unmarked car was pretty quiet. The only sound was the hiss of rubber over rain-slicked streets and Collins' pen scratching on his beat up notepad.

"So, kid, I guess the circle we checked out was a total fake?"

"Kinda," I said. "The symbols were right, they were just all out of place. And the outer ring was all wrong . . ." I let the sentence trail off.

Something was nagging at me, something I'd been trying to tell Collins last night. The images of the circles floated in front of my mind's eye, and I remembered Collins asking me where I'd been on certain dates, dates that were closer and closer together each time.

"Chance?" Dr. C asked.

"The outer symbols were wrong. Collins, I didn't get this until last night when I saw the circle. The dates . . . they've been following a pattern, I just couldn't see it! The next kid wasn't supposed to be abducted last night! If they're going to take another kid, it's going to happen tonight!" I turned around in the front seat to face Collins. "Whatever they're going to do, whatever this circle is for, the big finish is on Thursday! That's why they only wanted you to back off for three days. And they only need one more kid to do it."

"All right, kid. Now you're earning that 'consultant' title. Corwyn, drop me off here. At least my car's still in one piece. I owe you one, Fortunato." Collins barely waited for Dr. C to stop before he jumped out of the back seat and jogged to his car.

Dr. C pulled away and took a right.

"So, what are we really going to be doing, sir?" I asked a couple of minutes later.

"Well, you should be sleeping," he said, but I could hear in his voice that he didn't really believe that.

"I'll sleep in this weekend. I've only got until midnight tomorrow night to find the Maxilla, and in case you forgot, I haven't been making what you'd call stellar progress on that."

We pulled to one side to let a fire engine pass, then he got back out into traffic.

"If you insist, then we'll follow up on Lucas and Wanda's research today, and search in the area we think Sydney was in last," he said as we came to a stop light.

Another fire engine sped through the light before we made it through the intersection. I leaned my head back against the seat and closed my eyes to take the edge off of the headache, and promptly dozed off.

"Oh ye gods and little fishes," I heard Dr. C say.

My head came up and I blinked while I tried to get my bearings. We were across the street from the school. A police car and a couple of fire trucks were in the parking lot, with people in suits clustered around the cops and fire men well away from the front entrance. Then my eyes focused on the school itself, and I said something a lot worse than Dr. C did.

The walls were covered in something, and the only thing that came to my mind was *bugs*. It writhed and I swore I could hear the clicking of thousands of little legs against the brick. I shuddered.

Dr. C got out of the truck, and I opened my door a little more slowly. Instead of jumping down on the pavement, I stood up in the seat and held on to the top of the door. From there, I could see Shade, Lucas, and Wanda heading our way from the *Falcon.*

Wanda looked as freaked out as I did, but Lucas had a huge grin on his face. Lucas was in jeans and his denim trench, with a gray t-shirt that showed a dragon on the front. In red letters, it read "I slay dragons (on the internet)". Wanda had on a red and black plaid short skirt with red and black striped tights underneath. Her top was black, with a fanged Happy Bunny in white and red. The caption read "cute but kind of evil". Shade was still in the same outfit she'd had on when we left Dr. C's.

Dr. C gave me a "stay there" look and headed for the group of suits and cops.

"This is cool!" Lucas called out as he got closer. The horrified look on Wanda's face pretty much mirrored mine.

"Dude, you are seriously messed up," I said.

"It's happening all over town!" Wanda said, holding up her phone. "I got texts from friends at almost every other school. They say the same thing is happening! Bugs, birds, frogs, there's even lizards all over Lincoln Heights!"

"And we got bugs," I muttered.

"Actually, we got arachnids. These are pretty much all spiders and scorpions," Lucas said.

"Well, that works," I said as Shade put her arms around me and squeezed me tight.

"I was so worried," she said to me. She gave me a smile, as she looked over her shoulder at the walls of the school. "I don't think we're having class today." Her voice held the promise of all kinds of possibilities, and a lot of them ran through my mind.

"Yeah, it looks like you need the day off," Wanda said. "Have you even been home since you left Dr. C's place?"

"No, I had a rough night. Did you guys find anything useful?"

"Well, with the pollen and dirt on Mr. Chomsky's pants and boots, I managed to narrow it down to part of Mark Twain National Forest. That narrows it down to about sixty five thousand acres or so."

"Guess it's better than thirty thousand square miles. Okay, when Dr. C gets back, we'll figure out where we're going and stuff."

"Oh, it gets better. Remember, Alexis said she smelled fish? According to Dr. Corwyn, the gunk on his shoes was algae. So we know he walked through at least one stream. That narrows it down a lot more."

"Dude, you're a freakin' genius," I told him. "Maybe you need to be the detective."

"Nah, I'm more the forensics geek. I'll leave the getting beat up and knocked out part to you."

"Okay, kids, it looks like your worst academic nightmares are coming true. Classes are cancelled for today, and probably tomorrow," Dr. C said with mock seriousness.

"Damn," Lucas said. "I was so looking forward to a pop quiz today, too."

Dr. C pointed at him and Wanda. "You two, go home, get some rest. You've both done a lot more than was expected of you. I may need both of you tonight and I want you sharp. Now get."

They trooped off reluctantly, and only after getting a promise to call them if I found anything new.

"So, what are you guys going to be doing?" Shade asked.

"Legwork," Dr. C answered. "Lots and lots of legwork. You're welcome to tag along if you want, Alexis. I warn you, it's likely to be pretty boring. Lots of walking around in the woods, that kind of thing. You can ride with us if you want."

Her face lit up and she nodded.

"Can I stash my bike at your place?" she asked.

"Sure. We'll meet you there," he said with a smile. She gave me a quick kiss, then bounded off. I watched her bounce away for a few seconds, then turned back to Dr. C.

"So, why didn't you send her home like Lucas and Wanda?" I asked.

"Chancc, shc's your girlfriend, or she wants to be. And . . . I wanted to give you two some time together." His face fell a little, and I could see the sadness behind his eyes.

"Like normal kids, huh?" I said wistfully.

"You'll never be normal," he said after a moment. "Your life is going to be filled with problems other kids will never have. But it'll also be filled with magick, and wonder. I can't give you a normal day. But sometimes, I can give a good one. Maybe we can grab some stuff from my place, and you can have a romantic lunch out in the woods." He got in the truck and started it up. I climbed back in and closed my own door.

"You know, Dr. C, sometimes you can be okay," I told him a few minutes later as he navigated the streets toward his place.

"I try," he said with a slow smile. He was pretty damn cool most of the time, but there was no way I was going to tell him that. He was hard enough to deal with as it was.

Chapter 15

~ Details. It's all in the details. ~ Dwarven proverb.

I woke up in the back seat of Dr. Corwyn's Range Rover with a comfortable, warm weight on my chest and the half-remembered fragment of a sound in my ears. Shade was snuggled under my left arm, with her feet curled up under her and her left hand on my chest. Whatever I'd heard had woken me up, but Shade was still dozing, and I filed that under "Odd things that happened today." If anything, she should have been the one telling me she heard something.

I looked around, more than a little disoriented. The last thing I remembered was Dr. C pulling in to a gas station in a little town south of Springfield called Ozark. I was slumped up against the passenger side door in the back seat with the most beautiful girl I knew curled up under my arm. The sun had disappeared under ominous looking clouds, and we were parked in a gravel lot surrounded by forest. Through the front window, I could see Dr. C walking through waist-high brown grass with a pendulum swinging from his fingertips. I watched him walk a slow circle, then he lowered his hand and shook his head when he completed a circuit back to his starting point. He scribbled in a notebook that he pulled from his jacket pocket, then tucked it back away and walked a little further away.

The only other thing out here was the little Conservation Department bulletin board off to my right that had maps of the area, a bathroom and the boulders that blocked cars from driving across the field. None of that was likely to make noise and wake me up. Even the clouds just looked depressing and heavy with rain, without a hint of thunder or lightning.

Then I heard it again. A soft, plaintive moan came from Shade, and her hand clenched for a moment on my chest. Another, and this one was louder, more desperate. A nightmare. I was familiar with those. When she whimpered, I kissed the top of her head.

"It's okay, Shade," I said softly and slowly. "It's all right, I'm here. You're safe, everything's okay."

What I said was only half as important as how I said it. Calm, slow and reassuring, those were the things I wished for every time I woke up from my own nightmares. That, and a sudden case of amnesia. I slowly stroked her hair, and she let out a little sigh before she relaxed into my arms again.

"Goodnight my angel, time to close your eyes," I sang softly, "Save your questions for another day." The rest of the words were blurred in my head, a half-remembered Billy Joel song my mom had sung to me when I was three. Her breathing slowed again, and I savored the feel of her hair against my lips as I kissed her again. I tried not to imagine what she was dreaming about, but the image of her being pawed at by her old alpha, Dominic King, popped up in my head anyway. I'd literally knocked him off of her that night, but the image of her face turning to the side as he lay on top of her was one I would never forget. *Never again,* I thought.

She stirred in my arms a few minutes later, and I looked down to see sleepy gray eyes looking back up at me, with a curtain of red strands laying across her cheek and a dreamy smile spreading across her face.

"Dr. Corwyn's coming back," she said softly, her voice a little slurred with sleep. "I dreamed that you sang to me." Her smile melted my heart.

"You were having a bad dream," I told her. She nodded and looked down.

"I heard your voice." She looked up at me for a moment, then she kissed me, and the world went away for a few seconds. When she pulled back, I wanted to follow her, but I kept myself in place. "I felt safe again, when I heard your voice. Thank you." She smiled at me, and I tried to tell myself it wasn't because my face was turning red.

Dr. C saved me from having to fumble through a response when he opened his door and slid in behind the wheel. "Well, we're still south of where he went."

"Where are we?" I asked as he pored over his map.

"Just a little north of Bradleyville. Pretty much dead center in this section of the Mark Twain National Forest. And he was north of here. So, that cuts it down quite a lot."

"Shouldn't I be doing this, sir? Since I'm the Seeker, you know?" I asked.

He handed his pendulum over the seat to me with a gesture, and Shade and I climbed out of the back seat.

Divinations were usually divided into two different types among the mystic world: spirit summoning, and aetheric or *akashic.* The first relied on summoning a (hopefully) helpful entity to guide you to the answers you were looking for. There were hundreds of minor spirits that could be summoned, but it was a fifty-fifty shot at getting one that would help you unless you had a specific name. That was why Ouija boards were so damn dangerous. They weren't even real summoning tools. A game company had invented them back in the nineteenth century, but they were close enough to automatic writing to do the job. Using one for casual divination was a lot like opening your door in the middle of the night, leaving the lights on, and hoping that the first person who walked in the door wasn't going to rob your ass blind. Aside from being kind of iffy on the results, it was really easy for someone to find out what you were looking for when you used spirits to do your scrying. Most spirits, even the helpful ones, really didn't get things like loyalty or privacy, and the more helpful they were, the more likely they were to spill what they knew if someone summoned them and asked what you had been doing.

That was why people like Dr. C and me used the akashic form, which was more like accessing a huge, aetheric database. I'd tried to explain how that worked to Lucas once, and he'd instantly said it was like cloud computing, only more intuitive. Everything ever known or experienced was imprinted into the *akasha*, the primordial aether that touched everything. It was what the Four Elements came from, and what Alchemy called *quinta essentia,* or quintessence. According to Dr. C, when I opened my Third Eye, I was seeing the place where the physical world was affecting the quintessential.

Divination was more like watching a silent, foreign movie of what had happened. A silent, foreign film with mimes trying to act out a musical. The mind had to break it down into symbols or interpret it as images. That was why most people had to be in a trance state to do akashic divination, to make the left side of their brain shut the hell up and let the right brain finger paint like a kindergartener to show what it saw.

Using a pendulum took that to an even more basic level, bypassing the language part of the brain and using the part of the body's energy system that could touch the aether and interpret it directly as movement. Without a chart, pendulum divination, or *radiesthesia*, was limited to yes or no questions and pointing in a specific direction.

I stepped away from the Range Rover and into the grass. After I was a few yards away, I let my eyes close and concentrated on letting the energy centers in my body, what most people called *chakras*, open up. The crown, or *sahasrara* energy center was the first one, since it was like the antenna that let me touch the akasha, then the brow, or *ajna*, the part that let me interpret it. The central chakras were the ones most people knew about, but there were also minor chakras along the arms and legs, and I opened those up to act like a conducting wire for the energy I needed. My limb chakras were pretty messed up from all the times Dulka had broken my arms and legs, then healed them the next morning. Still, I felt the tingle of energy slide down my left arm and through the cord to the little crystal pendulum. Truth was, you could use almost anything, but crystal was the easiest for most people to work with, since it naturally conducted energy. I felt it quiver as the energy hit the end of the cord, then flowed back up as it completed the loop.

Almost immediately, the crystal started spinning in slow circles. I took a breath, held it, then let it out through my mouth to center myself. I started to concentrate on finding Mr. Chomsky's trail, but every time I tried to get my mind on the subject, the pendulum stopped spinning. I knew better than to fight it. Instead, I went from specific to general.

"Show me where I need to go," I said after a few seconds.

The words had barely come out of my mouth before it started swinging back and forth, almost in a straight line in front of me. But when I started forward, it started swinging side to side. My eyebrows collided as I turned around and walked the other way. That took me back toward the Range Rover. When I got to the driver's side window, I stopped and gestured at Dr. C to roll it down.

"Which direction am I facing?" I asked.

He pulled a black compass from his pocket and opened it, then looked back at me.

"Northwest. That's a lot more specific than what I got."

"That's funny, because I didn't get anything when I asked about Mr. Chomsky. I asked where I needed to go, and it started pointing this way. Can I see your map?" I asked.

He handed it to me as he got out.

Shade followed him as I laid the map on the hood of the Range Rover and held the pendulum over it.

Again, I focused my chakras, this time aligning the map in my head as the symbolic world to the pendulum, so that instead of trying to point to what I wanted in the world around me, it would show me where the right symbol on the map was for where I needed to be. Almost as soon as I set it to spinning above the map, it pulled tight against the chain. I let it draw my hand along, until the pull was straight down. Right over New Essex.

"Crap," I muttered. "We're missing something, sir. Whatever we need is back in New Essex." I tossed the pendulum down on the hood of the truck and took a step back. Between the slow headache that was creeping in behind my eyes and the dull ache of my busted ribs, I was feeling pretty cranky. It didn't help that I'd been feeling like this place was familiar, like I'd been in the woods recently.

"The trip isn't completely wasted, Chance. You had no way of knowing this was going to happen. Let's just stop someplace, get some lunch and make a day of it. We'll figure the rest out when we get back home."

Lunch ended up being at a place with wooden floors and bench seats in the lobby. License plates and state flags were all over, next to retro magazine covers, fishing tackle and antique tools. Shade and I let Dr. C talk us into getting the country-fried steak.

When they brought our food to us, I thought they were going to serve it straight from the frying pan on to our plates. Then it turned out the frying pans *were* our plates. And these weren't your normal skillets, either. Each pan had to be more than a foot wide, and the steak took up more than half of it. Between the full pound of batter-and-gravy covered steak, the baked potato and the bowl of corn, I barely finished the whole thing.

"I'm not gonna eat for a week," I moaned melodramatically on the way back to the truck.

Shade leaned against me. "Me, either," she said contentedly.

"I shouldn't have had the potatoes and onions they brought."

"Or the other three rolls," Dr. C added.

"They threw them at me, I swear."

"So, I've been giving some thought to what we're looking for," Dr. C said once we were in the Range Rover and Shade had snuggled back under my arm. "Maybe you should do some more general divination when we get home. Yours was the only good read we got today."

"Guess I should. It's my wyrd and all anyway, right? I just keep feeling like I'm missing something, and I don't know what it is. I should be closer to finding this damn thing."

"Don't let it bog you down, Chance. Remember, your emotions affect your magick. So do your doubts. You're an apprentice mage, and your words and your thoughts have power. Be gentle with yourself."

"Be gentle with myself?" I hissed. "I don't know if you missed this news flash or not, sir, but I'm not exactly battin' a thousand here. Hells, I'm not even a very good apprentice."

"Why do you think that?" he asked.

I wished I could believe the concern I heard in his voice, but there was just too much telling me it was so much bullshit.

"It only took you three days to make your first touchstone. Draeden only took a month. It took me more than two months to get one to hold. And I know exactly how far behind I am in the rest of my studies, too. I'm never going to catch up."

"Chance, being a mage isn't about what you know. It's about what you *do*. Your magick is in the way you talk, the way you live your life, in the way you treat other people. It isn't what's in your head that makes you a good mage. It's what lives in your heart. You're the best damn apprentice I could hope for."

"Then why does it take me so long to learn stuff?" I asked around the tightness in my throat.

"That's simple. I had a better teacher than you do."

"Now who's being hard on himself?" I asked, unable to resist the comeback.

"Sydney was a terrific teacher. I'm not so bad, but he was a lot better. So, you two relax, enjoy the ride back, and try not to steam up the windows, okay?"

"We'll behave," Shade said. She put her mouth close to my ear and whispered, "Mostly."

When we got back to Dr. C's place, Lucas and Wanda were waiting by the side door with Collins. Dr. C pulled into the garage at the back, and Shade and I tried to make it look like we hadn't been making out the whole way back while Dr. C grabbed his staff from the back. Technically, it was true. We'd only been making out *most* of the way back. My mom would have probably gone off on him if she knew about it, but I didn't think he was going to talk.

"Any luck?" Wanda asked as we opened the door.

"We narrowed it down to only a few thousand acres of forest, if you call that luck," Dr. C said. He set his staff by the door, then grabbed one of his Coke bottles from beside the refrigerator and slumped into the heavy wooden chair at the end of the kitchen table. Collins sat at the other end, and Lucas and Wanda took the pair of chairs next to the kitchen window, on the other side of the table from me after they grabbed their own sodas from the fridge. Shade sat down beside me, and sat a bottle between us.

"Demetrius, I could put on a pot of coffee if you'd like some," Dr. C said.

"Nah, I'm good. And you can call me Tré," he replied. "We been through too much shit to be all formal."

"So, what's next?" Lucas asked.

"Chance found out today that specific divinations are probably not working because we're looking for the wrong thing. So he's going to do some more general scrying to see what he can find."

"What about your visions?" Wanda asked me.

"You didn't mention any visions, Chance," Dr. C said.

"I forgot all about them. I've had a lot on my mind. I saw the first one in the alley with Dani, then I had one Saturday morning at the house. The last one I had was at Dani's house."

"What did you see?"

"A building, trees, and a sword. And there was a bell the last time."

"So, this girl was there when you had two of these visions," Dr. C said. "How is she connected, I wonder?"

"She said she was an empath, and she got really freaked out when she touched Chance. She almost fell out of her chair," Wanda added.

"Exposure to your psyche can be pretty jarring," Dr. C remarked. "Perhaps contact with her unlocks a latent talent in you, Chance. Why don't you do some general scrying, then go see her and try again, to see if you get better results."

"What about us?" Lucas asked with a gesture that included Wanda.

"Find Dani and Donovan," I told him. "Make sure she's free this afternoon."

"I need to make an appearance at home," Shade said. "And I need to make nice with Deek and check on the boys. I'll meet you back here after you talk to Dani." She took a drink from the Coke bottle, then leaned over and kissed me.

My lips were still tingling by the time she closed the door behind her.

"As for you, Tré, make yourself comfortable for a little bit. Once we do a few basic divinations, I have something that should make your visit to see Thraxus tonight a little easier." Dr. C gestured toward the front room as he stood up.

I followed him into the library, and grabbed my backpack from the hallway as we went. Once we were inside, I pulled my own pendulum from the outside pocket. Mine was an amethyst crystal wrapped in copper wire on a silver necklace. I'd used it to find Mr. Chomsky's killer, and it made sense to me to use it to find what he'd hidden. Since my last divination pointed us back to New Essex, I pulled a map of the city from the drawer of the reading table and spread it out on it. Almost as soon as I held the purple stone over the table, it started spinning.

"Where do I need to go now?" I asked. It was almost the same thing I'd asked back in the woods. The chain went tight as the pendulum swung from the center. I let my hand follow the pull until it was straight down, then let it drop down until the point touched the map.

"All right, either someone I need to meet is there, or the Universe thinks I really need cheesy bacon fries," I quipped.

"Where is that?" Dr. C asked.

"Dante's."

"So, you're sure that Dani is the next link here?" Lucas asked as we walked across the parking lot at Dante's.

The parking lot was pretty full, with school being out today. No one knew if we were going to have class tomorrow, but no one seemed to be betting on it. Lucas had found a space near the farthest reaches of parking Siberia, and now we were hiking in.

"Well, I asked where I needed to go next, and got led here. She's here. You do the math," I told Lucas.

"Remember what Dr. C said about spells, dude. Correlation doesn't always mean causality," Lucas reminded me as we got close to the door.

"I remember, man," I told him. "Keep my mind and my eyes open, because fortune favors the prepared mind."

"I thought he said that in his physics class," Wanda said.

I opened the door for her and let her and Lucas go in before me. The thump of the sound system hit us as we stepped into the darkened room. The switch from the cool spring air to the packed heat of Dante's was like a warm blanket on my skin.

"He says that in every class, but there's a lot of physics in magick," I called over the sound of the music. As packed as it was, it would have been hard for anyone to hear us over the music.

We made our way toward the back, jostling and squeezing until we hit the edge of the dance floor and the crowd opened up. Across the pool tables, I could see Donovan. He'd staked a claim on our regular table, and damn if people didn't give him a wider berth than they did me. Dani was dwarfed behind him, almost invisible in the back of our booth.

I grabbed a chair from the closest table and spun it around so the back was between me and the table, then straddled it.

"Are you the girl who reads minds?" I asked with a feeling of coming full circle.

Wanda and Lucas slid in to the seat across from them.

"I don't read minds," Dani snapped at me. There were dark circles under her eyes, and she had a haunted look to her face.

"Chill, Dani," Donovan said. "He's trying to help out."

"Since when did you become a fan?" she asked.

"Since I saw what he fights. Chance and I are on the same team, we just do things differently."

I gave Donovan an appraising glance, trying to see if he looked any different on the outside. The easy confidence seemed to have cracked a little, and the smug grin looked like it wasn't going to be making a showing any time soon.

"Great, while you boys were bonding, I haven't slept since Saturday night!" Dani barked. "While you've been putting on your capes and tights, or whatever, I've been dreaming about the things they do to Crystal!"

"Dani, I'm sorry," I told her. "I didn't know. Maybe your dreams can help me find her. That's what I came here for. When I've been around you, I've had these visions, and I think they can help me find Crystal."

She shoved against Donovan's side. "Let me out. I've had all the help from you I can take."

He slid out and held his hand out to her to help her to her feet.

As she pulled herself up against his arm, I felt my last chance at finding Crystal and the Maxilla walking out with her.

In desperation, I did the only thing I could. I reached out and grabbed her wrist.

My brain was instantly flooded with feelings and images that weren't mine. Kissing a dark-haired beauty in a darkened bedroom, trying to stay quiet so my parents wouldn't come in; listening to my father rant over dinner about people like me; hearing people talk about me behind my back; the way my heart raced when Crystal first told me she loved me; the way it broke when she freaked out; and the certain belief that she still loved me. Finally, I saw the dreams. Fear, pain, darkness. They were too raw and fresh to make much more than a fleeting, muddled impression.

Then the other images came. The Maxilla: a plain sword hanging in the air, the point up, hidden inside its own little pocket space. All it needed was the key to open the door. I tried to focus on the location, to find any clue about where it was, and I saw the same thing I'd seen before. A building made of rough wood, and I heard a bell. Only this time, I saw the bell. It was freestanding on a post, with a frayed rope dangling from the pull arm. My point of view got pulled back to the Maxilla, and I saw myself standing in the middle of a creekbed. If I were ever there, I would know it. Then I was thrown back into my own head as Donovan grabbed my wrist and pulled my hand away.

"You bastard!" Dani said. And then, she slapped me.

Wanda and Lucas tried to come out of their seat, but I put my hand up to stop them. The other went to my stinging cheek as I watched her head for the dance floor.

"Pretty sure I deserved that one, guys. Donovan, I need you to stay with her, man. Even if she doesn't like it, until she's behind a threshold, you stick to her like glue." He nodded and headed into the crowd.

"We need to head back to Dr. C's place," I told Lucas and Wanda.

"That's it? You got what you wanted, and now you're just leaving? Just like a guy!" Wanda said.

"She's the one who did the leaving," I told her. "I'm not gonna waste time making nice when I could be looking for her girlfriend." I turned and headed for the snack bar.

"And saving your own ass?" Lucas said as they joined me. "I'd be kinda partial to that if I was you."

I wasn't about to argue with him about that.

Chapter 16

~ Eating the messenger is bad form when accepting an invitation. ~ Vampire etiquette

When we got back to Dr. C's place, there was a low-slung black sports car parked in front of the house. Lucas was out of the car and around to the front of the house before I could even get out of the back seat. By the time I got to him, he was practically crowing in delight.

"Dude, do you know what this is?" he asked. He circled the car and looked across the top of it at me. "This . . . this is a Mercedes McLaren Roadster. I saw the episode they did on it on Top Gear. It costs like half a million dollars, and man is it fast! This one's been customized, and it's the convertible. See how it rides low because of the extra weight? Whoever drove this has some serious money!"

I looked down at the car. It barely came up to my elbow, and it looked like it was a couple of feet longer than the *Falcon.* Which was kind of funny to me, since it only had two seats.

"Then you probably can't wait to meet whoever drove it, can you?" I said.

Lucas' head snapped up at that, and his face broke out into a grin.

"Think they'll let me drive it?" He was practically bouncing as he came around the car.

"Doubt it," I said. "But I'm sure they'll let you drool on the keys or something like that." I gestured toward the front door, and he fell in beside me.

I opened the wards and let them through, then shut them behind us. The library door was open, and light spilled out into the hall. I headed that way, and ran right into someone soft and curvy the second I turned the corner.

She squealed and I grabbed for her, barely catching her.

"Sorry, ma'am," I said automatically.

She looked up at me, and I recognized the blond from the limo at Thraxus' place.

"Apology accepted," she purred.

I pulled my hands away from her, but she didn't move. Instead, she laid her hands against my chest and pressed most of the rest of her curves against me.

"I didn't get the opportunity to introduce myself the first time we met. I'm Chastity."

"Suuuure, you are," Wanda snarked from beside me.

"Jealousy doesn't suit you, little girl," Chastity said. "The offer for that . . . *ride* . . . is still on the table," she turned back to me.

"Again, I have to decline . . . for now. One, because I don't like owing vampires squat, and two, I don't do casual sex. With anyone." I pushed her away. I tried to keep my eyes on her face, but Powers help me, I'm still as human as the next guy. I looked. Okay, I stared. I might have even ogled.

She'd somehow poured herself into a black dress that started way north of her knees and stopped just far enough south of her shoulders to be legal. Black stockings did their best to make it all the way to the cover of the skirt hem, but they fell short, despite the help of her garter belt. Platform heels made her tall enough to reach my chin, but I had no idea how she managed to stay on her feet in them, as top heavy as she was.

She gave me a smile that promised lots of pleasant nasty and turned her attention to Lucas.

"Maybe you'll play with me tonight," she said as she pressed herself against his left side.

His eyes went wide, and I could see him start to shake as she ran one manicured black fingernail down the middle of his chest. Her tongue trailed across her upper lip before she turned a look on him that should have blistered his cheeks.

"Whoa . . . um . . . boobs . . . I'd love to . . . um . . . but I have to . . . uh . . . Wanda, a little help here? Chance?" he stammered.

"These aren't the breasts you're looking for," I said with a wave of my hand. "Crap, that only works on the weak-minded, doesn't it?" I turned toward Chastity to finish the joke, but Wanda was already stepping in.

"Back off, bitch," she hissed, and put her fingers against the buxom girl's left collarbone. When she straightened her arm, Chastity staggered back like she'd been punched, and fell on her ass.

"That hurt!" she cried, surprise in her voice.

"I warned you not to try that act with them," Dr. Corwyn said from behind his desk.

Collins had his butt half-perched on one corner of the desk, his arms folded across his chest. Both of them had matching smug grins on their faces.

"You knew this was gonna happen?" I demanded.

Chastity flowed to her feet more gracefully than most girls with her footwear ought to have been able to pull off.

"She tried the same thing on us when she first arrived," Dr. C said. "I guess Thraxus decided to keep her in reserve in case you took her up the ride she offered. I would imagine the poor girl's been more than a little bored."

"Why in the Nine Hells is she here anyway?"

"I came to deliver an invitation. For Chance Fortunato and a single guest, and for Detective Demetrius Collins, also allowing a single guest. Safe passage is guaranteed, but discretion in your choice of guests is expected." She pranced to one of the chairs facing Dr. C's desk and pulled a pair of envelopes from a slim black attaché case. She handed Collins one and brought the other over to me, managing to jiggle all the way.

I took it and ignored the stroke of her finger across mine on the underside of the envelope.

Thraxus had good taste in paper, that was for sure. Dr. C had been teaching me a lot about the quality of paper for making scrolls, and just enough had sunk in that I could tell this stuff was heavy and expensive. My name was hand-printed on the front in fancy calligraphy with enough flourish to make it look good, but not so much that it made it unreadable. I flipped it over and saw a thick black blob of wax impressed with a round seal of a dragon with wings spread over the flap. I reached for my balisong and found nothing in my pocket. I frowned, remembering that it was in evidence at the police station.

Dr. C opened one of his desk drawers and held out a wooden case.

I took it and popped it open to find a black folding knife nestled inside.

"Happy birthday," he said with a smile.

"Thanks," I said as I pulled it out and opened it with my thumb, then popped the seal on the envelope.

Inside was a card on equally heavy paper, written in the same script as the outside, only smaller, inviting me to visit Lord Thraxus this evening at my earliest possible pleasure to discuss redress for grievances committed against me. My eyes went to Dr. C as I handed him the invitation. In vampiric politics, this seemed almost as good as a confession, which made Thraxus look weak. His eyebrow went up and he gave me that slight head tilt that was his quizzical look.

"All right, I'm in," Collins said.

"I'm good with it," I told Dr. C.

He nodded, but I knew he didn't like it.

"Tell your Master we'll be there soon. And no . . . I do *not* need a ride out there tonight."

I saw Chastity's smile transform itself into a pout as she pranced up to me and handed me a business card.

"In case you come to your senses," she whispered sensually. She gave me a look that should have started fires nearby before she turned and flounced her way out in a clatter of stripper heels.

I shook my head.

"Boobs?" Wanda said to a red-faced Lucas, who looked like he was enjoying watching her leave.

"They were kinda hard to ignore . . . and you know how I get with girls," he said.

"*No one* knows how you get with girls," she shot back. "It's like Bigfoot or the Loch Ness Monster. Lots of stories, but no *hard* evidence."

"You two. Quiet," Dr. C said in his business tone.

They shut up and parked their backsides on chairs across from his desk. Even I didn't argue with him when he put the sharp edge on his voice like that.

"Tré, you're going to need this. I wanted to get this taken care of while the kids were gone, but Chastity's arrival shot that plan to Hell." He pulled a gunbelt from behind his desk and handed it to Collins.

Collins drew the heavy black revolver from the holster and held it up to look at it. The cylinder was huge, and what looked like a large tube ran below the barrel.

"Guess this means the silver rounds you gave me don't work on vampires," he said speculatively. "What the hell kind of gun is this? I don't think I've ever seen one like it before. This somethin' one of you wizards made?"

"That is a LeMat revolver, commonly known as a grape shot revolver for the sixteen-gauge lower barrel. It's a percussion cap pistol from the Civil War era, made for the Confederate Army. Originally, it held nine forty-two-caliber lead rounds in the cylinders, with the smooth bore under-barrel being loaded with grape shot, hence the name."

"What's it hold now?" Collins asked as he sighted down the barrel and tested the heft.

Dr. C came around the desk as he continued. "Nine rounds made from the lead of church roofs, each blessed and charged with an incendiary spell, with a special mixture of my own in the under-barrel called a Sunflare. Even a vampire as powerful as Thraxus won't be able to shrug that off. In cowan terms, it hits about like a rocket-propelled grenade. It's single action, and you move this lever on the hammer to fire the Sunflare round." He stepped back as Collins holstered the pistol.

"So, why do I need to carry this? I thought we were invited guests."

"To show Thraxus and everyone around him that you take him seriously enough to come loaded for bear. It helps him save a little face, which will put him further in your debt."

"He's gonna hate that," I remarked.

"You'll have to console yourself somehow," Dr. C said as he went back behind his desk. "You better arm up as well."

"I don't get a cool revolver?" I asked. "I'm gonna feel under-dressed."

"All you need is the Ariakon and your wand. You're the demon's apprentice; you beat your master and killed an alpha werewolf with less," Dr. C told me with a smile.

Outside, the sound of motorcycles drifted closer.

"That'll be Shade and the Pack," Wanda said as she and Lucas stood up. I grabbed my backpack and headed for the side door behind them. We made it to the gate as they pulled up and dismounted. Smaller by one with Brad going rogue, the Pack was tighter than ever. And even though we weren't Weres, they treated Lucas, Wanda, and me like family. That meant very physical greetings when we weren't in public. Contact was important to Weres, especially among pack members, and since the wolf spirit ran closer to its emotions, they enjoyed being able to show affection when they could. Here, we were treated to forearm-gripping handshakes that pulled into enthusiastic hugs, with growled warm greetings. Whether it had been an hour or a week since we'd seen each other, meeting with the pack outside of school always felt like meeting old friends you hadn't seen for years.

Once I made it through the wall of grinning, leather-clad Pack members, I went to Shade, who was still standing next to her bike.

Deek was beside her, and he had his hand on her wrist.

"I don't care; this kind of crap has got to stop. Humans are not pack," Deek hissed at her.

"They stood with us when no one else did, so they're part of *my* pack. Deal with it or get the hell out," she growled back.

"Someone needs to put you in your place, woman," Deek said.

Shade lost it. She pulled her wrist free and shoved him back, then came off her bike at him with her finger in his chest.

"I spent three *years* being put in my place by Dominic King, you smug little pureblood! I wasn't born this way. I got turned because a horny eighth grader wanted a permanent girlfriend! Where was your pretty little ass while I got raped every week? Where were you when he forced us to shake down humans and rob people? Where?" She had backed him up until he was at the curb on the other side of the road.

"That was his right, he was your alpha," Deek said.

"I'M the alpha now! ME! And this is the way it's gonna be." She turned her back on him and strode across the street toward me.

His eyes turned hard and he started after her.

"We'll see about that," he said.

I gave him a hard stare, and he stopped in his tracks for a second. The rest of the pack was behind me, and I could feel their hostility toward him.

Then, he plastered a smile on his face and sauntered our way.

"What's up tonight?" Shade said as she slipped her arm around my waist.

"Collins and I got an invite from Thraxus to come out and talk. We can each take one person with us. You can guess who I'm taking," I said.

Shade leaned in and grazed her teeth across my neck as I was talking, then smiled at me.

"Bryce?" she asked innocently. She even batted her eyelashes at me.

"I didn't think anyone knew," I quipped, and a round of chuckles went up.

"I'm going," Deek interjected.

"No, you're not," I said just as quickly.

"We've already been over this already. You can't stop me from coming with you."

"I don't have to. This time, it's invitation only, and you're not on the guest list. I'm taking Shade. Collins chooses his guest if he wants one. No one else allowed. Period."

Deek glared at me, then took a step back.

"I'm not taking anyone," Collins said from behind me. "You done layin' your dick down, there, Deek? Cuz the big kids got places to be."

I gave a quick chuckle as Shade and I headed over to his car and worked out the logistics. I would ride with Shade, and he'd follow us. It wasn't like he didn't know where Cromwell Manor was, but on paper, he was still keeping an eye on me. One of the guys, Riley, loaned me his helmet, not much more than a plastic bowl, and his riding goggles.

Before we got on her bike, Shade stopped and faced me, then pulled her collar aside and bared her neck to me. Without thinking, I pulled her to me and put my teeth to her throat and bit. The now-familiar tremble was harder than before, but when she looked at me again, her eyes were normal. I looked over her shoulder, and saw the rest of the pack nodding among themselves. This had been as much for their benefit as for her. And I wasn't above liking how much it pissed Deek off, either.

Chapter 17

~ Let your host believe that you fear him in his own house. ~
Infernal saying

The ride out was a pleasant blur of streetlights accompanied by the hum of the engine. Shade went easy on the way there, but I still held on like I was never letting go. The gates opened for us when we arrived, and we took the drive up.

"Why didn't we do this the last time we were here?" Shade asked once we got off the bike.

"We didn't have an invitation. The traditional version is that you don't presume on your host's stable. The cold-hearted, practical version? You don't leave your horse where your host can steal it."

Collins pulled up behind us and got out. He slid the gun belt around his hips and buckled it into place, then bent down and tied it down by his knee.

"I feel like Wyatt Earp or Cherokee Bill," he muttered as he straightened.

I followed his example and slid the paintball holster around my hips and buckled it to my left leg. My wand went into my front pocket on my right side, along with my touchstone. And, just in case, I tucked my new knife in my back pocket on the left side. Because I'd brought it, I probably wouldn't need it, and I was good with that. I wasn't ready to spend any more time unconscious this week. Absently, I wished I had a cinnamon Firebomb, but I'd eaten the last one hours ago. With my backpack settled on my back, and Shade at my side, we headed for the doors

They opened when we were about ten steps away, and the same doorman waited for us. He stepped aside and gestured for us to enter. We stepped in, and Collins head swiveled around, his gaze stopping on each of the vampires lounging about in the room. Instead of leading us toward the staircases, the doorman led us through the doors under the balcony, then turned to his right and led us down a carpeted hallway. The hall was dim, and the dark wood paneling only made it feel murkier as we went. Overhead, we could hear music and laughter for the first few yards, then silence descended like a shroud. The door-vamp turned to his left after a little ways in, and opened another set of double doors.

Inside was a room that looked big enough to hold a soccer game in, with a hardwood floor and floor to ceiling rows of windows that sliced the room into neat strips of red moonlight and darkness. We stepped in behind the doorman, and I could see the lone figure in the darkness, silhouetted in front of the pair of French doors set in the center of the opposite wall. The serrated look to the ears and the way the moonlight shone against his bare scalp revealed Thraxus to me. He turned to face us, and two crimson points of light blazed before us. Collins stopped in his tracks, but he kept his hand off his gun. Shade and I found each other's hand in the darkness, and I could feel her shoulders tensing up through her arms.

"Good evening, Detective Collins," Thraxus' smooth voice filtered through the room. "Apprentice Fortunato, Lady Shade, it's good to see you again, though I wish the circumstances were better."

As he spoke, the lights slowly came up to illuminate the room. Calling it a library fell way short. It had enough bookshelves, reading tables, and map tables to put Dr. C's to shame. But it didn't stop there. The wall to my left was bare of shelves, covered instead with glass display cases, armor stands, and weapon racks. Paintings covered the far wall, portraits of people I didn't know.

"I wish they were better, too," I told him after I finished giving the room the once over.

"Well, no matter how unfortunate the context of our meeting, good manners can smooth the way considerably. Perhaps you'd be so good as to make introductions, Apprentice Fortunato?" Thraxus gave me a smile that never parted his lips, and gestured with one too-long hand at Collins.

"Detective Demetrius Collins, this is Lord Thraxus, chief vampire of New Essex. Lord Thraxus, you seem to already know Detective Collins." I hoped I hadn't screwed that up too much.

Thraxus nodded, but kept his hand to himself.

“I do indeed,” Thraxus said smoothly. “First of all, Detective, I must offer my apologies for your ill treatment at the hands of my underling’s people. Overt use of force against public servants is forbidden by our oldest traditions.”

“And what keeps me from bustin’ you *and* your boy for assaulting a police officer?” Collins asked.

“Detective Collins, you could not hope to do more than inconvenience me briefly. The fallout of that inconvenience is what concerns us. If the existence of my kind were to be revealed as more than mere legend to the cowan, open warfare would result. The last time my kind warred openly with mortals, Lemuria and Atlantis were both above water at the outset. Your civilization has yet to recover even half the knowledge it lost. We two must avoid that at all costs.”

“And I’m supposed to be good with an apology?” Collins asked.

I hid a smile at that, but Shade didn’t look amused.

“No, Detective. Though you do not understand the value of even so small a thing from me, it is not all I bring to the table tonight. But there is more to be asked of you, I fear. When you first stepped into this world some months ago, you realized that many of the rules you held sacred no longer applied. I’m afraid you’re going to have to slaughter a few more of those sacred cows tonight.” Thraxus put his fingertips against each other and sat back.

“How the hell did you know about that?” Collins demanded a few seconds later.

“I have sources within the New Essex police department. And of course, when an alpha werewolf is killed, word spreads behind the Veil. And yet your report reads like a simple exchange of gunfire, it leaves no questions, and does not attempt to rationalize anything unusual. Clearly, a fabrication crafted to conceal the true course of events, something a man who was incapable of understanding the Veiled world would never think to do. Thus, I surmise that you are capable of bending the rules of the world you were born to. It is my estimation of you, Detective Collins, that where other men who wear a badge are men of the law, you are a man of justice.”

Collins gave him a hard stare, and I could see the emotions playing across his face. On the one hand, he wanted to play this straight, like a cop should. On the other, he knew that there was more at stake than due process. No matter which way he went, he was going to betray part of what he believed in. He either followed the rules that his badge said to enforce, or he avoided starting a potential war between vampires and humans. I pitied him until he turned to me.

"He tellin' the truth? About a war?" he asked.

"Well, the demons tell a different version, but yeah, story goes the humans tried to take pretty much everyone else on. Didn't end well for anyone," I told him. He nodded, then turned back to Thraxus.

"Okay, so apology accepted," he said with a little more of the confidence I usually saw from him. "Now what?" Thraxus gave him a closed mouthed smile that sent chills down my spine and made me wonder if we'd just played into something.

"I offer you what you desire most, Detective. Justice." Thraxus said it with the same relish as a hungry man describing a steak.

"That depends on whether we both think that's the same thing."

"Oh, I assure you, our definitions will coincide. Tell me, do you trust the boy?" he asked, with a nod toward me.

Collins shrugged. "Most of the time."

"Do not play at being coy, detective. When you entered the room, you checked the right side first, the side opposite the boy. When you didn't trust your own judgment, you turned to him. You treat him as a comrade in arms, in spite of your desire to see him as a child. Now, I ask you again. Do. You. Trust. The boy?" The vampire's last words hit like hammers, and Collins scowled at him.

"Yeah, I do. With my damn life."

"What of the lives of your nieces?" Thraxus asked.

Collins and I both took a step forward. Collins' hand fell to the butt of the pistol at his side, and my hand tightened around my wand. He looked back over his shoulder at me before he answered.

"I watched this kid kill a werewolf to protect his mom and his kid sister. He coulda backed down from your boy over a girl he don't even *know*, but he didn't, and he wouldn't go to a safehouse so he could keep looking for her. So, yeah, I trust him with my nieces' lives, too. Now get to the damn point!" His words ignited something in my heart, a feeling that only being Dee's hero had compared to.

"Well said, sir. The point is this. As an officer of the law, your actions are limited. As an apprentice mage, however tenuous his status may be, young Chance here still has considerably more leeway to act on both sides of the Veil. You do still have a claim to vengeance against Etienne. Were you to convey your claim to Chance, who also has a legitimate complaint against him, I would have no choice but to rescind my protection as his liege. You would not be acting in your official capacity as an officer of cowan law, and apprentice Fortunato would be saving the lives of both your families. Assuming he survived."

The feeling of pride deflated in my chest at his last sentence.

"Why the change of heart, Thraxus?" I asked.

"I will not speak of it here. Come with me, and you will see. The others must stay. What I am about to show you is not for their eyes." He glided around the desk and gestured for me to follow him as he made for the door. The double doors swung open wide when he was ten steps away. I gave Collins and Shade a nod before I followed him.

He led me down the hallway, and stopped by an alcove. Set inside was a narrow door with a keypad beside it, with a blinking red light at the top. His hand moved too quickly for me to follow it, and the little light at the top went from red to green. The door popped open, and he led me down a set of spiral stairs into darkness. If he hadn't guaranteed safe passage in writing, I would never have followed the scary master vampire down the dark stairway under the very old, very spooky house. In spite of that, I still had plenty of doubts gnawing at my spine.

Finally, we came to level ground, and followed the hallway to a heavy looking metal door set flush with the wall around it. There was no knob, no handle, no lock. All he did was put his hand against the door for a few seconds and it popped open. We went to a second door, this one an old style black vault door with gold trim around it and a heavy brass dial in the middle and a thick handle above it. He spun the combination so fast I could barely see when the dial stopped, and turned the handle to pull it open.

The room beyond the doorway was lit by a flickering blue light, and when he led me inside, I stopped and stared. Four heavy, black metal pieces hung against the back wall, each circled with a ring of blue-white fire. There was a gap on the right side, between the third and fourth pieces, where I guessed another one should have been. Even from across the room, I could feel the dark, heavy malevolence of them. With so many in one place, they pressed against my mystic senses, even though they were dormant.

"No cut is so deep as betrayal, nor any sting so sharp as that of treachery, no matter how many times I bear its scars. Even to admit to a mortal such as you that you were right loses much of its sting," Thraxus said heavily. "I discovered the loss of one of my fragments last night. Coupled with all that you have brought before me, I can come to no other conclusion than betrayal by the childe I sired."

"Yeah, your life must be one big suck-fest," I said flatly. "So, I guess you want me to stop Etienne's little power play for you. I'm already headed that way to hand him my own box of ass-kicking, so why not toss in a little something from dad, right?"

I tried to give the other four fragments a closer look without making it obvious. This was the largest single collection of G'Honn fragments I was likely to actually ever see with my own eyes, and each one had a wealth of magickal knowledge from the time of Atlantis and Lemuria. Most magi would sell body parts to get even one, and some had died trying.

"Perhaps a little something to sweeten the deal is in order. I will allow you fifteen minutes to study the fragments I still retain in exchange for recovering the one that was lost."

"An hour," I countered automatically.

"Are you attempting to haggle with me?" Thraxus asked incredulously.

"Do you have anyone else who can go put the beat down on Etienne?" I demanded.

"Twenty minutes. No more."

"Forty-five, or you send in the second string."

"Thirty minutes."

"I can live with half an hour. Alone."

I saw his upper lip start to creep up, but it stopped before the points of his teeth were exposed.

"Agreed," he growled. "Your time starts now." He turned his back and left.

When I heard the inner vault door shut, I shrugged my backpack off and unzipped it. My sketchbook came out, and the charcoal pencils Dr. C had insisted I buy to help with my visualization skills. I tore eight sheets out and headed for the first fragment. As I got close to it, I could feel the prickling sensation on the edge of my mystical senses that came from only one thing: Hellfire.

One of the few advantages to being able to summon Hellfire was the ability to temporarily dispel it. It wasn't something I could do in a fight, but with a spell like this one, that was set on a specific spot, I could disrupt it for a few minutes. For the umpteenth time, I wished for a cell phone with a camera, even if I wasn't sure the image would take. Old-school magick and electronics didn't always mix well.

I went to the first one on the left and held my right hand out until I could feel the phantom heat of the flames against my aura. Once I was familiar with how it felt, I moved my hand along the outside of the ring, until I found the tiny variance where the circle had been started and stopped.

"*Perturbare incaendium Infernum,*" I intoned.

The flames flickered, then chased themselves around the circle. I repeated the incantation three more times before it made it all the way around the circle and stayed out. The real trick to this was that I had no idea how long they would stay out. It was a terrific motivator to work fast. The paper was slightly smaller than the fragment, so I centered it on it and rubbed the length of the charcoal stick against the page until the whole thing was covered. Once that was done, I grabbed another sheet and did the edges in four vertical lines, with the sides labeled as carefully as I could with the little time I allowed myself.

After that, it was a repeat of the same thing with the other three. My hands got singed on the third one, and by the time I was done with the fourth, I was starting to sweat. The eight pages I'd torn out of my sketchpad were tucked into the leather-bound journal, with a page between them to keep them from smudging each other. Now all I had to do was convince Thraxus that I hadn't just cheated by taking rubbings of four closely guarded pieces of Lemurian lore. I risked a quick glance at my watch. Just under ten minutes left.

When Thraxus came in, I was sitting in front of the first fragment, sketching madly away. He frowned at me as he reached down and tore the page from the pad.

"I only gave you leave to study the fragments, not to draw a reproduction of them. I hope you remember what you drew," he said as he balled the page up and tossed it at the ring of Hellfire. It went up in a flash.

"I have a pretty good memory," I growled at him. Then I bowed and took on the formal tones of the Graces. "My apologies, Lord Thraxus, for abusing the privilege you granted me. I misunderstood the terms and intended no offense to your hospitality. I hope that the destruction of the offending sketch in some small way amends my error."

He gave me a gracious nod of his head. "Your apology is accepted. I believe that the loss is sufficient recompense for the offense." His tone was just as formal, though he made it sound more natural than I ever could. He turned for the door and gestured at me to follow him.

"You are most gracious, Lord Thraxus," I told him as the vault door closed behind us.

Shade and Collins came up out of the heavy leather chairs in front of Thraxus' desk when we came back in. Two nearly full glasses of wine and a pair of untouched plates of some kind of tiny pastry and cheese sat beside them. I gave Shade a smile, proud that she'd remembered what I'd told her last time we were here. Beside me, Thraxus gave a low laugh.

"Honored guests, you are here at my invitation. The obligation tonight is mine. You incur no debt by accepting my hospitality," he said with a smile.

I gave them a nod off their glances to me, and Shade reached behind her to take one of the little bite-sized offerings. Her eyes closed as she savored it, then she offered a contented moan.

"The canapés taste as good as they smell," she offered after she finished it.

Collins took one of his own, but he didn't offer an opinion on it.

"I'll convey your compliments to the kitchen staff," Thraxus said with a slight bow of his head. "Now, lest we forget our purpose here, Apprentice Fortunato accepts my reasons for withdrawing my protection. Detective Collins, do you convey your claim against Etienne to Apprentice Fortunato?"

"Yeah, I'll let him have my claim," Collins said.

"So be it, then. Apprentice Fortunato, given your previous complaint against Etienne, his further actions against you, and Detective Collins' claim that has been conferred in trust to you, I find that I can no longer offer him my protection as his sire in good faith. You have my leave to act against him as you see fit, coming the next setting of the sun."

"What?" Collins and I asked at the same time.

"Why tomorrow night?" Collins demanded.

"The forms must be followed. I must inform him of my decision, so that he has the opportunity to plead for mercy and amend his ways." The vampire's tone sounded so reasonable, but I was still fuming.

"You can't be serious!" I said.

"I am deadly serious, apprentice. I will not forsake the rules which have kept us safe and out of the public eye for millennia over a fifteen-year-old boy's protests. Officially, sunset is at ten minutes after seven. Until then, he is still under my protection. Have we an accord?"

"Yeah, we do," I grumbled.

Collins gave his yes a second later, and Thraxus nodded.

"Very well, then. Our business here is concluded, then. You're welcome to stay and enjoy the night's entertainments of course, but I doubt you will find much to your liking."

We didn't bother to agree with him out loud. After this visit, all I wanted was to be somewhere else.

Chapter 18

~ Long odds mean nothing to a mage. ~ Modern mage proverb

I came upstairs from the workroom in the basement less than fifteen minutes after we got back to Dr. C's place, and found Collins asleep on the sofa in the front room, with the borrowed pistol draped over the arm. I retrieved the gun belt and put it in the small storage space under the stairs until I could have Dr. Corwyn put it back wherever he stored it. I was just closing the door when Shade came down the stairs without a sound, a quilt in her arms. She stepped past me and laid it over Collins, then came back and put her arms around me. Our foreheads touched as we stood there quietly. My body loved having hers pressed against it, and the scent of her filled my nostrils as we stood there in the half-lit hallway. Under my hands, I could feel her tremble and shift slightly, and that set off a shift of my own.

"Penny for your thoughts," she whispered.

"I was wondering how you knew what those little things were that Thraxus served. Canopies?" I said.

"Canapés," she corrected me, saying the word slowly. "My parents work at Essex University; they go to mixers and cocktail parties all the time. And you're a terrible liar."

I shrugged in her embrace and gave her one of my lopsided smiles.

"You feel good in my arms," I said.

"Nothing else?" she said.

"Plenty else. Just nothing I want to say out loud yet."

"Yeah, me too," she whispered.

We stood there for a little longer, until it got too hard to keep my hands where they belonged.

"I . . . uh, I need to go tell Dr. C about tonight."

"And keep your hands to yourself," she whispered softly. "It's weird, you know? Being . . . well, having a guy in my life who isn't pawing at me all the time. Who treats me like . . ." Her words stopped with a little hiccup. I kissed the tip of her nose before I pulled her to me so she couldn't see my eyes water up. She squeezed me tight, and I gave an involuntary grunt as my ribs twinged. Reluctantly, she pulled back.

"I have to get back to the Pack anyway. If I'm gone too long, Deek might try to take over," she told me, and turned away.

I let her go, with a hundred things I wanted to say still on my tongue.

After the door closed, I headed upstairs to find Dr. C. He was standing in the doorway to Mr. Chomsky's room, with his hands in his pockets, his head down and his shoulders slumped. I stopped in my tracks and watched him for a few moments, unsure. He looked so defeated, worn down. If the smartest guy I'd ever met was feeling beat, how was I supposed to figure all of this out?

For a moment, everything came crashing down on me. The Ordeal, finding Crystal, beating Etienne. I was just a fifteen-year-old kid with a bad attitude and lots of issues. How was I supposed to do all that, when a full-fledged wizard couldn't figure how to handle even *one* of them? I didn't know what to do. The floor seemed to shift under my feet, and I wanted to run and hide. I might have been mad at Dr. C for what he'd pulled with my mom, but he'd still been the guy who knew what to do. He was my mentor, damn it! He wasn't allowed to fail.

I crept back down the stairs and slipped out the kitchen door. I needed to move, to be away from everything for a little while. I had no idea where I was going. I just walked.

Walking in a suburban neighborhood turned out to be a bad idea. At best, animals don't like me. They can see all the crap on my aura, and it scares them. Most of the time, they try to get as far away from me as they can. Walking through an area with a dog confined in almost every yard or house, once they got to the end of their space, all they could do was bark like mad and generally go nuts. Lights started coming on as I walked, and I decided I needed to get out of this neighborhood. A couple of streets over, I found myself near railroad tracks, which meant no houses, and no household pets dropping dead of fear-induced heart attacks.

I tried to get a handle on things, and figure out what was going on in my head. Feeling sorry for myself was something I tried not to do. It never fixed anything. But here I was, wandering down streets, pissed because I felt like I was on my own, like Dr. C had failed me somehow because he wasn't perfect. And I just couldn't shake that. That thought pissed me off even more, because I had never relied on anyone before, and it was turning out to be more trouble than it was worth. My thoughts kept going in circles, and I couldn't seem to get them moving in a different direction.

The sound of a dog yelping in pain brought me out of my own thoughts for a second. It was ahead of me, so it wasn't reacting to me. Besides, dogs usually barked at me, they didn't yelp like they were hurting. Before I knew it, I was jogging toward the sound with my wand out and all the mad I'd been feeling had a direction to go. It led me to the chain link gates of a junkyard, where I could hear men yelling over the dog's barking and whining. The lock was an easy pick with the TK wand, even if my mundane breaking and entering skills had gotten rusty, and I slipped inside. Only a couple of security lights on the outside of the cinderblock main office lit the front, but the sounds were coming from further in. I walked past the office to see racks of parts in rows leading to rows of half-disassembled cars. The rows made a path that led further back toward a smaller building. Light shone on the far side, and the voices seemed to be coming from there.

"Nah, hit him again!" one of the men said. "Just makes him meaner." There was a slap of something against skin, and another yelp came from the dog.

"Don't think it's gonna take with this one, Mac," a higher-pitched voice said amid a shuffling of feet.

"Damn well better. I got no use for a guard dog that don't earn his keep, and just barking ain't gonna cut it in my yard. Now hit 'im again!"

I came around the corner in time to see a skinny man in blue jeans, work boots and a vest over a t-shirt bring a strap of leather down on the flank of a rangy dog. Its short fur was mottled in brown and black, and it had a short, almost stubby muzzle with floppy ears. A short chain connected to a choke collar around its neck, and it held its whip of a tail low. The skinny guy turned as I came around the makeshift wall of tires that stretched from the building's edge to make a low fence. I saw that he had a baseball cap on over short, sandy hair. His narrow face was weathered from years of being out in the sun, and the look in his hazel eyes reminded me of a kid caught misbehaving.

Behind him was the other man, this one at least six feet tall, and pretty damn broad. If there was any fat on him, he hid it well. He wore black jeans and a tight black t-shirt that showed off arms like tree trunks. He had an almost chiseled jaw and cheekbones, and hard brown eyes under a pair of dark eyebrows that were pretty much the only hair on his head.

"Sic him, Buzzsaw!" the big guy yelled, and the dog leaped toward me. Unfortunately, the chain was way too short, and he drew up against the choker with a raspy bark. I knelt down in front of him, so our heads were at almost the same level, and he backed up a step. His thick head cocked to one side as I made myself less of a threat to him. Shade had been trying to teach me how wolves reacted, and a few lessons had stuck. Evidently, what worked for wolves worked for at least one dog, too. We looked at each other for a moment, and I noticed he had pale, almost white blue eyes.

For a second, our eyes locked, and I got a fleeting impression of him. A life of pain and abuse by his pack, constant beatings, and food only if he was subservient to the alpha human. Never understanding what the human wanted, or why he made other people come and beat him, never understanding what he did wrong, only knowing that he was hurt when his human brought other people around.

The connection between us broke, and I fell back on my ass. The bigger guy started toward me with a tire iron in his hand, and the dog turned to put himself between us. His head went down and a rumbling growl emerged from his throat. I struggled to my feet, and wondered if I'd just shared a Horus Gaze with a dog. The big guy took another step forward, and the dog jumped at him and barked savagely. He jumped back with a surprised look on his face, then turned his beady dark eyes on me.

"What'd you do to my dog, you little sumbitch?" he demanded.

With what I'd just seen, I wasn't about to waste my breath on an explanation. I just raised my wand and said "*Ictus*." The TK blast knocked him through the door of the shed behind him. His friend's eyes went wide as he turned back to face me.

"Hey, this wasn't my idea, man. He just had me come over and whip the dog to make 'im tougher, ya know?" he whined at me.

"Get the hell out of here, before I do the same thing to you." My voice was soft, and I even scared myself a little at the pure venom I put into it. Slim put feet to pavement, and scampered away. The dog watched him run, then came over to me and sat down. I squatted down in front of him and stayed still for a moment, so he didn't think I was going to hit him. He sniffed at me for a moment, then turned his head to one side and put a paw on my knee. It was the first time I'd been near a dog or any other animal for more than eight years.

"You're a good dog, you know that?" I said to him softly as I slipped the choker off. "I wish I could tell you that so you'd understand." I ruffled his ears and ran my hand down his side, relearning the simple pleasure of petting a dog. Ridges of old scar tissue ran in lines down his side, and I felt the rage from earlier tonight building again. "At least I could help you a little," I told him as I stood up. "Seems to be more than I can do for anyone else." When I turned to walk toward the front entrance, he followed, and I felt like my face was going to break in half because my grin was so big. I'd always wanted a dog, but I'd given up on that dream after Dulka bought me from my father. Big, fat tears of pure happy ran down my cheeks. If nothing else went right, this one thing did.

I had a dog.

My life still sucked as I walked back toward Dr. C's place, but with Junkyard beside me, all that seemed a little distant. At least for a couple of days, I had a dog. Somehow, that took the edge off all the suck that was going on in my life. For his own part, Junkyard seemed to care less that his new human might not be around by the end of the week. His tail wasn't down between his legs anymore; instead it stuck straight out and wagged every now and then.

Dr. C and Collins were coming out of the side door to his house when I walked up. His face clouded up when he saw me, and he headed for me like a storm on two feet, but I could almost see his feet skid on the sidewalk when Junkyard lunged in front of me and growled at him. I squatted down beside him and put my arm over his shoulders. I could feel him quivering, coiled to spring.

"It's okay, Junkyard," I said softly to him. "This is Dr. C. He's my friend. He's okay."

Dr. C squatted down too, and offered his hand. Junkyard leaned forward to sniff the air for a few seconds, then took a slow step forward to put his nose directly against Dr. C's knuckles. After a few more seconds of sniffing, he licked his hand, then sat back down and offered up a gruff little half-bark. I felt his tail hit my ankles a couple of times when I stood up and went to Collins to repeat the whole process.

"Not sure where to start now," Dr. C said after a few seconds. "First of all, are you okay? Second, how did you end up with a dog?"

"Yeah, I'm okay. The dog is . . . well, I'm not sure how that happened."

I laid out the story as we went inside, including the funky Horus Gaze Junkyard and I had shared. We ended up at the kitchen table, Dr. C and Collins on one side, me on the other, and the dog slurping water from a mixing bowl. When I finished, Dr. C put his head in his hand and shook it slowly.

"You assaulted a cowan with a witness around," he moaned. "At least you didn't try to alter their memories." His head came up with his eyebrows arched. "Right?"

“No, I made them both believe they were four-year-old girls who love Pretty Pretty Princess and ponies. Come on!” I snapped.

“I’m sorry. That wasn’t fair of me to assume,” he said with a hand raised in surrender. “It’s just been . . . a long day. For all of us. As for the *udjat* you shared with um, Junkyard, here, that was more of a familiar bond. I hadn’t covered that because we still had other things to overcome before I thought we’d have to deal with it.”

“Like my aura,” I interjected.

“Exactly. After that incident at the Humane Society, I figured it would be a long time before it came up. Remedial lesson: animals and magi often bond because they see the world in much the same way. Animals are sensitive to magick, and some magi think it’s a sign of our real duty. Stewards of the Earth and all that. Originally, familiars watched over us, protected us from harm, both physical and mystical.”

“So, why didn’t he run away from me?” I asked.

“Given what you described of his treatment, I don’t think one kind of aura was any different to him than another. Normal humans hurt him all the time, but you didn’t. All he had to go on was what you did.”

Junkyard put his wet chin on my leg and looked up at me with soulful doggy eyes. My eyes got misty again as I laid my hand on his head, and his tail thumped a few times against the table leg.

“Good boy,” I told him in a choked whisper. Rage and pain flashed through me again, and all I could do was stroke his fur and try to keep my cool.

“Chance,” Dr. C said softly. When I looked up, Collins’ chair was out and empty. “You’re normally not this emotional, and it isn’t like you to just take off, especially right now. What’s going on?” I took a shaky breath, and tried to tell him, and my mind just locked up.

“Want a list?” I managed after a second.

"It would be a start." His voice was calm, and he managed a smile.

"You're my mentor, you're supposed to know everything, and be all cryptic and shit."

"What shook your faith in my cryptic infallibility?" he asked after a few seconds.

"I saw you in Mr. Chomsky's doorway earlier, and you looked . . . I dunno . . ."

"Tired? Defeated? Sad? That's what I was feeling then."

"How am I supposed to do all the stuff I have to do if *your* ass is kicked? You're a wizard, damn it! You're supposed to be all smart, and just *know* stuff! I'm barely an apprentice!" My voice had risen and I paused as I heard myself. "Hells! Do I sound whiny or what?"

"You do have a lot on your plate, Chance. A hidden sword to find, a missing girl to rescue, a vampire to confront, and Gilder to frame for it," he said with a wan smile. "Frankly, you're swamped."

"Who's Gilder?" I asked, and he laughed.

"It's a movie line. We'll have to watch it this weekend."

"Assuming I'm around by then," I muttered.

"I am. Chance, I know things look pretty grim right now, and I can't say that I see a solution from here. Sometimes, you're going to face some pretty long odds, and if you try to take it all on at once, things can look pretty overwhelming. You can't control when it happens, all you can do is decide whether to face things head on or give up. You're the Seeker, which means your destiny is woven toward finding the Maxilla. It's been my experience that a wyrd doesn't attach itself to someone who isn't up to the task, so Someone has faith in you."

"Who would be stupid enough to believe in me?" I asked.

"Want a list?" he said, parroting me. "Your sister. Your mom. Dani. Alexis. Lucas. Wanda. Collins. Junkyard. Me. Every single one of us, you've put yourself in harm's way to help. It isn't in you to leave someone in a bad way. Because of that, a lot of people have faith in you, Chance, and that makes you powerful. It also makes you unpredictable, because you tend to do the right thing, instead of the smart thing sometimes. The important thing is to never give up. You never know when you'll find a way to turn things around."

Every name he gave me made my heart lurch as I realized exactly how many people actually *did* believe in me. My thoughts went to the one name he didn't put on that list, Dani's girlfriend Crystal. If Etienne had her, there was no telling what he was doing to her. And right now, I was the only person trying to do anything about it. For that matter, there were eleven other missing kids he might have. I knew I couldn't leave them in his hands, either. Damn, Dr. C was all kinds of right about me not doing the smart thing sometimes.

"You sound pretty confident that I'll be able to do that."

"We're magi, remember? We can bend the Universe to our will, and what we say is an expression of that will. When you talk, the Universe listens, so assume success, and never give the Universe an out. Now, speaking of not giving someone an out, tell me about the hour of quality time you spent with Thraxus tonight."

I laid out my time in the secure room with the G'Honn fragments, and watched his eyes get wider as I went on.

"I used the fixative on them to keep them from smudging, and they're downstairs in the workroom," I finished.

By then, Junkyard had moved around and was looking up at Dr. C. For his part, my mentor was looking more and more uncomfortable by the second.

"Do you know the kind of risk you put yourself in?" he asked sternly. "If he'd even suspected you'd done that, he would have ripped your head off! And that's if he was feeling charitable!"

"I let him catch me trying to make a sketch, and he chastised me, I apologized then kissed his ass a little. It was what he expected from a fifteen-year-old kid." I shrugged.

Dr. C, evidently thoroughly under the dog's thrall, got up and went to the refrigerator.

“So, Thraxus told you Etienne stole one of the G’Honn fragments. Any idea which one?” he asked as he pulled a white package out of the fridge.

Junkyard licked his chops and let out a little groan, and Dr. C shook his head.

“I think the five he has are sequential. I’m not sure exactly which ones they are, but if I could find a copy of the Medici Codex, I could make a damn good guess.”

“Sorry, fresh out of illegal tomes,” Dr. C remarked as he pulled a bowl out of the cabinet and unwrapped a batch of raw hamburger. Junkyard’s tail swept across the floor non-stop. “The Medici Codex was banned as soon as it was written. Pope Sixtus the Fourth ordered the assassination of Lorenzo and Giuliano de Medici for writing it.”

“I uh . . . might know where to get my hands on a copy . . . for a while.”

Dr. C’s left eyebrow went up at that, and he paused with the hamburger poised over the bowl.

“You know the Conclave would frown on that, to say the least.”

“What they don’t know . . .”

“Isn’t much,” he countered. “What would you have to do to get a look at a copy?”

“Pay the owner a ton of trade silver. Probably about a thousand ounces.”

“I could cover that,” Dr. C said.

“I’ve got it, it’s just in bearer chits. Which he’ll probably take. He’s one of the few merchants in the Hive who will.”

“Don’t worry about it. If you’re going to the Hive, then I’m coming with you.”

“I thought the Hive was supposed to be off limits to the Conclave.”

“It’s more of a strong suggestion. So long as we’re not recognized, we should be fine.”

Junkyard gave a little groan, then another of his short barks, as if to remind Dr. C that he was there.

“Sorry, Junkyard.” He dumped the meat into the bowl and set it in the microwave for a minute.

“I know someone who might be able to help with that, too. I just need to get a message to her.” Dr. C nodded, and we waited for the microwave to ding.

“I can handle the rest,” he said as he set the bowl down in front of Junkyard. “Avoiding the police watch, and the Sentinels,” he explained over the sound of a dog inhaling about a pound of hamburger.

I sat back in my chair and let myself relax a little. Dr. C was back to being mostly infallible, I had a plan for finding out what Etienne was up to with the G’Honn fragment, and the wyrd on me to find the Maxilla was probably going to be okay. I remembered the saying Master Draeden had quoted in his chamber Friday night. *'Wyrd often saves the undoomed man, so long as his courage holds.* Maybe I had a shot at all of this.

Chapter 19: (Wednesday morning. Last day before the Equinox)

~ Mistake not knowledge for wisdom. ~ Giovani de Medici, 1519

I woke up on the floor next to my borrowed bed with a warm, furry lump under my right arm. Junkyard was curled up next to me, with his head on my left arm. When I moved, he slowly got to his feet and stretched, then he came over and licked my chin before he trotted to the door and looked back at me. I stumbled to the door, and he headed for the stairs and to the kitchen door.

Dr. C was cooking something as I stumbled through the kitchen, and the smells of breakfast seemed to reach down my nose and into my stomach to wake it up. Junkyard went out into the yard and found a couple of trees to do his business on while I waited on the porch in my bare feet, sweat pants and t-shirt. Standing there in the early morning quiet, I was reminded that I hadn't been on my morning run for a few days. My legs were feeling stiff and I actually longed to feel the sidewalk pounding under my feet. Somehow, though, today didn't feel like a good day to run.

The morning was chill and gloomy again, and the clouds were low and heavy. They were red, and I wasn't sure if that was the early morning sun, or if there was a more ominous reason for it. In the distance, I heard a rumble of thunder, and Junkyard decided he'd explored as much of the yard as he needed to.

"Big baby," I muttered at him as he scampered up the steps and looked over his shoulder at me from beside the door. But I didn't waste any time getting inside, either. I tried to convince myself it was because I was hungry and my feet were cold.

Collins headed home after his relief showed up; Dr. C sent him on his way with a covered plate stacked with biscuits and gravy, scrambled eggs, and thick sliced bacon. Then we headed up for the workroom in the attic. I could feel the restrained power of the elaborate casting circled engraved in silver in the middle of the hardwood floor as we walked around it to the workbench set up on the right side of the room. It had taken me a couple of months to get into the habit of not crossing the circle's edge without a good reason, but now it came second nature. Dr. C had taught me a lot more respect for the tools of the trade than Dulka ever showed. I was pretty sure it had made my magick a little easier to use and a little stronger.

There were tall windows in each of the four walls, with benches and bookshelves scattered along each wall. On the wall behind us, at the rear of the house, was an angled table with a row of magickal reference books. Padrigal's *Essential Ephemeris* sat next to *The Collected Works of Jabir ibn Hayyad*, which leaned against the thick *Annotated Translation of Voynich's Ars Atlantea*. On the far side of the window was a mixing table for inks. On the wall to our left was the main alchemy lab, which also doubled as Dr. C's paintball reloading station. The front wall held all of the ritual tools: wands, chalices, ceremonial swords, robes, and a dozen other things. Incense was stored in jars, both the powdered and the stick forms, though Dr. C preferred the powders on charcoal for a cleaner burn.

The workbench we went to was used for crafting focuses, so it was covered with crafting tools, like knives, sandpaper, hammers and stuff like that. Above it was a rack with finished focuses. Some were medallions and rings, but there were stone animal shapes, chunks of cut and polished crystal, and a series of what looked like wooden framework birds.

Dr. C pulled one of the bird frames down and set it on the bench, then handed me a notepad and the stub of a carpenter's pencil. I wrote out a note and set it on the bench. Dr. C turned to me with the framework bird cupped in his hands. Up close, I could see it had a few feathers tied to it and little chunks of shiny black stone where its eyes went.

"Who are we sending this to?" he asked. "I need their name, and a description."

"Her name is Synreah. She's a cambion, red skin, black hair and eyes. She's about six-and-a-half feet tall and really hot looking." He nodded when I finished, held the bird up to his face and whispered a spell. Then, he pursed his lips and blew on it softly for several seconds. Feathers and skin seemed to fly onto it in reverse, going from the tail to the beak, traveling toward his face instead of away, like he was blowing the framework away to reveal the real bird on the inside. Finally, a pigeon rested in his hands, looking at him with black eyes and cooing softly.

"Seek Synreah, with red skin, black hair, black eyes, six-and-a-half feet tall. A cambion, pleasing of face and figure. Deliver this message to her, and your task be done."

He rolled the note into a tube and tied it to the bird's leg with a complex knot, then went to the window that faced the rear of the house and tilted it open. The pigeon took to the sky and he closed it up.

"How will we know when she gets the message?" I asked.

"I'll know. In the meantime, you need to practice on your touchstones," he said as he tossed a quartz crystal to me.

I fumbled it but managed to keep from dropping it on the floor. With a sigh, I went to the eastern edge of the circle and envisioned an opening in front of me, then stepped through. If I'd done that anywhere else, I would probably have gotten a little bit of feedback, which usually translated to minor shocks. Once I was inside, I imagined the doorway closing behind me and sat down in the center.

For most apprentices, the big challenge to getting a touchstone to work is actually getting the magick flowing into it, so for most of them, it's like trying to fill a glass with an eyedropper. My original lessons had relied on brute force and willpower to make magick work, so for me, touchstones were more like trying to fill a sippy cup with a firehose at first. Once I finally figured out how to see the matrix of the quartz crystal, and shape my magick to fit through it, I tended to shove too much into it too fast. The first ten literally blew up. Now that I was starting to get the hang of it, the worst I did was crack them. Forty-five minutes later, I had finished one and cracked a second when Dr. C signaled to me to open the circle.

"She got the message. Do you think she can get what we need in half an hour?" he asked as we headed down the stairs.

"Yeah. I don't think she'd have any other clients this early," I told him. I stopped at the second floor landing. "I need to grab my satchel. I'll be right down."

By the time I grabbed my satchel and backpack, Dr. C was waiting at the back door in khaki cargo pants, hiking boots and a fleece vest over a dark green button down shirt, staff in hand, with Junkyard wagging his tail beside him.

The sight of his staff tickled something in my brain, but I couldn't remember if it was important or not. I dismissed it, and figured if it was important, I'd remember it soon enough.

We slipped through the back yard and climbed into his Range Rover, carefully pulling the doors closed behind us once Junkyard had jumped into the backseat. Once we were in, he set a blob of modeling clay on the dash, then pulled a Matchbox car out of his pocket and set it in the clay. Finally, he carefully carved a couple of complex runes into the clay, and muttered a little. The air around us shimmered, and he sat back in his seat with a relieved grin on his face. To anyone outside the vehicle, we would look like the replica silver minivan he'd stuck in the modeling clay.

The cop watching the house was stationed where he could watch the front and the side of the house that actually abutted a neighbor's yard, so he couldn't see us pull out of the garage onto the side street, and we turned away from him when we hit Jackson. In the backseat, Junkyard had his nose pressed against the window, and I reached back to pet him for a few seconds. He leaned against my hand, and his tail thumped against the seat, then he decided there were things he needed to look at on the other side of the car, and stuck his nose against the far window.

Our first stop was at a pet store. I had to wait outside while Dr. C went in and picked up stuff for Junkyard. I'd given him the list of things I thought he needed, while Dr. C had a much shorter list of things he said he needed. In the end, he came out with all of his and most of mine. One thing neither of us had on our list was a collar. He pulled out of the parking lot as I handed Junkyard a thick strip of rawhide.

“So, Chance,” Dr. C said a little too casually a few minutes later. “What kind of clients does Synreah have?”

“Her owner pimps her out as a hooker.” I watched his face go hard at that. Even though I pretty much already knew he’d react that way, he still got major respect for not liking it. “When we get there, she might ask us for our discretion, if her owner doesn’t know we contacted her. She’s saving up for a contract.”

“Good,” he said. “I’m sure her owner won’t be happy to see her purchase her freedom back.”

“That isn’t a clause in her contract. He won’t survive the kind of contract she’s buying,” I said grimly.

“Even better,” he said with a feral smile that I shared. Most of the Conclave didn’t seem to give a damn one way or the other about the lesser races, especially half-bloods like cambions. They frowned on slavery for humans (unless there was a demon involved, evidently), but when it came to the lesser fae and demon-kin, you were on your own, unless you pissed them off. I was glad to see that Dr. C at least frowned on the idea of Synreah being a slave, and had no qualms about her buying a contract on her owner’s life, especially since she didn’t have a clause that let her buy her own freedom back.

We stopped at a parking garage a couple of blocks away from the Hive’s entrance and got out. Junkyard stayed at my side as we headed down the street for the side alley where I’d asked Synreah to meet us. We ducked into the narrow opening between two buildings, and took a second to let our eyes adjust to the gloom. Like I’d requested, there was a twine wrapped bundle waiting on the lid of one of the aluminum garbage cans. I cut the twine free and tossed a cloak and mask to Dr. C, then turned to the two figures who waited deeper in the alley as I slipped mine on.

It took more than a little effort to keep my cool, but I’d more than half expected her to have her owner with her. I’d gotten lucky the last time I’d come to the Hive, and caught her between tricks, before she’d been expected back. My note had just asked for escort services while in the Hive, and cloaks and masks for discretion’s sake near the Shadow Gate. That way, I figured, he wouldn't know we'd done business before.

Once Dr. Corwyn had the mask on and the cloak settled on his shoulders with the hood up, we headed for Synreah and her owner. It was obvious to me which was which, because she was the taller and curvier of the two. Her owner, as we got closer, looked more like a meth addict from one of my Health Ed books. Where she was tall with ample curves, he was stick thin and bony. Her face was framed by a mane of thick black hair, and her almond shaped eyes were all black. His fragile-looking hair was almost dust-colored and short, and seemed to be trying to go in every possible direction at once. But it was his eyes that made me want to look away. They were full of a desire to hurt something, like the world was nothing more than a playground to him, and he had elected himself head bully.

He stepped up to me when we got close, and stuck his gaunt face in mine, a clear challenge. Junkyard growled and barked at him, but backed off when I put a hand out to him.

"What's your name, boy?" he demanded.

The stench of intoxicants hit me like a wave, and I had no problem telling what he had smoked and drank last. Demanding a client's name was a serious breach of protocol in the Hive, especially for dodgy deals like hiring a cambion as an escort. Before I could come up with a smart reply, Dr. C spoke.

"Step back." The words were simple, and he didn't raise his voice above a casual, conversational level. But he filled it with enough command and power that I felt each word hit the pimp like physical things.

He stepped away from me, but slowly. Junkyard gave him a warning bark and stepped up to my side.

"You're not regulars, is all," he said. "Why'd you send a messenger straight to her, but not me?"

Dr. C nodded at me, as if giving me permission to answer for him.

“Biladon Garnet recommended her by name. Your name never came up,” I said, adding as much disdain as I could and trying to keep the formal cadence of the Veil in my voice. “My Master wishes to have a thing of beauty on his arm while he is here.” It bugged me to refer to Synreah like that, but it made sense for the role we were playing.

“A hundred trade ounces for an hour,” the pimp demanded.

“Five hundred for the day,” Dr. C countered.

I could see the greed in the little man’s eyes, and he looked to Synreah for a moment before he answered.

“Until the hour before sunset,” the pimp agreed.

Dr. C nodded and held out his hand. Laying on his palm was a square cut ruby, a little less than half an inch on a side.

“That will be sufficient,” he said as the man plucked the ruby from his hand and waved Synreah over to us.

Dr. C held his hand out to her, and she took it, then turned so that she was holding his hand and half-way wrapped around his arm at the same time. Everything about the move and her body language said she was completely his. Even covered mostly in a dark cloak, she made herself look hot. With a shrug of her shoulders, the cloak fell to the ground, and I got to see what she was wearing today. It looked like she’d taken a couple of pieces of fabric and turned them into a top and skirt without sewing anything. Her top was a blue piece that came down from the back of her neck, crossed over her breasts then went behind her back to turn itself into a bow. The skirt was the same color, just wrapped around her waist so that it was at an angle, higher on her left leg than on her right with a silver chain belt adorned with bandanas and cloth pouches on her hips. She wore a pair of blue canvas lace up boots that came halfway up her long calves, with heels that made me dizzy just to look at. They were laced with a paler blue ribbon. Her arms were wrapped in bands of blue that came up around her thumbs and crisscrossed starting at her wrists and going to her elbows, where she had them tied off to leave long streamers that flowed with her movements. She even had her hair done up with a blue band that ran up across the top of her forehead, and her tiny horns poked through it. I was sure she was violating some kind of fashion rule, but she broke it well.

"It was good to hear from you again," she said to me once we were out of earshot of her owner. Then she turned to Dr. C. "I am Synreah, and I'm yours for the day. Do you want me all to yourself, or did you plan on sharing?" She cast a hopeful glance at me and winked.

Dr. C laughed and said, "The boy doesn't need any distractions today." She gave a mocking pout and made a sympathetic sound as she pranced along at his side.

The ramp to the Shadow Gate dropped before us as we turned a corner. I avoided using the Shadow Gate when I could, and so did most people who didn't have a small army of bodyguards or a wizard with them. It was on the north side of the Hive, and it was underground, so full sunlight never hit the place. There were things lurking around it that you didn't want to run into on a sunny day, much less a red day like today.

Dr. C just kept going, his staff tapping against the stone as he went. With each step, a light glowed brighter and brighter from the top every time the tip hit the ground. Things recoiled into the darkness of the side tunnels as we approached the iron gate the marked the entrance to the underside of the Hive.

"Now that we're inside," Dr. C said warmly as we passed the gate, "I'd like to contract your services as a guide as well. Discreetly, of course."

Synreah's grin was hungry as she hugged his arm.

"I may be easy, but I'm not cheap," she purred.

"Neither am I. Let's say we pay you the same today as a guide as I just paid for your services as arm candy?" he said as he held out another ruby of similar size to the one he'd paid her pimp with. Unlike the previous transaction, though, he actually put it in her upturned hand instead of making her take it from him.

"Done," she said. "I like a generous man," she purred and pressed herself against him even further.

My jaw almost hit the ground. He'd just dropped a thousand trade ounces in less than five minutes without blinking. I had no idea how much he had, or where he got it, but he was either a *very* good actor, or he was loaded. Maybe both. I was even more impressed with him than I had been after the display with the pimp. He'd waited to make the deal for her services as a guide, which also told me he knew how to be more subtle than most magi I knew.

"So, what do you need guiding to?" she asked.

"I need to find Dead Leo," I told her.

She nodded and looked at Dr. C.

"You have the smell of true love on you," she said and pulled away from him and stepped closer to me. "And you have the scent of budding love about you. You're both going to be a temptation for me today, and I really hate resisting temptation."

She knelt in front of Junkyard and let him sniff at her hands, then pulled a red bandana from her belt and tied it loosely around his neck. "Now you look the proper rebel, like the human you chose," she said as she stood.

Without another word, she led us further into the underside of the Hive.

Dead Leo's place ended up being deep in the Hive, deeper than I'd ever been before. I tried to keep my eyes off Synreah's behind as she guided us further and further into the alleyways and side corridors. Junkyard seemed to take to the bandana as a badge of pride, and trotted along beside me with his tail a notch or two higher. Between Dr. C's staff and Junkyard at my side, anyone who saw us knew us for magi, but the cloaks and masks did their job well enough that no one seemed to recognize us. Even if they did, no one would say anything, either to our faces or behind our backs. Discretion was a commodity in the Hive, and silence was its chief export. Anyone who threatened those two things usually had a very messy death in their immediate future, most times a very public one, too.

"How is it you know about this man without knowing where he is?" Dr. C asked as we wound our way between dark alleyways and shrouded figures offering drugs or illegal curses from under their cloaks.

"He usually works with messengers and middlemen," I told him. "Half the forbidden books and lore you can buy in the Hive have his mark on them, but he never sells direct. What we need today, though, he'd never sell a copy of, so I need to buy some time in his library. So, how is it you know how to handle yourself in a place like this?" I asked.

"This isn't the only shady market in the world, you know. Although it's the biggest one I've seen in the U.S. I visited my fair share of them when I worked for the Sentinels as a troubleshooter."

"You were a Sentinel?" I asked softly.

"I quit after three weeks," he said calmly.

"Why?" I asked.

"I couldn't stand my boss. But, I was good at what I did, so they hire me to freelance sometimes when they need someone to do undercover work." Even as he said it, a brief flash of his memories played inside my head, of an argument between him and Polter, then just a wizard, and Dr. Corwyn a mage.

"Like find a rogue warlock?" I asked.

"No, Sydney was my mentor and friend. I did that on my own."

Synreah stopped and turned to face us. The building behind her was three stories tall, but the top story was gutted and the walls were an uneven line of crumbling brick, with the roof all but gone. I could see the red sky through the windows that faced the front of the building. A rickety set of stairs led up the side of the building, looking like they were still there more out of sheer stubbornness than any feat of engineering. A thick metal door sat in the middle of the lower story, and the lower windows were shuttered with metal panels. The windows in the upper story were covered with bars, and I couldn't even see the upstairs door.

"His place is upstairs," she said, tilting her head toward the upper story. "Stay close to the wall when you go up."

I gave her a longer look and wondered what kind of business she had with Dead Lorenzo before I headed up the steps with Junkyard at my side. I felt as much heard Dr. C on the steps behind me, and when I stopped at the heavy, iron-banded door, he was right beside me. Even under the mask, I could see his jaw was set, and his eyes were like cold steel. On my left side, Junkyard nuzzled my hand before he sat down.

"I've got this," I told him as I reached for the heavy knocker.

"You're my apprentice. It's my job to look out for you. You've been trying to do all this on your own, and, too often, I've had to let you. Right now, I *can* look out for you and damn it, that's what I'm going to do. Get over it."

I turned away a little and shook my head to hide the smile that was creeping across my face. It was kinda cool to have someone at my back that was a bigger badass in the magick department than I was. Even after six months living with my mom and having real friends, I was still getting used to the idea that someone might be there to come to *my* rescue. The reminder was nice. The sound of the knocker against the door didn't sound so ominous with that thought in my head.

A small panel about eye level opened and a pair of red-rimmed hazel eyes squinted out at us. "The Master doesn't sell his books or scrolls, least of all to the Conclave. Look somewhere else!" It all came out in a well-practiced rush, in a reedy, high-pitched voice. He pulled back, and started to slam the little panel shut, but Dr. C held his hand out in the gesture I kept trying so hard to imitate, with two fingers up, his ring and pinky finger bent down and his thumb bent just so. My mystic senses tingled as I felt a spell zip past me, and the panel stopped moving.

"Look at the boy, and tell me he works for the Conclave," he ordered. "And whether your Master is going to be pleased when he learns that we spent a thousand trade credits elsewhere when we could have spent two thousand here."

The eyes reappeared at the opening.

"Bold words, but empty," the voice said, then the eyes blinked and went slightly unfocused. "Right you are about the boy, though. What do you want?"

"A few hours among the stacks," Dr. C answered. He held up his left hand and pulled a round cut emerald from the small pile of gems on his palm.

The panel closed and the door opened. We stepped inside into a gloomy hallway that led straight back for about ten feet. The walls were almost completely covered in wards. Some I recognized, others I had to piece together from their component sigils. All of them were lethal, poison gases, spikes of telekinetic energy and frost wards. The reedy-voiced little guy we'd been talking to stood in front of us and held out his hand. Dr. C tossed the emerald his way casually, and I saw his hand snap forward and snatch it out of the air. As my eyes adjusted to the light, or, its absence, I could see that the little man wore a long, off white homespun robe with big, ink-stained sleeves.

"I am Inamosa," the little man said. "And I am at your service." His face was gaunt and pale, and his mouth never seemed to close all the way. Brown hair ringed his skull, and I could make out the recent growth where he'd shaved it. He looked like one of the monks from some of the old books I'd read when I worked for Dulka.

"I need a specific book," I said as Inamosa led us to the door at the other end of the hall.

He pulled a set of heavy keys from his pocket and started sorting through them.

"Of course you do," he said as he leaned with one hand against the door and stuck a key into the lock. The door creaked open, and he ushered us into another chamber. This room was furnished with a book-laden table that was flanked by a pair of leather-upholstered chairs that sat in front of a radiator heater. A love seat upholstered in red velvet faced the chairs. It was also better lit, with small clear globes scattered around it that each surrounded a single, bright flame, like an oversized candle. They hovered near the ceiling, and our host gestured at one. It floated over to hover over his right shoulder.

"Which particular tome of knowledge do you require?"

"The Medici Codex," I said.

He stared at me, and I was half afraid he was going to arch his back and hiss at me or make the sign of the cross.

"You don't ask for small favors, do you?" he finally said.

"It's worth it to you to grant this one," Dr. C said as he held up a tiny diamond.

Inamosa smiled and bowed his head regally before he answered.

"Indeed it is. The boy only. You are still Conclave, wizard, and still too much of a risk to admit to the reserve shelves."

They traded glares until Dr. C nodded.

"Chance, you'll need this," he said as he pulled a thick tube out of his pocket and tossed it across the room to me.

I caught it and gave him a frown from behind my mask.

"Is this . . . ?" I left the question unfinished.

His response was a smile, a nod, and a wink. Up to something he was, I found myself thinking in Lucas' painfully bad Yoda voice.

Inamosa gestured for me to follow him, and led me through the shelves filled with scrolls, loose pages, heavy leather-bound books, slim volumes, and some even made of metal, with hinged backs. We passed one shelf that held several heavy, rune-covered tablets on thick pallets. We came to a spiral staircase that led into darkness. The floating ball lit the way down past the first floor, into a moldy-smelling sublevel that was filled with shelves that were faced with heavy wire mesh over iron-framed doors. I finally found myself at a dust-covered wooden table that was made of planks thick enough to hold small buildings up. A sheaf of paper sat to the right of the high-backed chair, with a green glass ink bottle and a handful of copper-nibbed dip pens on a bed of faded strips of ribbon. As we got closer,

I could also see another globe set in a brass stand in the middle of the table.

Inamosa reached across the table and put his thumb against the globe, bringing it flickering to life. He gestured to the chair, then turned and wandered back among the bookshelves. I took the seat, and Junkyard laid down with his head on my feet.

A few minutes later, a heavy tome bound in some kind of black leather slid into view, pushed by a gaunt gray hand with blackened nails. Junkyard came to his feet when I started and came around behind the chair. I turned in the chair to face the newcomer, and tried to keep my cool. Standing over me was the corpse of a round-faced man in elaborate robes. A heavy gold crucifix dangled from his neck, and the smell of grave mold crept into my nose as he stared at me with milky white eyes. This had to be Dead Leo.

After a few-second-long eternity, his head turned slowly to look at Junkyard, then rotated back toward me. His dead-eyed gaze pinned me to the seat.

"Strewth, your familiar spirit fears me not," he croaked out finally. "'Tis passing strange. Moreso that he'll have aught to do with thee, with thy warlock's taint."

"He uh . . . normal people treated him like crap," I found myself explaining.

Every part of me wanted to be away from this dead thing, away from the power that kept him animated, that made my skin almost literally crawl. But if he was talking, the smart part of my mind, the part that regularly tricked my monkey brain into doing stupid shit, could convince itself that this was a normal conversation and ignore the part where he was supposed to be not walking around above ground and talking to me.

"I was the first person who was nice to him, I think."

His dry forehead wrinkled a little, then his lips split into a smile that made me look away before I heaved breakfast on his robes.

"My most sincere apologies, my young friend," he croaked from a few feet away. "I forget that to the living, I am naught but a cadaver that moves and speaks, an abomination before God. But I had to know who else sought out the Codex of the Medici. For centuries, it lay forgotten in my collection, and now, two seek it in less than the span of one year."

Something about the way he said the name of the book sounded odd, as if we saw the same book in two very different ways. But *what* he said made my mouth work faster than my brain.

"There was someone else who wanted to look at this book?" I asked.

"Aye, though I can not speak his name," he answered.

He put a little emphasis on the last word, as if that specific thing was important. I gave him a wolfish grin as I thought about what he *could* tell me. Proper etiquette was that I could ask three questions and still be considered polite. If I wanted to push it a little, I could ask one or two more, but I figured I didn't really want to piss off the really old dead guy.

"Did he come during the day or at night?" I asked, and he lifted a paper-thin eyebrow.

"During the day."

"Did he have a pulse?"

"When he first rang at my door, he did."

"How long ago?"

"After the Feast of St Dominic."

"And why are you letting this information . . . slip?" I asked, wary of a trap. Technically, I was still playing by the rules, since I wasn't asking a question about the same thing . . . well, not exactly.

"I felt the wyrd upon you as soon as you entered my home. And a thing I have not felt in a great many years . . . one of Samson's line has touched you. I may be an abomination before God, but I still may be the instrument of His will betimes."

He turned and limped into the darkness, and I still didn't hear him move. I reached down for Junkyard's back, and told myself he was nervous at watching me hold a conversation with a walking corpse, and he needed to be reassured and calmed down. He looked up at me as if he was checking to see if I was okay, and I gave him a mock serious look.

"Scaredy cat," I said.

He wagged his tail and gave me a big, slobbery grin before he went back to his spot under the table. If I was more reassured than annoyed by his head on my foot, I wasn't talking. My shoulders twitched as I turned to the book. It was hard to keep from looking over my shoulder to make sure Dead Leo wasn't going to come back and do something hideous and deforming to me. I was sitting in a creepy dead guy's basement, reading a forbidden tome, and I'd just had a conversation with said creepy dead guy. What was there to be paranoid about? I tried not to think about the fact that Dead Leo had also walked away from me in a different direction than the stairs.

It took me about an hour of reading and re-reading the first chapter before I noticed the narrow ribbons between pages. I flipped to the page with the first bookmark. It talked about the defeat of Mammon, and the symbols that the Atlantean mage-priests had used to seal him into his prison before exiling him for an eternity. In the margins, there was a note that magick avoided absolutes, like forever or never, because the conditions were impossible to keep, so the spell fizzled every time. It made me look at the term used: "an" eternity. A few pages deeper in, I learned that it meant 'one hundred times one hundred years,' the largest number the less literate kingdoms could understand and believe. It went on like that, outlining a recipe for Armageddon with each bookmarked page.

Eventually, I had to pull the rubbings I'd made out of the tube Dr. C had tossed me, and compared them to the descriptions on the page. Nothing was making sense, and I suspected that whoever had been reading this before me had missed something. It wasn't until I went to the first pages that detailed the G'Honn Tablets, when I saw the description of the reading room that I got it. My blood ran cold as I scanned back in the book until I found the section detailing rituals using the G'Honn formulae, and the consequences of failure. I reached for a sheet of paper from the pile on my right, and stopped as my fingers felt something on the paper itself. I set the page aside and grabbed another one, then snatched one of the pens from the jar.

My legs were shaky by the time Inamosa led me back up the stairs. Dr. C was sitting in one of the chairs with his staff standing unsupported beside him. He came to his feet when I leaned on the love seat for support. The staff snapped to his hand at his gesture, and he was at my side by the time I sat down.

"What's wrong, Chance?" he asked.

"I know too much for my own good, that's all, sir," I said with a wan smile. "Hey, Inamosa, when's the Feast of St. Dominic?" I asked the hovering little monk.

"August eighth," he said after a few seconds.

I nodded my thanks to him and got to my feet unsteadily.

Synreah joined us as we came down the steps, and Dr. C waited until we were out of sight of Dead Leo's place to give me the third degree.

"What did you learn, Chance?" he demanded.

"Too much. Etienne's not playing small. He's trying to open the seals on Mammon's prison so he can assume his mantle," I said, my voice still shaky.

"Mammon, as in one of the Seven Princes of the Abyss?" he asked softly.

I nodded.

"It gets worse, sir. The G'Honn fragments are all written backwards. Something about protecting mortal minds from the knowledge they hold. You have to read them with a mirror, or make an impression of them using soft clay to read them the right way. As far as I know, Etienne doesn't know that."

"How can you tell?" Dr. C asked me.

"He bookmarked the pages he read. And," I told him as I pulled a rolled page out of the tube, "he used a ballpoint pen to take notes." The page unfurled to reveal the shallow indentations of a pen in the page, made visible by the charcoal stick I'd rubbed across the face. "Either way, he's already very powerful, and he'll only need one more sacrifice to complete the ritual. Mr. Chomsky's journal mentioned a Seeker *and* a Wielder, right?"

His eyes closed for a moment.

"Come to think of it, it did," he said. "I thought he was referring to the same person."

"I'm not sure. We'll deal with that once we find it," I told him, but I already thought I knew the answer to that question. There had been one person who'd been around almost every time I'd seen a vision of the sword. It was a matter for another moment but things were starting to fall into place.

"I'll need to alert the Conclave. This is too big, Chance. Stay out of it. Concentrate on finding the Maxilla for now. The Sentinels will handle Etienne."

Thunder rumbled in the distance, and I felt the first heavy drops of rain hit the hood of my cloak. In front of us, people began looking around, and I saw panic begin to dawn in several faces. Merchants started packing up their stuff, and I held my own hand out to catch a couple of drops. Pale red splat marks colored my palm, and I turned to show Dr. C.

"I don't think so," I said as it began to rain blood.

Dr. Corwyn spent most of the drive home on his phone, alternately being diplomatic and yelling. He barely seemed to notice the watery red border his windshield wipers were making with every pass. Other people seemed to be staying off the roads, maybe afraid they'd get some blood-borne disease or something. The clock on his dash showed that it was coming up on six o'clock. I cursed at the loss of time, but for some reason, I felt almost optimistic, too. I felt like I was close to figuring out how to find the Maxilla, but I had no idea why.

A white limousine was waiting in front of the house, and I spotted four identical blue Crown Victorias parked up and down the main street. I looked down into one of them as we passed it and saw the Sentinel glare back at me. From the outside, it had a lot of the same things I'd seen on regular police cruisers. Nudge bars and a PIT bumper on the front, a wire mesh partition between the front and back seats, and tires made for the heavy duty suspension. I was willing to bet it had the same kind of high performance engine a law enforcement interceptor had as well. But regular police cruisers didn't have protection spells woven into the windshield, or aura glass. I felt the gaze of the Sentinel we had just passed hit my aura. Amplified by the aura glass, their aura gazing was like a spotlight; you could feel the heat from a long way off. Even when they didn't have their Third Eye open, they would have been able to see into the ethereal realm.

We drove past them and pulled into the garage. Junkyard and I got out on one side, and Dr. C pulled his staff from the back seat. As soon as we stepped out of the garage, car doors started opening up and down the street. Sixteen ankh-topped Sentinel *paramiir* staves popped up beside the blue Crown Vics, and a smooth white staff with a ruby tip emerged from the limo. I felt the glare start before Polter stepped into view, dressed immaculately in a dark blue suit. He glanced at the Sentinels, then turned to face us with the same smile I remembered from the other night. It reminded me of a shark, all teeth, no soul.

Polter's grin soured when T-Bone's Torino pulled into the driveway behind us, and Cross rode his Harley across the grass and parked it on the sidewalk. They still wore the same black outfits I'd seen them in last time, and I wondered if they had a closet full of identical black cargo pants, t-shirts and sweaters. They came over to Dr. C and me, Polter's face turned red. They shook hands with Dr. C, and Cross came over and put a hand on my shoulder.

"You doing all right, kid?" he asked.

I shrugged. "Not bad for the end of the world and all," I said.

"Not on our watch," T-Bone said from behind me.

Polter strode up as he finished and put his finger in the middle of Cross's chest.

"I didn't authorize this. Why did you abandon your post?" he demanded. Cross looked down at his hand, then back up at Polter. The pudgy wizard pulled his hand away but didn't give an inch.

"That's a good way to get your hand broken," T-Bone said.

"We don't answer to you," Cross said. His voice was a deep rumble, like thunder warning of a storm. He ignored Polter and turned to me. "Draeden asked us to come. Moon and Hardesty are watching over your family in our place."

"How are they? How's my sister?" I asked quickly. Polter sneered at me, but I was too busy hanging on T-Bone's answer to punch him like I wanted to.

"They're fine. Mostly bored." He stepped aside as Polter elbowed his way past me then stopped in his tracks as Junkyard planted his feet and growled up at him. The scene held for a second before Dr. C knelt down beside him.

"It's okay, Junkyard. You can bite him later," he told him. That earned him a lick on the face before Junkyard trotted over to me. I went to the side door to deactivate the wards while Junkyard greeted Cross and T-Bone. Unlike Polter and most every other human he met, he took right to them, further proof that my dog had good taste.

I watched the Sentinels converge on the house, then my eyes went to Dr. C and Polter standing on the sidewalk. Every single mage I'd seen lately had been carrying a staff. It was their status symbol, and one of the tools of power they wielded. The thing that had been bugging me for the past couple of days dropped into place in my head as I opened the door and invited Cross and T-Bone inside.

In less than ten minutes, Cross, T-bone, and I were cooling our heels in the kitchen while Dr. C was closeted with Polter and most of the Sentinels in his library. Four had been assigned to me, and had promptly disappeared. I was nursing the last bottle of Coke and trying to keep my mind off of the way Polter had started throwing orders around. This was Dr. C's house, damn it, and I hated that the overstuffed Master had been acting like he had been the one who'd figured everything out.

I was so hacked that I almost missed it when Junkyard's head came up off his paws and his nose turned toward the front door. Cross and T-Bone were on their feet and out the side door the second I heard Lucas' voice through the front door. I got up and made for the door at full speed a heartbeat later, with Junkyard on my heels.

The front door swung open to reveal Lucas in the clutches of two sentinels, one the girl who'd been guarding the elevator the night of my trial.

"This cowan has no business here," she said sternly. "He shouldn't even know of our world!"

"Well, if he didn't before, you just made sure he did," I snapped back at her. Her face went red at that.

"Dude, they took her!" Lucas cried, and I turned my attention back to him.

His lip was swollen, and he had a bruise along the side of his face that was just starting to turn purple. As if the black eye I'd given him wasn't enough, his other eye was nearly swollen shut now, and his shirt was torn at the right shoulder.

"They took her!" His voice was laced with combination of desperation, fear and anger.

I stepped out onto the porch and put my arm around his shoulder, in the process shoving the two Sentinels away from him. That earned me a black look, but Cross and T-Bone stepped up behind them and pulled them away. I pulled Lucas inside and up the stairs, trying to ignore the sounds of the pompous windbag in the library talking about 'his' conclusions. My ego took a back seat to the tears running down my friend's face.

"Who took who?" I asked him.

"Wanda!" he blurted out. "I don't know who they were, but they took Wanda!" The words stopped me in my tracks, and my eyes went to the line of silver staves lined up outside Dr. C's library, with Polter's at the end. We had a whole squad of Sentinels in this house, and one of my friends had still been kidnapped.

"I couldn't stop them," Lucas was saying. "I tried, but . . . they just kept hitting me, telling me to go tell you what they did."

"Did one of them have a hat?" I asked.

Lucas nodded as his cell phone played the chorus of "Cry Little Sister," the ringtone he'd set for Wanda. We exchanged looks: his hopeful, mine dismal. He pulled the phone out and hit the answer button. Wanda's cries came from the earpiece before he got it to his ear. They were abruptly cut off, and I could hear another, softer voice.

"I will," he said to whoever it was, then ended the call. He handed me the phone mutely and sat down on the stairs. It beeped a few seconds later, and the screen showed that there was an incoming video. I pressed the button to "View," and Wanda's tear-streaked face bounced across the screen for a second before it stabilized. A hand flew across the picture and smacked against her cheek, then pulled away quickly with a curse.

"Bitch!" the unseen speaker hissed.

The view pulled back to show her with her hands chained over her head. She had on a purple skirt with striped stockings that were torn at the knees. Her purple top was also ripped, exposing her bra and the pentacle that dangled just above the lace edge of it. It glowed blue, and I could see the guy who must have hit her cradling his hand next to his chest with tendrils of steam coming off of it. Streaks of mascara marked her puffy cheeks, and her lip was bleeding.

"Smile for the camera, bitch!" a familiar voice sneered. "Make sure he knows it's you."

Her head came up, and for a second, she looked almost composed.

"Chance," she said, and my stomach dropped to my toes.

Her pentacle glowed brighter, and the camera backed away. It turned and I saw Darth Fedora's smug face fill the screen as he walked through a doorway.

“Stay by the phone, warlock. Good boy!” He laughed and I heard several voices join him before the screen went black.

The dark, cold place in my mind woke up and ate the anger and pain I was feeling. When I met Lucas’ eyes, he flinched.

“Come on,” I told him as I headed up the stairs and toward the back of the house.

The last door at the end of the hallway led to a sunroom that faced to the south, and we closed the door behind us. I didn’t want Polter or his mage cops getting in the way of this. Karl had just made things personal, and there was no way I was going to let him walk away from this. The phone rang before the door clicked shut. I hit the button to put it on speaker before I hit the green answer button.

“What?” I answered.

“You know now that we have your little girlfriend,” Fedora chuckled. “Or are you screwing the leggy redhead?”

“The only person who’s gonna get fucked tonight, Darth Fedora,” I growled, “is you.”

“I don’t think so. You have defied my Master for the last time. You will stop prying into his business. You will not interfere. You will not even speak ill of him. You will swear to this right now, or she dies. Now, swear your obedience to my Master’s will!”

He was trying to put me over a barrel by making me swear a binding oath.

“Let her go, Darth,” I said softly as I tried to buy some time to think. “It’s the only way you’re gonna make it through the night in one piece.”

“Swear it!” he yelled into the phone.

“So long as you don’t hurt her, I swear that I won’t do any more digging into your Master’s business. I’m done trying to figure out what he’s up to. So long as she lives, I promise you that. Satisfied?” I asked as I felt the binding of the oath close around me.

“Yes. You finally understand your place in the world, worm.”

"Promise me you won't hurt her," I demanded.

"Why? You already promised me what I want, and you can't break it."

"Because my promise is only binding while Wanda's still alive and unharmed. And I promise you this, Karl. If you do hurt her, after I'm done with you, not even death will be mercy enough." I hit the end button and handed Lucas his phone back.

"What the hell did you just do?" he exclaimed angrily.

"Gave him an empty promise," I told him.

He shoved me away from the door and got in my face.

"You told him, no you *swore* you wouldn't interfere! You can't break that kind of promise!"

"Lucas, you know me better than that. I only promised him I wouldn't look into his Master's business. I told him I was done trying to figure out what he was doing because I already know. I never said I wasn't gonna fuck up his Master's world." Lucas took a step back and gave me a thoughtful look.

"Remind me never to make a deal with you, man," he said.

"You'll never have to. I don't make deals with my friends. I have a plan, but it's dangerous."

"More dangerous than getting chased through the woods by werewolves? More dangerous than an evil werewolf threatening to eat me?" he asked. I thought about that for a second.

"Probably."

"I'm still in, dude. This is Wanda we're talking about, there's no way I'm gonna sit this out. Especially not when you're about to put your ass on the line for her. You tell me what you need, and I'll do it. Unless I have to hit someone, 'cuz I kinda suck at that."

"No punches. But I need you to do a lot of stuff, and we don't have a lot of time. Come on," I said as I pulled him back into the hall.

Fifteen minutes later, we'd been through my room, the attic workroom and we were standing in the foyer. I opened the storage closet under the stairs and pulled out the pistol Dr. C had loaned Collins the night before. I wrapped the gunbelt around itself, stuffed it in my backpack and handed it to Lucas.

"Whoa, man! " he said softly. "A gun? Do you even know how to use that?"

"Dr. C taught me a few months ago. Gun safety, cleaning, maintenance, he even took me out to a range to let me fire a few rounds to make sure I hit what I was aiming at. It's a Texas thing, I guess. That and it bugged him that he'd sent me into the fight with King with a pistol I didn't know how to use."

"Did you? Hit what you were aiming at?" he asked with a grin.

"Not as often as he did, but yeah, if it's not moving and close enough, I can put a hole in it. Somewhere. Most of the time."

"So, is this everything?" he asked, hefting my backpack with a visible effort.

I nodded and pulled the *neglenom* charm out of the side pocket.

"Now you see it," I said as I tied it to the handle on the top.

"Now you don't," Lucas finished for me as it shimmered out of view. He shouldered it and gave me a determined look. "Okay, I have your gear, I know what I need to get, and who to talk to. Anything else?"

"Yeah, I need to borrow your phone again for a minute." He handed it over, and I dialed a number.

The voice that answered on the other end was familiar and hopeful.

"Chastity…about that ride."

Once Lucas was on his way, I turned around and faced the line of staves outside Dr. Corwyn's library door. Every mage had a staff. Dr. C took his almost everywhere with him. He'd been like a kid at

Christmas when his had arrived from Austin the week after I fought King. But I had never seen Mr. Chomsky's. Not even when he should have been using it to hold me against the wall in his classroom. If you were going to throw down on a warlock, it only made sense to use the best tools you had, but he'd used a rod instead of his staff. So where was it?

I headed for the doors and pushed them both open. Twelve heads swiveled in my direction from around Dr. C's desk. Polter was beside Dr. C behind it, and the Sentinels were in a loose ring around it.

"Where is Sydney's staff?" I asked him. It felt weird using Mr. Chomsky's first name, but it was how Dr. C knew him, and I needed him to try to answer without having to think about it.

"It was . . ." he faltered. "It's . . . I have no idea," he admitted.

"What is the meaning of this?" Polter snapped. "Get out!"

"Shut up, Polter," Dr. C said as he came around from behind his desk. "I never thought about it for some reason. I haven't seen it since I came back. Is this about the Maxilla?"

I nodded. "I think it's the key to finding it . . . and getting it. And I think I know where it might be."

I turned and headed for the stairs. Dr. C was right on my heels as I opened the door the Mr. Chomsky's room and stepped inside. I went to the dresser and held my hand over the spare change and assorted junk in the silver bowl on the top. When I felt a gentle pressure and warmth against my palm, I reached down and picked up the quartz crystal, and realized that my memories of picking it up a couple of days ago were fuzzy and hard to reach until I picked it up again. I closed my eyes and tried again to imagine what happened the night he'd hidden the Maxilla.

Chomsky steps into the room. He's in a hurry. He has less than an hour to get changed and get to the school for first period. Conference period. He goes to the wardrobe to get out of his dirty clothes . . . he sets something in the narrow space between it and the wall before he takes his shoes off and peels his clothes off. Even he isn't sure where he's been.

I stepped up to the wardrobe and reached into the narrow gap between it and the wall.

The second my fingers came into contact with the smooth warm wood, I saw the entire night play out in front of my eyes like a video played at high speed. If I concentrated, I could slow parts down, and I could make out details. I watched him drive past Springfield, stop in Ozark and get gas, then backtrack a little north until he made a turn by a National Forest sign. I concentrated on it, and read the words "Blue Hole" under the logo. As he went, he looked at landmarks, as if he was trying to make sure he could find his way back. A chimney from a ruined building, a fork in the road, a building . . . a bell with a frayed rope. He got out of his car and walked through a camping area, followed a trail to a creek bed, and sloshed his way to a brush covered strip of land where the stream parted and rejoined itself a few yards later. As he stood on the islet, I saw him turn, like he was facing me, and smiled, almost as if he was expecting me.

I stumbled back from the wardrobe, with his staff in my hand and tears streaming down my face. A quick swipe of my left hand across my cheeks took care of the tears, but when I turned around, I knew Dr. C wasn't fooled.

"I need a ride. I know where it is," I told him. "And I need to borrow your phone."

Chapter 20

~ I'm never going to use it. ~

Every kid ever about math.

If I'd expected to just get in the car and go, I would have been really disappointed. It took almost an hour for Dr. C to get Polter out of his house. In the end, the only way he'd go was if the Sentinels came with us.

"Once you have the Maxilla, you are to deliver it straight to the Council," Polter said as the Sentinels gathered their staves. "If you go anywhere else, the Sentinels have orders to pursue and apprehend you. In the meantime, Corwyn, I'll be trying to talk some sense into Draeden. Make sure he brings the sword back quickly. You have just as much to lose as he does."

"Pompous windbag," muttered Dr. C as the Sentinels trooped out after him.

Junkyard roused himself from his spot under the kitchen table and trotted over to join us. We went out after them, and re-set the wards before we both headed for the garage, this time with both of us carrying a staff.

Four blue Crown Victorias pulled out behind us while Polter's limousine took the first turn we came to and headed off in a different direction. Cross and T-Bone pulled in behind the Sentinels, and we headed for the freeway.

"Draeden vetoed an attack on Etienne," he said as we came off the ramp onto Highway 44. "At least until we can get permission from Thraxus to act."

"Which I already have. Bet that pisses Polter off."

"Somehow, I forgot to mention that part," he said. "If he knew, it would chap his hide that a kid, a warlock at that, was two steps ahead of him. And if he knew, he'd have done everything in his power to keep you from leaving the house."

"Thanks, sir. For not telling him, I mean. And . . . well, you know, for all the other stuff." I had to fight my own urge to just tell him what I had in mind, to tell him Etienne had Wanda, just hear him tell me everything would be all right.

"Look, Chance, once the Council has the Maxilla, they'll take care of Etienne. He's too powerful now to go after him without it. Between that, and the rubbings of the G'honn fragments, and you figuring out what he was up to, there's really no way the Council can vote against you. Not without losing their seats."

"They'll still try to find a way," I said.

"Some of them will try, probably. If it comes down to a vote, though, I want to give you a bit of advice. Before a mage or an apprentice faces judgment, they have the right to bequeath their tools and possessions to someone, usually family. In your case, I'd suggest, and strongly, that you choose your sister."

"Why Dee?" I asked. "Why not you or my mom?"

"Because of the way I think certain members of the Council will react. I can't go into much more detail. You'll just have to trust me on this."

"Okay," I said. "But the next time I do something that seems stupid, you know I'm gonna use this against you, right?"

"I'll try to live with the knowledge," he laughed.

A black sport bike passed us on the left, crossed the lane in front of us and took the exit for a small town called Fidelity. As we went over the overpass, I saw a group of motorcycles pull out of the parking lot of a convenience store and head for the onramp. The next hour and a half was the hardest time of the past week, as I fought to keep my big mouth shut for once. Once we got to Ozark, I had to start giving Dr. C directions, and that kept my mind off wanting to blurt the truth out to him.

Eventually, we came around the last of what felt like a thousand curves to find the sign for Blue Hole waiting for us. Dr. C took the turn in, and our six-vehicle escort followed. The Range Rover stopped, and Dr. C turned the engine off.

Ahead of us was a chain across the dirt road, with a red sign dangling from the center of it that read "Closed". A few feet beyond it, I could see the reason why. With the rain we'd had today, the dirt road had turned into a mud pit. Deep tire tracks ran to the edge of the asphalt, and a thick trail of mud picked up from there, telling the story of a vehicle trapped in the mud and pulled to the safety of pavement.

We got out, Junkyard obviously excited to be someplace he'd never peed before. The first thing he did was find a tree to fix that. He trotted back to me with his tail wagging, obviously happy to have claimed the particular part of the world for his very own.

One of the Sentinels went up to the chained-off road, took a quick look and went back to join the knot of his blue-cloaked brethren. I pulled Mr. Chomsky's staff out of the back and turned back to our escort to see them shedding their cloaks and stowing them in their cars. Without their cloaks, they looked a lot less intimidating. Not that they weren't still pretty scary without them. Every single one of them carried two pistols, one of them I figured had to be a paintball gun like Dr. C's and mine. I saw paired shoulder holsters, paired thigh rigs with tactical holsters, a couple with a shoulder holster and a hip holster on the same side. One of them was buckling on a pair of holsters that rode at the back of his belt. And then, as if they hadn't gone far enough in the cool gear department, they took their staves and twisted the ankh on the top, and the bottom of the staff went shimmery and got sucked up into the base of the ankh. It was one of the cool things about their *paramiir* staves. I'd heard that they also turned into swords on command. That was a trick I really didn't want to see tonight. They clipped them to their belts or tucked them into pouches, and came our way. Most of them wore some kind of hiking boots, jeans or cargo pants, and either a t-shirt or a work shirt. Nothing fancy, and nothing that they'd mind getting dirty.

"He isn't worthy to be carrying a wizard's staff," one of the Sentinels said. This guy was older, with a few streaks of grey in his short brown hair. He had the square jaw and broad features that belonged on an action hero, and arms that begged for the word 'thews' or something just as barbaric sounding to describe them.

"Chill the hell out, Carter," T-Bone said as he and Cross passed them. "There's a reason he's carrying it." He shot me a look, and I nodded.

"Mr. Chomsky's staff is the key to getting the Maxilla," I said. "Believe me, I'm the last guy to go acting like I'm a mage when I'm not. The place we're heading for is about a mile up this road. Maybe two."

Dr. C handed me a flashlight and gave everyone a few tips on hiking after a rainstorm, then gestured for me to lead the way. We marched along in the darkness for a while, silently following the beams of our flashlights. Behind us, I could hear the occasional curse after one of the Sentinels missed their footing. Between the darkness, the hills and the mud, it took us almost an hour to get to the open field that bordered the campsite I was looking for. I stopped at a particularly deep puddle and pointed my light into it. It was brown with dirt, but there wasn't a trace of red in it.

"We're close," Dr. Corwyn said. "The Maxilla's influence kept the plagues away from this area. We should have thought to look for that."

I gave him a shrug.

"We didn't know there was a connection then." I stood up and headed for the broad trail.

Around us, the night went quiet.

"Now that isn't ominous or anything," Dr. C said softly as he pulled his pistol.

Junkyard sniffed the air, then barked once. I kept going. About twenty yards further on, the sound of the creek reached my ears. I broke into a trot until I felt rocks shift under my boots. A few steps later, and my feet were splashing through the water. By now, the staff felt like it was pulling me forward as much as I was carrying it, and the water was over my knees before I knew it. Then I was stumbling across dry land, or at least ground that wasn't completely under water. Dr. C was a few yards behind me as I made my way to the circle of saplings that sat in the center of the island. I pointed my flashlight at the ground in the middle of them, and saw a small circle of stones, each marked with a rune that I wasn't familiar with. I doubted Mr. Chomsky had known them either when he carved them on to the rocks. A dozen beams of light filtered through the trees as the Sentinels slogged their way into the water. I only had seconds to do what I needed to do.

I raised the staff above my head and brought the tip down in the center of the circle of stones. The ground gave under the wood like water, and I felt a wave of magick wash over my skin as the spell released itself, and physics took over. I heard Dr. C curse a split second before he hit the ground and I found myself at ground zero as a ten-foot sphere of nothing popped back into existence over my head.

When you make a speck of nothing turn into a ten foot bubble of something in a microsecond, you have over twelve hundred square feet of area pushing everything around it to make room for the more than four thousand cubic feet inside it. Even if it's nothing but air, that's a lot of cubic feet to move around all at once. It was like a bomb going off a foot from my head. Of course, Mr. Chomsky had thought of that and he'd planned for it. The only problem was that you had to know you needed it. As the sphere popped into place, the tip of the staff glowed bright blue, and a cone of light formed around the top of it like an umbrella opening. I dropped to my knees and hugged the staff hard. Even doing that, I felt like I'd just been kicked in the chest and back at the same time by two giant mules. Giant mules with elephant feet. For a few seconds there was no air in my lungs, and it felt like there wasn't any nearby, either. When I finally could breathe, I stood up and realized that math had just saved my life.

I was standing in a blast shadow about four feet wide. Beyond that four-foot circle, very little was still upright. In the sudden moment of moonlight, I could even see the ripples spreading across the stream in a widening circle. I looked up to see a hole in the clouds overhead. It wasn't a perfect circle, at least not anymore, but I had to wonder if I'd done that, too. Then the shimmer of air in front of my face caught my eye. I put my hand up and let it touch the ripple in the air, and the illusion peeled away like cloth.

Hanging a foot over my head was the Maxilla. As swords went, it looked pretty plain. It had a straight blade etched in an alphabet I couldn't place. The handle looked like a long leather wrapped jawbone that ran up both sides of the blade's base to make a sort of hand guard, though someone had also put straight quillons as well. That was why the sword's full name was *Maxilla Asini*. The jawbone of an ass. Literally. I reached for it.

When my fingers wrapped around the handle, the blade flared white, and I couldn't see anything for a few seconds. When I could see again, I was standing face to face with the most beautiful woman in the world. Her cheekbones and nose reminded me of my mom and my sister, but her eyes and mouth made me think of Shade. When she smiled at me, I would have done anything to make sure she never stopped. Beside her stood a man in a horned headdress, silent and radiating primal power. His silence seemed to speak as loudly as her words.

"Chance Fortunato," she said.

It was like she'd been calling my name all my life, and I'd just never been able to understand it until just then, as if I'd never known who I was until she said it. The sound of her voice was gentle and fierce at the same time, and it sounded familiar to me, like I'd been hearing it from the day I was born.

"One of My children calls out to Me in her hour of need. It is your name she calls, you who embody her faith in Me. She prays not for herself, but for those around her who suffer as she does. I will not let her prayer go unheeded while you carry the instrument of My Will in your hand."

Her frown made me want to cower and beg for mercy, but I knew she wasn't angry at me. She was feeling the same rage I was, only on a scale my brain would never be able to understand. I could feel the depths of love she felt for Wanda, and somehow even for me, driving her fury. Her hair took on Shade's red coloring, and her features became sharper as her eyes flared red. The horned man beside her bared his teeth, and I felt their rage like a fire in my own heart.

When she spoke again, I could hear thunder and fire in her voice.

"Bring My comfort to her, and be My answer to her prayer. Deliver My child from her captors, and pour out My wrath among them as if from Mine own terrible hand"

Wrath I could get behind. Wrath I knew how to do. The rest . . . well, I'd wing it.

The horned man smiled at me as if he understood what I was thinking, and it seemed to make sense that he would.

"I promise you, I will," I said, and I felt the power of that promise like no other I'd made before. I wanted to keep it like nothing else, and I knew I'd die before I failed to deliver on it. It didn't feel so much like it bound me as I bound it to myself. I felt like I'd only just now understood what it meant to give my word.

She smiled at me, and I was in love with her.

"I know you will. Go with My gifts, freely given. I give you My daughter's faith in Me. I give you My comfort to deliver to those who need it. I give you My Wrath as both sword and shield among your foes. And I give you words from a friend. Sydney Chomsky is proud of you, and of your mentor, Trevor. He thanks you for seeking justice on his behalf. Now, go My child. Our wills are one tonight."

One perfect hand touched my forehead, and I learned the meaning of benediction.

I knelt on the stony spit of land, overwhelmed and awed by the presence of a God and Goddess. Not just a single Goddess, but every Goddess ever. Every God ever named. Tears streamed down my face, but I was trembling in rage. I held the Maxilla in my hand, but in front of me was a belt and a simple scabbard. I sheathed the sword and got to my feet.

Dr. Corwyn was stirring when I got to him. His eyes opened when I rolled him over, and to my relief, they focused on me. Nearby, I could see and hear the rest of the Sentinels moving, too.

"Etienne has Wanda, Dr. C. I'm sorry I didn't tell you about this before, but . . . well, you would have just tried to stop me. I have a promise to a friend to keep."

I stood up and slung the sword belt over my shoulder and looked around. Shade and the rest of the pack came out of the woods by the creek's edge in their wolf form. Junkyard bounded around Shade, dwarfed by her but completely undaunted. I started for the woods.

"Chance, wait!" Dr. C called out.

I turned and looked over my shoulder at him. Several of the Sentinels had turned toward his voice, and I saw hands move for holsters.

"You'll just have to trust me on this," I told him as I pulled my wand out of my pocket. Then I ran.

Half a dozen potion balls splatted against my shield almost as soon as the word "*Obex!*" left my mouth. I jumped the narrow part of the stream and landed next to Shade. More paintballs zipped by, but only a couple hit my shield.

"I need to get back to the cars before they do!" I cried out as I ran into the cover of the trees.

Without a sound, eight wolves turned and headed into the brush in different directions, and Shade looked over her shoulder at me with glowing gold eyes, then took off at a run. I followed her, blessing every inch of pavement Dr. C had made me cover in my morning runs. The path she led me on wasn't the straightest, but it was the smoothest and I figured the fastest.

I heard a few of the Sentinels crashing through the brush behind me, and a couple of paintballs zipped through the woods somewhere to my right. Amid the shouting and curses from the Sentinels, I could also swear I heard someone laughing. Finally, I heard their voices fade behind me. When I looked over my shoulder for signs of pursuit, I saw the bobbing beams of a dozen flashlights moving along the road. A hill loomed in front of me, and while it was going to try to kick my ass, it probably took half a mile off our route back to the cars.

Shade barked as she leaped a barbed wire fence, and I put my hand on one of the thick wooden posts and vaulted over it without half the grace of her jump. I hit the ground and found myself on the edge of an open field. With no trees to dodge, I could really open my stride and just flat run. Shade matched my stride, and the pack came out of the trees like so many lupine ghosts on my right and left. They formed up in a loose group around us, four in front, and two to either side, with Junkyard bounding along beside me with his tongue hanging out like a doggy grin. My lungs were burning and my legs felt like so much lead, but I caught my second wind about halfway across the field. I only saw the next fence as the pack vaulted over it. This one had the narrow steel posts that I couldn't vault over, so I had to slip between the strands. Junkyard just belly crawled under the bottom strand and waited for me, then turned and sprinted into the brush behind Shade.

We broke from cover a few minutes later, and I could see the parking lot about thirty yards ahead. Beside me, Shade started changing, her arms and legs elongating and her torso shifting to its normal shape. Her stride became a sort of front to back leg bound for a few steps until she went to her back feet and completed the changed from her hybrid form to human. The rest of the pack was changing as well, and by the time we hit the asphalt, they were running barefoot and naked. I tried to look away and spare Shade's modesty while I caught my breath, but she took advantage of the gesture to ambush me.

One moment, I was trying not to look at the naked girl five feet away from me, and the next, all five feet five of her was pressed up against me, and she had her mouth glued to mine. My arms listened to my monkey brain, and wrapped around her. She put one leg around my waist as I pulled her close, and dropped her hand to my ass. Not one to waste the moment, I let my hands run down her back, then brought my left hand up to wrap in her hair. It took a little effort to pull her mouth from mine, but as soon as I got my teeth on her neck, she arched her back and gasped. The soft sound of pleasure that she uttered cracked my concentration, but I pulled away after a few more seconds.

"God you're hot," I panted in her hear. "But we need to stay on target."

Our hands came away from each other's butt cheeks at the same time, and she took a step back, then shook her head. I damned the darkness for hiding her from me, then slapped monkey brain down. I had a friend to rescue.

The good-natured chuckles of the rest of the pack followed me as I went to Dr. C's Range Rover and opened the passenger door. Junkyard got in obediently, then turned around. He accepted the few affectionate strokes I could spare, then sat down like he expected to stay there.

"Good boy," I whispered, "Stay with Dr. C for now."

He made a sound in the back of his throat and cocked his head a little as I closed the door.

I had to force myself to head over to Steve's bike. Lucas waited with him, my backpack on his back and a duffle bag in his hand. Steve wore a blue leather jacket, jeans, and a black t-shirt with a red Love N' Chains logo on it. He hefted a thick metal bar as I came up and offered me a hungry grin.

"I see you found a stick you won't break," I said. He hefted it and nodded.

"Yeah, it just gets all bendy if I hit stuff too hard."

"Guess you're gonna have to make do with smackin' on vampires then. Did you get everything?" I asked Lucas.

He reached into the duffel bag and pulled out a bag of cinnamon candies.

“Yup. I even brought your Scooby snacks,” he said as he tossed the bag to me.

“Thanks, Shaggy,” I said as I turned and headed for the dark shape that lurked behind a park sign. “I brought something for you, too.”

I pulled the tarp away to reveal the black sports car that had been parked in front of Dr. C’s place the night before. His jaw dropped, and if his eyes could have popped out of his head like in the cartoons, I think they would have. As he gawked and made sounds like speech, I lifted the door open and pulled the keys out of the ignition to dangle them in front of him.

“Who’s your best friend?”

“Wanda. You, man, are a GOD!” he shouted as he snatched them from my hand.

From down the road, I saw the beams of the Sentinels’ flashlights.

“Get in the car, and drive it like you stole it.” I didn’t have to tell him twice. I heard the whine of the pack’s bikes starting up as I lifted my door, and the low cough of Steve’s BMW. He pulled his bike over to Lucas’s side of the car and hefted the bat.

“You want me to keep them from following us?” he asked over the top of the car with a smile.

“No. We actually need them.”

Shade pulled up on next to me and gave me a lingering look.

“I’m glad you’re with me tonight,” I told her.

“So am I. Be careful.”

I answered her with a quick kiss. “Don’t know how. It’s why you like me.”

She put her helmet on and leaned over the handlebars, then gunned the bike.

I dropped into the McLaren’s seat and pulled the door down. Lucas laid down a layer of rubber before the tires got traction, and the car shot forward with a deep-throated roar. He passed Shade in under a minute, and took the first turn tight and hard.

"This," he said as he sped into the next turn, "I can do." His bruised face was a mask of determination as we headed for Ozark.

"How fast can you get me back to New Essex?" I asked him as I checked the clock on the dashboard. It was after ten thirty.

"In this thing? Under an hour, if I don't care about losing my license."

"Do you?" I asked as we blazed through the first little town.

"Not as much as I care about Wanda. There's Gatorade in the bag, and some snacks. You always eat like a horse after you do magick, so I figured you'd want to stock up. Now do me a favor and shut up so I can drive."

I shut up and grabbed the bottle of Gatorade.

We blazed through two more towns in as many minutes before we hit Ozark. Lucas slowed down to the speed limit while we drove through the little town, but as soon as we hit the onramp to Highway 65, I heard the engine growl and felt the acceleration press me back into the seat. As the speedometer topped one hundred, we saw the first blue strobes light up our rear window. I looked back through the rear window and saw four sets of lights. Traffic slowed and pulled over ahead of them, and Lucas shot me a disbelieving look.

"Cops? Already? What do you want me to do?" he asked.

"Keep going. Those aren't cops. Not real cops, anyway. That's the Sentinels. Just keep them in your rear view mirror. I don't want to lose them."

He nodded and gave the car more gas. Even in the fast lane, we had to weave around slower cars to keep from losing speed. Still, Lucas slowed down if he couldn't pass safely. It kept the Sentinels on our tail, but it was too close for comfort. I left the driving to Lucas as I got ready for the rest of the night's fun.

When we hit Route 44, Lucas darted into the far left lane and pressed the pedal down all the way, and the needle climbed toward the two hundred mark. I glanced at the dash clock. Between the delay at Dr. Corwyn's, the trip to Blue Hole and the walk to the creek, I'd lost most of the night. The blue numbers jumped to eleven oh eight as we hit the halfway mark between Springfield and New Essex.

"Dude, you're not gonna be able to save Wanda and get the sword back in time," Lucas said as it hit eleven fifteen. We were still fifteen miles from New Essex, but not even a speed machine like the McLaren could get across New Essex in under half an hour.

"Shut up and drive," I told him.

"Uh-oh," he said a couple of minutes later.

I looked ahead to see a trio of cars backing up behind a pair of semis. The cars were in the right lane, and it looked like one of the eighteen-wheelers was trying to stay even with the other.

"Do those mage cops have CB radios?" he asked.

"Probably. Why?"

"They're getting the semis to set up a rolling road block."

As if to confirm what he was saying, blue lights lit up the rear window again, this time only fifty yards behind us. Between the cars and the semis, we were effectively blocked in with the Sentinels behind us. My heart sank as the first sign for our exit slid by overhead.

My disappointment only lasted for a moment, until a black sport bike sped past us and shot between the two eighteen-wheelers, then pulled in front of the one on the right. Brake lights lit up on the back of the truck, even as we passed the one-mile marker for our exit. The truck on the left slowed down before a gap opened between the other cab and the rear of his trailer. We slowed down to almost forty-five miles an hour, and Lucas cursed.

"Damn it!" I added. "We're not gonna make it!"

Lucas reached down and flipped a switch on the dash. The roof of the car lifted up and back, and I looked at him as we pulled up beside the right hand semi, a heavy-duty log hauler with three large trees supporting themselves between the front and rear wheels.

"Yes we are!" he said over the wind and freeway noise. "Hang on . . . and get ready to take out the barrier!"

He sped up, and the pack fell in behind us, cutting off the lead Sentinel. We pulled up beside the semi on the right, and the left-hand truck's brake lights came on. Lucas looked to the right, then up ahead, and I watched his hands tense on the wheel. I gripped my wand and wondered what he was about to do.

He turned to me and yelled, "Duck!"

My head dropped instinctively, and he hit the gas. When we were near the front of the trailer, he yanked the wheel to the right and we slid under the heavy trunks. There was a scraping sound and bark flew from the top of the windshield as I watched Shade lean down over her handlebars and follow us.

Then the yellow crash barriers were looming in front of us, and I put my wand over the windshield and cried, "*Ictus latior!*"

The wave of force slammed into the barrels and sent water spraying into the air as they collapsed like they were supposed to. We caught air as we came off the edge of the road, and the front end of the McLaren clipped one of the flattened barrels and sent it bouncing back toward the freeway to bounce off the side of the semi. I looked over my shoulder to see the rest of the pack and Donovan slipping between the slowing cars to hit the offramp behind us.

Meanwhile, the Sentinels were forced to keep going by the traffic that had backed up behind them. Dr. C's Range Rover was at the rear of the line of vehicles, and came to a stop at the top of the overpass with Cross and T-Bone bracketing him. Lucas hit the bottom of the ramp and slid to a stop at the light. He looked left and right as I watched Dr. C get out of his truck and go to the rail. Lucas gunned the McLaren through the intersection, and Dr. C gave me a thumbs-up. Then we were zooming under the freeway and headed for Inferno with Shade and the pack behind us. Seconds later, the flashing blue lights of the Sentinels' vehicles came into view.

"Good thing you didn't want to lose these guys," Lucas joked as we sped down the street.

In town, the McLaren's advantage in speed was lost, and it looked like they were going to catch up to us in a few seconds.

"Yeah, but I didn't count on them being up our ass when we got to Inferno," I told him as I grabbed the sword belt. "I wanted you to just drop me off and drive away. I needed to be inside when they showed up."

"Yeah, how's that workin' for ya?" he said. "Because I don't think that's happening."

One of the Crown Victorias pulled up alongside us on Lucas' side, and another was sliding up on mine.

"I think you're right," I agreed.

"You just need to be inside, right?" Lucas asked. "Because, you know, I've already taken a couple of insane risks tonight, so I figure, hey, what's one more?"

"Luuucaaas!" I yelled as he hit the gas again.

The two Sentinels fell behind as he skidded through the left turn, then yanked the wheel back to the right and gunned it again. We went airborne for the second time that night when he hit the angled entrance, then bounced hard on the asphalt. He stomped on the brakes and yanked the wheel to the left less than twenty feet from the side of the club. I barely had enough time to aim a TK blast at the front window before we slammed into it.

I got fleeting glimpses of tables and chairs flying as we spun across the floor. When the McLaren finally came to a stop, there was a ring of pissed-off vampires in a ragged circle around us. To my left, Lucas had a death grip on the wheel as he took deep breaths. Off to my right, I could see Shade and the boys sprinting across the lot as the blue Crown Vics screeched to a stop outside the hole we'd made. And in front of me, a crowd of vampires were closing in for a snack.

Gone was their human look. Their gray skin was drawn tight against their faces, making the strange jaw structure stand out, and their arms and legs were all bony and misshapen as they took on the appearance of the dead things they really were. The young ones were the most dangerous, because they barely had control of their blood-thirst at the best of times. In a fight, they'd lose control and suck you dry faster than a six year old with a juice box.

Above them I could see the long row of angled floor-to-ceiling windows of an office. Standing in it was a vampire in a business suit. He glared down at me, and his lips curled away from his fangs in a snarl. I wasn't sure if it was the long hair that brushed his shoulders in perfect curls or the face that was more pretty than handsome that made me sure that this was Etienne. All I was certain of was that he and I were going to see each other up close and personal before the end of the night, and that one of us wasn't going to walk away. He turned away and slid his jacket off his shoulders, leaving me to face the closing ring of his minions.

My brilliant plan was shot to all Nine Hells. I hadn't counted on Lucas being inside with me, and I hadn't counted on the vampires and the Sentinels seeing each other until after I was already inside. It was time to improvise. I tossed the duffel bag to Lucas, then popped the door and climbed to my feet. As the crowd of bloodsucking fiends closed in on me, I pointed to the fourteen blue robed magi gathering at the new door we'd made. Inhuman faces turned to look where I was pointing.

"It's the Sentinels!" I called out. "They're here to stop you!"

Surprisingly, a fight broke out.

Chapter 21

~ Fight dirty. Fight to win. ~ TS Cross, Left Hand of Death

There is a reason warlocks fear Sentinels. Mostly, because they're badasses. Dozens of vampires swarmed fourteen Sentinels. Half of them died before they could get close. The girl with the ponytail brought her hand up, and a red beam lanced from her fingertip. She swept her hand in a narrow arc, and four fiery vampire heads fell to the ground. It was kind of moot, because their bodies burst into flame, too. The biggest Sentinel, Carter, pushed his hand out and knocked several of them sprawling as the boom of magickally compressed air flattened them like a cannon. Another one thrust his hands forward, and an arc of electricity jumped from him to one of the vampires, then to two more before it died out and left three smoking bodies in its wake. Then they were on them, and the Sentinels drew the ankhs from their belts and got down to some serious vampire slaughter.

Lucas and I saw this in the split second before we bolted for the bar. Then we had vampires of our own to deal with. The first one made a flying leap at us from behind the bar, fangs bared and claws out. I nailed him with a wide TK blast and sent him back over the bar. Three more of his buddies hopped up on the bar and crouched for a jump of their own. That was when Lucas got his first licks in.

One of the goodies he'd pulled from the duffel bag was the watergun filled with true blessed-on-consecrated-ground holy water. For younger vampires, it was like getting hosed down with sulfuric acid that was on fire. If they'd been older than a few decades, it might not have worked, but these guys were new enough, they were still wearing this year's clothes. One of the benefits of having a normal childhood, it seemed, was being pretty damn accurate with a watergun, because Lucas hit all three of them in the face with one steady stream. Hey, if you're gonna douse someone with flaming acid, that's the place to light up. As if that wasn't enough, he arced it back across their torsos, too. They lit up and did the natural thing: they jumped back, away from the deadly stream . . . right into the bottles of flammable liquor. Fire, along with either a stake through the heart or decapitation, was one of best ways to kill a young vampire.

As the bar exploded, I grabbed Lucas and shoved him down under my body until the bits of flaming glass stopped raining down on us.

"Damn!" Lucas said when I let him up.

"Congratulations on your first arson!" I called out over the sound of the fight. "At least this one isn't all *my* fault!"

I heard the hollow *thunk!* of metal on flesh and bone, and a vampire hit the floor like a wet rag and slid past us. A quick glance over my shoulder let me see Steve, Shade, and the rest of the pack fighting their way toward us. The Sentinels weren't far behind, but catching me seemed to be further down on their "to-do" list than staying alive.

Through the boiling mass of combat, I saw Deek's face still at the hole in the wall, outside and watching as my friends fought their way to me.

I pulled the paintball gun, checked to make sure I had the hopper with red tape on it and pointed at the knot of vamps surrounding Shade and Steve. Lucas got the idea and pumped up the water gun, then gave me a nod. I aimed left and pumped a couple of rounds from the Ariakon into two vampires in sport coats and slacks. The red paintballs were supposed to be filled with an incendiary, but when the rounds hit, the two vampires' chests just disappeared. They fell in two pieces and started to wither. Lucas had doused four more with the holy water, and they were busy writhing in pain on the floor while Steve made short work of the two that were still between us and the pack with a swing from his club that sent them flying for the far wall, and into the group of vampires that had emerged from behind the club's stage.

"Man, you know how to make an entrance," Steve said with a grin as he made it to us.

"Yeah, it's the exit I need to work on," I said as the rest of the pack joined us.

I turned to head for the door behind the bar, and found another half-dozen vampires coming out of it. Lucas screamed and soaked the first one in holy water, then turned the water gun on the second one. The water gun gave a spurt of mostly air and spat a few drops, then went dry. I hit the second one with a paintball, but the next one landed on me and knocked me flat. The Ariakon and my wand went spinning, and it was all I could do to get my forearm against the vamp's throat before he ripped mine out. I fumbled with my right hand for the LeMat as he grabbed my shoulders and pulled, trying to overcome leverage with sheer inhuman strength. Just when I thought my arm was going to break or my shoulder was going to pop out of its socket, the pressure on my arm disappeared, and the vamp screamed. Then he got pulled off of me, and I saw Shade hurl his armless body into the group that was running at her.

She leaped on the nearest one as Steve waded into them with his club flying. As she twisted the head off one, Steve knocked the head of another off by sheer force, and I dove for the Ariakon. My wand was nowhere in sight, so I turned the ring on my right hand around and cried out "*Vocare!*"

My wand came flying from under the McLaren, drawn to the summoning ring's quartz setting. I made a note to thank Lucas for all the ideas he'd given me by making me watch all six of the *Star Wars* movies last year as I turned back to the brief fight for the door.

Shade had one by the neck and was busy swinging him into another while Steve drove his club down through the skull of the last of them.

"Who's next?" he called out.

The door opened and six-and-a-half feet of vampire stepped out in jeans and a black t-shirt. This guy gave him a toothy grin and a 'Come here' gesture, and Steve lunged forward. I barely saw the other vamp's hand move as he slammed it into Steve's chest and sent him sliding across the floor toward me. Shade hunkered down into a fighting stance and circled him warily. She lunged in with a punch that he blocked with his forearm, then reeled back as he backhanded her. I holstered the Ariakon, drew the LeMat and thumbed the hammer back.

"Hey!" I said as I walked toward him.

Both his and Shade's heads turned toward me.

"No one hits my girl, asshole," I growled to keep him off balance.

As he tried to size me up, I pointed the wand at him and hissed "*Ictus!*"

The blast knocked him back through the door and into the kitchen behind it. I heard him hit something metal and heavy, then there was a curse. I lifted the LeMat and fired at the empty door. The trick to fighting bad guys with superhuman speed and reflexes, Dr. C had taught me, was thinking ahead. The bullet arrived at the door about the same time the vampire did. After that, it wasn't very pretty.

I offered Steve a hand up as the vampire in the doorway screamed and writhed on the floor.

"Damn, conservation of ninjitsu works!" he moaned as we made for the door.

"Huh?" I said as he picked up his club.

"It isn't the hundred ninjas you have to worry about, it's the one guy who steps up. Only so much badass to go around," Lucas explained as we went through the stainless steel and white tile maze that was Inferno's kitchen.

Shade turned to her left and pointed at a wooden door.

"I smell them. They're back there," she said. She grabbed my shoulder and kissed me hard for a split second. "For calling me your girl," she said before she turned to follow the others.

Steve didn't bother to use the knob to open the door. The vampire on the other side had a split second to be surprised before he was slammed against the brick wall behind it, and skewered by half a dozen shards of wood. One of them must have hit his heart, because he just slid down the wall and started melting.

"I thought they were supposed to . . . you know . . ." Lucas said as we stepped over the spreading pool of goo.

“They all die differently for some reason,” I explained.

We followed Shade and the boys down the steps, letting their noses lead us to where we needed to be. We ended up in the building’s basement, in a room that looked like it used to be bar of its own a long time ago.

Of course, it was a trap.

Vampires vaulted over the bar and dropped from the ceiling. One landed next to Steve and got backhanded away. Another landed on Shade and one of the boys. The one who landed on Shade got flipped over her shoulder, while the one that had vaulted onto Tyler went stiff as Tyler’s fist erupted from his back with its pulped heart oozing in his grip. It burst into bloody chunks a second later, and Tyler rolled over and puked.

Another one landed in front of me, and I reflexively pulled the trigger on the LeMat. It flinched, then we both looked down at the gun, inert in my hand. I’d forgotten to pull the hammer back. Its grey skin pulled back from inch long fangs as it smiled at me hideously.

“Duck!” Donovan yelled, and I hit the floor.

His bat caught the vamp in the chest and flung him across the room. It flattened against the wall for a moment, then slid to the ground. I pulled the hammer back on the LeMat and took aim at its chest as it shook its head, then pulled the trigger as its eyes met mine. Even from across the room, I should have been able to hit it, but the bullet just made a fist sized hole in the wall beside it, and it leaped for me with a grin on its face. Halfway across the room, one of the pack caught it in mid-flight and slammed it against the wall.

I thumbed the hammer back again as another one grabbed me from behind. My first instinct was to put the gun in his face and pull the trigger, but his hand caught the gun by the barrel. I heard him chuckle from behind me and slammed my head back into his face. Fire erupted on my scalp where I hit him, but he let go of the gun and me long enough that I could turn and jam the gun against his chest and pull the trigger. The left side of his chest exploded and I saw one of his buddies take the flaming round just below the ribs. He got a wide-eyed look just before he burst into flames. Then the only sound was the wet *thump* of a vampire's head being slammed into the wall again and again.

I walked past Shade, heading for the heavy steel door on the far side of the room. Set into the brick wall, it looked like it would hold up against the worst I'd seen Steve and Shade dish out. That was where magick and a little applied physics came in. From the front of the Ariakon's holster, I pulled a spare hopper, this one marked with a strip of blue and white tape. As I changed it out, Lucas' phone played Wanda's ringtone. He pulled it out with a sheepish look and put it to his ear.

"He wants to talk to you," he said after a few seconds.

I took the phone from him.

"Honey, I told you never to call this phone," I said, my voice flat.

"I know you're outside the door," Darth Fedora's voice hissed over the line. "If you so much as knock, I'm going to blow her pretty little head off. Her faith may be strong, but it won't stop a bullet."

"Hey, little piggy, let me in," I said as I brought the paintball gun up and pulled the trigger.

The first pellet hit the center of the door. A web of frost covered the surface and I could feel the cold even from fifteen feet away, but it didn't cover enough of the door. I put another pellet in each of the four corners, and I heard the steel start to groan as it contracted in on itself from the intense cold.

Darth laughed at me as I holstered the gun.

"Or what? Are you gonna huff and puff and blow my house down?" he asked.

I ended the call and gestured for everyone to get back.

"Something like that, asshole," I muttered as I raised my wand and gripped the touchstone.

I pictured Wanda on the other side of the door, and I remembered that she had been praying to her Goddess for me. She had faith in me, and I was not going to let her down. Darth Fedora and his crew had taken her, and I could imagine what they were trying to do to her. I could almost feel the vampires and servants on the other side of the door, waiting for her faith to fail so they could have their fun with her. I let my own anger build, and felt the touch of the dark Goddess and the horned God's rage as well. I let it form a core of power inside me, and with the release word of my spell, I delivered the wrath of an angry Goddess.

Extreme cold makes steel very brittle. The door shattered under the impact of the TK bolt I'd just hit it with, and sent Darth Fedora and several of his cronies flying across the room. I stepped into the open doorway, gun and wand in my hands, with Steve and Shade beside me and a pack of angry teen werewolves behind us.

Thirteen kids were chained to the wall on our right, each one in front of a circle of Lemurian glyphs. The blackened metal of the stolen G'Honn fragment sat on a table in the back of the vault. At least a dozen vampires and just as many wanna-bes were picking themselves up off the ground, and thirteen heads were turning our way along the wall. Wanda's head raised last, and I could see that they'd found a way to hurt her without touching her. Several, from the looks of her swollen eyes and bruised cheeks. Blood ran down her face from her hair, and her lips were swollen and bleeding.

"Chance?" she slurred as she tried to focus on me.

"You prayed to your Goddess with unwavering devotion," I heard myself saying, "and I am come, your faith rewarded." The words weren't mine, even though they came out of my mouth. They sounded right, though. So very right. And even if they weren't mine, Wanda smiled, and I was grateful they'd been given to me for her sake.

"Kill them!" Darth Fedora yelled, breaking the moment.

Vampires and hopefuls ran toward us, but they never made it. As they started our way, I saw a glow start from Wanda's pentacle, then spread from her entire body and the whole room was suddenly lit up with a blinding white light. When it faded, all that was left of the vampires was their clothes, and the vampire groupies were screaming in agony on the floor.

“What was that?” Shade asked.

“Faith,” I said softly. “All her hopes rewarded, and her fears quieted in the presence of that which her Goddess sent to comfort and aid her.” Again, words that were not mine were coming out of my mouth, but they still felt right. “However unworthy the vessel,” I whispered. Somehow, I got the impression someone was laughing at that, but it wasn’t me.

“Can I get a ‘Blessed be’?” Lucas joked in a shaky voice.

“Amen, brother,” Steve said.

“Keep an eye on them,” I told Steve as I headed over to Wanda.

I pointed the paintball gun at the chains holding Wanda’s hands over her head and pulled the trigger. Links shattered under Wanda’s weight, and she fell into my arms. I laid her gently down as Lucas knelt beside her. Tears ran down his face as he saw the extent of her injuries.

“I prayed that you’d come,” she said to us.

“I know. She told me.”

“You saw Her?” Her split lips stretched into a pained smile, and my heart wrenched at the thought that the Goddess had appeared to me instead of her. If anyone deserved a vision like that, it was Wanda.

“I did,” I said softly as I felt my hand start to get warm. “She gave me a gift for you.”

I put my palm on her cheek, and I felt the warmth flow from me into her. The bruises and swelling faded, and her face glowed as her eyes closed in relief. When she opened them again, her face was back to normal, and she put her hand on my face.

“I saw Her. She’s beautiful. Thank you, Chance.”

“It wasn’t me,” I said as I turned my face away. “It was all Her. I just carried it for a while. It’s yours now,” I said, not sure of how I knew that. Maybe it was because the warm place that it had taken up in my head was gone, or maybe it was because all that was left was the rage of the Horned God who stood behind her. What I *did* know was that Wanda was the one to give comfort to those who needed it. My job involved a lot more bloodshed.

There was still a lot to do before the night was over, though, and I had more than one more promise to keep. One at least was going to be easy. It only took a few steps to retrieve the G'Honn fragment from the floor and slip it into my backpack. I turned to Lucas and Shade and pressed my backpack into Lucas' hands.

"Stay with Wanda. Shade, can you get the rest of them out of here? Lucas, hang on to this. There're extra hoppers for the Ariakon in there. Just don't give it to anyone else but me, okay?"

Lucas nodded and dug the extra hoppers out and stuffed them into his pocket. The rest of the pack started working on the chains holding the other kids up. I looked them over as they pulled them down. All of them were outcasts, outsiders. Crystal wore skinny jeans, a black shirt with a band called Kill Hannah on the front, and had piercings on each eyebrow, her nose, and one through her lip. Another wore black strappy pants with a mesh shirt and had the sides of his head shaved. Another girl closer to Wanda had the remains of a spiky Mohawk drooping over her head. A couple looked like the invisible kids everyone talked about but never to, one with a headband that Lucas had told me was part of an anime character's costume. Of the thirteen, only four of them were white. The rest were as diverse as New Essex: black, Asian, Hispanic, and Arabic faces looked back at me, and my mother's Romany blood boiled in my veins. Between their race and their differences, they were the kids people would be least likely to go looking for. The ones the cops would be less likely to connect as part of a pattern. The ones too many people thought didn't matter.

"What did you do to me?" Karl cried out to me.

I went over to him and squatted down in front of him. His legs didn't seem to be working, and both of his eyes were red like they were filled with blood. He only seemed to have partial use of his left hand, too. Bruises stretched along his face and neck.

"Me? Nothing. But I'm guessing all that vampire blood you've been sucking just got purged. Bet that hurt."

"I'll kill you!" he screamed.

"No, you won't," I told him. "Do you remember what I promised you would happen if you hurt Wanda?"

"Fuck you!" he snarled.

"No. I promised you even death wasn't going to be mercy enough if you hurt Wanda. And while this hurts, it's nothing compared to what I'm going to do next." I stood and headed for Steve.

"You're too weak!" he crowed. "You can't kill me, you don't have the balls!"

I gestured for Steve to come with me, then turned to look at Darth Fedora over my shoulder.

"I don't have to kill you to hurt you. I'm going to go kill your master." We left the room to the sound of his impotent screams.

"You're a cold-hearted bastard," Steve said as we walked through the old bar.

"You say that like it's a bad thing," I said coldly.

"Maybe not right now. So, what's the plan for this Etienne guy?" he asked as we took the steps.

"We kill him."

"Yeah, I got that part. But how?"

"Violence."

"I'm good with that."

Chapter 22

~ The worthy always refuse power when first offered. ~ Merlin.

When we got back up to the first floor, Dr. C, T-Bone, and Cross had joined the fight and the Sentinels, down by five from what I could tell, were starting to turn the tide of the fight with their help. By now, they held the middle of the main floor. It was still twelve against more than fifty, so I figured it was going to take a lot of time, and that wasn't something we had a lot of.

Steve and I crept up the spiral staircase as Cross went toe to toe with another vamp carrying a pair of blades, and T-Bone put bullets into vampires so fast that the sound of his pistol was more a single roar than a series of shots. Cross's sword barely seemed to move as he parried the twin blades, and when T-Bone's gun went empty, he dropped the clip and had another one in before the spent magazine hit the ground.

Dr. Corwyn knelt over one of the fallen Sentinels with his staff in one hand and his own pistol in the other. He fired at a charging vamp and the slide locked back. As the disintegrating corpse slid toward him, he holstered his gun, got to his feet and started to spin his staff. Each end lit up with a blue white fire, and the staff wove a pattern of light in the air in front of him. A pair of vamps tried to rush him from opposite sides, but they'd underestimated what a badass my mentor was. He spun around to slam the tip against the face of the one on his right, then kept going and planted the other end in the chest of the one on his left. Another tried to rush him and he spun the staff to spear it in the chest, then brought the length up into another charging blood-sucker's face. As it reeled back in a spray of broken teeth, he brought the staff around his body and started weaving it through the crowd that had closed around him. As we slipped through the door, I saw Cross' blade slip forward and impale his opponent as one of the paired blades took him in the shoulder.

The hallway we were in was carpeted in green, with a flowery pattern running down the middle of it. Halfway down, a pair of double doors waited, carved with ornate designs and covered with gold accents. The door closed behind us, and the sound of the fight downstairs disappeared. I almost expected to hear elevator music. We stopped outside of the double doors and looked at them.

I glanced over at Steve. He'd picked up a few bruises and cuts, and one sleeve of his t-shirt had been ripped away. I was down to my wand, one touchstone, six rounds in the LeMat's cylinder plus the Sunflare, and the Maxilla. All Steve had was that metal club of his, and it was looking pretty bendy.

"Your stick's looking pretty bad," I told him. "You want the sword?"

He shook his head and grabbed the end of the length of metal with one hand. Muscles in each arm flexed, and the bar slowly straightened.

"Nah, I'm good. Thanks though. Maybe later." He hefted the club and tapped it against his palm. I smiled, happy that at least one thing was going the way it was supposed to.

"So, I kicked in the last big door. You want this one?" I offered.

"What if we just knocked?" he asked with a mocking grin.

"Sends the wrong message."

"Good point." He leaned back and planted his foot along the center-line of the doors. Wood splintered and they flew off the hinges, and we stood there like a couple of action heroes. Facing us from across the room was the pretty vampire I'd seen in the window earlier. His shirt was gone now, and the lack did his narrow, pale chest no favors. Behind him I could see matching Lemurian circle glyphs for the ones in the basement. They went as far around the wall as I could see, and I was betting they went all the way around the room.

"Welcome, little warlock," he said. "You've chosen a good night to die."

I didn't bother with a snappy comeback. Instead, I pulled the sword and charged across the room at him. He stayed still until I swung the blade at his head, then he was gone, and I was stumbling through the follow-through. I turned to see him duck under Steve's swing and return the favor with a casual looking backhand that sent him flying into the wall beside the door. Then he turned back to me, and started slowly walking across the room.

"You need not die tonight," he said as I braced myself to swing again. "Not by my hand, and I can see to it that you need never fear the Conclave's judgment. We two are too much alike to waste such symmetry."

"Not seeing the similarities here, Etienne. I've got a pulse, you don't. That's a hard one to get past."

"Nonsense," he said with a smile, and I could feel the compulsion trying to work its way into my mind. Even as amped up as he was, he wasn't in either Dulka's or Thraxus' league and his compulsion buckled on my defenses. "We've both been enslaved to an uncaring master, and like you, I've found a way to throw off the yoke of my servitude."

"By assuming the mantle of Mammon," I said and straightened. I let my right hand fall away from the sword's grip, and the point dropped to the floor slowly.

"Correct. With Mammon's power, I will become far greater than my Master, and reshape the world to my liking. Those whom I have sired will share in my power, and those I favor will be granted all that they desire. You could be one of those favored few."

"I could be," I said slowly, as if the charm was working. He stepped closer, almost within arm's reach.

"You would enjoy such power," he suggested. His hand slowly reached for my throat.

"No," I said and swung the blade up from the floor.

He almost dodged it completely, but the tip scraped his chest and left a line of fire as he spun to my right and backed away. I drew the blade up over my head in a two handed grip and sent it spinning across the room at him. He barely moved as it swept by him, but when he turned back to face me, I could see the blisters on his skin that close proximity to the Maxilla had raised. The blade stuck in the wall a few feet from Steve's limp form, and my best weapon was gone. Now all I had was faith, treachery and my barbed wit.

"You've lost the only weapon you had that could hurt me," Etienne said.

"It wasn't mine to begin with," I said as he took another step closer to me, bringing him just within reach. I let my eyes slide into aura sight, and saw the unhealthy black and putrid green of his aura. Even the undead had one, and just like living people theirs broadcast their intentions if you knew what to look for. His went red around his right fist.

Before I even saw him move, I was ducking, and his hand swept past over my head. Another flare of red appeared around his hand. I dodged to my left and felt the wind of his fist right before it hit the wall. When I hit the floor, I rolled to me feet with my wand out and fired off a TK blast at him. It caught him as he pulled his fist free of the wall and threw him to the rear of the office.

When he bounced off the wall and landed in a crouch, I knew I was in deeper trouble than I was going to be able to dig myself out of alone. He stood slowly and closed his eyes. His chest seemed to expand, then his body turned gray and contorted. Bloody bone erupted from his shoulders, then stretched away from his body with strands of muscle and flesh growing along its length until it became a pair of leathery black wings. His legs and arms seemed to break and twist, then expanded, with horns and spikes bursting from his skin. It looked like it should have hurt like all Hell, but he was laughing as it happened.

The circle behind him started to glow, then the two on either side began to glow faintly. As the center circle got brighter, the two beside it did as well, and the two beside them started to glow. If he managed to activate all of them, the spell would be complete, and all Hell would break loose. Literally.

I pulled the LeMat and aimed it at him with a trembling hand before thumbing the hammer back. He saw the movement and started across the room toward me. I pulled the trigger and the round caught him in the chest. He barely slowed down long enough to brush the flaming ball of lead off his chest. He didn't even try to dodge the TK blast I sent at him, and waded through it like it wasn't stronger than a stiff breeze. I threw another TK blast at him and followed it up with a shot from the LeMat, and that did stagger him. Three more wand and bullet combos bought me a few more seconds, then his hand was around my throat and I was pinned to the window. I could feel the prickly, crawling sensation of the Lemurian glyph circle on my skin even through my jacket and shirt. His gaze hammered at me, and I felt his thoughts pressing against mine. Someone had just taken a couple of levels of badass.

"So much rage, little warlock," he said softly, almost tenderly. "And so little of it for the world I seek to destroy. Your heart burns for the lambs I must slaughter. They are nothing. Even if it were not me who ended their pathetic lives, no one would miss them. They are awkward and ugly. Why do you care for them? There are sheep, made for slaughter. Nothing more."

"Because when I look at them, I see myself in their eyes," I told him, yielding a little more to the compulsion than I liked. "And they're not sheep. They have the balls to be different, not to be what asshats like you want them to be. That's why you're nothing like me."

"Then there is no hope for you, little warlock. You are not the first human I have killed, nor will you be the last. Perhaps you will be one of the more memorable, though, and that is honor enough. You are one of the few who fought me to the last, instead of trying to run."

"Believe me, I wanted to. I just needed your undivided attention for a few seconds," I said as Steve rose up behind him and drove the Maxilla into his back.

Even being struck from behind, his reflexes were fast enough that he turned before Steve could drive the glowing blade all the way into his heart. I ended up flying into Steve as Etienne screamed and arched his back. He spun around a few times as he tried to reach the sword, but Steve had managed to hit a spot between his wings that his arms wouldn't bend far enough to get to. I looked at the walls and saw that the glow had spread halfway along the wall to the three circles etched in the glass. Even as I picked myself up, another pair of them lit up on either side, and I could feel reality warping around me. Etienne stopped his thrashing and looked at the purplish-black glow from the circles and realized what I had known since yesterday: this spell wasn't going to go down the way he thought it would.

"We've got to finish this quick!" I told Steve as I pulled him to his feet.

"He's too fast!" he said.

"Be ready to follow my lead, then," I said as I slipped the wand under my pinky and middle fingers, and over my ring and index fingers.

Etienne let out an agonized roar as his attention came back to his more immediate problems, then spat a gout of fire at us.

"*Obex*!" I spat, holding my hand up to keep the shield at an angle.

Most of the heat slid off to my right, away from Steve and me, but enough of it made it through that my right hand and the right side of my face felt like they were going to blister up. Then the heat let up, and I could hear Etienne cursing us.

"I will flay the flesh from your bones, and slaughter your families!" he bellowed as he took a step toward us. "You cannot stop me, not even with the holy little toothpick!"

I lifted my reddened right hand and pointed at him with my index and middle finger, and pulled the deepest voice I could from my throat.

"I find your lack of faith disturbing," I intoned.

The last pair of glyphs on the walls started to glow as the telekinetic ring closed around his throat. Only three left before the ritual was complete. I lifted him into the air and started forward with Steve only a couple of steps behind me. Etienne's wings flared as he moved toward the glass wall, and slowed him down. I pointed at the heavy desk and Steve stepped to the left and shoved it toward

Etienne. It caught him behind the knees just as I spun him around, and pinned him to the glass as the two outer glyph circles started to glow faintly. Etienne's claws scraped against the glass with a sound that made fingernails on a chalkboard sound almost angelic as I jumped on the desk, planted my right knee in Etienne's back and drew the LeMat. Steve followed me up and grabbed the Maxilla's handle as I pressed the gun's barrel to the glass and thumbed the lever on the hammer down before I pulled it back. The sword glowed even brighter as he tried to thrust it deeper. The edges of the glyph beneath us started to brighten, and we were out of time. I pulled the trigger.

When Dr. C had named the round in the LeMat's lower barrel the Sunflare, he hadn't been kidding. It melted through the glass and sent a tongue of white-hot fire belching down toward the McLaren. The glass Steve, Etienne, and I were pressed up against didn't so much break as it melted and shattered. We plummeted toward the ground, and I saw the long stream expanded out from the middle to make an oblong of superheated fire that scorched the paint off the car and made half a dozen vamps taking cover near it burst into flame.

Behind us, the room exploded, raining bits of wood, steel, and glass on us as we fell. I had a split second to see all that happen, then we hit the burning remains of the bar. Even with the bulk of Etienne to break our fall, it hurt when we hit.

I came to my senses to see Steve stumbling to his feet and backing away from the shining blade that was stuck far enough through Etienne that I figured the tip was several inches into the floor. I rolled away myself, because the demonic vampire was starting to burn in places, and if he was as powerful as I thought he'd become, this wasn't going to be pretty or safe to watch from too close. He screamed and thrashed as a brilliant flare burst through his skin, and I could feel the heat through my jacket. The skin around it started to melt and drip upward. More and more holes burned through, and it was like watching magnesium burn, only upside down. His screams reverberated through the room, and every piece of glass in the room shattered. I dropped the LeMat to clap my hands over my ears, and almost everyone with a pulse in the room did, too. The vampires were too busy dying to worry about their eardrums. When the last bits of Etienne flew toward the ceiling, the Maxilla dimmed and the last of the vampires crumbled to dust, shattered, or exploded into gooey chunks.

I shook my head and turned to take stock of things and a wall of knuckles slammed into my jaw and knocked me on my ass. I sat up and saw a pair of Sentinel Carters looking at his fist in disbelief. Just as my eyes started to focus, he started forward again, only to find himself facing a wall of people. Lucas was at the front, with Steve and Shade flanking him. The rest of the pack poured in behind them, and behind them I saw the kids we'd just rescued.

"Move aside. The punishment for aiding a warlock is death," Carter said.

As if to make his point, he held up his ankh and extended the paramiir's blade from the circle at the top. Magick-enhanced steel glowed as he held it in front of himself. I tried to pull myself to my feet and keep someone from getting killed when Cross appeared at my side and hauled me up with his good hand.

"You okay, kid?" he asked quietly.

"I just got sucker punched by a freight train, but other than that, yeah, I'm doing great," I managed to slur.

"Back off, Carter," I heard T-Bone say as I tried to stumble toward the Sentinel.

Cross helped me along, and I saw T-Bone step between my friends and the super-sized mage cop.

"I don't answer to you, Hand," Carter sneered. "We were charged with bringing the warlock in if he tried to take the artifact anywhere but to the Council. That's exactly what I plan to do, and no one is going to stand in our way."

"I'm standin' in your way," T-Bone said calmly. "You think you got a chance of goin' through me?" Carter's determined expression cracked, and I saw doubt on his face. I stepped forward.

"I'll go with you on my own," I said. Doubt turned to outright disbelief on Carter's face. T-Bone just turned and nodded at me. "I just need to get the Maxilla."

"The sword is no longer your concern," he announced. "We will return it to the Council."

"You're welcome to try," I said with a wave toward the sword.

He waved a dismissive hand at me as he went over to where the sword was stuck in the floor, retracting the paramiir as he went. He grabbed the hilt and tried to pull it free, then yanked his hands away with a cry of pain. Steam rose from the handle, but it didn't look as if it was hot.

"Looks like it's in there pretty good," Steve said from beside me as Carter glared at the sword.

"Yeah. You sure you don't want it?" I asked. For a moment, the heavy weight that had been on my soul seemed to shift as I offered the blade to him.

"I've got enough on my plate as it is. I don't need to be adding a magic sword to my problems."

"Guess I'll have to hang on to it for now, huh?" I said.

"Dude, you're welcome to it," he chuckled. The burden on my soul settled back on my shoulders, both a disappointment and a relief as he inadvertently reaffirmed my duty to carry the Maxilla.

I stepped forward and gave Carter a smile. "Told ya," I said before I grabbed the handle and pulled it out of the floor easily. I gave him a smile and shucked the scabbard from my back to sheathe it. "Now I'll go with you," I said to him.

He put a pair of spellbinders on my wrists and led me out of Inferno as it burned behind us.

In the distance, we could hear the sound of sirens.

Chapter 23:(Equinox)

~ The Seeker's true task is not finding the Maxilla. The sword will see to that itself. The Seeker is burdened with a worthier task. ~ Sydney Chomsky.

Somewhere along the way, midnight passed, signaling the start of the Spring Equinox and my birthday. I'd made it to sixteen, but odds were stacked against me seeing seventeen. They'd blindfolded me and put me in spellbinders as soon as I turned myself over to them. They kept me in them during the ride, and while I sat and waited in a little room. I had no idea how long they made me sit there, but I was sure I dozed off at least twice. Finally, they came for me and led me to face the Council.

"This is most irregular! I call for a vote!" I heard Polter demand stridently.

"Really, Andrew, do you really want to squander the remaining influence you have on something so petty, or do you fear the presence of witnesses so much?" Draeden's calm voice said. There was a mix of grumbling and laughter, then I was announced by one of the Sentinels and led into the middle of the floor.

"Master Draeden!" the voice I thought belonged to Hardesty called out. "This is an outrage! Allowing a warlock to come armed? Sentinels, relieve him of that weapon!"

"We can't Madame Hardesty," Carter said sourly from beside me. "He's the only person who can pick it up or carry it. He came peacefully and gave an oath not to resist over the sword itself. I found it sufficient, given what we saw tonight."

"We will see if this Council agrees," Polter said. "For your sake, I hope that it does, but I wouldn't hold my breath."

"Chance Fortunato, you have been called to face the justice of this Council. You have been given an Ordeal, one which you appear to have failed. What do you have to say in your defense before the Council passes judgment?" another voice called out.

"I have a lot to say, but I'd prefer to say it when I can see the Council."

"Remove the blindfold and the restraints," Draeden ordered. "Unless anyone here thinks a fifteen-year-old warlock is too powerful for the gathered Council to face."

No one said anything, and a few seconds later, I was facing the Council with my hands free. I could see Dr. C, Shade, Lucas, Wanda, and Steve in the crowd, and I felt a little less alone. They were probably what had Polter's panties in a wad. I wished my Mom was there, but I felt better knowing she was somewhere safe.

"Speak your piece, then," Draeden ordered.

"First, sir, I think there is the matter of what to do with my tools and my other property?" Several members of the Council nodded. "I'd like to bequeath my wand and my working tools, and all of my other possessions to my sister, Dierdre Murathy."

"Preposterous!" Polter bellowed. "Tools like that are too dangerous to give to a child, especially from a warlock! An eight-year-old girl is not capable of using such things responsibly! Your request is denied! The Council will decide what is to be done with your property."

Several heads nodded in agreement, though Draeden's remained still. His eyes narrowed and I thought I could see the faint beginnings of a smile.

"Then why do you think that I was capable of making life and death decisions when I was seven?" I demanded, catching the direction Dr. C had wanted Polter to go. "If my eight-year-old sister is too young to be trusted with a wand, then how was I supposed to be better prepared for facing a demon? Make up your mind!"

"That point is irrelevant," Polter sneered. "You agreed to the Ordeal, and you failed miserably."

"The Ordeal was to return the Maxilla, and fulfill the fate set by my wyrd. I did that almost an hour ago." That made the whole chamber erupt. Liar was the kindest thing they called me. It went on for a couple of minutes, until Draeden raised his staff and slammed it down with a boom that I felt in my feet.

"Explain yourself," he demanded.

"The wyrd on me was to find the Maxilla, which I did around eleven, and to return it, which I did just before midnight. I even managed to do it right."

"You lie!" Polter exclaimed.

"Speak out of turn again, Andrew, and I will have you removed from these proceedings," Draeden said. The edge of his voice was so sharp I was sure thousands of air molecules went screaming to their death just being too close his mouth. He nodded to me.

"Thank you sir. I was never supposed to return it to you. The Maxilla doesn't belong to you. It's a responsibility, and it chooses who guards it and who carries it, not you. It was never stolen, and Dr. Corwyn never had it. Sydney Chomsky hid it before he died, but he kept the case at his house so everyone would keep going after it instead of looking for where he hid the sword."

"How do you know all of this?" Moon asked me.

"The night I fought Dominic King, I found the Page of Swords card and a note with the case saying that Mr. Chomsky had hidden it. I never told anyone because I thought it was safer if everyone thought someone else had it, so no one would start looking in the right direction. I think that was why the Maxilla chose me to be the Seeker. But that's the thing; I'm just the Seeker, the Page of Swords. The Maxilla also chose a Wielder, a Knight of Swords. My wyrd wasn't to find the Maxilla. My wyrd was to find the Wielder, and I did that a while back, I just didn't know it."

"With respect to the Council, Master Draeden, this tale is becoming increasingly hard to believe!" one of the Council members who'd voted with Polter before blurted.

"Have you some way of proving what you say?" Draeden asked.

"I do sir," I said. "I need to draw the sword to do it." Draeden nodded.

The sword slid free of the scabbard with a metallic hiss, and I held it up for a second so everyone could see it. With everyone's eyes on it, I took it in both hands, turned it with the point down, and decided to be a little dramatic. I thrust down hard, and drove the point into the floor. There was a sound like a bass string being plucked, and it felt like the whole world rippled in its wake. I turned to face the crowd.

"No one can pull this blade free except for the Wielder and me."

"You don't mind if we test that, do you?" Moon said.

I shook my head. "No, I don't. That's exactly what I need you to do."

"Master Clay, you voted to have this boy executed. Why don't you try it?" Moon said.

The wizard three places from the right end of the line of Masters flinched at that, but he pulled his hood back to reveal a handsome face and salt and pepper hair. He came down and pulled his sleeves back a little and put his hands to the leather of the handle, and almost immediately snatched them away. His palms were red and a wisp of steam rose from his right hand.

"I can barely touch it," he admitted.

I gave Draeden and Moon a glance, and they nodded. I turned and faced the one person who'd been there for almost every vision of the sword, the one person who had the birthright to carry the sword I'd just busted my ass to find. The man I'd offered the blade to twice, and who had refused it two of the three times required.

"Steve Donovan," I said simply. He stepped out of the crowd and looked at me like I'd just passed sentence on him. "Your turn."

His steps were slow, reluctant, as he walked toward the sword sticking up out of the floor. When he got within arm's reach, he put his right hand out and gripped the handle. With barely an effort, he pulled it free, then he turned and handed it to me.

"You take it. I don't want it," he said, refusing it the third time. "This . . . it's too big. I barely understand what I am. I can't do this too."

"Steve," I said gently as I reversed the blade and offered it to him again. "This is yours to carry. It was never mine. My duty was to find it, and deliver it to you. Nothing more. You're one of the line of Samson, a Nazarite, sworn to serve a higher purpose. A Divine Warrior. You, my friend, are the Maxilla's Wielder. You're what you are because you were born for this."

I handed the Maxilla to him, and the blade blazed for a second before it faded and went back to normal. His eyes had the faraway look I imagined mine had right after I first touched the sword.

"Thrice offered, thrice refused," I said, once again saying things I wasn't sure how I knew to say. "You, my friend, are worthy to carry it."

"This is all very impressive, but it comes too late," Polter said from behind me.

"It isn't the first time Donovan's held the sword," Cross rumbled from my left. "Nine Sentinels, T-Bone, and I all saw him use it to kill Etienne and disrupt the ritual he was trying to perform. I say that the sword was returned before the Equinox, Master Draeden. I will attest that the Ordeal has been completed."

"Me, too," T-Bone said.

"I saw Donovan use the sword as well," Carter said from his place on the staircase.

One at a time, eight other voices backed me up, even if they didn't all sound happy about it. I turned to face the Council and waited for their decision. I wasn't holding my breath. Slowly, almost every member of the Council nodded. Polter's head remained locked in place.

"Your Ordeal is completed," Draeden said. "By your actions, you've proven to this Council that you are not a warlock, Chance Fortunato. The accusations against Wizard Corwyn are thus void. Though you still have much to answer for, this is not the forum for that. Now, we come to you, Mr. Donovan. The first Wielder the Maxilla has chosen in more than a century. You'll be given the best instruction in its use we have to offer, of course, and tutored in your role."

"With all due respect to you, sir, you can all go piss up a rope," Steve said. That brought a lot of gasps and exclamations. He forged ahead as if they hadn't said a word. "You people are the best the Conclave has to offer? I'd rather eat broken glass than listen to you."

"Those are some harsh words, young man," Moon said. "You mind explaining yourself?"

"All this week, I've seen Chance bust his ass to do what you people are *supposed* to be doing!" Steve said, his finger pointing at the Council. "He's been looking for a girl who was kidnapped by a vampire, trying to keep his own family safe from the guy who took her, *and* looking for this sword. While he's trying to do all that, he's under this Ordeal, trying to prove himself to you so you don't kill him! And tonight? When it came down to saving his own ass or helping someone else, he chose to save his friend and twelve other kids: kids *you* should have been looking for, instead of sitting on your lazy butts judging my friend. If you ask me, he shouldn't have had to choose between kissing your collective ass to save his own life and doing the right thing. He did the right thing even when you might have killed him for it, and frankly, I'll follow his example over yours any day of the week."

In the silence that followed his rant, I looked at him with a new respect.

"I believe," Moon said after a few moments, "that we've been rebuked, Master Draeden."

"Justly so," Draeden said as he pulled his hood back. "And while you speak from ignorance, Mr. Donovan, you raise an excellent point. No man should have to choose between the Council's displeasure and doing the right thing. And in spite of Wizard Polter's dismissal of his argument, your friend Chance has raised a valid argument, in that we expected more of him as a child than we had a right to. Our offer remains open to you, Mr. Donovan. We hope that you will look upon us in a better light in days to come. Both of you. Our business here is done. We open this circle."

"Let it remain unbroken," the crowd responded, and the Council turned and filed back through the doors behind them.

A pair of long, slender arms wrapped around me from behind, and I felt Shade's lips against my neck. I put my right hand on her wrist and turned my head to kiss her full on the lips before I turned to wrap my arms around her and give her a serious kiss.

"That's for standing up for me at Inferno," I said when our lips parted.

She kissed me hard back."That's for saving the world tonight," she whispered.

Not to be outdone, I kissed her again."That's for . . . oh, Hell with it," I said as I found her lips again.

Someone cleared their throat, and we came up for air again and favored them with a double dose of a harsh look. Carter stood out of easy reach, impervious to our best glares. Damn mages.

"Master Draeden respectfully asks you to join him," he said.

I left the circle of Shade's embrace after I gave her another kiss, and followed Carter. After a series of turns, I found myself being led down a hall to a familiar looking set of doors.

Draeden sat behind a table on the raised dais in the middle of the dining room I'd first met him in. There were two place settings at the table, and he was already sipping a pale wine from one of the glasses in front of him. My jacket and both holsters were laid on another table, along with my wand and the bag of candy Lucas had given me. He gestured toward the seat across from him, and this time, I hurt too much not to take it.

"You look a bit the worse for wear since our last visit," he commented.

"It's been a long week," I agreed.

A waiter appeared from behind me and filled one of the glasses in front of me with water. I reached for it as soon as he pulled the pitcher away.

"And it appears that you've been a busy young man. I would have asked why you didn't tell Polter that you had Thraxus' leave to confront Etienne, but such concessions don't come with a guest list. Making the Sentinels chase you into Inferno was a rather inspired way around that. We were able to make the case that they were following you in the course of their duties, and Thraxus was . . . mollified. I gather that was your intent?" he asked.

I looked up from the cloth-covered basket that the waiter had just set on the table and nodded, because if I opened my mouth, I was going to drool from the smell of fresh baked bread. Draeden flipped the cloth back and took one of the rolls under it, and I grabbed one of my own.

"I thought as much," he said as he took one of his knives and ran it across the scoop of butter in the little ceramic bowl beside the breadbasket.

I copied him, even though my stomach was demanding that I ignore the damn etiquette and get some food down my throat *now*.

"Of course, Andrew was rather vague about how he learned of the threat Etienne posed. Odd, too that the first call about it that I received came from Trevor. I have to wonder however, who it was who really discovered it. And how. Very few of us are well-versed in Lemurian rituals. In fact, the last copy of the Medici Codex disappeared in 1521, shortly after the death of Pope Leo the Tenth, and they were banned because they were so detailed on the G'Honn Tablets and Lemurian lore. Trevor is quite talented at undercover work, but even he doesn't have the extensive contacts among the less savory of our ilk here in New Essex to find such information. Polter, of course, would not deign to dirty his hands with something so beneath his dignity. However, a young man who once worked for a demon, however reluctantly, might know where to go, who to talk to and who to pay for such things."

The last bite of my roll scraped its way down a suddenly dry throat as I looked at him.

"He might," I admitted.

"Such a young man might also be precisely what the Conclave needs in the days to come. If he were trained properly."

He slid a thick, cream-colored envelope across the table toward me. The seal was in blue wax, and over it was a crest in blue and white. I picked it up by the corner, almost like it might bite me. The crest had a key in the upper right hand white section, and a book on the lower left hand side. At the top, a ribbon read "per virtus, libertatum" *Through virtue, freedom.* At the bottom, another ribbon read "Franklin Academy, Est.1787."

"What's this?" I asked.

"One of the privileges I enjoy as head of the High Council is the authority to grant an appointment for deserving young apprentices to attend the Franklin Academy under the Lincoln Fellowship. After what you suffered due to the Council's lack of action, it seems that the least we can do to make amends to you is to see to your education."

I dropped the envelope back on the table.

"You're sending me to magick school? What about Dr. C? I'm his apprentice, and I like that just fine."

"You will continue to be his apprentice. He will help assign your classes, and advise you when he is able to. I think you'll find that a diploma from the Franklin Academy will do much to dispel the . . . stigma of your previous associations. To say nothing of opening doors which will allow you to make your family's life much easier."

I looked down at the envelope. Going to school to learn magick sounded really cool, but I also liked the way things were. I had friends here, and my family. Some place with a name like the Franklin Academy and a motto in Latin sounded like it would be somewhere in New England.

"Can I think about it?" I asked.

"Only if you're trying to find a good reason to say yes. Let me give you one. By agreeing to attend the Franklin Academy, you will forestall disciplinary action against your mentor for concealing your apprenticeship. It will be considered that he is acting in good faith by allowing you to be tutored in a more . . . structured environment." His smile turned frosty, and my gaze went hot.

"Some place easier to keep me under your thumb," I challenged.

"Some might see it that way. I prefer a more mutually beneficial outlook. You get the benefit of the best magickal training in the U.S., and I am spared the unpleasantness of having to discipline a very talented wizard."

"So, I'm saying yes whether I want to or not," I said, my voice just edging to a growl. He'd played me like a chump by pressing all the buttons I couldn't help but react to.

"Glad to hear it. You'll begin during the fall semester, to make your transition a little smoother. The Academy will also want to assess your skill level before you start, so expect a visit. Now that we've taken care of that bit of business, I've ordered filet mignon. After the night you've had, I'm sure nothing less than a steak will do."

He gestured for the waiter, as I slid my chair back and stood up.

"With all due respect, Master Draeden, I'd rather not. I haven't seen my mom and my sister since Sunday," I said. His smile was as sincere as my respect as he nodded.

"Of course, my boy. Perhaps another time. Don't forget your letter," he gestured to the envelope still lying on the table.

I put my jacket on and gathered my gear. I slung both gunbelts over my shoulder, then pulled one of the cinnamon candies out and popped it in my mouth before I scooped up the envelope and tucked it into my back pocket.

He waited until I was almost to the door before he spoke.

"It's been a long time since anyone has rebuked the Council openly. It was long overdue. You and your friend Mr. Donovan opened some eyes tonight." He sipped his wine as I turned back to face him.

"Careful, sir. You almost sound like you approve," I told him.

"I do approve. Times are changing, Chance, and we have fallen behind them. I think that the Franklin Academy is going to benefit as much from your rather disruptive presence there as you will from its discipline and structure."

“I’ll try not to disappoint,” I told him as I reached for the door.

“I’m sure you won’t. I’m curious though. When did you realize it was Donovan that the sword was meant for?”

“I wasn’t certain until last night, when I remembered that Steve had been there almost every time I’d had a vision of the Maxilla.”

“Well done. Oh, and Chance? Happy birthday.”

I found everyone in the parking lot, in a circle around Shade and Deek. The two of them were squared off, both with their jackets off. Shade’s bare arms were tensed, and I could see the rips and tears in her t-shirt, compared to Deek’s pristine band shirt. On the ground behind Shade was Tyler, shaking his head and slowly getting to his feet. The rest of the pack was tensed, but their eyes kept going from Shade to Tyler. I knew they wanted to help their pack brother up, but I figured it was a pride thing not to make him look weak. By the same token, it looked like Deek had just hit Tyler, and they all wanted a piece of him.

“It’s my right as a beta to slap down any lesser wolf!” he said to Shade as I reached the edge of the circle. “Especially if he’s disrespectful.”

I could see Shade was fighting her wolf down hard, and if I’d been in her shoes, they’d be awfully small on my feet, but I’d also want to rip Deek’s throat out. But then again, that was why she had me. I pulled the LeMat and stepped into the circle. The sound of the hammer clicking back might as well have been a cannon going off.

“The lesser wolf here,” I said as I took my place beside Shade, “is the beta who pissed his pants and hid at Inferno tonight.”

“Your word against mine, human,” Deek sneered.

Shade’s hand moved, or at least I think it did, because I heard the crack of her palm on his cheek, but all I saw was the blur that went from her shoulder to his face.

“You will treat my *gothi* with respect,” she snarled. “He’s right. Lucas has bigger balls than you. If anyone should have run for the door, it was him; he stuck with us all the way, and all he had was a *watergun*. You didn't even come inside. You're a coward, and you're not welcome here. You have no status with my pack, and if you want to challenge anyone, you start with my *gothi.*"

"He's no challenge," Deek sneered. "Do you think I won't call him out because he's so far beneath me?"

"You haven't seen my *gothi* fight," Shade said with a cold smile. The laughter behind us made Deek's eyes narrow. "If you'd had the balls to stand with us tonight, you'd know that. Go."

The word was more threat than command, and Deek was on his bike in seconds. My heart felt a little lighter as the sound of his bike faded. I turned to Shade and my friends.

"It's my birthday, guys. I want you all there to help me celebrate it." I had a chorus of yeses, except for Steve, who looked uncertain.

"I, uh," he started.

"We just killed a major bad guy, man. Cake is the least I can do."

Epilogue:

Shade's body was pressed up against mine as we stood under the big oak tree in my backyard. Over by the grill, Dr. C was keeping watch over burgers and steaks, with Junkyard keeping an alert nose and eye out for the occasional scraps that just happened to get dropped. He'd claimed that manning the barbecue was his duty as a Texan, over Mom's halfhearted protests. He'd done it right after Collins brought Mom and Dee home, so she didn't figure out that he'd relieved her of most of the cooking until after we'd spent two hours catching up.

She still insisted on making a cake and cookies and Goddess knew what else. Dr. C had brought a long folding table and several extra chairs from somewhere, and Steve was regaling everyone else with the story of our fight upstairs. The rest of the pack sat protectively around Lucas, Wanda and their guests, Dani and Crystal. Crystal was curled up in Dani's arms, and every now and then I watched them kiss or share a gentle touch.

"You helped make that happen," Shade said softly as Dani pressed her lips to Crystal's.

"So did you," I reminded her.

She smiled and shrugged as she reached up and touched Wanda's pentacle where it lay on my chest, her birthday gift to me. Dr. C had given me the LeMat, though unless I needed it, it stayed at his house until I turned eighteen. Lucas had given me a thick set of leather bound books, Tolkien's *The Hobbit* and the *Lord of the Rings* trilogy as a set, and a promise to repair my poor backpack.

"I want to give you something for your birthday," she said softly.

I recognized the heat in her voice, and cocked my head.

"It's . . . as much for me as it's for you. I mean, it's . . . it isn't like the night . . . when I tried to," she stammered to a stop and her cheeks turned red before she dipped her head to hide her face.

"I know what you mean," I said softly. "It's okay."

She took a deep breath and looked back up at me. Her eyes weren't full of desire so much as raw need.

"I need your touch," she said.

I put my hand to her cheek gently, but she turned her face away and took my hand in hers. Slowly, gently, her trembling hand put mine over the first gentle rise of her breast, then brought my palm to her lips and kissed it, almost like a blessing.

"Soon. Please?"

I nodded. Her gift wasn't her body; it was her trust. All I could do was nod, because words seemed too small for the job. I pulled her to me and kissed her gently, then wrapped her in my arms.

"Chance, your necklace is glowing," I heard her whisper a moment later.

My eyes snapped open to see a man in the alley, looking straight at me. His face wasn't remarkable to look at, in spite of the square jaw and high cheekbones. All of that was boring when it had to compete with the void of his eyes. I recognized those eyes, even if the face was completely different.

"I'll be right back," I said.

A few moments later, I was standing at the back fence with a heavy, cloth-wrapped burden in my hands that I couldn't wait to get rid of.

The man came over to me and looked at my pentacle with open disdain.

"Remove that obnoxious bauble from my sight," Thraxus demanded.

"My house, my rules. You don't like it, you can go."

"When did you gain faith?" he asked.

I shrugged.

"It was a gift. Sorry about the car by the way," I said insincerely as I handed the fragment over to him. As soon as he took it, I felt the last burden I'd taken on seem to fall from my shoulders.

“It served its purpose. As did you.”

“Did Etienne?” I asked.

He looked at me with a smile.

“What ever do you mean?” he asked. Butter wouldn’t have melted in his mouth.

“Even if he hadn’t crossed the line with Collins, you already had that story with the fragment ready. The ritual he was doing took months to pull off, and there’s no way he could have started it unless he had it. There’s no way you went six months without missing it.”

“An interesting theory. One I have no doubt you will amuse yourself with for many nights to come as you try to understand why I would have wanted him to fail at the last possible moment, and how I could have predicted events so precisely as I did. When you comprehend that, I beg you, let me know of my great skill, because it eludes me as to how I would have accomplished it.” He turned and walked away, and my pentacle slowly faded.

“Arrogant prick,” Dr. C said from over my shoulder.

“How’d you know?” I asked.

“Wanda felt him. I think you’re right, by the way. He used Etienne as much as he used us. Not that I have any sympathy for the bastard. We’ll figure out what he was up to, don’t worry.”

“Hard not to,” I said as I turned to face the house and the impromptu party.

“Well, let me help take your mind off things,” he said as he reached into his pocket and pulled out a set of keys. “Happy birthday.”

“What’s this?” I asked.

The end of one of the keys was square, the other rounded. Both of them had the image of a running horse on one side, and the Ford logo on the other side.

“It’s a set of car keys. They’re for my old Mustang.” He smiled like he was about to tell the punch line of the funniest joke ever.

"A car? You're kidding! Where is it?" I exclaimed.

"San Angelo. It's yours on two conditions."

"Name it!" I pretty much bounced.

"One, you ace Driver's Ed. Two, get it running."

"You got it. Your burgers are burning." I smiled as he took off across the yard.

Shade came over and took my hand, and we leaned against the fence, basking in what passed for normal with us. A werewolf pack in my back yard, a wizard grilling steaks, and two lovers reunited because of what we'd done.

"Penny for your thoughts," she offered.

"Just trying to figure out why saving the world doesn't seem as cool as all this," I said as I gestured at the impromptu party. "You know. Surviving my birthday. Saving my friend. Getting the hot girl. Looking the Goddess in the face is like . . . cool and all, but this," I said as I kissed her lips. "Way better."

"The little things are what make the big things worth fighting for," Shade said softly.

She pulled me toward the table as Dr. C started serving up food, and I realized she was right. More than she knew, she was right. Being a mage wasn't about saving the world. It was about making the world worth hanging onto. That, I could do.

Dear Readers,

Thanks for picking up Page of Swords. I hope you enjoyed walking around in Chance's world again. I know I certainly liked coming back to see some familiar faces and meeting some new folks as well. When I re-released The Demon's Apprentice, the response was amazing and far better than I had ever imagined. I love seeing your reviews, as well as hearing from you through my website, www.chancefortunato.com and author page on Facebook and through Twitter (@TheOneTrueBen).

Page of Swords was a very involved book for me, since it starts to address some of the issues Chance is dealing with from his past and his relationships with his friends and family. As well, we start to see the larger world behind the Veil, and learn that it isn't all that squeaky clean. I especially enjoyed writing Chance and Shade's complicated relationship and I'm looking forward to seeing that continue to grow.

As always, I love to know what YOU think. In fact, as a writer, I need to know what my readers think, and what you want to see next. Leave a review, drop me a line or leave a comment on my web page.

Finally, if you love high fantasy, steampunk or want some more urban fantasy, drop by the Irrational Worlds website at www.irrationalworlds.com. Turn the page to check out some of my fellow authors' work.

Best regards,

Ben Reeder

From Irrational Worlds:

The Herald of Autumn

There are things unseen in the world of men, strange things that live in the secret cracks between places. Hungry monstrosities that the sons of man cannot fathom. It is The Herald's place to hunt them, protecting us from the darkness that we cannot see.

Every year, with the death of summer, Tommy Maple, the Herald of Autumn, awakens to again wander the land. Wherever he goes, red and golden leaves follow him, and he hunts the twisted creatures in the darkness.

This Autumn, however, is different from those in the past.

Tommy awakens to the taunting of a depraved enemy, a mysterious and elusive shaman. Tommy is powerless before his strange, bent magics, and knows that the old man has slaughtered his kind in the past. He is the last person the Herald should trust.

And yet, Tommy is forced to listen.

Soon, a sinister tale unfolds- a story that spans centuries and the entire continent. A story made from the whispering of forgotten legends that ends with a dark revelation. A story that Tommy has always been part of, even though he didn't know it.

Now the Herald faces an ancient abomination, unlike anything he has ever known before. For once, the hunter is the one that is hunted, chased through a misbegotten wood by a creature who seems to be little more than darkness and feckless hunger.

The behemoth is pure horror, and can unmake everything Tommy is.

As the Herald faces a foe unlike any other, will he fall to the darkness that haunts our world? Will the shadows of a lost age devour him, causing him to be reborn as one of the world's terrors? Or can he trust the shaman, a creature spun from little more than trickery, malevolence and deceit?

What are people saying about
"The Herald of Autumn?"

"Beautiful. It whisks you along with all the grace and power of an autumn wind, biting at times with its chill and whispering always at more to come. The blend of myth and modern, action and love, was superbly done. Definitely want to read more."

"The story is compelling. It is brisk. It hints at other and deeper stories. It is, in all the senses of the word, captivating. If you don't think you like myth, legend and stories, this one - with ancient roots but a modern touch in the telling - might be a nice place to start."

"I can honestly say this is one of my favorite books that I have read this year - and it's November so I've read a good many books. The Herald of Autumn earns a place on a very exclusive bookshelf - the one with books I will read over and over. I suspect each time I read it, I will find more I did not perceive before. There is no doubt that I will be buying more books by this author."

On The Matter of the Red Hand

All Thom wants is to drink a few rounds with his friend and play some bar games, or maybe make friends with that new serving girl- but that's not in the cards. No, Thom has a problem- a problem that may get him killed.

Or worse.

Tonight, it is raining. Thom stands in the shadows as strange visions run through his head like molten silver- visions that show dark injustices, hidden behind strange inexplicable symbols.

It's enough to make a man want a drink.

Thom is on duty, however. These visions have brought him to the door of a madman- Santiago Il Ladren. Santiago is a monster, rumored to have his enemies tortured to death- that is, the ones that don't simply vanish.

It is possible that Santiago will have Thom killed, just for asking the wrong questions.

Soon, the mystery takes a sharp turn. There is a missing girl- and it happens that Santiago is her brother. Each is another step down a twisted road that leads to forbidden alchemies and experiments in horror, hidden in plain sight. Every move Thom takes leads him further into strange shadows, until finally he is confronted with truths that he never wanted to face.

Some nights, it's just not worth the trouble it takes to stay out of the taverns.

Rationality Zero

The world is not what it seems.

Michael Bishop is an Asset of the Facility- a job that comes with many strange perks. He is a man who never gets ill, who never pays taxes. He is effortlessly fit, and has a different woman every night of the week.

That is, when he is not on assignment.

When activated, Michael becomes Asset 108, an enhanced human who stands against the strange darkness that lurks at the edge of our world. Armed with equipment that most would find impossible to comprehend, he is sent on missions both strange and deadly. Each dossier pits him against irrational creatures and beings- most with the power to unravel his sanity, or reality itself. It's never a simple job.

This job, however, is more complex than most. Mysterious unknown targets are fracturing reality, somewhere in the middle of the Mojave desert.

The Facility has no other Assets in the area, and their telemetry is spotty at best. Without knowing what to expect, Bishop is activated, assigned to a cadre, and sent to the middle of nowhere.

What he finds there is both the beginning and the end.
This is a stanza from THE PAEAN OF SUNDERED DREAMS.

Made in the USA
Middletown, DE
20 August 2016